Hans Christian Andersen

was born in 1805 in Odense, Denmark. His father was a poor cobbler of unfulfilled intellectual ambitions; his mother a nearly illiterate woman of the people. The young Andersen grew up solitary, dreamy, enamored of literature and the theater. At fourteen, armed with little more than sheer determination, he went to Copenhagen, where he succeeded in winning the patronage of several prominent citizens, and acquired a limited amount of formal schooling. In 1829, his poems, plays, and travel sketches began to appear; in 1835, his first novel, *The Improvisatore*, met with considerable success. That same year, he published his first collection of tales, to be followed over the years by further creations in a genre he made singularly his own. His life was marked by extensive travels, enormous popularity, the friendship of many leading personalities of the era, and the highest honors of his native land. By the time of his death in 1875, this gauche, awkward figure, born in the humblest of circumstances, who set out alone to win fame and fortune, had enjoyed a career that might well have come out of one of his most imaginative tales.

Andersen's Fairy Tales

Hans Christian Andersen

SELECTED AND TRANSLATED
WITH AN AFTERWORD BY
Pat Shaw Iversen

ILLUSTRATED BY
Sheila Greenwald

A SIGNET CLASSIC

SIGNET CLASSIC
Published by New American Library, a division of
Penguin Putnam Inc., 375 Hudson Street,
New York, New York 10014, U.S.A.
Penguin Books Ltd, 27 Wrights Lane,
London W8 5TZ, England
Penguin Books Australia Ltd, Ringwood,
Victoria, Australia
Penguin Books Canada Ltd, 10 Alcorn Avenue,
Toronto, Ontario, Canada M4V 3B2
Penguin Books (N.Z.) Ltd, 182–190 Wairau Road,
Auckland 10, New Zealand

Penguin Books Ltd, Registered Offices:
Harmondsworth, Middlesex, England

Published by Signet Classic, an imprint of New American Library,
a division of Penguin Putnam Inc.

This book previously appeared in a somewhat different form,
as *The Snow Queen and Other Tales*.

First Signet Classic Printing (New Edition), June 1987
11

 REGISTERED TRADEMARK—MARCA REGISTRADA

Library of Congress Catalog Card Number: 86-63383

Printed in the United States of America

BOOKS ARE AVAILABLE AT QUANTITY DISCOUNTS WHEN USED TO PROMOTE PROD-
UCTS OR SERVICES. FOR INFORMATION PLEASE WRITE TO PREMIUM MARKETING DIVI-
SION, PENGUIN PUTNAM INC., 375 HUDSON STREET, NEW YORK, NEW YORK 10014.

Contents

The Tinderbox

A SOLDIER came marching along the highway: One, two! One, two! He had his knapsack on his back and a sword at his side, for he had been to war and now he was on his way home. Then he met an old witch on the highway. She was hideous, and her lower lip hung right down to her chest.

She said, "Good evening, soldier! My, what a pretty sword and a big knapsack you have! You're a real soldier! Now you shall have as much money as you'd like to have!"

"Thanks, old witch!" said the soldier.

"Do you see that big tree?" said the witch, and pointed to a tree beside them. "It's quite hollow inside. You're to climb up to the top. Then you'll see a hole you can slide through, and you'll come down way inside the tree! I'll tie a rope around your waist so I can pull you up again when you call me."

"What'll I do down in the tree, then?" asked the soldier.

"Fetch money!" said the witch. "Now I'll tell you: when you're down at the bottom of the tree, you'll find yourself in a great hall. It's quite light, for over a hundred lamps are burning there. Then you'll see three doors. You can open them: the keys are in them. If you go into the first chamber, you'll see a big chest in the middle of the floor. On top of it sits a dog with a pair of eyes as big as teacups.

7

But you needn't pay any attention to that. I'll give you my blue-checked apron, which you can spread out on the floor. Then go over quickly and get the dog, put him on my apron, open the chest, and take as many shillings as you like! They're all of copper. But if you'd rather have silver, then go into the next room. There sits a dog with a pair of eyes as big as mill wheels! But you needn't pay any attention to that. Put him on my apron and take the money. On the other hand, if you'd rather have gold, you can also have that, and as much as you can carry, if you just go into the third chamber. But the dog sitting on the money chest here has a pair of eyes each one as big as the Round Tower! That's a real dog, I'll have you know! But you needn't pay any attention to that. Just put him on my apron, so he won't do you any harm, and take as much gold as you like from the chest."

"There's nothing wrong with that!" said the soldier. "But what'll I get for you, old witch? For I daresay you want something too!"

"No," said the witch, "not a single shilling will I have! You can just bring me an old tinderbox, which my grandmother forgot the last time she was down there."

"Well, put the rope around my waist," said the soldier.

"Here it is," said the witch, "and here's my blue-checked apron."

Then the soldier climbed up into the tree, let himself drop down through the hole, and stood now, as the old witch had said, down in the great hall where the many hundreds of lamps were burning.

Now he unlocked the first door. Ugh! There sat the dog with eyes as big as teacups, and it glowered at him.

"You're a pretty fellow!" said the soldier; he put the dog on the witch's apron and then took as many copper shillings as he could get in his pocket. Then he closed the chest, put the dog on it again, and went into the second chamber. Yeow! There sat the dog with eyes as big as mill wheels.

"You shouldn't look at me so hard," said the soldier; "it might strain your eyes!" Then he put the dog on the witch's apron, but when he saw all the silver coins in the chest, he got rid of all the copper money he had and filled his pocket and his knapsack with silver only. Now he went into the third chamber! My, how hideous it was! The dog in there really did have two eyes each as big as the Round Tower, and they rolled around in his head like wheels!

"Good evening," said the soldier, and touched his cap, for he had never seen a dog like that before. But after he had looked at it for a while, he thought, "Now that's enough," and lifted it down to the floor and opened the chest. Well, heaven be praised! What a lot of gold there was! He could buy all of Copenhagen with it, and the sugar pigs of the cake wives, and all the tin soldiers and whips and rocking horses in the world! Yes, that was really a lot of money! Now the soldier threw away all the silver shillings in his pocket and knapsack and took gold instead. Yes, he filled all his pockets and his knapsack, and his cap and boots were so full that he could hardly walk! Now he had money! He put the dog on the chest, shut the door, and then shouted up through the tree: "Pull me up now, old witch."

"Do you have the tinderbox with you?" asked the witch.

"That's right," said the soldier. "I'd clean forgotten it." And then he went and got it. The witch pulled him up, and now he was standing on the highway again with his pockets, boots, knapsack, and cap full of money.

"What do you want that tinderbox for?" asked the soldier.

"That's none of your business!" said the witch. "Why, you've got the money now. Just give me the tinderbox!"

"Fiddlesticks!" said the soldier. "Tell me at once what you want it for, or I'll draw my sword and chop off your head!"

"No!" said the witch.

Then the soldier chopped off her head. There she lay! But he tied all his money in her apron, carried it like a pack on his back, put the tinderbox in his pocket, and went straight to the town.

It was a lovely town, and he put up at the finest inn and demanded the very best rooms and all the food he liked, for he was rich, now that he had so much money.

The servant who was to polish his boots thought, of course, that they were queer old boots for such a rich gentleman to have, for he hadn't bought any new ones yet. The next day he got boots to walk in and pretty clothes. Now the soldier had become a fine gentleman, and they told him about all the things to do in their town, and about their king, and what a lovely princess his daughter was.

"Where can she be seen?" asked the soldier.

"She can't be seen at all," they said. "She lives in a big copper castle with many walls and towers around it. No one but the king is allowed to go in and out, for it has been prophesied that she will be married to a common soldier, and the king can't stand that one bit!"

"I'd like to see her, all right," thought the soldier, but this he wasn't allowed to do at all.

Now he lived merrily and well, went to the theater, drove in the royal park, and gave lots of money away to the poor; and that was well done! He remembered very well from the old days how bad it was to be penniless! Now he was rich and had fine clothes and many friends, who all said what a nice fellow he was, a real cavalier; and the soldier certainly didn't mind hearing that. But as he spent money every day and didn't get any back at all, it happened that at last he had no more than two shillings left and had to move from the nice rooms where he had lived to a tiny little room way up under the roof, and he had to brush his boots himself and mend them with a needle; and none of his friends came to see him, for there were so many stairs to climb.

One evening it was quite dark and he couldn't buy even a candle, but then he remembered there was a little stub in the tinderbox he had taken out of the hollow tree where the witch had helped him. He took out the tinderbox and the candle stub, but just as he struck a light and the sparks flew from the flint, the door flew open and the dog with eyes as big as teacups, which he had seen down under the tree, stood before him and said, "What does my master command?"

"What's that?" said the soldier. "Why, this is a funny tinderbox if I can get whatever I like! Get me some money," he said to the dog. And whoops! It was gone! Whoops! It was back again, holding a bag full of coins in its mouth.

Now the soldier understood what a marvelous tinderbox it was. If he struck it once, the dog that sat on the chest full of copper money came; if he struck it twice, the one with the silver money came; and if he struck it three times, the one with the gold came. Now the soldier moved back down to the lovely rooms again, put on the fine clothing, and then all his friends knew him again right away, and they were so fond of him.

Then one day he thought: "Now, it's really quite odd that no one is allowed to see the princess. Everyone says she's supposed to be so lovely. But what's the good of it when she always has to sit inside that big copper castle with all the towers? Can't I even get to see her at all? Now, where's my tinderbox?" And then he struck a light, and whoops! There stood the dog with eyes as big as teacups.

"I know it's the middle of the night," said the soldier, "but I'd so like to see the princess, just for a tiny moment."

The dog was out of the door at once, and before the soldier had given it a thought, it was back again with the princess. She sat on the dog's back and was asleep, and she was so lovely that anyone could see that she was a real princess. The soldier couldn't resist; he had to kiss her, for he was a real soldier.

Then the dog ran back again with the princess. But in the morning, when the king and queen were having their tea, the princess said that she had dreamed such a remarkable dream last night about a dog and a soldier. She had ridden on the dog, and the soldier had kissed her.

"That was a pretty story, indeed!" said the queen.

Now, one of the old ladies-in-waiting was to keep watch by the princess' bed the next night to see if it really were a dream or what it could be.

The soldier wanted very much to see the lovely princess again, and so the dog came during the night, took her, and ran as fast as it could, but the old lady-in-waiting pulled on a pair of rubber boots and ran after it just as fast. When she saw that they disappeared inside a big house, she drew a big cross on the door with a piece of chalk. Then she went home and went to bed, and the dog came back with the princess. But when it saw that a cross had been made on the door, it also took a piece of chalk and made crosses on all the doors in the city, and that was wise, for now, of course, the lady-in-waiting couldn't find the right door when there was a cross on every single one.

Early the next morning the king and the queen, the old lady-in-waiting, and all the officers came to see where the Princess had been.

"There it is!" said the king when he saw the first door with a cross on it.

"No, *there* it is, my dear husband," said the queen, who saw the second door with a cross on it.

"But there's one and there's one!" they all said. No matter where they looked, there was a cross on the door. So then they could see that there was no use searching one bit.

But the queen was a very wise woman, who knew about more than just riding in the royal coach. She took her big golden scissors, cut up a large piece of silk, and sewed a lovely little bag. This she filled with small, fine grains of buckwheat, tied it to the princess' back, and when that was done, clipped a tiny hole in the bag so the grain could dribble out all along the way, wherever the princess went.

That night, the dog came again, took the princess on his back, and carried her straight to the soldier, who had fallen in love with her and gladly would have been a prince so he could make her his wife.

The dog didn't notice at all how the grains dribbled out all the way from the castle to the soldier's window, where it ran up the wall with the princess. In the morning the king and queen saw where their daughter had been, all right, and so they took the soldier and put him in jail. There he sat! Ugh! How dark and dreary it was! And then they said to him, "Tomorrow you're to be hanged!" That wasn't a nice thing to hear, and he had forgotten his tinderbox back at the inn. In the morning, through the bars in the tiny window, he could see the people hurrying out of the city to see him hanged. He heard drums and saw the soldiers marching. Everybody was rushing out, including a shoemaker's apprentice in his leather apron and slippers, who was in such a hurry that one of his slippers flew off and landed nearby the wall where the soldier sat peering out through the iron bars.

"Hey there, shoemaker's boy, you needn't be in such a hurry," said the soldier. "Nothing will happen until I get there. But if you'll run to my lodgings and fetch my tinderbox, you'll get four shillings. But then you must really run." The shoemaker's boy was only too glad to have four shillings, and he scurried away after the tinderbox and gave it to the soldier, and—yes, now we shall hear:

Outside the city a big gallows had been built; around it stood the soldiers and many hundreds of thousands of people. The king and the queen sat on a lovely throne right above the judge and the whole court. The soldier was already on the ladder, but as they were going to put the noose around his neck he said—oh, yes, a sinner is always granted one little innocent wish before he receives his punishment—he would so like to smoke a pipeful of tobacco. After all, it would be the last pipe he'd have in this world.

The king couldn't really say no to that, and so the soldier took out his tinderbox and struck a light: One! Two! Three! And there stood all the dogs: the first with eyes as big as teacups, the second with eyes as big as mill wheels, and the third with eyes each as big as the Round Tower.

"Help me now, so I won't be hanged!" said the soldier. And then the dogs flew right at the judge and the whole court, took one by the legs and one by the nose, and tossed them many miles up in the air so they fell down and broke into pieces.

"I won't!" said the king, but the biggest dog took both him and the queen and threw them after all the others. Then the soldiers were frightened, and all the people shouted: "Little soldier, you shall be our king and have the lovely princess!"

Then they put the soldier in the king's coach, and all three dogs danced in front and shouted, "Hurrah!" And all the boys whistled through their fingers, and the soldiers presented arms. The princess came out of the copper castle, and was made queen, and that she liked very well. The wedding party lasted eight days, and the dogs sat at the table and made eyes at everybody.

Little Claus
and Big Claus

❖   ❖   ❖

IN one town there were two men who had the very
same name: they were both called Claus, but one of
them owned four horses and the other only a single horse:
and so, in order to tell them apart, the one who had four
horses was called Big Claus, and the one who had only
one horse, Little Claus. Now we shall hear how the two
got along, for this is a true story!

All week long Little Claus had to plow for Big Claus and
lend him his one horse. Then Big Claus helped him in
return with all four of his horses, but only once a week,
and that was on Sunday. Huzzah! How Little Claus cracked
his whip over all five horses; after all, they were as good as
his on that one day. The sun was shining so delightfully,
and all the bells in the church tower were ringing for church.
People were all dressed up and walked by with their hymn
books under their arms, on their way to hear the parson
preach. And they looked at Little Claus, who was plowing
with five horses, and he was so contented that he cracked
his whip again and shouted: "Gee up, all my horses!"

"You mustn't say that," said Big Claus. "After all, only
one of the horses is yours!"

But when somebody went by again on the way to church,
Little Claus forgot that he mustn't say it, and so he shouted:
"Gee up, all my horses!"

"Well, now, I'm telling you to stop that!" said Big Claus. "If you say it just one more time, I'll strike your horse on the forehead so he'll be lying dead on the spot, and that'll be the end of him!"

"I certainly won't say it anymore," said Little Claus. But when people went by, nodding and saying, "Good day," he became so contented, thinking it looked so grand for him to have five horses to plow his field with, that he cracked his whip and shouted: "Gee up, all my horses!"

"I'll gee up your horse!" said Big Claus, and he took the tethering mallet and gave Little Claus's horse such a blow on the forehead that it fell down quite dead.

"Oh, woe! Now I haven't got any horse at all!" said Little Claus, and started to cry. Later he flayed the horse, took the hide, and let it dry well in the wind; and then, putting it in a bag that he carried on his back, he went to town to sell his horsehide.

He had such a long way to go, through a deep, dark forest, and now a terrible storm blew up; he completely lost his way, and before he had got back on the right path again it was evening and much too far both from town and from home to arrive at either before nightfall.

Close to the road stood a big farmhouse. The outside shutters were closed, but the light still shone out at the top. "I hope I'll be allowed to spend the night here," thought Little Claus, and went over to knock at the door.

The farmer's wife opened it, but when she heard what he wanted, she told him to be on his way. Her husband wasn't home, and she didn't take in strangers.

"Well, I'll have to sleep outside, then," said Little Claus, and the farmer's wife shut the door on him.

Nearby stood a big haystack, and between that and the house a little shed had been put up, with a flat thatched roof.

"I can lie up there," said Little Claus when he saw the roof. "After all, it's a lovely bed. I daresay the stork won't fly down and bite me in the legs!" For a real live stork was standing on the roof, where it had its nest.

Now Little Claus crawled onto the shed, where he lay twisting and turning in order to make himself comfortable. The wooden shutters in front of the windows didn't go all the way up to the top, and so he could see right into the parlor.

A big table had been laid with wine and a roast and such a delicious fish. The farmer's wife and the parish clerk were sitting at the table, and no one else at all was there. And she poured him a drink, and he prodded the fish, for that was something he liked.

"If only I could have some too!" said Little Claus, and stretched his head all the way over to the window. Heavens! What a lovely cake he could see standing there. That was quite a feast.

Now he heard someone riding along the road toward the house—it was the woman's husband who was coming.

He was such a good man, but he had the singular affliction of not being able to bear the sight of a parish clerk! If he laid eyes on a parish clerk, he would fly into a terrible rage. This was also the reason why the parish clerk had dropped in to pay his respects to the wife when he knew that the husband wasn't at home, and the good wife set before him the most delicious food she had. Now, when they heard the husband coming, they were so terrified that the wife bade the parish clerk crawl down inside a big empty chest that was standing over in the corner. This he did, for he knew, of course, that the poor husband couldn't bear the sight of a parish clerk! The wife quickly hid all the delicious food and wine in her oven, because if the husband had seen it, he certainly would have asked what it was all about.

"Oh, woe!" sighed Little Claus on the shed when he saw all the food disappear.

"Is there someone up there?" asked the farmer, and

peered up at Little Claus. "Why are you lying there? Come in the house with me instead!"

Then Little Claus told how he had lost his way, and he asked if he could spend the night there.

"Why, of course!" said the farmer. "But first we're going to have a bite to eat!"

The wife welcomed them both very warmly, laid a long table, and gave them a big bowl of porridge. The farmer was hungry and ate with a good appetite, but Little Claus couldn't stop thinking about the lovely roast and fish and cake that he knew were standing in the oven.

Under the table at his feet he had put his bag with the horsehide in it—for we know that he had brought it from home to sell in town. He wouldn't enjoy the porridge at all, and so he trod on his bag, and the dry hide inside gave out quite a loud creak.

"Hush!" said Little Claus to his bag, but trod on it again, making it creak louder than before.

"Why, what do you have in your bag?" asked the farmer.

"Oh, it's a sorcerer!" said Little Claus. "He says we shouldn't eat porridge; he's conjured the whole oven full of a roast and fish and cake."

"What's that?" said the farmer, and he quickly opened the oven and saw all the delicious food the wife had hidden, but which he now believed had been conjured up for them by the sorcerer in the bag. The wife dared not say a thing but put the food on the table at once, and then they both ate the fish and the roast and the cake. Without delay Little Claus trod on his bag again so the hide creaked.

"What does he say now?" asked the farmer.

"He says," said Little Claus, "that he has also conjured up three bottles of wine for us, and they're standing in the oven too!" Now the wife had to take out the wine she had hidden, and the farmer drank and became quite merry; he'd be only too willing to own a sorcerer like the one Little Claus had in his bag.

"Can he conjure up the devil too?" asked the farmer. "I'd really like to see him, for now I feel so merry!"

"Yes," said Little Claus. "My sorcerer can do anything I ask him to. Can't you?" he asked, and trod on the bag so it creaked. "Can you hear? He says, 'Of course!' But the devil looks so terrible that it's better not to look at him!"

"Oh, I'm not afraid at all. How do you think he'll look?"

"Well, he'll appear in the shape of a parish clerk!"

"Whew!" said the farmer. "That's awful! You've got to know that I can't bear the sight of parish clerks! But no matter! After all, I know it's the devil, so I guess I'll just have to put up with it. I've got courage now! But he mustn't come too close!"

"Now I'm going to ask my sorcerer," said Little Claus, treading on the bag and holding his ear to it.

"What does he say?"

"He says that you can go over and open the chest standing in the corner, and then you'll see the devil mop-ing inside. But you've got to hold onto the lid so he doesn't get out!"

"Will you help me to hold it?" said the farmer, and went over to the chest where the wife had hidden the real parish clerk, who sat there scared to death.

The farmer lifted the lid a crack and peered in under it. "Yeow!" he shrieked, jumping back. "Yes, now I saw him; he looked just like our parish clerk! My, that was dreadful!"

They had to have a drink after this, and then they kept on drinking far into the night.

"You've got to sell that sorcerer to me!" said the farmer. "Ask whatever you like! Yes, I'll give you a whole bushel of money right away."

"No, I can't do that," said Little Claus. "Think of how much use that sorcerer is to me."

"Oh, I'd so like to have it," said the farmer, and kept on begging.

"Well," said Little Claus at last, "since you've been so kind as to put me up for the night, it's all right. You shall have the sorcerer for a bushel of money, but it has to be heaping full!"

"You shall have it!" said the farmer. "But you'll have to take that chest over there with you. I won't have it in the house another hour—you never can tell if he's still sitting in there."

Little Claus gave the farmer his bag with the dry hide inside, and was given a whole bushel of money—and heaping full, at that. And the farmer even gave him a big wheelbarrow on which to carry the money and the chest.

"Farewell!" said Little Claus, and then off he went with his money and the big chest with the parish clerk still sitting inside.

On the other side of the forest there was a big, deep river; it flowed so fast that one could hardly swim against the current. A large new bridge had been built across it. Little Claus stopped right in the middle of it and said quite loudly, so the parish clerk inside the chest could hear it: "Well, whatever am I going to do with that silly chest? It's as heavy as if it were full of stones. I'm getting quite tired of driving it any farther, so I'm going to throw it out in the river! If it sails home to me, then it's all very well; and if it doesn't, then it doesn't matter."

And taking hold of the chest with one hand, he lifted it up as if he were going to throw it in the water.

"No, stop! Don't do that!" shouted the parish clerk inside the chest. "Just let me come out!"

"Yeow!" said Little Claus, pretending to be afraid. "He's still sitting in there! I've got to throw it in the river right away so he can drown!"

"Oh, no! Oh, no!" shouted the parish clerk. "I'll give you a whole bushel of money if you don't!"

"Well, that's another story!" said Little Claus, and opened the chest. The parish clerk crawled out at once, shoved the empty chest into the water, and then went to his home, where Little Claus received a whole bushel of money—he had already gotten one from the farmer—and now his wheelbarrow was full of money.

"See, I got quite a good price for that horse," he said to himself when he came home to his cottage; then he emptied his bag in the middle of the floor and put all the money into a big pile. "That will annoy Big Claus when he finds out how rich I've become with my one horse. But I'm not going to tell him outright!"

Now he sent a boy over to Big Claus to borrow a bushel measure.

"I wonder what he wants that for!" thought Big Claus, and he smeared the bottom with tar so that a little of what was measured would stick fast. And so it did, too, for when he got the measure back, three new silver florins were stuck to it.

"What's this?" said Big Claus, and ran to Little Claus at once. "Where did you get all that money from?"

"Oh, that's for my horsehide. I sold it yesterday evening."

"I'll say you were well paid!" said Big Claus. He ran home, took an ax, struck all four of his horses on the forehead, flayed them, and drove to town with their hides.

"Hides! Hides! Who'll buy my hides?" he shouted through the streets.

All the shoemakers and tanners came running and asked how much he wanted for them.

"A bushel of money for each one!" said Big Claus.

"Are you mad!" they all said. "Do you think we have tons of money?"

"Hides! Hides! Who'll buy my hides?" he shouted again, but to everyone who asked what the hides cost he replied, "A bushel of money!"

"He's trying to make fun of us!" they all said, and then the shoemakers took their straps and the tanners their leather aprons and started to give Big Claus a thrashing.

"Hides! Hides!" they mimicked him. "Yes, we'll give you a hiding until you look like a flayed pig! Out of town with him!" they shouted, and Big Claus had to get moving as fast as he could. He'd never had such a thrashing before.

"Aha!" he said when he came back home. "I'll get even with Little Claus for this! I'm going to kill him!"

But meanwhile Little Claus's old grandmother had died at his home. To be sure, she had been quite shrewish and nasty to him, but he was still very sad, and taking the old woman, he laid her in his warm bed to see if he could bring her back to life again. She was to lie there all night while he was going to sit over in the corner and sleep on a chair, as he had done before.

Now as he was sitting there during the night the door opened, and Big Claus came in with his ax. He knew very well where Little Claus had his bed, and walking straight over to it, he struck the old grandmother on the forehead, thinking it was Little Claus.

"There now!" he said. "You're not going to fool me again!" And then he went back home again.

"Why, that nasty, wicked man!" said Little Claus. "He wanted to kill me! Still, it was a good thing old Granny was already dead, or else he'd have done away with her!"

Now he dressed old Granny in her Sunday best, borrowed a horse from his neighbor, hitched it to the wagon, and sat the old woman up in the back seat so she couldn't fall out when he was driving, and then they rolled away through the forest. When the sun came up they were outside a big inn. Here Little Claus stopped and went in to get a bite to eat.

The innkeeper had so very very much money; he was also a very good man but as hot-tempered as if he were full of pepper and snuff inside.

"Good morning," he said to Little Claus. "You're up early today in your Sunday best."

"Yes," said Little Claus. "I'm on my way to town with my old grandmother. She's sitting out there in the wagon. I can't get her to come inside. Won't you take a glass of mead out to her? But you'll have to speak quite loudly, as she can't hear very well."

"Indeed I shall," said the innkeeper, and poured out a big glass of mead, which he took out to the dead grandmother, who had been set up in the wagon.

"Here's a glass of mead from your grandson!" said the innkeeper, but the dead woman sat quite still and didn't say a word.

"Don't you hear!" shouted the innkeeper as loud as he could. "HERE'S A GLASS OF MEAD FROM YOUR GRANDSON!"

He shouted the same thing again, and once more after that, but when she didn't budge an inch he flew into a rage and threw the glass right in her face, so the mead ran down over her nose, and she fell over backward in the wagon, for she had only been propped up and not tied fast.

"GOOD LORD!" shouted Little Claus, running out of the door and grabbing the innkeeper by the collar. "You've killed my grandmother! Just look, there's a big hole in her forehead!"

"Oh, it was an accident!" cried the innkeeper, wringing his hands. "It's all because of my hot temper! Dear Little Claus, I'll give you a whole bushel of money if only you'll keep quiet about it, for otherwise they'll chop off my head, and that's so disgusting!"

So Little Claus got a whole bushel of money, and the innkeeper buried the grandmother as if she had been his own.

When Little Claus came back home with all the money, he sent his boy right over to Big Claus to ask if he could borrow a bushel measure.

"What's that?" said Big Claus. "Didn't I kill him? I'll have to go see for myself." And then he took the bushel measure to Little Claus.

"Why, where did you get all this money from?" he asked, his eyes opening wide at the sight of all this additional money that had come in.

"It was my grandmother and not me that you killed!" said Little Claus. "And now I've sold her for a bushel of money."

"You were really well paid!" said Big Claus, and hurrying home, he took an ax and killed his old grandmother straightaway; and putting her in the wagon, he drove off to town, where the apothecary lived, and asked if he wanted to buy a dead body.

"Whose is it, and where did you get it from?" asked the apothecary.

"It's my grandmother," said Big Claus. "I killed her for a bushel of money!"

"Good Lord!" said the apothecary. "You're talking nonsense! But you mustn't say a thing like that, or you can lose your head!" And then he told him what a really wicked deed he had done, and what a terrible man he was, and that he ought to be punished. Big Claus became so terrified at this that he ran right out of the apothecary's shop, right out to the wagon, whipped the horses, and rushed home. But the apothecary and everybody else thought he was mad, and so they let him drive wherever he liked.

"I'll get even with you for that!" said Big Claus when he was out on the highway. "Yes, I'll get even with you for that, Little Claus!" And as soon as he came home he took the biggest sack he could find, went to Little Claus, and said, "Now you've fooled me again! First I killed my horses and then my old grandmother! It's all your fault, but you're never going to fool me again!" And then he grabbed Little Claus by the waist, put him in his sack, threw him on his back, and shouted, "Now I'm going to drown you!"

He had a long way to go before he came to the river, and Little Claus wasn't such a light burden. The road ran by the church; the organ was playing and people were singing so beautifully inside. Then Big Claus placed his sack, with Little Claus in it, close to the church door, and thought it would be a good idea to go in and listen to a hymn first before he went on. After all, Little Claus couldn't get out and everybody else was inside the church, so he went in.

"Oh, woe! Oh, woe!" sighed Little Claus inside the sack. He turned this way and that, but he couldn't open the sack. At that very moment an old cattle drover, with chalk-white hair and a big staff in his hand, came along. He was driving a whole herd of cows and bulls ahead of him; they ran against the sack in which Little Claus was sitting, and it turned over.

"Oh, woe!" said Little Claus. "I'm so young, and I'm going to heaven already!"

"And I, poor soul," said the drover, "am so old and can't get there yet!"

"Open the sack!" shouted Little Claus. "Crawl in, in my place, and you'll get to heaven right away!"

"Yes, I'd be glad to!" said the drover, and untied the sack for Little Claus, who jumped out at once.

"Will you mind the cattle?" said the old man, and crawled down in the sack, which Little Claus tied up and then went on his way with all the cows and bulls.

A little later Big Claus came out of the church and put the sack on his back. Of course he thought it had grown lighter, for the old drover didn't weigh half as much as Little Claus did. "How light he's grown! Yes, I daresay it's because I've listened to a hymn!" Then he went over to the river, which was deep and wide, threw the sack with the old cattle drover in it, into the water, and shouted after him—for of course he thought it was Little Claus: "That's that! You're not going to trick me anymore!"

Then he started for home, but when he came to the crossroads he met Little Claus driving along all his cattle.

"What's that?" said Big Claus. "Didn't I drown you?"

"Yes indeed!" said Little Claus. "You threw me in the river not quite half an hour ago!"

"But where did you get all these fine cattle from?" asked Big Claus.

"They're sea cattle!" said Little Claus. "I'll tell you the whole story, and thanks for drowning me too! Now I'm on top! I'm really rich, I'll have you know! I was so frightened when I was lying in the sack, and the wind whistled about my ears when you threw me down from the bridge into that cold water. I sank straight to the bottom, but I didn't hurt myself, for down there grows the finest soft grass. There I fell, and at once the bag was opened, and the loveliest maiden, in chalk-white clothes and with a green garland on her wet hair, took me by the hand and said, 'Is that you, Little Claus? First of all, here's some cattle! A mile up the road is another herd, which I'm going to give you.' Then I saw that the river was a great highway for the sea people. On the bottom they walked and drove right up from the sea and all the way to land, where the river ends. The flowers there were so lovely and the grass so fresh, and the fish swimming in the water darted past my ears just the way the birds do up here in the air. What handsome people they were, and what a lot of cattle were walking by the fences and in the ditches!"

"But why did you come back up here so fast?" asked Big Claus. "I wouldn't have done that if it was so fine down there!"

"Oh, yes!" said Little Claus. "That was the shrewdest thing I could have done! You'll understand, of course, when I tell you: The mermaid said that about a mile up the road—and by the road she meant the river, of course, because she can't go anywhere else—another herd of cattle is waiting for me. But I know how the river twists and turns, first this way and then that. It's a long detour. Well, you can make it shorter by coming up here on land and driving straight across to the river again. Then I save almost half a mile and come to my sea cattle all the faster."

"Oh, you're a lucky man!" said Big Claus. "Do you think I would get some sea cattle if I went down to the bottom of the sea?"

"Oh, yes, I should think you would!" said Little Claus. "But I can't carry you to the river in the sack. You're too heavy for me. But if you'll walk over there yourself and then crawl into the sack, I'll throw you in with the greatest of pleasure!"

"Thank's a lot!" said Big Claus. "But if I don't get any sea cattle when I get down there, I'll give you a beating, I want you to know!"

"Oh, no! Don't be so mean!" And then they went to the

river. The cattle were thirsty, and when they saw the water they ran as fast as they could so as to have a drink.

"See how they hurry!" said Little Claus. "They're longing to go down to the bottom again!"

"Well, just help me first!" said Big Claus. "Or else you'll get a beating!" And then he crawled into the big sack, which had been lying across the back of one of the bulls. "Put a stone in it, or else I'm afraid I won't sink!" said Big Claus.

"You'll sink, all right!" said Little Claus, but nonetheless he put a big stone in the sack, tied it up tight, and then gave it a push. Plop! There was Big Claus in the water, and he sank to the bottom without delay.

"I'm afraid he won't find the cattle!" said Little Claus, and then he drove home what he had.

The Princess on the Pea

❖ ❖ ❖

THERE was once a prince. He wanted a princess, but it had to be a true princess! So he journeyed all around the world to find one, but no matter where he went, something was wrong. There were plenty of princesses, but whether or not they were true princesses he couldn't find out. There was always something that wasn't quite right. So he came home again and was very sad, for he wanted a true princess so very much.

One evening there was a terrible storm. The lightning flashed, the thunder boomed, and the rain poured down! It was really frightful! Then somebody knocked at the city gate, and the old king went out to open it.

A princess was standing outside, but heavens, how she looked from the rain and the bad weather! Water poured off her hair and clothes and ran in at the toe of her shoe and out at the heel, but she said she was a true princess!

"Well, we'll soon find that out!" thought the old queen, but she didn't say anything. She went into the bedroom, took off all the bedding, and put a pea on the bottom of the bed. Then she took twenty mattresses and laid them on top of the pea and then put twenty eiderdown quilts on top of the mattresses. There the princess was to sleep that night.

In the morning they asked her how she had slept.

"Oh, just miserably!" said the princess. "I've hardly closed my eyes all night! Heaven knows what was in my bed! I've been lying on something so hard that I'm black and blue all over! It's simply dreadful!"

Then they could tell that this was a true princess, because through the twenty mattresses and the twenty eiderdown quilts she had felt the pea. Only a true princess could have such delicate skin.

So the prince took her for his wife, for now he knew that he had a true princess, and the pea was put into the museum, where it can still be seen, if no one has taken it! See, this was a true story!

The Fable Alludes to You

❖ ❖ ❖

THE Sages of Antiquity kindly invented a way of telling people the truth without being rude to their faces: they held before them a singular mirror in which all kinds of animals and strange things came into view, and produced a spectacle as entertaining as it was edifying. They called it "A Fable," and whatever foolish or intelligent thing the animals performed there, the human beings had but to apply it to themselves and thereby think: the fable alludes to you. Let us take an example.

There were two high mountains, and on the very top of each mountain stood a castle. Down in the valley a dog was running. It sniffed along the ground as if, to stay its hunger, it were searching for mice or partridges. Suddenly, from one of the castles the trumpet sounded announcing that dinner was ready. At once the dog started running up the mountain to get a little, too. But just as it had come halfway, the trumpeter stopped blowing, and a trumpet from the other castle began. Then the dog thought, "They will have finished eating here before I come, but over there they will have just begun." And so down it went and ran up the other mountain. But now the trumpet at the first castle started blowing again, whereas the other had stopped. Once more the dog ran down one mountain and up the other, and he kept on in this way until both trumpets were at last silent and the meal would be at an end no matter to which place the dog came.

Guess now what the Sages of Antiquity wish to imply by this fable and which of us it alludes to, who wears himself out in this fashion without winning either here or there.

The Talisman

A PRINCE and a princess were still on their honeymoon. They felt so extremely happy. Only one thought disturbed them; it was this: will we always be as happy as we are now? And so they wanted to own a talisman that would protect them against every disappointment in marriage.

Now, they had often heard of a man who lived in the forest, and who was held in high esteem by everyone for his wisdom. He knew how to give the best advice for every hardship and misery. The prince and the princess went to him and told him what was troubling them.

When the wise man had heard it, he replied, "Journey through all the lands in the world, and when you meet a truly contented married couple, ask them for a little piece of the linen they wear next to their skin. When you get it, always carry it with you. That is an effective remedy."

The prince and the princess rode off, and soon they heard of a knight who, with his wife, was said to live the happiest of lives. They came up to the castle and asked them, themselves, whether in their marriage they were as extremely happy as rumor would have it.

"Of course!" was the reply. "Except for one thing: we have no children!"

Here, then, the talisman was not to be found, and the

prince and the princess had to continue on their journey to seek out the most perfectly contented married couple.

Next they came to a city in which, they heard, an honest burgher lived with his wife in the greatest harmony and contentment. They went to him, too, and asked whether he really were as happy in his marriage as people said.

"Yes, indeed I am!" replied the man. "My wife and I live the best of lives together. If only we didn't have so many children. They cause us so much sorrow and anxiety!"

The talisman was not to be found with him, either, and the prince and the princess journeyed on through the land and inquired everywhere after contented married couples.

But not one came forward.

One day, as they were riding along fields and meadows, they noticed a shepherd who was playing quite merrily on a shawm. At the same time they saw a woman come over to him with a child on her arm and leading a little boy by the hand. As soon as the shepherd saw her, he went to

meet her. He greeted her and took the child, which he
kissed and caressed. The shepherd's dog came over to the
boy, licked his little hand, and barked and jumped up and
down with joy. In the meantime the wife made ready the
pot that she had brought with her and said, "Papa, come
now and eat."

The man sat down and helped himself to the dishes. But
the first bite went to the little child and he divided the
second between the boy and the dog. All this the prince
and the princess saw and heard. Now they went closer,
talked with them, and said, "Are you truly what might be
called a happy and contented married couple?"

"Yes, indeed we are!" replied the man. "Praise be to
God! No prince or princess could be happier than we are."

"Then listen," said the prince. "Do us a favor that you
will not come to regret. Give us a tiny piece of the linen
that you wear next to your skin."

At this request the shepherd and his wife looked strangely
at each other. At last he said, "Heaven knows we would
gladly give it to you, and not just a tiny piece but the
whole shirt and petticoat if only we had them. But we
don't own a thread!"

So the prince and the princess continued on their journey without any success. At last they grew tired of this
long, fruitless wandering, and so they headed for home.
When they now came to the wise man's hut, they scolded
him for having given them such poor advice. He listened
to the whole story of their journey.

Then the wise man smiled and said, "Has your journey
really been so fruitless? Didn't you come home rich in
experience?"

"Yes," said the prince. "I have learned that contentment is a rare blessing on this earth."

"And I have learned," said the princess, "that in order
to be content, you need nothing more than just that—to
be content."

Then the prince gave the princess his hand. They gazed at each other with an expression of the deepest love. And the wise man gave them his blessing and said, "In your hearts you have found the true talisman. Guard it carefully, and never will the evil spirit of discontent gain power over you!"

The Little Mermaid

❖ ❖ ❖

F AR out to sea the water is as blue as the petals on the loveliest cornflower and as clear as the purest glass. But it is very deep, deeper than any anchor rope can reach. Many church steeples would have to be placed one on top of the other to reach from the bottom up to the surface of the water. Down there live the mermen.

Now, it certainly shouldn't be thought that the bottom is only bare and sandy. No, down there grow the strangest trees and plants, which have such flexible stalks and leaves that the slightest movement of the water sets them in motion as if they were alive. All the fish, big and small, slip in and out among the branches just the way the birds do up here in the air. At the very deepest spot lies the castle of the king of the sea. The walls are of coral, and the long tapering windows are of the clearest amber. But the roof is of mussel shells, which open and close with the flow of the water. The effect is lovely, for in each one there is a beautiful pearl, any of which would be highly prized in a queen's crown.

For many years the king of the sea had been a widower, and his old mother kept house for him. She was a wise woman and proud of her royal birth, and so she wore twelve oysters on her tail; the others of noble birth had to content themselves with only six. Otherwise she deserved much praise, especially because she was so fond of the little princesses, her grandchildren. They were six lovely children, but the youngest was the fairest of them all. Her skin was as clear and opalescent as a rose petal. Her eyes were as blue as the deepest sea. But like all the others, she had no feet. Her body ended in a fishtail.

All day long they could play down in the castle in the great halls where living flowers grew out of the walls. The big amber windows were opened, and then the fish swam into them just as on land the swallows fly in when we open our windows. But the fish swam right over to the little princesses, ate out of their hands, and allowed themselves to be petted.

Outside the castle was a large garden with trees as red as fire and as blue as night. The fruit shone like gold, and the flowers looked like burning flames, for their stalks and leaves were always in motion. The ground itself was the finest sand, but blue like the flame of brimstone. A strange blue sheen lay over everything down there. It was more like standing high up in the air and seeing only sky above and below than like being at the bottom of the sea. In a dead calm the sun could be glimpsed. It looked like a purple flower from whose chalice the light streamed out.

Each of the little princesses had her own tiny plot in the garden, where she could dig and plant just as she wished. One made her flower bed in the shape of a whale. Another preferred hers to resemble a little mermaid. But the youngest made hers quite round like the sun and had only flowers that shone red the way it did. She was a strange child, quiet and pensive, and while the other sisters decorated their gardens with the strangest things they had found from wrecked ships, the only thing she wanted, besides the rosy-red flowers that resembled the sun high above, was a beautiful marble statue. It was a handsome boy carved out of clear white stone, and in the shipwreck it had come down to the bottom of the sea. By the pedestal she had planted a rose-colored weeping willow. It grew magnificently, and its fresh branches hung out over the statue and down toward the blue, sandy bottom, where its shadow appeared violet and moved just like the branches. It looked as if the top and roots played at kissing each other.

Nothing pleased her more than to hear about the world of mortals up above. The old grandmother had to tell everything she knew about ships and cities, mortals and animals. To her it seemed especially wonderful and lovely that on the earth the flowers gave off a fragrance, since they didn't at the bottom of the sea, and that the forests were green and those fish that were seen among the branches there could sing so loud and sweet that it was a pleasure. What the grandmother called fish were the little birds, for otherwise the princesses wouldn't have understood her, as they had never seen a bird.

"When you reach the age of fifteen," said the grandmother, "you shall be permitted to go to the surface of the water, sit in the moonlight on the rocks, and look at the great ships sailing by. You will see forests and cities too."

The next year the first sister would be fifteen, but the others—yes, each one was a year younger than the other; so the youngest still had five years left before she might come up from the bottom of the sea and find out how it looked in our world. But each one promised to tell the others what she had seen on that first day and what she had found to be the most wonderful thing, for their grandmother hadn't told them enough—there was so much they had to find out.

No one was as full of longing as the youngest, the one who had to wait the longest and who was so quiet and pensive. Many a night she stood by the open window and looked up through the dark blue water where the fish flipped their fins and tails. She could see the moon and stars. To be sure, they shone quite pale, but through the

water they looked much bigger than they do to our eyes.
If it seemed as though a black shadow glided slowly under
them, then she knew it was either a whale that swam over
her or else it was a ship with many mortals on board. It
certainly never occurred to them that a lovely little mermaid was standing down below stretching her white hands
up toward the keel.

Now the eldest princess was fifteen and was permitted
to go up to the surface of the water.

When she came back, she had hundreds of things to tell
about. But the most wonderful thing of all, she said, was
to lie in the moonlight on a sandbank in the calm sea and
to look at the big city close to the shore, where the lights
twinkled like hundreds of stars, and to listen to the music
and the noise and commotion of carriages and mortals, to
see the many church steeples and spires, and to hear the
chimes ring. And just because the youngest sister couldn't
go up there, she longed for all this the most.

Oh, how the little mermaid listened. And later in the
evening, when she was standing by the open window and
looking up through the dark blue water, she thought of
the great city with all the noise and commotion, and then
it seemed to her that she could hear the church bells
ringing down to her.

The next year the second sister was allowed to rise up
through the water and swim wherever she liked. She
came up just as the sun was setting, and she found this
sight the loveliest. The whole sky looked like gold, she
said—and the clouds. Well, she couldn't describe their
beauty enough. Crimson and violet, they had sailed over
her. But even faster than the clouds, like a long white
veil, a flock of wild swans had flown over the water into
the sun. She swam toward it, but it sank, and the rosy
glow went out on the sea and on the clouds.

The next year the third sister came up. She was the
boldest of them all, and so she swam up a broad river that

emptied into the sea. She saw lovely green hills covered with grapevines. Castles and farms peeped out among great forests. She heard how all the birds sang, and the sun shone so hot that she had to dive under the water to cool her burning face. In a little bay she came upon a whole flock of little children. Quite naked, they ran and splashed in the water. She wanted to play with them, but they ran away terrified. And then a little black animal came; it was a dog, but she had never seen a dog before. It barked at her so furiously that she grew frightened and made for the open sea. But never could she forget the great forests, the green hills, and the lovely children who could swim in the water despite the fact that they had no fishtails.

The fourth sister was not so bold. She stayed out in the middle of the rolling sea and said that this was the loveliest of all. She could see for many miles all around her, and the sky was just like a big glass bell. She had seen ships, but far away. They looked like sea gulls. The funny dolphins had turned somersaults, and the big whales had spouted water through their nostrils so it had looked like hundreds of fountains all around.

Now it was the turn of the fifth sister. Her birthday was in winter, so she saw what the others hadn't seen. The sea looked quite green, and huge icebergs were swimming all around. Each one looked like a pearl, she said, although they were certainly much bigger than the church steeples built by mortals. They appeared in the strangest shapes and sparkled like diamonds. She had sat on one of the biggest, and all the ships sailed, terrified, around where she sat with her long hair flying in the breeze. But in the evening the sky was covered with clouds. The lightning flashed and the thunder boomed while the black sea lifted the huge icebergs up high, where they glittered in the bright flashes of light. On all the ships they took in the sails, and they were anxious and afraid. But she sat calmly on her floating iceberg and watched the blue streaks of lightning zigzag into the sea.

Each time one of the sisters came to the surface of the water for the first time she was always enchanted by the new and wonderful things she had seen. But now that, as grown girls, they were permitted to go up there whenever they liked, it no longer mattered to them. They longed again for home. And after a month they said it was most beautiful down there where they lived and that home was the best of all.

Many an evening the five sisters rose up arm in arm to the surface of the water. They had beautiful voices, sweeter than those of any mortals, and whenever a storm was nigh and they thought a ship might be wrecked, they swam ahead of the ship and sang so sweetly about how beautiful it was at the bottom of the sea and bade the sailors not to be afraid of coming down there. But the sailors couldn't understand the words. They thought it was the storm. Nor were they able to see the wonders down there either, for when the ship sank, the mortals drowned and came only as corpses to the castle of the king of the sea.

Now, in the evening, when the sisters rose up arm in arm through the sea, the little sister was left behind quite alone, looking after them and as if she were going to cry. But a mermaid has no tears, and so she suffers even more.

"Oh, if only I were fifteen," she said. "I know that I will truly come to love that world and the mortals who build and dwell up there."

At last she too was fifteen.

"See, now it is your turn!" said her grandmother, the old dowager queen. "Come now, let me adorn you just like your other sisters." And she put a wreath of white lilies on her hair. But each flower petal was half a pearl. And the old queen had eight oysters squeeze themselves tightly to the princess' tail to who her high rank.

"It hurts so much!" said the little mermaid.

"Yes, you must suffer a bit to look pretty!" said the old queen.

Oh, how happy she would have been to shake off all this magnificence, to take off the heavy wreath. Her red flowers in her garden were more becoming to her, but she dared not do otherwise now. "Farewell," she said and rose as easily and as lightly as a bubble up through the water.

The sun had just gone down as she raised her head out of the water, but all the clouds still shone like roses and gold, and in the middle of the pink sky the evening star shone clear and lovely. The air was mild and fresh, and the sea was as smooth as glass. There lay a big ship with three masts. Only a single sail was up, for not a breeze was blowing, and around in the ropes and masts sailors were sitting. There was music and song, and as the evening grew darker hundreds of many-colored lanterns were lit. It looked as if the flags of all nations were waving in the air. The little mermaid swam right over to the cabin window, and every time the water lifted her high in the air she could see in through the glass panes to where many finely dressed mortals were standing. But the handsomest by far was the young prince with the big dark eyes, who was certainly not more than sixteen. It was his birthday, and this was why all the festivities were taking place. The sailors danced on deck, and when the young prince came out, more than a hundred rockets rose into the air. They shone as bright as day, so the little mermaid became quite frightened and ducked down under the water. But she soon stuck her head out again, and then it was as if all the stars in the sky were falling down to her. Never before had she seen such fireworks. Huge suns whirled around, magnificent flaming fish swung in the blue air, and everything was reflected in the clear, calm sea. The ship itself was so lit up that every little rope was visible, not to mention mortals. Oh, how handsome the young prince was, and he shook everybody by the hand and laughed and smiled while the wonderful night was filled with music.

It grew late, but the little mermaid couldn't tear her eyes away from the ship or the handsome prince. The many-colored lanterns were put out. The rockets no longer climbed into the air, nor were any more salutes fired from the cannons, either. But deep down in the sea it rumbled and grumbled. All the while she sat bobbing up and down on the water so she could see into the cabin. But now the ship went faster, and one sail after the other spread out. Now the waves were rougher, great clouds rolled up, and in the distance there was lightning. Oh, there was going to be a terrible storm, so the sailors took in the sails. The ship rocked at top speed over the raging sea. The water rose like huge black mountains that wanted to pour over the mast, but the ship dived down like a swan among the high billows and let itself be lifted high again on the towering water. The little mermaid thought this speed was pleasant, but the sailors didn't think so. The ship creaked and cracked and the thick planks buckled under the heavy blows. Waves poured in over the ship, the mast snapped in the middle just like a reed, and the ship rolled over on its side while the water poured into the hold. Now the little mermaid saw they were in danger. She herself had to beware of planks and bits of wreckage floating on the water. For a moment it was so pitch black that she could not see a thing, but when the lightning flashed, it was again so bright that she could make out everyone on the ship. They were all floundering and struggling for their lives. She looked especially for the young prince, and as the ship broke apart she saw him sink down into the depths. At first she was quite pleased, for now he would come down to her. But then she remembered that mortals could not live in the water and that only as a corpse could he come down to her father's castle. No, die he mustn't! And so she swam among beams and planks that floated on the sea, quite forgetting that they could have crushed her. She dived deep down in the water and rose up high among the waves, and thus she came at last to the young prince, who could hardly swim any longer in the stormy sea. His arms and legs were growing weak; his beautiful eyes were closed. He would have died had the little mermaid not arrived. She held his head up above the water and thus let the waves carry them wherever they liked.

In the morning the storm was over. Of the ship there wasn't a chip to be seen. The sun climbed, red and shining, out of the water; it was as if it brought life into the prince's cheeks, but his eyes remained closed. The mermaid kissed his high, handsome forehead and stroked back his wet hair. She thought he resembled the marble statue down in her little garden. She kissed him again and wished for him to live.

Now she saw the mainland ahead of her, high blue mountains on whose peaks the white snow shone as if swans were lying there. Down by the coast were lovely green forests, and ahead lay a church or a convent. Which, she didn't rightly know, but it was a building. Lemon and orange trees were growing there in the garden, and in front of the gate stood high palm trees. The sea had made a little bay here, which was calm but very deep all the way over to the rock where the fine white sand had been washed ashore. Here she swam with the handsome prince and put him on the sand, but especially she saw to it that his head was raised in the sunshine.

Now the bells rang in the big white building, and many young girls came out through the gate to the garden. Then the little mermaid swam farther out behind some big rocks that jutted up out of the water, covered her hair and breast with sea foam so no one could see her little face, and then kept watch to see who came out to the unfortunate prince.

It wasn't long before a young girl came over to where he lay. She seemed to be quite frightened, but only for a moment. Then she fetched several mortals, and the mermaid saw that the prince revived and that he smiled at everyone around him. But he didn't smile out to her, for he didn't know at all that she had saved him. She was so unhappy. And when he was carried into the big building, she dived down sorrowfully in the water and found her way home to her father's castle.

She had always been silent and pensive, but now she was more so than ever. Her sisters asked about what she had seen the first time she was up there, but she told them nothing.

Many an evening and morning she swam up to where she had left the prince. She saw that the fruits in the garden ripened and were picked. She saw that the snow melted on the high mountains, but she didn't see the prince, and so she returned home even sadder than before. Her only comfort was to sit in the little garden and throw her arms around the pretty marble statue that resembled the prince. But she didn't take care of her flowers. As in a jungle, they grew out over the paths, with their long stalks and leaves intertwined with the branches of the trees, until it was quite dark.

At last she couldn't hold out any longer, but told one of her sisters. And then all the others found out at once, but no more than they, and a few other mermaids, who didn't tell anyone except their closest friends. One of them knew who the prince was. She had also seen the festivities on the ship and knew where he was from and where his kingdom lay.

"Come, little sister," said the other princesses, and with their arms around one another's shoulders they came up to the surface of the water in a long row in front of the spot where they knew the prince's castle stood.

It was made of a pale yellow, shiny kind of stone, with great stairways—one went right down to the water. Magnificent gilded domes soared above the roof, and among the pillars that went around the whole building stood marble statues that looked as if they were alive. Through the clear glass in the high windows one could see into the most magnificent halls, where costly silken curtains and tapestries were hanging, and all of the walls were adorned with large paintings that were a joy to behold. In the middle of the biggest hall splashed a great fountain. Streams of water shot up high toward the glass dome in the roof, through which the sun shone on the water and all the lovely plants growing in the big pool.

Now she knew where he lived, and many an evening and night she came there over the water. She swam much closer to land than any of the others had dared. Yes, she went all the way up the little canal, under the magnificent marble balcony that cast a long shadow on the water. Here she sat and looked at the young prince, who thought he was quite alone in the clear moonlight.

Many an evening she saw him sail to the sound of music in the splendid boat on which the flags were waving. She peeped out from among the green rushes and caught the wind in her long silvery white veil, and if anyone saw it, he thought it was a swan spreading its wings.

Many a night, when the fishermen were fishing by torchlight in the sea, she heard them tell so many good things about the young prince that she was glad she had saved his life when he was drifting about half dead on the waves. And she thought of how fervently she had kissed him then. He knew nothing about it at all, couldn't even dream of her once.

She grew fonder and fonder of mortals, wished more and more that she could rise up among them. She thought their world was far bigger than hers. Why, they could fly over the sea in ships and climb the high mountains way above the clouds, and their lands with forests and fields stretched farther than she could see. There was so much she wanted to find out, but her sisters didn't know the answers to everything, and so she asked her old grandmother, and *she* knew the upper world well, which she quite rightly called The Lands Above the Sea.

"If mortals don't drown," the little mermaid asked, "do they live forever? Don't they die the way we do down here in the sea?"

"Why, yes," said the old queen, "they must also die, and their lifetime is much shorter than ours. We can live to be three hundred years old, but when we stop existing here, we only turn into foam upon the water. We don't even have a grave down here among our loved ones. We have no immortal soul; we never have life again. We are like the green rushes: once they are cut they can never be green again. Mortals, on the other hand, have a soul, which lives forever after the body has turned to dust. It mounts up through the clear air to all the shining stars. Just as we come to the surface of the water and see the land of the mortals, so do they come up to lovely unknown places that we will never see."

"Why didn't we get an immortal soul?" asked the little mermaid sadly. "I'd gladly give all my hundreds of years just to be a mortal for one day and afterward to be able to share in the heavenly world."

"You mustn't go and think about that," said the old queen. "We are much better off than the mortals up there."

"I too shall die and float as foam upon the sea, not hear the music of the waves or see the lovely flowers and the red sun. Isn't there anything at all I can do to win an immortal soul?"

"No," said the old queen. "Only if a mortal fell so much in love with you that you were dearer to him than a father and mother; only if you remained in all his thoughts and he was so deeply attached to you that he let the priest place his right hand in yours with a vow of faithfulness now and forever; only then would his soul float over into your body, and you would also share in the happiness of mortals. He would give you a soul and still keep his own. But that never can happen. The very thing that is so lovely here in the sea, your fishtail, they find so disgusting up there on the earth. They don't know any better. Up there one has to have two clumsy stumps, which they call legs, to be beautiful!"

Then the little mermaid sighed and looked sadly at her fishtail.

"Let us be satisfied," said the old queen. "We will frisk and frolic in the three hundred years we have to live in. That's plenty of time indeed. Afterward one can rest in one's grave all the more happily. This evening we are going to have a court ball!"

Now, this was a splendor not to be seen on earth. Walls and ceiling in the great ballroom were of thick but clear glass. Several hundred gigantic mussel shells, rosy-red and green as grass, stood in rows on each side with a blue flame, which lit up the whole ballroom and shone out through the walls so the sea too was brightly illuminated. One could see the countless fish that swam over to the glass wall. On some the scales shone purple; on others they seemed to be silver and gold. Through the middle of the ballroom flowed a broad stream, and in this the mermen and mermaids danced to the music of their own lovely songs. No mortals on earth have such beautiful voices. The little mermaid had the loveliest voice of all, and they clapped their hands for her. And for a moment her heart was filled with joy, for she knew that she had the most beautiful voice of all on this earth and in the sea. But soon she started thinking again of the world above her. She couldn't forget the handsome prince and her sorrow at not possessing, like him, an immortal soul. And so she slipped out of her father's castle unnoticed, and while everything inside was merriment and song she sat sadly in her little garden. Then she heard a horn ring down through the water, and she thought: "Now he is sailing up there, the one I love more than a father or a mother, the one who remains in all my thoughts and in whose hand I would place all my life's happiness. I would risk everything to win him and an immortal soul. I will go to the sea witch. I have always been so afraid of her, but maybe she can advise and help me."

Now the little mermaid went out of her garden toward the roaring maelstroms behind which the sea witch lived. She had never gone that way before. Here grew no flowers, no sea grass. Only the bare, gray, sandy bottom stretched on toward the maelstroms, which, like roaring mill wheels, whirled around and dragged everything that came their way down with them into the depths. In between these crushing whirlpools she had to go to enter the realm of the sea witch, and for a long way there was no other road than over hot bubbling mire that the sea witch called her peat bog. In back of it lay her house, right in the midst of an eerie forest. All the trees and bushes were polyps—half animal, half plant. They looked like hundred-headed serpents growing out of the earth. All the branches were long slimy arms with fingers like sinuous worms, and joint by joint they moved from the roots to the outermost tips. Whatever they could grab in the sea they wound their arms around it and never let it go. Terrified, the little mermaid remained standing outside the forest. Her heart was pounding with fright. She almost turned back, but then she thought of the prince and of an immortal soul, and it gave her courage. She bound her long, flowing hair around her head so the polyps could not grab her by it. She crossed both hands upon her breast and then off she flew, the way the fish can fly through the water, in among the loathsome polyps that reached out their arms and fingers after her. She saw where each of them had something it had seized; hundreds of small arms held onto it like strong iron bands. Rows of white bones of mortals who had drowned at sea and sunk all the way down there peered forth from the polyps' arms. Ships' wheels and chests they held tightly, skeletons of land animals, and—most terrifying of all—a little mermaid that they had captured and strangled.

Now she came to a large slimy opening in the forest where big fat water snakes gamboled, revealing their ugly yellowish-white bellies. In the middle of the opening had been erected a house made of the bones of shipwrecked mortals. There sat the sea witch letting a toad eat from her mouth, just the way mortals permit a little canary bird to eat sugar. She called the fat, hideous water snakes her little chickens and let them tumble on her big spongy breasts.

"I know what you want, all right," said the sea witch. "It's stupid of you to do it. Nonetheless, you shall have your way, for it will bring you misfortune, my lovely princess! You want to get rid of your fishtail and have two stumps to walk on instead, just like mortals, so the young

prince can fall in love with you, and you can win him and
an immortal soul." Just then the sea witch let out such a
loud and hideous laugh that the toad and the water snakes
fell down to the ground and writhed there. "You've come
just in the nick of time," said the witch. "Tomorrow, after
the sun rises, I couldn't help you until another year was
over. I shall make you a potion, and before the sun rises
you shall take it and swim to land, seat yourself on the
shore there, and drink it. Then your tail will split and
shrink into what mortals call lovely legs. But it hurts. It is
like being pierced through by a sharp sword. Everyone
who sees you will say you are the loveliest mortal child he
has ever seen. You will keep your grace of movement. No
dancer will ever float the way you do, but each step you
take will be like treading on a sharp knife so your blood
will flow! If you want to suffer all this, then I will help
you."

"Yes," said the little mermaid in a trembling voice,
thinking of the prince and of winning an immortal soul.

"But remember," said the witch, "once you have been
given a mortal shape, you can never become a mermaid
again. You can never sink down through the water to your
sisters and to your father's castle. And if you do not win
the love of the prince so that for your sake he forgets his
father and mother and never puts you out of his thoughts
and lets the priest place your hand in his so you become
man and wife, you will not win an immortal soul. The first
morning after he is married to another, your heart will
break and you will turn into foam upon the water."

"This I want!" said the little mermaid and turned deathly
pale.

"But you must also pay me," said the witch, "and what I
demand is no small thing. You have the loveliest voice of
all down here at the bottom of the sea, and you probably
think you're going to enchant him with it. But that voice
you shall give to me. I want the best thing you have for

my precious drink. Why, I must put my very own blood in it so it will be as sharp as a two-edged sword."

"But if you take my voice," said the little mermaid, "what will I have left?"

"Your lovely figure," said the witch, "your grace of movement, and your sparkling eyes. With them you can enchant a mortal heart, all right! Stick out your little tongue so I can cut it off in payment, and you shall have the potent drink!"

"So be it!" said the little mermaid, and the witch put her kettle on to brew the magic potion. "Cleanliness is a good thing," she said, and scoured her kettle with her water snakes, which she knotted together. Now she cut her breast and let the black blood drip into the kettle. The steam made strange shapes that were terrifying and dreadful to see. Every moment the witch put something new into the kettle, and when it had cooked properly, it was like crocodile tears. At last the drink was ready, and it was as clear as water.

"There it is," said the witch, and cut out the little mermaid's tongue. Now she was mute and could neither speak nor sing.

"If any of the polyps should grab you when you go back through my forest," said the witch, "just throw one drop of this drink on them and their arms and fingers will burst into a thousand pieces." But the little mermaid didn't have to do that. The polyps drew back in terror when they saw the shining drink that glowed in her hand like a glittering star. And she soon came through the forest, the bog, and the roaring maelstroms.

She could see her father's castle. The torches had been extinguished in the great ballroom. They were probably all asleep inside there, but she dared not look for them now that she was mute and was going to leave them forever. It was as though her heart would break with grief. She stole into the garden, took a flower from each of her sisters' flower beds, threw hundreds of kisses toward the castle, and rose up through the dark blue sea.

The sun had not yet risen when she saw the prince's castle and went up the magnificent marble stairway. The moon shone bright and clear. The little mermaid drank the strong, burning drink, and it was as if a two-edged sword were going through her delicate body. At that she fainted and lay as if dead. When the sun was shining high on the sea, she awoke and felt a piercing pain, but right in front of her stood the handsome prince. He fixed his coal-black eyes upon her so that she had to cast down her own, and then she saw that her fishtail was gone, and she had the prettiest little white legs that any young girl could have, but she was quite naked. And so she enveloped herself in her thick long hair. The prince asked who she was and how she had come there, and she looked at him softly yet sadly with her dark blue eyes, for of course she could not speak. Each step she took was, as the witch had said, like stepping on pointed awls and sharp knives. But she endured this willingly. At the prince's side she rose as easily as a bubble, and he and everyone else marveled at her graceful, flowing movements.

She was given costly gowns of silk and muslin to wear. In the castle she was the fairest of all. But she was mute; she could neither sing nor speak. Lovely slave girls, dressed in silk and gold, came forth and sang for the prince and his royal parents. One of them sang more sweetly than all the others, and the prince clapped his hands and smiled at her. Then the little mermaid was sad. She knew that she herself had sung far more beautifully, and she thought, "Oh, if only he knew that to be with him I have given away my voice for all eternity."

Now the slave girls danced in graceful, floating movements to the accompaniment of the loveliest music. Then the little mermaid raised her beautiful white arms, stood up on her toes, and glided across the floor. She danced as no one had ever danced before. With each movement, her beauty became even more apparent, and her eyes spoke more deeply to the heart than the slave girl's song.

Everyone was enchanted by her, especially the prince, who called her his little foundling, and she danced on and on despite the fact that each time her feet touched the ground it was like treading on sharp knives. The prince said she was to stay with him forever, and she was allowed to sleep outside his door on a velvet cushion.

He had boys' clothes made for her so she could accompany him on horseback. They rode through the fragrant forests, where the green branches brushed her shoulders and the little birds sang within the fresh leaves. With the prince she climbed up the high mountains, and despite the fact that her delicate feet bled so the others could see it, she laughed at this and followed him until they could see the clouds sailing far below them like a flock of birds on their way to distant lands.

Back at the prince's castle, at night while the others slept, she went down the marble stairway and cooled her burning feet by standing in the cold sea water. And then she thought of those down there in the depths.

One night her sisters came arm in arm. They sang so mournfully as they swam over the water, and she waved to them. They recognized her and told her how unhappy she had made them all. After this they visited her every night, and one night far out she saw her old grandmother, who had not been to the surface of the water for many years, and the king of the sea with his crown upon his head. They stretched out their arms to her but dared not come as close to land as her sisters.

Day by day the prince grew fonder of her. He loved her the way one loves a dear, good child, but to make her his queen did not occur to him at all. And she would have to become his wife if she were to live, or else she would have no immortal soul and would turn into foam upon the sea on the morning after his wedding.

"Don't you love me most of all?" the eyes of the little mermaid seemed to say when he took her in his arms and kissed her beautiful forehead.

"Of course I love you best," said the prince, "for you have the kindest heart of all. You are devoted to me, and you resemble a young girl I once saw but will certainly never find again. I was on a ship that was wrecked. The waves carried me ashore near a holy temple to which several young maidens had been consecrated. The youngest of them found me on the shore and saved my life. I only saw her twice. She was the only one I could love in this world. But you look like her and you have almost replaced her image in my soul. She belongs to the holy temple, and so good fortune has sent you to me. We shall never be parted!"

"Alas! He doesn't know that I saved his life!" thought the little mermaid. "I carried him over the sea to the forest where the temple stands. I hid under the foam and waited to see if any mortals would come. I saw that beautiful girl, whom he loves more than me." And the mermaid sighed deeply, for she couldn't cry. "The girl is consecrated to the holy temple, he said. She will never come out into the world. They will never meet again, but I am with him and see him every day. I will take care of him, love him, lay down my life for him!"

But now people were saying that the prince was going to be married to the lovely daughter of the neighboring king. That was why he was equipping so magnificent a ship. It was given out that the prince is to travel to see the country of the neighboring king, but actually it is to see his daughter. He is to have a great retinue with him.

But the little mermaid shook her head and laughed. She knew the prince's thoughts far better than all the rest. "I have to go," he had told her. "I have to look at the lovely princess. My parents insist upon it. But they won't be able to force me to bring her home as my bride. I cannot love her. She doesn't look like the beautiful girl in the temple, whom you resemble. If I should ever choose a bride, you would be the more likely one, my mute little foundling with the speaking eyes!" And he kissed her rosy mouth, played with her long hair, and rested his head upon her heart, which dreamed of mortal happiness and an immortal soul.

"You're not afraid of the sea, are you, my mute little child!" he said as they stood on the deck of the magnificent ship that was taking him to the country of the neighboring king. And he told her of storms and calms and of strange fish in the depths and of what the divers had seen down there. And she smiled at his story, for of course she knew about the bottom of the sea far better than anyone else.

In the moonlit night, when everyone was asleep—even the sailor at the wheel—she sat by the railing of the ship and stared down through the clear water, and it seemed to her that she could see her father's castle. At the very top stood her old grandmother with her silver crown on her head, staring up through the strong currents at the keel of the ship. Then her sisters came up to the surface of the water. They gazed at her sadly and wrung their white hands. She waved to them and smiled and was going to tell them that all was well with her and that she was happy, but the ship's boy approached and her sisters dived down, so he thought the white he had seen was foam upon the sea.

The next morning the ship sailed into the harbor of the neighboring king's capital. All the church bells were ringing, and from the high towers trumpets were blowing, while the soldiers stood with waving banners and glittering bayonets. Every day there was a feast. Balls and parties followed one after the other, but the princess had not yet come. She was being educated far away in a holy temple, they said; there she was learning all the royal virtues. At last she arrived.

The little mermaid was waiting eagerly to see how beautiful she was, and she had to confess that she had never seen a lovelier creature. Her skin was delicate and soft, and from under her long dark eyelashes smiled a pair of dark blue faithful eyes.

"It is you!" said the prince. "You, who saved me when I lay as if dead on the shore!" And he took his blushing bride into his arms. "Oh, I am far too happy," he said to the little mermaid. "The best I could ever dare hope for has at last come true! You will be overjoyed at my good fortune, for you love me best of all." And the little mermaid kissed his hand, but already she seemed to feel her heart breaking. His wedding morning would indeed bring her death and change her into foam upon the sea.

All the church bells were ringing. The heralds rode through the streets and proclaimed the betrothal. On all the altars fragrant oils burned in costly silver lamps. The priests swung censers, and the bride and bridegroom gave each other their hands and received the blessing of the bishop. The little mermaid, dressed in silk and gold, stood holding the bride's train, but her ears did not hear the festive music nor did her eyes see the sacred ceremony. She thought of the morning of her death, of everything she had lost in this world.

The very same evening the bride and bridegroom went on board the ship. Cannons fired salutes, all the flags were waving, and in the middle of the deck a majestic purple and gold pavilion with the softest cushions had been erected. Here the bridal pair was to sleep in the still, cool night. The breeze filled the sails, and the ship glided easily and gently over the clear sea.

When it started to get dark, many-colored lanterns were lighted and the sailors danced merrily on deck. It made the little mermaid think of the first time she had come to the surface of the water and seen the same splendor and festivity. And she whirled along in the dance, floating as the swallow soars when it is being pursued, and everyone applauded her and cried out in admiration. Never had she danced so magnificently. It was as though sharp knives were cutting her delicate feet, but she didn't feel it. The pain in her heart was even greater. She knew this was the last evening she would see the one for whom she had left her family and her home, sacrificed her beautiful voice, and daily suffered endless agony without his ever realizing it. It was the last night she would breathe the same air as he, see the deep sea and the starry sky. An endless night without thoughts or dreams awaited her—she who neither had a soul nor could ever win one. And there was gaiety and merriment on the ship until long past midnight. She laughed and danced, with the thought of death in her heart. The prince kissed his lovely bride and she played with his dark hair, and arm in arm they went to bed in the magnificent pavilion.

It grew silent and still on the ship. Only the helmsman stood at the wheel. The little mermaid leaned her white arms on the railing and looked toward the east for the dawn, for the first rays of the sun, which she knew would kill her. Then she saw her sisters come to the surface of the water. They were as pale as she was. Their long beautiful hair no longer floated in the breeze. It had been cut off.

"We have given it to the witch so she could help you, so you needn't die tonight. She has given us a knife; here it is. See how sharp it is? Before the sun rises, you must plunge it into the prince's heart! And when his warm blood spatters your feet, they will grow together into a fishtail, and you will become a mermaid again and can sink down into the water to us, and live your three hundred years before you turn into the lifeless, salty sea foam.

Hurry! Either you or he must die before the sun rises. Our old grandmother has grieved so much that her hair has fallen out, as ours has fallen under the witch's scissors. Kill the prince and return to us! Hurry! Do you see that red streak on the horizon? In a few moments the sun will rise, and then you must die!" And they uttered a strange, deep sigh and sank beneath the waves.

The little mermaid drew the purple curtain back from the pavilion and looked at the lovely bride asleep with her head on the prince's chest. She bent down and kissed his handsome forehead; looked at the sky, which grew rosier and rosier; looked at the sharp knife; and again fastened her eyes on the prince, who murmured the name of his bride in his dreams. She alone was in his thoughts, and the knife glittered in the mermaid's hand. But then she threw it far out into the waves. They shone red where it fell, as if drops of blood were bubbling up through the water. Once more she gazed at the prince with dimming eyes, then plunged from the ship down into the sea. And she felt her body dissolving into foam.

Now the sun rose out of the sea. The mild, warm rays fell on the deathly cold sea foam, and the little mermaid did not feel death. She saw the clear sun, and up above her floated hundreds of lovely transparent creatures. Through them she could see the white sails of the ship and the rosy clouds in the sky. Their voices were melodious but so ethereal that no mortal ear could hear them, just as no mortal eye could perceive them. Without wings, they floated through the air by their own lightness. The little mermaid saw that she had a body like theirs. It rose higher and higher out of the foam.

"To whom do I come?" she said, and her voice, like that of the others, rang so ethereally that no earthly music can reproduce it.

"To the daughters of the air," replied the others. "A mermaid has no immortal soul and can never have one

unless she wins the love of a mortal. Her immortality
depends on an unknown power. The daughters of the air
have no immortal souls, either, but by good deeds they
can create one for themselves. We fly to the hot countries,
where the humid, pestilential air kills mortals. There we

waft cooling breezes. We spread the fragrance of flowers through the air and send refreshment and healing. After striving for three hundred years to do what good we can, we then receive an immortal soul and share in the eternal happiness of mortals. Poor little mermaid, with all your heart you have striven for the same goal. You have suffered and endured and have risen to the world of the spirits of the air. Now by good deeds you can create an immortal soul for yourself after three hundred years."

And the little mermaid raised her transparent arms up toward God's sun, and for the first time she felt tears. On the ship there was again life and movement. She saw the prince with his lovely bride searching for her. Sorrowfully they stared at the bubbling foam, as if they knew she had thrown herself into the sea. Invisible, she kissed the bride's forehead, smiled at the prince, and with the other children of the air rose up onto the pink cloud that sailed through the air.

"In three hundred years we will float like this into the kingdom of God!"

"We can come there earlier," whispered one. "Unseen we float into the houses of mortals where there are children, and for every day that we find a good child who makes his parents happy and deserves their love, God shortens our period of trial. The child does not know when we fly through the room, and when we smile over it with joy a year is taken from the three hundred. But if we see a naughty and wicked child, we must weep tears of sorrow, and each tear adds a day to our period of trial!"

The Emperor's New Clothes

❖   ❖   ❖

MANY years ago there lived an emperor who was so exceedingly fond of beautiful new clothes that he spent all his money just on dressing up. He paid no attention to his soldiers, nor did he care about plays or taking drives in the woods except for the sole purpose of showing off his new clothes. He had a robe for every hour of the day, and just as it is said of a king that he is "in council," so they always said here: "The emperor is in the clothes closet!"

In the great city where he lived everybody had a very good time. Many visitors came there every day. One day two charlatans came. They passed themselves off as weavers and said that they knew how to weave the most exquisite cloth imaginable. Not only were the colors and the pattern uncommonly beautiful but also the clothes that were made from the cloth had the singular quality of being invisible to every person who was unfit for his post or else was inadmissably stupid.

"Well, these are some splendid clothes," thought the emperor. "With them on I could find out which men in my kingdom were not suited for the posts they have; I can tell the wise ones from the stupid! Yes, that cloth must be woven for me at once!" And he gave the two charlatans lots of money in advance so they could begin their work.

They put up two looms, all right, and pretended to be working, but they had nothing whatsoever on the looms. Without ceremony they demanded the finest silk and the most magnificent gold thread. This they put in their own pockets and worked at the empty looms until far into the night.

"Now I'd like to see how far they've come with the cloth!" thought the emperor. But it made him feel a little uneasy to think that anyone who was stupid or unfit for his post couldn't see it. Of course he didn't believe that he himself needed to be afraid. Nonetheless he wanted to send someone else first to see how things stood. The whole city knew of the remarkable powers possessed by the cloth, and everyone was eager to see how bad or stupid his neighbor was.

"I'll send my honest old minister to the weavers," thought the emperor. "He's the best one to see how the cloth looks, for he has brains and no one is better fitted for his post than he is!"

Now the harmless old minister went into the hall where the two charlatans sat working at the empty looms.

"Heaven help us!" thought the old minister, his eyes opening wide. "Why, I can't see a thing!" But he didn't say so.

Both the charlatans asked him to please step closer and asked if it didn't have a beautiful pattern and lovely colors. Then they pointed to the empty loom, and the poor old minister kept opening his eyes wider. But he couldn't see a thing, for there was nothing there.

"Good Lord!" he thought. "Am I supposed to be stupid? I never thought so, and not a soul must find it out! Am I unfit for my post? No, it'll never do for me to say that I can't see the cloth!"

"Well, you're not saying anything about it!" said the one who was weaving.

"Oh, it's nice! Quite charming!" said the old minister,

and peered through his spectacles. "This pattern and these colors! Yes, I shall tell the emperor that it pleases me highly!"

"Well, we're delighted to hear it!" said both the weavers, and now they named the colors by name and described the singular pattern. The old minister paid close attention so he could repeat it all when he came back to the emperor. And this he did.

Now the charlatans demanded more money for more silk and gold thread, which they were going to use for the weaving. They stuffed everything into their own pockets. Not a thread went onto the looms, but they kept on weaving on the empty looms as before.

Soon afterward the emperor sent another harmless official there to see how the weaving was coming along and if the cloth should soon be ready. The same thing happened to him as to the minister. He looked and he looked, but as there was nothing there but the empty looms, he couldn't see a thing.

"Well, isn't it a beautiful piece of cloth?" both the charlatans said, and showed and explained the lovely pattern that wasn't there at all.

"Well, I'm not stupid!" thought the man. "Then it's my good position that I'm unfit for? That is strange enough, but I must be careful not to show it!" And so he praised the cloth he didn't see and assured them how delighted he was with the beautiful colors and the lovely pattern. "Yes, it's quite charming!" he said to the emperor.

All the people in the city were talking about the magnificent cloth.

Now the emperor himself wanted to see it while it was still on the loom. With a whole crowd of hand-picked men, among them the two harmless old officials who had been there before, he went to where the two sly charlatans were now weaving with all their might, but without a stitch or a thread.

"Yes, isn't it *magnifique?*" said the two honest officials. "Will your majesty look—what a pattern, what colors!" And then they pointed to the empty looms, for they thought that the others were certainly able to see the cloth.

"What's this?" thought the emperor. "I don't see anything! Why, this is dreadful! Am I stupid? Am I not fit to be emperor? This is the most horrible thing that could happen to me!"

"Oh, it's quite beautiful!" said the emperor. "It has my highest approval!" And he nodded contentedly and regarded the empty looms. He didn't want to say that he couldn't see a thing. The entire company he had brought with him looked and looked, but they weren't able to make any more out of it than the others. Yet, like the emperor, they said, "Oh, it's quite beautiful!" And they advised him to have clothes made of the magnificent new cloth in time for the great procession that was forthcoming.

"It is *magnifique!* Exquisite! Excellent!" passed from mouth to mouth. And every one of them was so fervently delighted with it. Upon each of the charlatans the emperor bestowed a badge of knighthood to hang in his buttonhole, and the title of "Weaver-Junker."

All night long, before the morning of the procession, the charlatans sat up with more than sixteen candles burning. People could see that they were busy finishing the emperor's new clothes. They acted as if they were taking the cloth from the looms, they clipped in the air with big scissors, they sewed with needles without thread, and at last they said, "See, now the clothes are ready!"

With his highest gentlemen-in-waiting the emperor came there himself and both the charlatans lifted an arm in the air as if they were holding something and said, "See, here are the knee breeches! Here's the tailcoat! Here's the cloak!" And so on.

"It's as light as a spider's web! You'd think you had nothing on, but that's the beauty of it!"

"Yes," said all the gentlemen-in-waiting, but they couldn't see a thing, for there was nothing there.

"Now, if your majesty would most graciously consent to take off your clothes," said the charlatans, "we will help you on with the new ones here in front of the big mirror!"

The emperor took off all his clothes, and the charlatans

acted as if they were handing him each of the new garments that had supposedly been sewed. And they put their arms around his waist as if they were tying something on—that was the train—and the emperor turned and twisted in front of the mirror.

"Heavens, how well it becomes you! How splendidly it fits!" they all said. "What a pattern! What colors! That's a magnificent outfit!"

"They're waiting outside with the canopy that is to be carried over your majesty in the procession," said the chief master of ceremonies.

"Well, I'm ready!" said the emperor. "Isn't it a nice fit?"

And then he turned around in front of the mirror just one more time, so it should really look as if he were regarding his finery.

The gentlemen-in-waiting, who were to carry the train, fumbled down on the floor with their hands just as if they were picking up the train. They walked and held their arms high in the air. They dared not let it appear as if they couldn't see a thing.

And then the emperor walked in the procession under the beautiful canopy. And all the people in the street and at the windows said, "Heavens, how wonderful the emperor's new clothes are! What a lovely train he has on the robe! What a marvelous fit!" No one wanted it to appear that he couldn't see anything, for then of course he would have been unfit for his position or very stupid. None of the emperor's clothes had ever been such a success.

"But he doesn't have anything on!" said a little child.

"Heavens, listen to the innocent's voice!" said the father, and then the child's words were whispered from one to another.

"He doesn't have anything on! That's what a little child is saying—he doesn't have anything on!"

"He doesn't have anything on!" the whole populace shouted at last. And the emperor shuddered, for it seemed to him that they were right. But then he thought, "Now I must go through with the procession." And he carried himself more proudly than ever, and the gentlemen-in-waiting carried the train that wasn't there at all.

The Steadfast Tin Soldier

❖   ❖   ❖

THERE were once five-and-twenty tin soldiers; they were all brothers, for they had been born of an old tin spoon. They shouldered their arms, they faced straight ahead, and their uniforms—red and blue—were ever so lovely. The very first thing they heard in this world, when the lid was taken off the box in which they were lying, were the words: "Tin soldiers!" It was shouted by a little boy, and he clapped his hands. They had been given to him for his birthday, and now he was lining them up on the table. Each soldier looked exactly like the other. Only one was slightly different: he had but one leg, for he was the last one to be cast and there hadn't been enough tin. And yet he stood just as firmly on his one leg as the others did on their two, and he is the very one who turns out to be unique.

On the table where they had been lined up there were many other playthings, but the one that stood out most was a lovely paper castle. Through the tiny windows you could look right into the halls. Outside were tiny trees standing around a little mirror that was supposed to look like a lake. Wax swans were swimming on it and being reflected there. It was all lovely, and yet the loveliest of all was a little maiden who was standing in the open door of the castle. She too had been cut out of paper, but she was wearing a skirt of the sheerest lawn and a narrow ribbon over her shoulder just like a drapery; in the very center of it was a shining spangle as big as her whole face. The little maiden was stretching out both her arms, for she was a dancer, and then she had raised one leg so high in the air that the tin soldier couldn't find it at all, and he thought she had but one leg, just like himself.

"That's the wife for me!" he thought. "But she's very highborn. She lives in a castle and I have only a box, and then it must do for five-and-twenty of us—that's no place for her. Still, I must see about making her acquaintance!" And then he stretched out at full length behind a snuffbox that stood on the table. From here he could look right at the little highborn lady, who continued to stand on one leg without losing her balance.

Later in the evening all the other tin soldiers went back in their box, and the people of the house went to bed. Now the toys began to play—at "Visitors," waging war, and holding balls. The tin soldiers rattled in their box because they wanted to join in, but they couldn't get the lid off. The nutcracker turned somersaults, and the slate pencil did monkeyshines on the slate; there was such a racket that the canary bird woke up and joined in the talk—and in verse, at that! The only two who didn't budge an inch were the tin soldier and the little dancer. She held herself erect on the tip of her toe and with both arms outstretched; he was just as steadfast on his one leg and his eyes never left her for a moment.

Now the clock struck twelve, and crash! The lid of the snuffbox flew off, but there wasn't any snuff in there—no, but a little black troll, and that was quite a trick.

"Tin soldier!" said the troll. "Will you keep your eyes to yourself!"

But the tin soldier pretended not to hear.

"Well, wait until tomorrow!" said the troll.

Now, when it was morning and the children got up, the

tin soldier was placed over in the window; and whether it
was caused by the troll or the draft, the window suddenly
flew open and the tin soldier went headlong out from the
third floor with a terrible speed. He turned his leg up in
the air and landed on his cap, with his bayonet stuck
between the paving stones.

The maid and the little boy went right down to look for
him, but despite the fact that they nearly stepped on him,
they couldn't see him. If the tin soldier had shouted
"Here I am!" they would have found him, all right. But he
didn't think it proper to shout when he was in uniform.

Now it started to rain; the drops fell thick and fast. It
turned into a regular downpour. When it was over, two
street urchins came along.

"Look!" said the first. "There's a tin soldier. He's going
out sailing!"

And so they made a boat out of a newspaper and put the
tin soldier in the middle of it, and now he sailed down the
gutter. Both the boys ran alongside and clapped their
hands. Heaven help us! What waves there were in that
gutter and what a current! But, then, the rain had poured
down. The paper boat bobbed up and down, and now and
then it turned around, sending a shudder through the tin
soldier. But he was just as steadfast, didn't bat an eyelash,
looked straight ahead, and shouldered his gun.

All at once the boat drifted in under a long gutter plank;
it was just as dark as if he were in his box.

"I wonder where I'm going now," he thought. "Well,
well, it's the fault of the troll. Alas, if only the little
maiden were sitting here in the boat, then it could be
twice as dark for all I'd care!"

At the same moment a big water rat came along, who
lived under the gutter plank.

"Do you have a passport?" asked the rat. "Hand over
your passport!"

But the tin soldier remained silent and held the gun

even tighter. The boat flew away with the rat right behind it. Whew! How it gnashed its teeth and shouted to sticks and straws: "Stop him! Stop him! He hasn't paid the toll! He hasn't shown his passport!"

But the current grew stronger and stronger; the tin soldier could already see daylight ahead where the gutter plank ended, but he could also hear a roaring sound that was enough to frighten a brave man. Just think, where the gutter plank ended, the gutter poured right out into a big canal! It was just as dangerous for him as it would be for us to sail down a great waterfall.

Now he was already so close to it that he couldn't stop. The boat shot out; the poor tin soldier held himself as stiffly as he could. No one was going to say that he had blinked his eyes. The boat whirled around three or four times and filled with water right up to the edge. It had to sink. The tin soldier stood in water up to his neck. The boat sank deeper and deeper; the paper grew soggier and soggier. Now the water went over the tin soldier's head. Then he thought of the lovely little dancer, whom he would never see again, and in the ears of the tin soldier rang the song:

> Fare forth! Fare forth, warrior!
> Thou shalt suffer death!

Now the paper was torn to pieces and the tin soldier plunged through—but at the same moment he was gobbled up by a big fish.

My, how dark it was in there! It was even worse than under the gutter plank, and then too it was so cramped! But the tin soldier was steadfast and lay at full length, shouldering his gun.

The fish darted about; it made the most terrible movements. At last it was quite still. It was as if a flash of

lightning had streaked through it. The light was shining quite brightly and someone shouted: "A tin soldier!"

The fish had been caught, taken to market, and sold, and had ended up in the kitchen, where the maid had cut it open with a big knife. With two fingers she picked the tin soldier up by the middle and carried him into the parlor, where they all wanted to see this remarkable man who had journeyed about in the stomach of a fish. But the tin soldier wasn't proud at all. They stood him up on the table, and there—my, what strange things can happen in this world! The tin soldier was in the very same room he had been in before! He saw the very same children and the playthings standing on the table, and the lovely castle with the beautiful little dancer. She was still standing on one leg and holding the other high in the air—she was steadfast too. The tin soldier was so moved that he could have cried tears of tin, but it wasn't proper! He looked at her and she looked at him, but they didn't say anything.

At the same moment one of the little boys took the tin soldier and threw him right into the tiled stove without giving any reason for doing so. It was decidedly the troll in the box who was to blame.

The tin soldier stood all aglow and felt the terrible heat—but whether it was from the real fire or from love, he didn't know. His colors were all gone, but whether that had happened on the journey or from sorrow, no one could tell. He looked at the little maiden, she looked at him, and he felt he was melting. But still he stood steadfast and shouldered his gun. Then a door opened, the wind took the dancer, and like a sylphid she flew right into the tiled stove to the tin soldier, blazed up, and was gone. Then the tin soldier melted to a clump, and when the maid took out the ashes the next day, she found him in the shape of a little tin heart. Of the dancer, on the other hand, only the spangle was left, and that was burned as black as coal.

The Garden of Paradise

❖   ❖   ❖

THERE was once a king's son. No one had so many or such beautiful books as he had. He was able to read about everything that had taken place in this world and see it depicted in magnificent pictures. He was able to learn about every nation and every land. But about where the Garden of Paradise was to be found there wasn't a word, and that was the very thing he thought of most.

When he was still quite young, but was going to start his schooling, his grandmother had told him that every flower in the Garden of Paradise was the sweetest cake, and the filaments were the choicest wine. On one flower was written "History," on another "Geography" or "Tables." You had only to eat cake and you knew your lesson. Indeed, the more you ate, the more history or geography or tables you knew.

He believed it then, but as he grew bigger and learned more and became much wiser he understood very well that there had to be far different delights in the Garden of Paradise.

"Oh, why did Eve pick from the Tree of Knowledge? Why did Adam partake of the forbidden fruit? It should have been me, then it would never have happened! Never would sin have entered the world!"

He said it then, and he was still saying it when he was seventeen. The Garden of Paradise filled his thoughts.

One day he went into the forest; he went alone, for that gave him the greatest pleasure.

It grew dark, the sky clouded over, and then it began to rain as if the whole sky were one big sluice from which the water was pouring. It was as dark as it usually is at night in the deepest well. Now he was slipping on the wet grass, now he was falling over the bare stones that jutted out of the rocky ground. Everything was wringing wet. There wasn't a dry stitch left on the unfortunate prince. He had to crawl up over huge blocks of stone, where the water seeped out of the deep moss. He was just about to drop when he heard a strange rushing sound, and ahead of him he saw a huge brightly lit cave. In the middle burned a fire big enough to roast a stag by, and this was being done too. The most magnificent stag, with its high antlers, had been stuck on a spit and was being slowly turned around between two felled fir trees. An elderly woman, tall and husky like a man in disguise, was sitting by the fire throwing on one piece of wood after another.

"Just come closer!" she said. "Sit by the fire so you can dry your clothes!"

"There's a terrible draft here!" said the prince, and sat down on the floor.

"It'll be even worse when my sons come home!" answered the woman. "You're in the Cave of the Winds; my sons are the Four Winds of the world. Can you grasp that?"

"Where are your sons?" asked the prince.

"Well, it's not so easy to give an answer when you ask a stupid question!" said the woman. "My sons are on their own. They're playing ball with the clouds up there in the parlor!" And then she pointed up in the air.

"Oh, is that so!" said the prince. "By the way, you speak

quite harshly and not so gently as the womenfolk I usually see about me."

"Well, as likely as not, they don't have anything else to do! I've got to be harsh if I'm to keep my boys under control! But I can do it, even if they are pigheaded! Do you see those four sacks hanging on the wall? They're just as afraid of them as you were of the rod behind the mirror. I can double the boys up, I'll have you know, and then into the sack they go. No fuss about it! There they sit, and they don't come out to go gallivanting until I see fit! But here comes one of them!"

It was the North Wind, who strode in with an icy chill. Huge hailstones bounced across the floor and snowflakes whirled about. He was clad in bearskin pants and jacket, a sealskin hood went down over his ears, long icicles hung from his beard, and one hailstone after another slid down from the collar of his jacket.

"Don't go over to the fire right away," said the prince. "You can easily get chilblains on your face and hands."

"Chilblains!" said the North Wind, and gave quite a loud laugh. "Chilblains! Why, that's just what I enjoy most! But what sort of a milksop are you? How did you get into the Cave of the Winds?"

"He's my guest!" said the old woman. "And if you don't like that explanation, you can just go in the sack! You're familiar with my judgment!"

See, it helped, and now the North Wind told where he had come from and where he had been for almost a whole month.

"I come from the Arctic Ocean," he said. "I've been on Bering Island with the Russian walrus hunters. I sat and slept at the helm when they sailed out from the North Cape. Now and then, when I woke up for a little while, the stormy petrel was flying about my legs. That's a funny bird: it gives a quick flap of the wings and then holds them outstretched, motionless, and now it has enough speed."

"Just don't make it so long-drawn-out!" said the Mother of the Winds. "And then you came to Bering Island!"

"It's lovely there! There's a floor to dance on as flat as a plate, half-thawed snow and moss, and sharp stones with skeletons of walruses and polar bears, lay there. They looked like the arms and legs of giants, moldy and green. You'd think the sun had never shone on them. I blew on the fog a little to get a glimpse of the hut. It was a house built of wreckage and covered with walrus hide, the fleshy side turned out—it was all red and green. A live polar bear was sitting on the roof growling. I went to the shore, looked at the birds' nests, looked at the bald nestlings shrieking and gaping. I blew into the thousands of throats, and they learned how to shut their mouths. Down below, the walruses were tumbling about like living entrails or giant maggots with heads of pigs and teeth a yard long!"

"You tell the story well, my boy," said the mother. "It makes my mouth water to listen to you."

"Then the hunt began! The harpoon was plunged into the breast of the walrus so the steaming jet of blood spurted onto the ice like a fountain. Then I also thought of my game. I started to blow and let my sailing ships—the icebergs as high as a cliff—crush the boats. Whew! How the men sniveled and how they shrieked, but I shrieked louder! They had to unload the whale carcasses, the chests, and the ropes onto the ice. I shook the snowflakes over them and let them drift south in the wedged-in vessels to have a taste of salt water. They'll never come back to Bering Island!"

"Then you've been up to mischief!" said the Mother of the Winds.

"The others can tell you of the good I've done," he said. "But there's my brother from the West. I like him best of all—he smacks of the sea and brings a heavenly chill along with him."

"Is that little Zephyrus?" asked the prince.

"Yes, that's Zephyrus, all right!" said the old woman. "But he's not so little after all. In the old days he was a handsome boy, but that's over now!"

He looked like a wild man, but he had on a baby's cap so as not to hurt himself. In his hand he carried a mahogany club, chopped down in the mahogany forests of America. It could be no less!

"Where do you come from?" asked his mother.

"From the forest wilderness," he said, "where the thorny lianas make a fence between each tree, where the water snake lies in the grass and mankind seems to be unnecessary."

"What were you doing there?"

"I was looking at the deep river and saw how it plunged down from the cliff, turned to spray, and flew up to the clouds to carry the rainbow. I was watching the wild buffalo swimming in the river, but the current dragged him along with it, and he drifted with a flock of wild ducks that flew in the air where the water went over the edge. The buffalo had to go over. I liked that, so I blew up a storm so the ancient trees went sailing and were dashed to shavings."

"And you haven't done anything else?" asked the old woman.

"I've been turning somersaults in the savannas, and I've been patting the wild horse and shaking down coconuts. Oh, yes, I've got stories to tell, but one shouldn't tell everything one knows. You're well aware of that, old lady!" And then he gave his mother such a kiss that she almost fell over backward. He was really a wild boy.

Now the South Wind came in, wearing a turban and a flowing burnoose.

"It's mighty cold in here!" he said, throwing a log on the fire. "It's easy to tell that North Wind has come first."

"It's hot enough to roast a polar bear in here!" said the North Wind.

"You're a polar bear yourself!" said the South Wind.

"Do you want to be put in the sack?" asked the old woman. "Sit down on that stone and tell us where you've been."

"In Africa, Mother!" he replied. "I was hunting lions with the Hottentots in the land of the Kaffirs. My, what grass is growing on the plain there, as green as an olive! There the gnu was dancing and the ostrich ran races with me, but I'm still more nimble-footed. I came to the desert, to the golden sand that looks like the bottom of the sea. I met a caravan. They were butchering their last camel to get water to drink, but they got only a little. The sun blazed up above, and the sand roasted down below. The vast desert has no boundaries. Then I frolicked about in the fine loose sand and whirled it up into tall pillars! What a dance that was! You should have seen how dispiritedly the dromedary stood and how the merchant drew his caftan over his head. He prostrated himself before me, as before Allah, his god. Now they're buried. A pyramid of sand stands over them all. Someday, when I blow it away, the sun will bleach their bones. Then the travelers will be able to see that people have been here before; otherwise you wouldn't think so in the desert!"

"Then you've just been doing harm too!" said the mother. "March into the sack!" And before he knew it, she had the South Wind by the middle and into the sack! It rolled about on the floor, but she sat on it and then it had to lie still.

"You've got some lively boys here, I must say!" said the prince.

"Yes, so I have," she replied, "but I know how to handle them! There's the fourth!"

It was the East Wind. He was clad like a Chinese.

"So, you've come from that direction!" she said. "I thought you'd been to the Garden of Paradise."

"I'm not flying there until morning. It'll be a hundred

years tomorrow since I was there! Now I've just come from China, where I've been dancing on the porcelain tower so all the bells tinkled. Down in the street the officials were being flogged. Bamboo poles were being worn out on their shoulders, and they were people from the first to the ninth rank. They shrieked, "Many thanks, my fatherly benefactor!" But they didn't mean a thing by it; and I tinkled the bells and sang 'Tsing tsang tsu!' "

"You're a wild one!" said the old woman. "It's a good thing you're going to the Garden of Paradise tomorrow. That always improves your manners. Drink deeply of the Spring of Wisdom, and bring home a little flaskful for me."

"That I'll do!" said the East Wind. "But why did you put my brother from the South down in the sack? Out with him! He's going to tell me about the Phoenix. The princess in the Garden of Paradise always wants to hear about that bird when I pay a visit every hundred years. Open the sack, that's my sweet mother, and I'll make you a present of two pocketsful of tea, as green and fresh as it was on the spot where I picked it."

"Well, for the sake of the tea and because you're mother's darling, I'll open the sack!" And so she did! And the South Wind crawled out, but he looked quite crestfallen because the strange prince had seen it.

"Here's a palm leaf for you to give to the princess!" said the South Wind. "That leaf has been given to me by the old Phoenix, the only one in the world. With his beak he has scratched on it the whole account of his life, the hundred years he has lived; now she can read it for herself. I saw how the Phoenix himself set fire to his nest, sat on it, and burned up like the Hindu's widow. My, how the dry branches crackled, what smoke and fragrance there was! At last it all went up in flames. The old Phoenix turned to ashes, but his egg lay red in the fire. It cracked with a loud bang and the youngster flew out. Now he's the ruler of all the birds and the only Phoenix in the world. He has bitten a hole in the palm leaf I gave you. That's his greeting to the princess."

"What about a bit to eat!" said the Mother of the Winds, and then they all sat down to dine on the roasted stag. The prince sat beside the East Wind, and thus they soon became good friends.

"Listen, tell me now," said the prince, "just who is this princess there has been so much talk about, and where is the Garden of Paradise?"

"Ho! Ho!" said the East Wind. "If you'd like to go there, just fly with me tomorrow. But otherwise I'd better tell you that no mortal has been there since the time of Adam and Eve. I daresay you know about them from your Scriptures!"

"Yes, of course!" said the prince.

"At the time they were driven out, the Garden of Paradise sank into the earth. But it kept its warm sunshine, its gentle breeze, and all its splendor. The queen of the fairies dwells there. There lies the Isle of Bliss, where Death never comes; it's a delightful place to be. Sit on my back tomorrow and I'll take you with me. I daresay it can be done! But now you mustn't talk anymore, for I want to go to sleep!"

And then they all went to sleep.

Early in the morning the prince woke up, and he was not a little dumbfounded to find himself already high above the clouds. He was sitting on the back of the East Wind, who was holding onto him quite squarely. They were so high in the sky that forests and fields, rivers and lakes, looked like an enormous illustrated map.

"Good morning," said the East Wind. "You could just as well have slept a little longer; there's not much to look at on the flatland beneath us unless you like to count churches! They stand out like pricks of chalk on the green board down there." The fields and meadows were what he called "the green board."

"It was very impolite of me not to say good-bye to your mother and your brothers," said the prince.

"Allowances are made for one who's sleeping," said the East Wind, and then they flew faster than ever. You could tell by the treetops in the forest that they were rushing over them: all the leaves and branches rustled; you could tell by the seas and lakes, for wherever they flew, the waves rolled higher and the great ships curtsied deep down in the water like floating swans.

Toward evening, as it was growing dark, the big cities were a delight to behold: the lights were burning, now here, now there—just as when someone burns a piece of paper and sees the myriads of tiny sparks, like children on their way from school! And the prince clapped his hands, but the East Wind told him to stop that and hang on tight instead, or else he could easily fall down and find himself hanging on a church spire.

The eagle from the dark forest flew quite easily, but the East Wind flew easier still. The cossack on his horse dashed along over the steppes, but the prince was dashing along in another fashion.

"Now you can see the Himalayas!" said the East Wind. "They're the highest mountains in Asia. We should be coming to the Garden of Paradise soon!" Then they veered in a more southerly direction, and soon there was the scent of spices and flowers. Figs and pomegranates were growing wild, and the wild grapevines had blue and red grapes. Here they both came down and stretched out in the soft grass, where the flowers nodded to the wind as if they wanted to say, "Welcome back!"

"Are we in the Garden of Paradise now?" asked the prince.

"No, not at all!" replied the East Wind. "But we should be there soon. Do you see that wall of rock there, and the big grotto with the grapevines hanging around it like a huge green curtain? We're going in through there! Wrap yourself up in your cloak. The sun is scorching hot here, but one step away and it's as cold as ice. The bird that sweeps past that grotto has one wing out here in the heat of summer and the other in there in the cold of winter!"

"So that's the way to the Garden of Paradise?" asked the prince.

Now they went into the grotto. Whew! How icy cold it was! But it didn't last long. The East Wind spread out his wings, and they shone like the brightest fire. My, what a grotto that was! Huge blocks of stone, from which water dripped, hung over them in the most fantastic shapes. Now the grotto was so narrow that they had to crawl on their hands and knees; now it was as high and spacious as if they were out in the open. It looked like a sepulchral chapel with mute organ pipes and petrified banners.

"I daresay we're taking the Road of Death to the Garden of Paradise," said the prince, but the East Wind didn't answer a word; he pointed ahead, and the loveliest blue light was shining at them. The blocks of stone overhead were fading more and more into a haze that at last was as bright as a white cloud in the moonlight. Now they were in the loveliest gentle breeze, as refreshing as in the mountains, as fragrant as in a valley of roses.

A river was flowing there, as clear as the air itself, and the fish were like silver and gold. Violet eels, which shot off blue sparks at every turn, were frolicking down in the water, and the broad leaves of the water lily were colors of the rainbow. The flower itself was a reddish-yellow burning flame, which was fed by the water, just as oil constantly keeps the lamp burning. A massive bridge of marble—but as remarkably and delicately carved as if it were of lace and glass beads—spanned the water to the Isle of Bliss, where the Garden of Paradise was blooming.

The East Wind took the prince in his arms and carried him across. There the flowers and leaves were singing the most beautiful songs from his childhood, but in swelling tones more delightful than any human voice can sing.

Were they palm trees or huge water plants that were growing here? The prince had never seen such lush and enormous trees before. There, in long garlands, hung the most remarkable twining vines, such as are to be found only in gold and color in the margins of the ancient books about the saints or threading in and out of the initial letters. It was the strangest combination of birds, flowers, and flourishes. Nearby, in the grass, stood a flock of pea-cocks with outspread, iridescent tails. Of course, that's just what they were! But no, when the prince touched them, he realized that they weren't animals but plants; they were huge dock plants that were as radiant here as the peacock's lovely tail. The lion and tiger were gambol-ing about like supple cats among the green hedges, which had a fragrance of olive blossoms, and the lion and the tiger were tame. The wild wood pigeon, as lustrous as the most beautiful pearl, flapped the lion's mane with its wings and the antelope, which is usually so timid, stood nodding its head as if it too wanted to join in the play.

Now the Fairy of Paradise came; her raiment shone like the sun and her face was as mild as that of a happy mother whose child has brought her joy. She was so young and fair, and attending her were the loveliest maidens, each with a shining star in her hair.

The East Wind gave her the inscribed leaf from the Phoenix, and her eyes sparkled with joy. She took the prince by the hand and led him into her castle, where the walls were the color of the most magnificent tulip petal when held up to the sun; the ceiling itself was one big lustrous flower, and indeed, the more you stared into it, the deeper its calyx seemed to be. The prince stepped over to the window and looked through one of the panes.

Then he saw the Tree of Knowledge with the serpent, and Adam and Eve were standing nearby. "Weren't they driven out?" he asked. And the Fairy smiled and explained to him that Time had thus burned its picture onto every pane, but not the way one usually saw it. No, there was life in it, the leaves on the trees moved. The people came and went, as in a reflected image. And he looked through another pane, and there was Jacob's dream, with the ladder going straight up to heaven, and the angels with big wings were hovering up and down. Yes, everything that had happened in this world was living and moving in the panes of glass. Time alone could burn such remarkable pictures.

The Fairy smiled and led him into a huge, lofty hall. Its walls seemed to be transparent paintings, with each face lovelier than the next. There were millions of happy faces that smiled and sang until it blended into a single melody. The ones at the very top were so tiny that they appeared to be tinier than the tiniest rosebud when it is drawn as a dot on the paper. And in the middle of the hall stood a huge tree, with luxuriant, hanging branches; golden apples, big and small, hung like oranges among the green leaves. This was the Tree of Knowledge, of whose fruit Adam and Eve had partaken. From each leaf dripped a glistening red drop of dew! It was as if the tree were crying tears of blood.

"Now let us get the boat," said the Fairy. "There we will enjoy refreshments out on the billowing water. The boat rocks, and yet it doesn't budge from the spot. But all the lands of the world will glide past our eyes." And it was strange to see how the whole coast moved. Here came the high snow-capped Alps, with clouds and black fir trees. The horn rang out, deep and melancholic, and the shepherd yodeled prettily in the valley. Now the banana trees bent their long drooping branches over the boat, coal-black swans were swimming on the water, and the most curious animals and flowers came into sight on the shore. This was New Holland, the fifth continent, that was gliding past and offering a view of the blue mountains; you could hear the chants of the priests and see the wild men dance to the sound of drums and bone pipes. The pyramids of Egypt, soaring to the clouds, and overturned columns and sphinxes half buried in the sand sailed past. The Aurora Borealis blazed over the glaciers of the North; it was a display of fireworks that none could match. The prince was so blissful. And indeed, he saw a hundred times more than we have described here.

"And can I stay here always?" he asked.

"That depends on yourself!" answered the Fairy. "If you don't, like Adam, allow yourself to be tempted to do what is forbidden, then you can always stay here."

"I won't touch the apples on the Tree of Knowedge!" said the prince. "Why, there're thousands of fruits here as lovely as they are."

"Test yourself, and if you're not strong enough, then go back with the East Wind, who brought you; he is flying back now and won't be coming here again for a hundred years. The time here in this place will pass for you as though it were only a hundred hours, but that's a long time for temptation and sin. Every evening, when I leave you, I must call out to you: 'Follow me!' I must beckon to you with my hand—but remain where you are. Don't come with me, for with every step your yearning will increase. You will enter the hall where the Tree of Knowledge grows. I sleep beneath its fragrant, drooping boughs. You will bend over me and I must smile. But if you press one kiss upon my lips, Paradise will then sink deep into the earth and be lost to you. The biting wind of the desert will whistle around you, the cold rain will drip from your hair. Trial and tribulation will be your lot."

"I'm staying here!" said the prince. And the East Wind kissed his forehead and said, "Be strong, and we'll meet

here again in a hundred years. Farewell! Farewell!" And
the East Wind spread out his mighty wings; they shone
like heat lightning in the summer, or the Northern Lights
in the cold winter. "Farewell! Farewell!" came the echo
from flowers and trees. Storks and pelicans flew in rows
like fluttering streamers and accompanied him to the boundary of the garden.

"Now our dance begins," said the Fairy. "At the end,
when I dance with you, you will see me beckoning to you
as the sun goes down; you will hear me calling you:
'Follow me!' But don't do it! For a hundred years I must
repeat it every evening. Every time that hour is past you
will gain more strength; at last you will never think of it
again. This evening is the first time. Now I have warned
you."

And the Fairy led him into a great hall of white transparent lilies. The yellow filament of each was a tiny harp of
gold, which rang out with the sound of strings and flutes.
The most beautiful maidens, graceful and willowy, clad in
billowing gauze that revealed their lovely limbs, hovered
in the dance and sang of how delightful it is to live, of how
they would never die, and of how the Garden of Paradise
would bloom in all eternity.

As the sun went down the entire sky turned a golden
hue that tinged the lilies like the loveliest roses. And the
prince drank of the sparkling wine handed to him by the
maidens, and he felt a bliss he had never known before.
He saw how the back of the hall opened, and the Tree of
Knowledge stood in a radiance that blinded his eyes! The
song coming from it was soft and lovely, like his mother's
voice, and it was as if she were singing, "My child, my
beloved child!"

Then the Fairy beckoned and called so affectionately,
"Follow me! Follow me!" And he plunged toward her,
forgetting his vow, forgetting it already on the very first
evening. And she beckoned and smiled. The fragrance,

the spicy fragrance all around, grew headier; the harps rang out far more beautifully; and the millions of smiling heads in the hall where the tree was growing seemed to be nodding and singing: "One should know everything! Man is the lord of the earth!" And they were no longer tears of blood that fell from the leaves of the Tree of Knowledge; they were red, twinkling stars, it seemed to him. "Follow me! Follow me!" echoed the tremulous strains, and at every step the prince's cheeks burned hotter and his blood flowed faster. "I must!" he said. "Why, that's no sin. It can't be! Why not follow beauty and happiness! I will look at her asleep. After all, nothing is lost as long as I don't kiss her, and I won't do that, I am strong! I have a strong will!"

And the Fairy let drop her dazzling raiment, bent back the branches, and a moment later was hidden inside.

"I haven't sinned yet!" said the prince. "And I'm not

going to, either." And then he drew the branches aside. She was already asleep, as lovely as only the Fairy in the Garden of Paradise can be. She smiled in her dreams. He bent over her and saw the tears welling up between her eyelashes.

"Are you crying over me?" he whispered. "Don't cry, you lovely woman! Only now do I comprehend the happiness of Paradise! It pours through my blood and through my thoughts. I can feel the might of cherubs and of eternal life in my mortal limbs! Let there be everlasting night for me; one moment such as this is riches enough!" And he kissed the tears away from her eyes, and his lips touched hers. . . .

Then there was a thunderclap louder and more dreadful than had ever been heard before, and everything fell down: the lovely Fairy and the blossoming Paradise sank. It sank so deep, so deep. The prince saw it sink in the black night; like a tiny gleaming star, it sparkled far away. A deathly chill went through his limbs; he closed his eyes and lay as if dead for a long time.

The cold rain was falling on his face and the biting wind was blowing about his head when he regained his thoughts. "What have I done?" he sighed. "I have sinned like Adam! Sinned so that Paradise has sunk deep down there!" And he opened his eyes. He could still see the star in the distance, the star that twinkled like the sunken Paradise—it was the Morning Star in the sky.

He got up and found that he was in the great forest close to the Cave of the Winds, and the Mother of the Winds was sitting by his side. She looked angry, and she lifted her arm in the air. "Already on the very first evening!" she said. "I thought as much! Yes, if you were my boy, you'd go down in the sack now!"

"That's where he's going," said Death; he was a strong old man with a scythe in one hand and with huge black wings. "He'll be laid in a coffin, but not now. I'll just mark

94 *Hans Christian Andersen*

him and then let him wander about the world for a while, atone for his sin, grow better and improve! I'll come one day. When he least expects it, I'll put him in the black coffin, place it on my head, and fly up toward the star. The Garden of Paradise is blooming there too. And if he is good and pious, he shall enter there; but if his thoughts are evil and his heart is still full of sin, he will sink in the coffin deeper than Paradise sank and only once every thousand years will I fetch him up again, so that he may sink deeper or remain on the star, the twinkling star on high!"

The Flying Trunk

❖ ❖ ❖

THERE was once a merchant; he was so rich that he could pave the whole street, and most of a little alleyway too, with silver money. But he didn't do it; he knew of other ways to use his money. If he spent a shilling, he got back a daler. That's the sort of merchant he was—and then he died.

Now the son got all this money, and he lived merrily—going to masquerade balls every night, making paper kites out of rixdaler bills, and playing ducks and drakes on the lake with golden coins instead of stones. So I daresay the money could go, and go it did. At last he had no more than four shillings left, and he had no other clothes than a pair of slippers and an old bathrobe. His friends no longer bothered about him now, as, indeed, they couldn't walk down the street together. But one of them, who was kind, sent him an old trunk and said, "Pack it!" Now, that was all very well, but he had nothing to pack, and so he seated himself in the trunk.

It was a funny trunk. As soon as you pressed the lock, the trunk could fly—and fly it did! Whoops! It flew up through the chimney with him, high above the clouds, farther and farther away. The bottom creaked, and he was afraid it would go to pieces, for then he would have made quite a big *jolt!* Heaven help us! And then he came to the land of the Turks. He hid the trunk in the woods under the dried leaves and then went into the town. He could do this easily, for among the Turks everyone, of course, walked around like he did, in a bathrobe and slippers. Then he met a nurse with a baby.

"Listen, you Turkish nurse," he said, "what big castle is this close to the city? The windows are so high!"

"The king's daughter lives there!" she said. "It has been prophesied that a sweetheart is going to make her very unhappy, so no one can come in to see her unless the king and the queen are there!"

"Thanks!" said the merchant's son. And then he went out in the woods, seated himself in his trunk, flew up on the roof, and crawled in through the window to the princess.

She was lying on the sofa asleep. She was so lovely that the merchant's son had to kiss her. She woke up and was quite terrified, but he said that he was the God of the Turks, who had come down to her through the air, and she liked that very much.

Then they sat next to each other, and he told her tales about her eyes: they were the loveliest dark pools, and her thoughts swam about there like mermaids. And he told her about her forehead: it was a snow-capped mountain with the most magnificent halls and pictures. And he told her about the stork that brings the sweet little babies.

Yes, those were some lovely tales! Then he proposed to the princess, and she said yes right away.

"But you must come here on Saturday," she said. "Then the king and the queen will be here with me for tea! They will be very proud that I am getting the God of the Turks. But see to it that you know a really lovely story, for my parents are especially fond of them. My mother likes it to be moral and decorous, while my father likes it jolly, so you can laugh!"

"Well, I'm bringing no other wedding present than a story!" he said, and then they parted. But the princess gave him a saber that was encrusted with golden coins—and he could particularly use those.

Now he flew away, bought himself a new bathrobe, and then sat out in the woods and started making up a story. It had to be ready by Saturday, and that's not at all easy.

Then he was ready, and then it was Saturday.

The king and the queen and the whole court were waiting with tea at the princess'. He was given such a nice reception!

"Now, will you tell a story!" said the queen. "One that is profound and imparts a moral."

"But one that can still make you laugh!" said the king.

"Yes, of course!" he said, and started his tale. And now you must listen very carefully.

"There was once a bunch of matches that were so exceedingly proud of their high descent. Their family tree—that is to say, the big fir tree of which each one was a tiny stick—had been a huge old tree in the forest. The matches were now lying on the shelf between a tinderbox and an old iron pot, and they were telling them about their youth.

" 'Yes, when we lived high on the green branch,' they said, 'we were really living high! Every morning and evening, diamond tea—that was the dew. All day we had sunshine—when the sun was shining—and all the little birds had to tell us stories. We were very well aware that we were rich too, for the leafy trees were clad only in the summer, but our family could afford green clothes both summer and winter. But then came the woodcutters—that was the Great Revolution—and our family was split up. The head of the family was given a post as the mainmast on a splendid ship that could sail around the world—if it wanted to. The other branches ended up in other places, and it is now our task to provide light for the rank and file. That's why people of rank like ourselves happen to be in the kitchen.'

" 'Well, it's been different with me!' said the iron pot, which was lying beside the matches. 'Ever since I came out into the world, I've been scoured and boiled many times! I attend to the substantial things, and as a matter of fact, I really come first in this house. My only joy—next to the table—is to lie nice and clean on the shelf and carry on a sensible chat with my companions. But—with the exception of the water pail, which occasionally goes down in the yard—we always live indoors. Our only news bringer is the market basket, but it talks so alarmingly about the government and the people. Yes, the other day an elderly pot was so upset by it all that it fell down and broke to bits! That's liberalism, I tell you!'

" 'Now you're talking too much!' said the tinderbox, and the steel struck the flint so the sparks flew. 'Weren't we going to have a cheerful evening?'

" 'Yes, let's talk about which of us is the most aristocratic!' said the matches.

" 'No, I don't enjoy talking about myself!' said the earthenware pot. 'Let's have an evening's *divertissement*. I'll begin. I'm going to tell about the sort of thing each one of us has experienced; you can enter into it so nicely, and that's such a delight. On the Baltic Sea, by the Danish beeches! . . .'

" 'That's a delightful beginning!' said all the plates. 'This is decidedly going to be the kind of story I like!'

" 'Well, there I spent my youth with a quiet family. The furniture was polished, the floors washed; clean curtains were put up every fourteen days!'

" 'My, what an interesting storyteller you are!' said the mop. 'You can tell right away that it's being told by a lady. Such cleanliness pervades!'

" 'Yes, you can feel it!' said the water pail, and then it gave a little hop for joy, so it went splash on the floor.

"And the pot went on with the story, and the end was just as good as the beginning.

"All the plates rattled with delight, and the mop took green parsley out of the sand bin and crowned the pot with it, for it knew this would irritate the others. 'And if I crown her today,' it said, 'then she'll crown me tomorrow!'

" 'Well, I want to dance,' said the fire tongs, and dance she did. Yes, heaven help us, how she could lift one leg up in the air! The old chair cover over in the corner split just from looking at it. 'May I be crowned too?' said the fire tongs, and then she was.

" 'All the same, they're only rabble!' thought the matches.

"Now the samovar was to sing, but it had a cold, it said—it couldn't unless it was boiling. But that was plain snobbishness; it wouldn't sing except when it was standing on the table in the room with the family.

"Over in the window sat an old quill pen, which the maid usually wrote with. There was nothing exceptional about it except that it had been dipped too far down in the inkwell. But because of this it now put on airs. 'If the samovar won't sing,' it said, 'then it needn't. Hanging outside in a cage is a nightingale. It can sing. To be sure, it hasn't been taught anything, but we won't malign it this evening!'

" 'I find it highly improper,' said the tea kettle, who was a kitchen singer and half sister to the samovar, 'that such an alien bird is to be heard! Is that patriotic? I'll let the market basket be the judge!'

" 'I'm simply vexed!' said the market basket. 'I'm as deeply vexed as anyone can imagine! Is this a fitting way to spend an evening? Wouldn't it be better to put the house to rights? Then everyone would find his place, and I'd run the whole caboodle! Then there'd be another song and dance!'

" 'Yes, let's raise a rumpus!' they all said. At the same moment the door opened. It was the maid, and so they stood still. There wasn't a peep out of anyone. But there wasn't a pot there that didn't know what it was capable of doing or how distinguished it was.

" 'Yes, if only I'd wanted to,' each thought, 'it really would have been a lively evening!'

"The maid took the matches and made a fire with them! Heavens, how they sputtered and burst into flames!

" 'Now,' they thought, 'everyone can see that we're the first! What a radiance we have! What a light!' And then they were burned out."

"That was a delightful story!" said the queen. "I felt just as if I were in the kitchen with the matches! Yes, now thou shalt have our daughter!"

"Certainly!" said the king. "Thou shalt have our daughter on Monday!" They said "thou" to him now that he was going to be one of the family.

And thus the wedding was decided; on the evening before, the entire city was illuminated. Buns and cakes were thrown out to be scrambled for. The street urchins stood on tiptoe, shouted "Hurrah!" and whistled through their fingers.

It was truly magnificent.

"Well, I guess I'd better see about doing something too," thought the merchant's son, and then he bought rockets, torpedoes, and all the fireworks you can imagine, put them in his trunk, and flew up in the air with them.

SWOOOOOOOOSH! How they went off! And how they popped!

It made all the Turks hop in the air so their slippers flew about their ears. They'd never seen a vision like this before. Now they could tell that it was the God of the Turks himself who was going to marry the princess.

As soon as the merchant's son had come back down in the forest again with his trunk, he thought, "I'll just go into the city to find out how it looked!" And of course it was only reasonable that he wanted to do that.

My, how people were talking! Every last person he asked had seen it, in his own fashion, but they all thought it had been delightful!

"I saw the God of the Turks himself!" said one. "He had eyes like shining stars and a beard like frothy water!"

"He flew in a fiery robe!" said another. "The loveliest cherubs were peeking out from among the folds!"

Indeed, those were delightful things he heard, and on the following day he was to be married.

Now he went back to the forest to seat himself in the trunk—but where was it?

The trunk had burned up! A spark from the fireworks had remained and set it on fire, and the trunk was in

ashes. No longer could he fly, no longer could he come to his bride.

She stood all day on the roof and waited. She's waiting still while he's wandering about the world telling stories. But they're no longer as gay as the one he told about the matches.

The Rose Elf

❖   ❖   ❖

IN the middle of a garden there grew a rosebush. It was quite full of roses, and in one of these, the most beautiful of them all, there dwelled an elf. He was so teeny-weeny that no human eye could see him; behind each petal of the rose he had a bedchamber. He was as well shaped and delightful as any child could be, and he had wings from his shoulders all the way down to his feet. Oh, what a fragrance there was in his chamber, and how bright and lovely were the walls! After all, they were the pale red, delicate rose petals.

All day long he amused himself in the warm sunshine flying from flower to flower, dancing on the wings of the fluttering butterfly, and counting the number of steps he had to take to run across all the highways and paths to be found on a single linden leaf. He regarded what we call the veins of the leaf as highways and paths, and indeed they were endless roads to him. Before he had finished, the sun had gone down, but then he had started so late.

It grew so cold; the dew was falling and the wind was blowing. The best thing to do now was to go home! He hurried as fast as he could, but the rose had closed and he wasn't able to come in—not a single rose was open; the poor little elf became so frightened, for he had never been out at night before and had always slept so soundly behind the sheltered rose petals. Oh, this would certainly be the death of him!

At the other end of the garden, he knew, there was a bower of lovely honeysuckle. The flowers looked like big painted horns; he would climb into one of these and sleep until morning.

He flew there. Shhhh! Two people were inside: a hand-

some young man and the loveliest of maidens. They were sitting side by side, wishing that they would never be parted. They were so much in love with each other, much more than the best of children can love his father and mother.

"And yet we must part!" said the young man. "Your brother has it in for us, so he's sending me on an errand far away over the mountains and seas! Farewell, my sweet bride, for that is what you are to me!"

And then they kissed each other, and the young maiden

wept and gave him a rose. But before she handed it to him she pressed so firm and fervent a kiss upon it that the flower opened. Then the little elf flew inside and leaned his head against the delicate, fragrant walls. But he could hear very well that they were saying: "Farewell! Farewell!" And he could feel the rose being placed at the young man's breast. Oh, how his heart was pounding inside! The little elf couldn't fall asleep, it was pounding so!

The rose didn't remain at the young man's breast long. He took it off, and as he walked alone through the dark forest he kissed the flower so often and so fervently that the little elf came close to being crushed to death. He could feel through the petals how the young man's lips were burning, and the rose had opened as in the heat of the strongest noonday sun.

Now came another man, dark and angry. He was the lovely maiden's evil brother. He drew a big sharp knife, and as the other was kissing the rose the evil man stabbed him to death, cut off his head, and buried it with the body in the soft earth under a linden tree.

"Now he's gone and forgotten!" thought the evil brother. "He'll never come back again. He was going to take a long journey over mountains and seas. Then it's easy to lose one's life, and so he has! He won't be back, and my sister will never dare to ask me about him!"

Then with his foot he scattered withered leaves over the upturned earth and went back home in the dark night. But he didn't go alone as he thought—the little elf went with him. He was sitting in a withered, curled-up linden leaf that had fallen on the hair of the evil man as he was digging the grave. The hat had been placed over him now. It was so dark in there, and the elf was trembling with fright and rage at that odious deed.

The evil man came home at daybreak; he took off his hat and went into his sister's bedroom. There lay the lovely maiden, in the bloom of youth, dreaming about the one she loved so much, and who she now thought was going over mountains and through forests. And the evil brother leaned over her, laughing nastily as only a devil can laugh. Then the withered leaf fell out of his hair and onto the cover, but he didn't notice it and went out, to get a little sleep in the early-morning hours. But the elf popped out of the withered leaf, went into the sleeping girl's ear, told her—as if in a dream—about the horrible murder, described the spot to her where the brother had killed him and left his body, told about the blossoming linden tree close by, and said, "So that you do not think what I have told you is a dream, you will find a withered leaf on your bed." And this is what she found when she awoke.

Oh, how she cried salt tears now! And she dared not confide her grief in anyone. The window stood open all day; the little elf could easily have gone out into the garden to the roses and all the other flowers, but he didn't have the heart to leave the grief-stricken girl. In the window was standing a bush of monthly roses. He seated himself in one of the flowers and looked at the poor girl. Her brother came into the room many times, and he was merry and evil, but she dared not say a word about her broken heart.

As soon as it was night she slipped out of the house, went into the forest to the spot where the linden tree stood, swept the leaves away from the dirt, dug down in it, and found at once the one who had been killed. Oh, how she wept and prayed to the Lord to let her die soon.

She wanted to take the body home with her, but she wasn't able to do it. But then she picked up the pale head with the closed eyes, kissed the cold lips, and shook the dirt out of his beautiful hair.

"I want this!" she said, and after covering the dead body with dirt and leaves, she took home with her the head and a little twig of the jasmine that blossomed in the forest where he had been killed.

As soon as she was in her room, she fetched the biggest flowerpot she could find, and putting the dead man's head in it, she covered it with earth and then planted the twig of jasmine in the pot.

"Farewell! Farewell!" whispered the little elf. He could no longer bear to see so much grief, and so he flew out into the garden to his rose. But it had withered, and only a few pale petals were hanging to the green hip.

"Alas, how soon everything that is beautiful and good comes to an end!" sighed the elf. At last he found another rose. This became his dwelling, behind its delicate, fragrant petals he could stay.

Every morning he flew over to the window of the unfortunate girl, and she was always standing there crying by the flowerpot. The salt tears fell on the jasmine branch, and for every day that she grew paler and paler, the branch became fresher and greener; one shoot after the other grew out; little white buds turned into blossoms and she kissed them. But the evil brother scolded her and asked if she weren't being silly; he didn't like it, nor could he know whose eyes had been closed and whose red lips had turned to dust. And she rested her head against the flowerpot, and the little elf from the rose found her dozing there. Then he climbed into her ear and told her about the evening in the bower, about the fragrance of the roses, and the love of the elves. She had such a sweet dream, and as she was dreaming her life faded away. She had died a peaceful death; she was in heaven with the one she loved.

And the jasmine blossoms opened their big white bells and shed a strange fragrance; this was their only way of weeping for the dead.

But the evil brother looked at the beautiful flowering tree and took it for himself as an inheritance. He put it in his room next to his bed, for it was so lovely to look at and the fragrance was so sweet and delicious. The little rose elf went along too, flying from blossom to blossom. In each one dwelled a tiny soul, and he told them all about the murdered young man, whose head had now turned to dust, and about the evil brother and the unfortunate sister.

"We know it," said all the souls in the blossoms. "We know it! Haven't we sprung forth from the dead man's eyes and lips? We know it! We know it!" And they nodded their heads in such a curious fashion.

The rose elf couldn't understand how they could remain so calm, and he flew out to the bees, who were gathering honey, and told them the story about the evil brother. And the bees told their queen, who ordered them all to kill the murderer the next morning.

But that night—it was the first night after the sister's death—as the brother was sleeping in his bed next to the fragrant jasmine tree, each flower opened its cup; and invisible, but with a poisonous spear, each flower soul climbed out. First they sat by his ear and told him bad dreams, and then they flew over his lips and stuck his tongue with the poisonous spears. "Now we have avenged the dead!" they said, and returned to the jasmine's white bells.

In the morning, when the window to the bedroom was suddenly thrown open, the rose elf and the queen bee with the whole swarm of bees flew in to kill him.

But he was already dead. People were standing around the bed, and they said, "The jasmine odor has killed him!"

Then the rose elf understood the revenge of the flowers. And he told the queen bee, and she and the whole swarm flew buzzing around the flowerpot. The bees were not to be ousted. Then a man took the flowerpot away, but one of the bees stung him on the hand, making him drop the pot, and it broke.

Then they saw the white skull and knew that the dead man in the bed was a murderer.

And the queen bee buzzed in the air and sang about the revenge of the flowers and about the rose elf, and that behind each tiny petal there dwells one who knows how to reveal and to avenge evil.

The Evil Prince
(A Legend)

❖ ❖ ❖

THERE was once an evil and overbearing prince whose only thought was to conquer all the lands of the world and strike terror with his name; he fared forth with fire and sword; his soldiers trampled down the grain in the field; they set fire to the farmer's house and saw the red flame lick the leaves from the trees and the fruit hang scorched on the black, charred branches. Many a poor mother hid with her naked, nursing babe behind the smoking wall, and the soldiers hunted for her; and if they found her and the child, their fiendish pleasures began. Evil spirits could not have behaved worse; but the prince thought that this was just as it should be. Day by day his power grew; his name was feared by everyone and success followed him in all his deeds. From the conquered cities he took gold and great treasures. In his royal residence were amassed riches, the like of which was nowhere to be found. Now he had erected magnificent castles, churches, and arches, and everyone who saw these splendors said, "What a great prince!" They did not think of the misery he had brought upon other lands; they did not hear the sighs and the wails that went up from the scorched cities.

The prince looked at his gold, looked at his magnificent buildings, and thought, as the mob, "What a great prince! But I must have more! Much more! No power must be

110

mentioned as equal to mine, much less greater!" And he went to war against all his neighbors and conquered them all. He had the vanquished kings fettered to his carriage with golden chains as he drove through the streets, and when he sat down at the table, they had to lie at his feet and at the feet of his courtiers and take the pieces of bread that were thrown to them.

Now the prince had his statue erected in the squares and in the royal palace. Yes, he even wanted it to stand in the churches before the altar of the Lord. But the priests said, "Prince, you are mighty, but God is mightier. We dare not do it."

"Well," said the evil prince, "then I am going to conquer God too!" And with overweening pride and folly in his heart, he had a remarkable ship built that he could fly through the air with. It was as brightly colored as the tail of a peacock and appeared to be encrusted with a thousand eyes. But each eye was the barrel of a gun. The prince sat in the middle of the ship; he had only to push a spring and a thousand bullets flew out, and the guns were again loaded as before. A hundred strong eagles were attached to the front of the ship, and in this fashion he flew up toward the sun. The earth lay far below; at first, with its mountains and forests, it resembled a plowed-up field where the green peeps forth from the overturned turf. Then it looked like a flat map, and soon it was quite hidden in fog and clouds. Higher and higher flew the eagles. Then God dispatched a single one of his myriads of angels, and the evil prince let fly a thousand bullets at him. But the bullets fell off the angel's shining wings like hail. A drop of blood—only a single one—dripped from the wing feather, and this drop fell on the ship in which the prince was sitting. It burned itself fast; it was as heavy as a thousand hundredweights of lead and swept the ship down toward the earth at breakneck speed. The strong wings of the eagles were broken, the wind rushed around

the prince's head, and the clouds that were all around—
after all, they were from the burned cities—took on threatening shapes, like mile-long crayfish that stretched out
their strong claws after him, like rolling boulders or fire-
spouting dragons. Half dead, he lay in the ship, which was
caught at last among the thick branches of the forest.

"I will vanquish God!" he said. "I have sworn it; my will
shall be done!" And for seven years he had remarkable
ships constructed that would fly through the air. He had
thunderbolts forged from the hardest steel, because he
wanted to blow up the fortress of heaven. From all his
lands he gathered a great army, which covered a radius of
several miles when the men stood lined up. They climbed
into the remarkable ships. The prince himself was ap-
proaching his when God sent out a swarm of mosquitoes, a

little swarm of mosquitoes. They buzzed around the prince and bit him on the face and hands. In a rage he drew his sword, but struck out at the empty air. He couldn't touch the mosquitoes. Then he ordered costly carpets to be brought. They were to be wrapped around him—no mosquito could penetrate them with its sting—and this was done as he ordered. But a single mosquito was sitting on the innermost carpet. It crawled into the prince's ear and bit him there. It seared like fire; the poison surged up to his brain. He tore himself loose, yanked off the carpets, ripped his clothes to shreds, and danced naked in front of the brutal, barbarous soldiers that were now mocking the mad prince, who wanted to pester God and was vanquished by a single little mosquito.

The Swineherd

❖   ❖   ❖

THERE was once a poor prince. He had a kingdom that was quite small, but then it was big enough to get married on, and marry he would.

Now it was, of course, a bit presumptuous of him to dare to say to the emperor's daughter: "Will you have me?" But that he dared, all right, for his name was known far and wide, and there were hundreds of princesses who would have been glad to have him. But see if she was!

Now we shall hear.

On the grave of the prince's father there grew a rose-bush. Oh, such a lovely rosebush! It bore flowers every fifth year, and then only a single rose. But it was a rose that smelled so sweet that by smelling it one forgot all one's cares and woes. And then he had a nightingale that could sing as though all the lovely melodies in the world were in its little throat. That rose and that nightingale the princess was to have, and so they were put into two big silver cases and sent to her.

The emperor had them brought in before him to the great hall, where the princess was playing "Visitors" with her ladies-in-waiting—they had nothing else to do—and when she saw the big cases with the presents inside, she clapped her hands for joy.

"If only it were a little pussycat!" she said—but then out came the lovely rose.

"My, how nicely it has been made!" said all the ladies-in-waiting.

"It is more than nice," said the emperor, "it is beautiful!"

But the princess touched it, and then she was on the verge of tears.

"Fie, Papa!" she said. "It's not artificial! It's real."

"Fie!" said all the ladies-in-waiting. "It's real!"

"Now, let us first see what is in the other case before we lose our tempers," thought the emperor, and then the nightingale came out. It sang so sweetly that to begin with no one could find fault with it.

"*Superbe! Charmante!*" said the ladies-in-waiting, for they all spoke French, each one worse than the other.

"How that bird reminds me of the late-lamented empress' music box," said one old courtier. "Ahhh yes, it is quite the same tune, the same rendering."

"Yes," said the emperor, and then he cried like a little baby.

"I should hardly like to think that it's real," said the princess.

"Why, yes, it is a real bird," said the people who had brought it.

"Well, then, let that bird go!" said the princess, and she would in no way permit the prince to come.

But he didn't lose heart. He stained his face brown and black, and pulling his cap down over his eyes, he knocked at the door.

"Good morning, Emperor!" he said. "Can't you take me into your service here at the palace?"

"Well, there are so many who apply here," said the emperor. "But—let me see—I need someone to keep the pigs, for we have a lot of them."

And so the prince was hired as the imperial swineherd. He was given a wretched little room down by the pigsty, and there he had to stay. But the whole day he sat working, and by the time it was evening he had made a pretty little pot. Around it were bells, and as soon as the pot boiled they started ringing delightfully and played an old tune:

> *Ach, du lieber Augustin,*
> *Alles ist weg! Weg! Weg!*[1]

But the most curious thing of all, however, was that anyone holding his finger in the steam from the pot could smell at once what food was cooking on every stove in the town, so that was certainly a far cry from a rose.

Now the princess came walking along with all her ladies-in-waiting, and when she heard the tune, she stood still and looked very pleased, for she could also play "Ach, du lieber Augustin." It was the only tune she knew, and she played it with one finger.

"Why, that's the tune I can play!" she said. "This must be a cultivated swineherd! Listen! Go in and ask him what that instrument costs."

And then one of the ladies-in-waiting had to run in, but she put on wooden shoes.

"What will you have for that pot?" said the lady-in-waiting.

"I want ten kisses from the princess," said the swineherd.

"Heaven help us!" said the lady-in-waiting.

"Well, it can't be less," said the swineherd.

"Now! What does he say?" asked the princess.

"That I really can't tell you!" said the lady-in-waiting. "It is too horrible!"

"Then you can whisper!" And so she whispered.

"Why, how rude he is!" said the princess, and left at once. But when she had gone a little way, the bells tinkled so prettily:

---

[1] Ah, dear Augustine,
 All is over and done! Done! Done!

Ach, du lieber Augustin,
Alles ist weg! Weg! Weg!

"Listen," said the princess. "Ask him if he will take ten kisses from my ladies-in-waiting."

"No, thanks!" said the swineherd. "Ten kisses from the princess, or else I keep the pot."

"How really vexatious!" said the princess. "But then you must stand around me so that no one sees it."

And the ladies-in-waiting lined up in front of her and spread out their skirts, and then the swineherd got the ten kisses and she got the pot.

Oh, what fun they had! All that evening and the next day the pot had to boil. They knew what was cooking on every stove in the whole town, whether at the chamberlain's or at the shoemaker's. The ladies-in-waiting danced and clapped their hands.

"We know who's going to have fruit soup and pancakes! We know who's going to have porridge and meatballs! Oh, how interesting!"

"Extremely interesting," said the mistress of the robes.

"Yes, but keep it a secret, for I am the emperor's daughter!"

"Heaven help us!" they all said.

The swineherd—that is to say, the prince, but they didn't know, of course, that he was anything but a real swineherd—didn't let the next day pass before he had made something else, and this time he made a rattle. Whenever anyone swung it around, it played all the waltzes and quadrilles and polkas that were known since the creation of the world.

"But that is *superbe!*" said the princess as she went by. "I have never heard a lovelier composition! Listen, go in and ask what that instrument costs. But no kissing!"

"He wants a hundred kisses from the princess!" said the lady-in-waiting who had been inside to ask.

"I do believe he's mad!" said the princess. And then she left. But after she had gone a little way, she stopped. "One should encourage the arts!" she said. "I *am* the emperor's daughter. Tell him he shall get ten kisses just like yesterday. The rest he can take from my ladies-in-waiting."

"Yes, but not unless we have to!" said the ladies-in-waiting.

"That's just talk!" said the princess. "If I can kiss him, then you can too! Remember, I give you board and wages!" And then the lady-in-waiting had to go in to him again.

"One hundred kisses from the princess," he said, "or else each keeps what he has!"

"Stand in front!" she said. So all the ladies-in-waiting lined up in front of her, and then he started kissing.

"What can all that commotion be down by the pigsty?" said the emperor, who had stepped out onto the balcony. He rubbed his eyes and put on his glasses. "Why, it's the ladies-in-waiting! They're up to something. I certainly must go down to them!" And then he pulled his slippers up in back, for they were shoes that he had worn down at the heel.

My, how he hurried!

As soon as he came down into the courtyard he walked quite softly, and the ladies-in-waiting were so busy counting the kisses to make sure there was fair play—so he shouldn't get too many, but not too few, either—that they didn't notice the emperor at all. He stood up on tiptoe.

"What on earth!" he said when he saw them kissing, and then he hit them on the head with his slipper just as the swineherd got the eighty-sixth kiss. "*Heraus!*"[2] said the emperor, for he was furious, and both the swineherd and the princess were put out of his empire.

There she stood now and cried, the swineherd swore, and the rain poured down.

----

[2] "Get out!"

"Ohhhh, what a miserable soul I am," said the princess. "If only I'd taken that lovely prince! Ohhhh, how unhappy I am!"

And the swineherd went behind a tree, wiped away the brown and black from his face, threw away the ugly clothes, and stepped forth in his prince's clothing, looking so handsome that the princess had to curtsy to him.

"I have come to despise you," he said. "You wouldn't have an honest prince! You didn't understand about the rose and the nightingale, but you could kiss the swineherd for a mechanical music box! Now it serves you right!"

And then he went into his kingdom and closed and bolted the door, so she really could stand outside and sing:

> *"Ach, du lieber Augustin,*
> *Alles ist weg! Weg! Weg!"*

The Nightingale

❖   ❖   ❖

I N China, you know of course, the emperor is Chinese, and everyone he has around him is Chinese too. Now this happened many years ago, but that is just why the story is worth hearing, before it is forgotten. The emperor's palace was the most magnificent in the world. It was made entirely of fine porcelain, so precious and so fragile and delicate that one really had to watch one's step. In the garden the most unusual flowers were to be seen, and the most beautiful had fastened to them silver bells that tinkled so that no one would go past without noticing them. Yes, everything had been very well thought out in the emperor's garden, and it stretched so far that even the gardener didn't know where it stopped. If one kept on walking, one came to the loveliest forest with great trees and deep lakes. The forest stretched all the way down to the sea, which was blue and so deep that great ships could sail right in under the branches. And in these branches lived a nightingale that sang so sweetly that even the poor fisherman, who had so many other things to keep him busy, lay still and listened when he was out at night pulling in his net.

"Good heavens! How beautiful!" he said. But then he had to look after his net and forgot the bird, although the next night, when it sang again and the fisherman came out there, he said the same thing: "Good heavens! How beautiful!"

From every land in the world travelers came to the emperor's city. They admired the city, the palace, and the garden. But when they heard the nightingale, they all said: "But this is really the best thing of all!" And the travelers told about it when they got home, and scholars wrote many books about the city, the palace, and the garden. But they didn't forget the nightingale—it was given the highest place of all. And those who were poets wrote the loveliest poems, each one about the nightingale in the forest by the sea.

These books went around the world, and once some of them came to the emperor. He sat in his golden chair, reading and reading and nodding his head, for he was pleased by the lovely descriptions of the city, the palace, and the garden. "But the nightingale is really the best thing of all"—there it stood in print.

"What's that?" said the emperor. "The nightingale? Why, I don't know anything about it! Is there such a bird in my empire, in my very own garden? I have never heard of it before! Fancy having to find this out from a book!"

And then he summoned his chamberlain, who was so grand that if anyone of lower rank dared speak to him or ask about something, he would only say: "P!" And that doesn't mean anything at all.

"There is supposed to be a highly remarkable bird here called a nightingale!" said the emperor. "They say it's the very best thing of all in my great kingdom! Why hasn't anyone ever told me about it?"

"I have never heard it mentioned before!" said the chamberlain. "It has never been presented at court!"

"I want it to come here this evening and sing for me," said the emperor. "The whole world knows what I have, and I don't!"

"I have never heard it mentioned before!" said the chamberlain. "I shall look for it! I shall find it!"

But where was it to be found? The chamberlain ran up and down all the stairs, through great halls and corridors. But no one he met had ever heard of the nightingale, and the chamberlain ran back again to the emperor and said it was probably a fable made up by the people who write books. "Your Imperial Majesty shouldn't believe what is written in them. They are inventions and belong to something called black magic!"

"But the book in which I read it was sent to me by the mighty emperor of Japan, so it cannot be false. I will hear the nightingale! It shall be here this evening! I bestow my highest patronage upon it! And if it doesn't come, I'll have the whole court thumped on their stomachs after they have eaten supper!"

"Tsing-pe!" said the chamberlain, and again ran up and down all the stairs and through all the great halls and corridors. And half the court ran with him, for they weren't at all willing to be thumped on their stomachs. They asked and asked about the remarkable nightingale that was known to the whole world but not to the court.

Finally they met a little peasant girl in the kitchen. She said, "The nightingale? Heavens! I know it well. Yes, how it can sing! Every evening I'm permitted to take a few scraps from the table home to my poor sick mother—she lives down by the shore. And on my way back, when I'm tired and stop to rest in the forest, I can hear the nightingale sing. It brings tears to my eyes. It's just as though my mother were kissing me."

"Little kitchen maid!" said the chamberlain. "You shall have a permanent position in the kitchen and permission to stand and watch the emperor eating if you can lead us to the nightingale. It has been summoned to appear at court this evening."

And so they all set out for the part of the forest where

the nightingale usually sang. Half the court went with them. As they were walking along at a fast pace a cow started mooing.

"Oh!" said a courtier. "There it is! Indeed, what remarkable force for so tiny an animal. I am certain I have heard it before."

"No, that's the cow mooing," said the little kitchen maid. "We're still quite a long way from the spot."

Now the frogs started croaking in the marsh.

"Lovely," said the Chinese imperial chaplain. "Now I can hear her. It's just like tiny church bells."

"No, that's the frogs!" said the little kitchen maid. "But now I think we'll soon hear it."

Then the nightingale started to sing.

"That's it!" said the little girl. "Listen! Listen! There it sits!" And then she pointed to a little gray bird up in the branches.

"Is it possible?" said the chamberlain. "I had never imagined it like this. How ordinary it looks! No doubt seeing so many fine people has made it lose its *couleur!*"

"Little nightingale," shouted the little kitchen maid quite loud, "our gracious emperor would so like you to sing for him!"

"With the greatest pleasure," said the nightingale, and sang in a way to warm one's heart.

"It is just like glass bells!" said the chamberlain. "And look at that tiny throat. How it vibrates! It's remarkable that we have never heard it before. It will be a great success at court."

"Shall I sing for the emperor again?" said the nightingale, who thought the emperor was there.

"My enchanting little nightingale," said the chamberlain, "it gives me the greatest pleasure to command you to appear at a court celebration this evening, where you will delight his High Imperial Eminence with your *charmante* song!"

"It sounds best out of doors," said the nightingale, but it followed them gladly when it heard it was the emperor's wish.

The palace had been properly polished up. Walls and floors, which were of porcelain, glowed from the lights of thousands of golden lamps. The loveliest flowers, which really could tinkle, had been lined up in the halls. There was such a running back and forth that it caused a draft that made all the bells tinkle so one couldn't hear oneself think.

In the middle of the great hall, where the emperor sat, a golden perch had been placed for the nightingale to sit on. The whole court was there, and the little kitchen maid had been given permission to stand behind the door, for now she really did have the title of kitchen maid. Everyone was wearing his most splendid attire. They all looked at the little gray bird, to which the emperor was nodding.

And the nightingale sang so sweetly that tears came to the emperor's eyes and rolled down his cheeks. And then the nightingale sang even more sweetly. It went straight to one's heart. And the emperor was so pleased that he said the nightingale was to have his golden slipper to wear around its neck. But the nightingale said no, thank you—it had been rewarded enough.

"I have seen tears in the emperor's eyes. To me, that is the richest treasure. An emperor's tears have a wondrous power. Heaven knows I have been rewarded enough!" And then it sang again with its sweet and blessed voice.

"That is the most adorable *coquetterie* I know of," said the ladies standing around. And then they put water in their mouths so they could gurgle whenever anyone spoke to them, for now they thought that they were nightingales too. Yes, even the lackeys and chambermaids let it be known that they were also satisfied, and that was saying a lot, for they are the hardest to please. Yes indeed, the nightingale had really been a success.

Now it was to remain at court and have its own cage as well as freedom to take a walk outside twice during the day and once at night. It was given twelve servants, too, each one holding tightly to a silken ribbon fastened to its leg. That kind of walk was no pleasure at all.

The whole city talked about the remarkable bird, and whenever two people met, the first merely said "Night!" and the other said "Gale!" And then they sighed and understood each other! Yes, eleven shopkeepers' children were named after it, but not one of them could ever sing a note in his life!

One day a big package came for the emperor. On the outside was written "Nightingale."

"Here's a new book about our famous bird," said the emperor. But it was no book, it was a little work of art in a case: an artificial nightingale made to resemble the real one, except that it was encrusted with diamonds and rubies and sapphires! As soon as the artificial bird was wound up it could sing one of the melodies the real one sang, and then its tail bobbed up and down, glittering with gold and silver. Around its neck hung a ribbon, and on it was written: "The emperor of Japan's nightingale is poor compared to the emperor of China's."

"How lovely!" said everyone. And the person who had brought the artificial nightingale immediately had the title of chief-imperial-nightingale-bringer bestowed upon him.

"Now they must sing together! What a duet that will be!"

And then they had to sing together, but it didn't really come off because the real nightingale sang in its own way and the artificial bird worked mechanically.

"It is not to blame," said the music master. "It keeps time perfectly and according to the rules of my own system!" Then the artificial bird had to sing alone. It was as much of a success as the real one, and besides, it was so much more beautiful to look at: it glittered like bracelets and brooches.

Thirty-three times it sang one and the same melody, and still it wasn't tired. People were only too willing to hear it from the beginning again, but the emperor thought that now the living nightingale should also sing a little. But where was it? No one had noticed it fly out of the open window, away to its green forest.

"But what kind of behavior is that?" said the emperor. And all the courtiers berated it and said the nightingale was a most ungrateful bird.

"We still have the best bird," they said, and again the artificial bird had to sing. And it was the thirty-fourth time they had heard the same tune, but they didn't know it all the way through yet, for it was so hard. And the music master praised the bird very highly—yes, even assured them that it was better than the real nightingale, not only as far as its clothes and the many diamonds were concerned, but internally as well.

"You see, my lords and ladies, and your Imperial Majesty above all! You can never figure out what the real nightingale will sing, but with the artificial bird everything has already been decided. This is the way it will be, and not otherwise. It can be accounted for; it can be opened up to reveal the human logic that has gone into the arrangement of the works, how they operate and how they turn one after the other!"

"Those are my thoughts precisely!" they all said. And on the following Sunday the music master was allowed to show the bird to the people. They were also going to hear it sing, said the emperor. And they heard it and were as happy as if they had all drunk themselves merry on tea, for that is so very Chinese. And then they all said "Oh" and held their index fingers high in the air and nodded. But the poor fisherman, who had heard the real nightingale, said: "It sounds pretty enough, and it is similar too. But something is missing. I don't know what it is."

The real nightingale was banished from the land.

The artificial bird had its place on a silken pillow close to the emperor's bed. All the gifts it had received, gold and precious stones, lay around it, and its title had risen to high-imperial-bedside-table-singer. It ranked Number One on the left, for the emperor considered the side where the heart lies to be the most important. And the heart of an emperor is on the left side too. The music master wrote a treatise in twenty-five volumes about the artificial bird. It was very learned and very long and contained the biggest Chinese words, and all the people said they had read and understood it, for otherwise they would have been considered stupid and would have been thumped on their stomachs.

It went on like this for a whole year. The emperor, the

court, and all the other Chinese knew every little "cluck" in the song of the artificial bird by heart. But this is why they prized it so highly now: they could sing along with it themselves, and this they did! The street boys sang "Zizizi! Cluck-cluck-cluck!" And the emperor sang it too. Yes, it was certainly lovely.

But one evening, as the artificial bird was singing away and the emperor was lying in bed listening to it, something went "Pop!" inside the bird. "Whirrrrrrrrrrr!" All the wheels went around, and then the music stopped.

The emperor sprang out of bed and had his personal physician summoned. But what good was he? Then they summoned the watchmaker, and after much talk and many examinations of the bird he put it more or less in order again. But he said it must be used as sparingly as possible. The cogs were so worn down that it wasn't possible to put in new ones in a way that would be sure to make music. What a great affliction this was! Only once a year did they dare let the artificial bird sing, and even that was hard on it. But then the music master made a little speech, with big words, and said it was just as good as new, and then it *was* just as good as new.

Five years passed, and then a great sorrow fell upon the land. They were all fond of their emperor, but now he was sick and it was said he could not live. A new emperor had already been picked out, and people stood out in the street and asked the chamberlain how their emperor was.

"P!" he said, and shook his head.

Cold and pale, the emperor lay in his great magnificent bed. The whole court thought he was dead, and they all ran off to greet the new emperor. The lackeys ran out to talk about it, and the chambermaids had a big tea party. Cloths had been put down in all the halls and corridors to deaden the sound of footsteps. And now it was so quiet, so quiet. But the emperor was not yet dead. Stiff and pale, he lay in the magnificent bed with the long velvet curtains and the heavy gold tassels. High above him a window stood open, and the moon shone in on the emperor and the artificial bird.

The poor emperor could hardly breathe. It was as though something heavy were sitting on his chest. He opened his eyes and then he saw that Death was sitting on his chest. He had put on his golden crown and was holding the emperor's golden sword in one hand and his magnificent banner in the other. All around from the folds of the velvet curtains strange faces were peering out. Some were quite hideous, others so kindly and mild. These were all the emperor's good and wicked deeds that were looking at him now that Death was sitting on his heart.

"Do you remember that?" whispered one after the other. "Do you remember that?" And then they told him so much that the sweat stood out on his forehead.

"I never knew that!" said the emperor. "Music! Music! The big Chinese drum!" he shouted. "So I don't have to hear all the things they're saying!"

But they kept it up, and Death nodded, just the way the Chinese do, at everything that was being said.

"Music! Music!" shrieked the emperor. "Blessed little golden bird, sing now! Sing! I've given you gold and costly presents. I myself hung my golden slipper around your neck. Sing now! Sing!"

But the bird kept silent. There was no one to wind it up, so it didn't sing. But Death kept on looking at the emperor out of his big empty sockets, and it was so quiet, so terribly quiet.

Suddenly the loveliest song could be heard close to the window. It was the little real nightingale sitting on the branch outside. It had heard of the emperor's need and had come to sing him comfort and hope. And as it sang the face became paler and paler, and the blood started flowing faster and faster in the emperor's weak body, and Death himself listened and said, "Keep on, little nightingale, keep on!"

"If you will give me the magnificent golden sword! If you will give me the rich banner! If you will give me the emperor's crown!"

And Death gave each treasure for a song, and the nightingale kept on singing. And it sang about the quiet churchyard where the white roses grow and the scent of the elder tree perfumes the air and where the fresh grass is watered by the tears of the bereaved. Then Death was filled with longing for his garden and drifted like a cold, white mist out of the window.

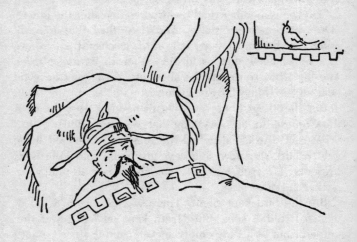

"Thank you, thank you!" said the emperor. "Heavenly little bird, I know you, all right. I have driven you out of my land and empire, and still you have sung the bad visions away from my bed and removed Death from my heart! How can I reward you?"

"You have already rewarded me!" said the nightingale. "You gave me the tears from your eyes the first time I

sang. I will never forget that. Those are the jewels that do
a singer's heart good. But sleep now, and get well and
strong. I shall sing for you."

And it sang, and the emperor fell into a sweet sleep,
which was calm and beneficial.

The sun was shining in on him through the windows
when he awoke, refreshed and healthy. None of his servants had returned yet, for they thought he was dead, but
the nightingale still sat there and sang.

"You must always stay with me," said the emperor.
"You shall sing only when you yourself want to, and I shall
break the artificial bird into a thousand bits!"

"Don't do that!" said the nightingale. "Why, it has done
what good it could. Keep it as before. I cannot build my
nest and live at the palace, but let me come whenever I
want to. Then in the evening I will sit on the branch here
by the window and sing for you. I shall sing about those
who are happy and those who suffer. I shall sing of good
and evil, which is kept hidden from you. The little songbird flies far, to the poor fisherman, to the farmer's roof,
to everyone who is far from you and your court. I love
your heart more than your crown, and yet your crown has
an odor of sanctity about it. I will come. I will sing for
you. But you must promise me one thing!"

"Everything!" said the emperor, standing there in his
imperial robe, which he himself had put on, and holding
the heavy golden sword up to his heart.

"One thing I beg of you. Tell no one that you have a
little bird that tells you everything! Then things will go
even better!"

And then the nightingale flew away.

The servants came in to have a look at their dead
emperor. Yes, there they stood, and the emperor said,
"Good morning!"

The Sweethearts
(The Top and the Ball)

❖　　❖　　❖

THE top and the ball were lying in a drawer together
among other playthings, and so the top said to the
ball, "Shouldn't we be sweethearts, as long as we're lying
in a drawer together?"

But the ball, who had been sewn of morocco leather and
who put on just as many airs as a fashionable young lady,
would not reply to such a thing.

The next day the little boy who owned the playthings
came. He painted over the top red and gold, and ham-

mered a brass nail right in the middle. It was a magnificent sight when the top spun around.

"Look at me!" he said to the ball. "What do you say now? Shouldn't we be sweethearts? We go so well together. You spring and I dance! Happier than we no two could ever be!"

"So that's what you think!" said the ball. "I daresay you're unaware that my father and mother have been morocco leather slippers and that I have a cork inside!"

"Yes, but I am made of mahogany wood!" said the top. "And the bailiff himself has turned me out! He has his own lathe, and it afforded him great pleasure!"

"Indeed! Can I rely on that?" said the ball.

"May I never be whipped again if I'm lying!" said the top.

"You speak up quite well for yourself," said the ball, "but I can't, all the same. I'm as good as half engaged to a swallow. Every time I go up in the air he sticks his head out of the nest and says, 'Will you? Will you?' And now I've said yes to myself, and that's as good as being half engaged. But I promise I shall never forget you!"

"Well, that'll be a great help!" said the top, and then they stopped speaking to each other.

The next day the ball was taken out. The top saw how she flew high up in the air, just like a bird. At last she couldn't be seen at all. She came back again every time, but she always made a high jump when she touched the ground. And this came either from longing or because she had a cork inside. The ninth time the ball disappeared and didn't come back again. The boy searched and searched, but gone she was.

"I know where she is, all right," sighed the top. "She's in the swallow's nest and is married to the swallow!"

Indeed, the more the top thought about it, the more infatuated he became with the ball. Just because he couldn't have her, love began. And the queer thing about it was the fact that she had taken another! And the top danced and spun around, but he was always thinking of the ball, who, in his imagination, grew lovelier and lovelier. Thus many years passed—and then it was an old love affair.

And the top was no longer young! But one day he was gilded over. Never had he looked so lovely! Now he was a golden top, and he whirled until he hummed. Indeed, that was something! But all at once he whirled too high, and gone he was!

They searched and searched, even down in the cellar, but still he was nowhere to be found.

Where was he?

He had hopped up into the trash can, where all kinds of things were lying: cabbage stalks, sweepings, and rubble that had fallen down from the drainpipe.

"A fine place for me to be lying in, I must say! The gilding will soon come off. And what sort of rabble have I come among?" And then it stole a look at a long cabbage stalk that had come much too close and at a strange round thing that looked like an old apple. But it wasn't an apple. It was an old ball that had been lying in the drainpipe for many years, and through which the water had been oozing.

"Heaven be praised! Here comes one of my own kind that I can talk to!" said the ball, and regarded the gilded top. "I'm really of morocco leather, sewn by the hands of a maiden, and I have a cork inside! But no one can tell that by looking at me! I was just going to marry a swallow when I fell in the drainpipe, and there I've been lying for five years oozing water. For a maiden that's a long time, believe me!"

But the top didn't say a thing! He was thinking of his old sweetheart. And indeed, the more he listened, the more certain he became that this was she.

Then the serving girl came to empty the trash can. "Hey, now! There's the gold top!" she said.

And the top came back in the house, to high esteem and

honor. But no one heard anything about the ball, and the top never spoke about his old sweetheart again. That goes over when the sweetheart has been lying in a drainpipe oozing water for five years. Indeed, you never recognize her again if you meet her in the trash can!

The Ugly Duckling

❖　　❖　　❖

IT was so lovely out in the country—it was summer. The wheat stood golden, the oats green. The hay had been piled in stacks down in the green meadows, and there the stork went about on his long red legs and spoke Egyptian, for that is the language he had learned from his mother. Around the fields and meadows were great forests, and in the midst of the forests were deep lakes. Yes, it really was lovely out there in the country.

Squarely in the sunshine stood an old manor house with a deep moat all around it, and from the walls down to the water grew huge dock leaves that were so high that little children could stand upright under the biggest. It was as dense in there as in the deepest forest, and here sat a duck on her nest. She was about to hatch out her little ducklings, but now she had just about had enough of it because it was taking so long and she seldom had a visitor. The other ducks were fonder of swimming about in the moat than of running up and sitting under a dock leaf to chatter with her.

Finally one egg after the other started cracking. "Cheep! Cheep!" they said. All the egg yolks had come to life and stuck out their heads.

"Quack! Quack!" she said, and then they quacked as hard as they could and peered about on all sides under the green leaves. And their mother let them look about as much as they liked, for green is good for the eyes.

"My, how big the world is!" said all the youngsters, for now, of course, they had far more room than when they were inside the eggs.

"Do you think this is the whole world?" said the mother. "It stretches all the way to the other side of the garden, right into the parson's meadow. But I've never been there! Well, you're all here now, aren't you?" And then she got up. "No, I don't have them all! The biggest egg is still there. How long will it take? Now I'll soon get tired of it!" And then she settled down again.

"Well, how's it going?" said an old duck who had come to pay her a visit.

"One egg is taking so long!" said the duck who was hatching. "It won't crack! But now you shall see the others. They're the prettiest ducklings I've seen. They all look just like their father, the wretch! He doesn't even come to visit me."

"Let me see that egg that won't crack!" said the old duck. "You can be certain it's a turkey egg! I was fooled like that myself once. And I had my sorrows and troubles with those youngsters, for they're afraid of the water, I can tell you! I couldn't get them out in it! I quacked and I snapped, but it didn't help! Let me have a look at that egg! Yes, it's a turkey egg, all right. You just let it lie there and teach the other children how to swim."

"Oh, I still want to sit on it a little longer," said the duck. "I've been sitting on it for so long that I can just as well wait a little longer!"

"Suit yourself!" said the old duck, and then she left.

Finally the big egg cracked. "Cheep! Cheep!" said the youngster, and tumbled out. He was very big and ugly. The duck looked at him.

"Now, that's a terribly big duckling!" she said. "None of the others looks like that! Could he be a turkey chick after all? Well, we'll soon find out. Into the water he'll go if I have to kick him out into it myself!"

The next day the weather was perfect. The sun shone on all the green dock leaves. The mother duck came down to the moat with her whole family. Splash! She jumped into the water. "Quack! Quack!" she said, and one duckling after the other plumped in. The water washed over their heads, but they came up again at once and floated splendidly. Their feet moved of themselves, and they were all out in the water. Even the ugly gray youngster was swimming too.

"That's no turkey," she said. "See how splendidly he uses his legs, how straight he holds himself. That's my own child! As a matter of fact, he is quite handsome when one looks at him in the right way. Quack! Quack! Now come with me, and I'll take you out in the world and present you to the duck yard. But always keep close to me so that no one steps on you. And keep an eye out for the cat!"

And then they came to the duck yard. There was a terrible commotion, for two families were fighting over an eel's head, and then the cat got it, of course.

"See, that's the way it goes in this world," said the mother duck, and smacked her bill, for she would have liked to have had the eel's head herself. "Now use your legs," she said. "See if you can't step lively and bow your necks to that old duck over there. She's the most aristocratic of anyone here: she has Spanish blood in her veins. That's why she's so fat. And see? She has a red rag around her leg. That is something very special and is the highest honor any duck can receive. It means that no one wants to get rid of her and that she is to be recognized by animals and men! Be quick! Out with your toes! A well-brought-up duck places his feet wide apart, just like his father and mother. Now, then! Bow your necks and say 'Quack!' "

This they did, but the other ducks all around looked at

them and said quite loudly, "Look there! Now we're to have one more batch, as if there weren't enough of us already! And fie, how that duckling looks! We won't put up with him!" And at once a duck flew over and bit him in the neck.

"Leave him alone!" said the mother. "He's not bothering anyone."

"Yes, but he's too big and queer!" said the duck who had bitten him. "So he has to be pushed around."

"Those are pretty children the mother has," said the old duck with the rag around her leg. "They're all pretty except that one; he didn't turn out right. I do wish she could make him over again."

"That can't be, your grace," said the mother duck. "He's not pretty, but he has an exceedingly good disposition, and he swims as well as any of the others; yes, I might venture to say a bit better. I do believe he'll grow prettier or in time a little smaller. He's lain in the egg too long, so he hasn't got the right shape!" And then she ruffled his feathers and smoothed them down. "Besides, he's a drake, so it doesn't matter very much. I think he'll grow much stronger. He'll get along all right."

"The other ducklings are lovely," said the old duck. "Just make yourselves at home, and if you can find an eel's head, you may bring it to me!"

And so they made themselves quite at home.

But the poor duckling, who had been the last one out of the egg and looked so ugly, was bitten and shoved and ridiculed by both the ducks and the hens. "He's too big!" they all said. And the turkey cock, who had been born with spurs on and so believed himself to be an emperor, puffed himself up like a ship in full sail, went right up to him, and gobbled until he got quite red in the face. The poor duckling didn't know whether to stay or go. He was miserable because he was so ugly and was the laughingstock of the whole duck yard.

So the first day passed, but afterward it grew worse and worse. The poor duckling was chased by everyone. Even his brothers and sisters were nasty to him and were always saying: "If only the cat would get you, you ugly wretch!" And his mother said, "If only you were far away!" And the ducks bit him, and the hens pecked him, and the girl who fed the poultry kicked at him.

Then he ran and flew over the hedge. The little birds in the bushes flew up in fright. "It's because I'm so ugly!" thought the duckling, and shut his eyes, but he still kept on running. Then he came out into the big marsh where the wild ducks lived. He was so exhausted and unhappy that he lay there all night.

In the morning the wild ducks flew up and looked at their new comrade. "What kind of a duck are you?" they asked, and the duckling turned from one side to the other and greeted them as best he could.

"How ugly you are!" said the wild ducks. "But it makes no difference to us as long as you don't marry into our family!"

Poor thing! He certainly wasn't thinking about marriage. All he wanted was to be allowed to lie in the rushes and to drink a little water from the marsh.

There he lay for two whole days, and then there came two wild geese, or rather two wild ganders, for they were both males, not long out of the egg, and therefore they were quite saucy.

"Listen, comrade!" they said. "You're so ugly that you appeal to us. Want to come along and be a bird of passage? In another marsh close by are some sweet lovely wild geese, every single one unmarried, who can say 'Quack!' You're in a position to make your fortune, ugly as you are!"

Bang! Bang! Shots suddenly rang out above them, and both the wild geese fell down dead in the rushes, and the water was red with blood. Bang! Bang! It sounded again, and whole flocks of wild geese flew up out of the rushes, and the guns cracked again. A great hunt was on. The hunters lay around the marsh. Yes, some were even sitting up in the branches of the trees that hung over the water. The blue smoke drifted in among the dark trees and hovered over the water. Into the mud came the hunting dogs. Splash! Splash! Reeds and rushes swayed on all sides. The poor duckling was terrified. He turned his head to put it under his wing and at the same moment found himself standing face to face with a terribly big dog! Its tongue was hanging way out of its mouth, and its eyes gleamed horribly. It opened its jaws over the duckling, showed its sharp teeth, and—splash!—went on without touching him.

"Oh, heaven be praised!" sighed the duckling. "I'm so ugly that even the dog doesn't care to bite me!"

And then he lay quite still while the buckshot whistled through the rushes and shot after shot resounded.

Not until late in the day did it become quiet, but even then the poor duckling didn't dare get up. He waited several hours before he looked around, and then he hurried out of the marsh as fast as he could. He ran over field and meadows, and there was such a wind that the going was hard.

Toward evening he came to a wretched little house. It was so ramshackle that it didn't know which way to fall, and so it remained standing. The wind blew so hard around the duckling that he had to sit on his tail to keep from blowing away. Then he noticed that the door was off one of its hinges and hung so crookedly that he could slip into the house through the crack, and this he did.

Here lived an old woman with her cat and her hen. And the cat, whom she called Sonny, could arch his back and purr, and he even gave off sparks, but only if one stroked him the wrong way. The hen had quite short tiny legs, so she was called Chicky Low Legs. She laid good eggs, and the old woman was as fond of her as if she were her own child.

In the morning the strange duckling was noticed at once, and the cat started to purr and the hen to cluck. "What's that?" said the old woman, and looked around, but she couldn't see very well, so she thought the duckling was a fat duck that had lost its way. "Why, that was a fine catch!" she said. "Now I can get duck eggs, if only it's not a drake. That we'll have to try!"

So the duckling was accepted on trial for three weeks, but no eggs came. And the cat was master of the house, and the hen madam. And they always said, "We and the world," for they believed that they were half of the world, and the very best half, at that. The duckling thought there might be another opinion, but the hen wouldn't stand for that.

"Can you lay eggs?" she asked.

"No!"

"Then keep your mouth shut!"

And the cat said, "Can you arch your back, purr, and give off sparks?"

"No!"

"Well, then keep your opinion to yourself when sensible folks are speaking."

And the duckling sat in the corner in low spirits. Then he started thinking of the fresh air and the sunshine. He had such a strange desire to float on the water. At last he couldn't help himself; he had to tell it to the hen.

"What's wrong with you?" she asked. "You have nothing to do. That's why you're putting on these airs! Lay eggs or purr, then it'll go over."

"But it's so lovely to float on the water!" said the duckling. "So lovely to get it over your head and duck down to the bottom."

"Yes, a great pleasure, I daresay!" said the hen. "You've gone quite mad. Ask the cat, he's the wisest one I know, if *he* likes to float on the water or duck under it. Not to mention myself. Ask our mistress, the old woman; there is no one wiser than she in the whole world. Do you think she wants to float and get water over her head?"

"You don't understand me," said the duckling.

"Well, if we don't understand you, who would? Indeed, you'll never be wiser than the cat and the old woman, not to mention myself. Don't put on airs, my child! And thank your Creator for all the good that has been done for you. Haven't you come into a warm house, into a circle from which you can learn something? But you're a fool, and it's no fun associating with you! Believe you me! When I tell you harsh truths it's for your own good, and this way one can know one's true friends. See to it now that you start laying eggs or learn to purr and give off sparks."

"I think I'll go out into the wide world!" said the duckling.

"Yes, just do that!" said the hen.

So the duckling went out. He floated on the water and dived down to the bottom, but he was shunned by all the animals because of his ugliness.

Now it was autumn. The leaves in the forest turned golden and brown. The wind took hold of them and they danced about. The sky looked cold, and the clouds hung heavy with hail and snow. A raven stood on the fence and shrieked "Off! Off!" just from the cold. Merely thinking of it could make one freeze. The poor duckling was really in a bad way.

One evening as the sun was setting in all its splendor, a great flock of beautiful large birds came out of the bushes. The duckling had never seen anything so lovely. They were shining white, with long supple necks. They were

swans, and uttering a strange cry, they spread their splendid broad wings and flew away from the cold meadows to
warmer lands and open seas. They rose so high, so high,
and the ugly little duckling had such a strange feeling. He
moved around and around in the water like a wheel,
stretching his neck high in the air after them and uttering
a cry so shrill and strange that he frightened even himself.
Oh, he couldn't forget those lovely birds, those happy
birds; and when he could no longer see them, he dived
right down to the bottom, and when he came up again he
was quite beside himself. He didn't know what those birds
were called or where they were flying, but he was fonder
of them than he had ever been of anyone before. He
didn't envy them in the least. How could it occur to him
to wish for such loveliness for himself? He would have
been glad if only the ducks had tolerated him in their
midst—the poor ugly bird.

And the winter was so cold, so cold. The duckling had
to swim about in the water to keep from freezing. But
each night the hole in which he swam became smaller and
smaller; it froze so the crust of the ice creaked. The
duckling had to keep his legs moving so the hole wouldn't
close, but at last he grew tired, lay quite still, and froze
fast in the ice.

Early in the morning a farmer came along. He saw the
duckling, went out and made a hole in the ice with his
wooden shoe, and then carried him home to his wife.
There he was brought back to life.

The children wanted to play with him, but the duckling
thought they wanted to hurt him, and in his fright he flew
into the milk dish so the milk splashed out in the room.
The woman shrieked and waved her arms. Then he flew
into the butter trough and down into the flour barrel and
out again. My, how he looked now! The woman screamed
and hit at him with the tongs, and the children knocked
each other over trying to capture him, and they laughed

and shrieked. It was a good thing the door was standing open. Out flew the duckling among the bushes, into the newly fallen snow, and he lay there as if stunned.

But it would be far too sad to tell of all the suffering and misery he had to go through during that hard winter. He was lying in the marsh among the rushes when the sun began to shine warmly again. The larks sang—it was a beautiful spring.

Then all at once he raised his wings. They beat more strongly than before and powerfully carried him away. And before he knew it, he was in a large garden where the apple trees were in bloom and the fragrance of lilacs filled the air, where they hung on the long green branches right

down to the winding canal. Oh, it was so lovely here with the freshness of spring. And straight ahead, out of the thicket came three beautiful swans. They ruffled their feathers and floated so lightly on the water. The duckling recognized the magnificent birds and was filled with a strange melancholy.

"I will fly straight to them, those royal birds, and they

will peck me to death because I am so ugly and yet dare approach them. But it doesn't matter. Better to be killed by them than to be bitten by the ducks, pecked by the hens, kicked by the girl who takes care of the poultry yard, or suffer such hardships during the winter!" And he flew out into the water and swam over toward the magnificent swans. They saw him and hurried toward him with ruffled feathers.

"Just kill me," said the poor creature, and bowed down his head toward the surface of the water and awaited his death. But what did he see in the clear water? Under him he saw his own reflection, but he was no longer a clumsy, grayish-black bird, ugly and disgusting. He was a swan himself!

Being born in a duck yard doesn't matter if one has lain in a swan's egg!

He felt quite happy about all the hardships and suffering he had undergone. Now he could really appreciate his happiness and all the beauty that greeted him. And the big swans swam around him and stroked him with their bills.

Some little children came down to the garden and threw bread and seeds out into the water, and the smallest one cried, "There's a new one!" And the other children joined in, shouting jubilantly, "Yes, a new one has come!" And they all clapped their hands and danced for joy and ran to get their father and mother. And bread and cake were thrown into the water, and they all said, "The new one is the prettiest! So young and lovely!" And the old swans bowed to him.

Then he felt very shy and put his head under his wing—he didn't know why. He was much too happy, but not proud at all, for a good heart is never proud. He thought of how he had been persecuted and ridiculed, and now he heard everyone saying that he was the loveliest of all the lovely birds. And the lilacs bowed their branches right down to the water to him, and the sun shone so warm and bright. Then he ruffled his feathers, lifted his slender neck, and from the depths of his heart said joyously:

"I never dreamed of so much happiness when I was the ugly duckling."

The Snow Queen
(An Adventure in Seven Tales)

❖ ❖ ❖

FIRST TALE:
WHICH IS ABOUT THE MIRROR
AND THE FRAGMENTS

SEE, there! Now we're going to begin. When we come to the end of the tale, we'll know more than we do now, because of an evil troll! He was one of the worst of all, he was the "Devil." One day he was in a really good humor because he had made a mirror that had the quality of making everything good and fair that was reflected in it dwindle to almost nothing, but whatever was worthless and ugly stood out and grew even worse. The loveliest landscapes looked like boiled spinach in it, and the best people became nasty or stood on their heads without stomachs; the faces became so distorted that they were unrecognizable, and if you had a freckle, you could be certain that it spread over nose and mouth. "That was highly entertaining," said the Devil. Now, if a person had a good, pious thought, a grin would appear in the mirror, and the troll Devil had to laugh at his curious invention. Everyone who went to the troll school—for he ran a school for trolls—spread the word that a miracle had occurred: now, for the first time, they believed, you could see how the world and mortals really looked. They ran about with the mirror, and at last there wasn't a land or a person that hadn't been distorted in it. Now they also wanted to fly up to Heaven itself, to make fun of the angels and Our Lord. Indeed, the higher they flew with the mirror, the harder it grinned! They could hardly hold onto it. Higher and higher they flew, nearer to God and the angels. Then the mirror quivered so dreadfully in its grin that it shot out of their hands and plunged down to the earth, where it broke into a hundred million billion—and even more—fragments. And now it did much greater harm than before, for some of the fragments were scarcely bigger than a grain of sand; and these flew about in the wide world, and wherever they got into someone's eyes, they remained there; and then these people saw everything wrong or had eyes only for what was bad with a thing—for each tiny particle of the mirror had retained the same power as the whole mirror. Some people even got a little fragment of the mirror in their hearts, and this was quite horrible—the heart became just like a lump of ice. Some of the fragments of the mirror were so big that they were used as windowpanes, but it wasn't advisable to look at one's friends through those panes. Other fragments came into spectacles, and when people put these spectacles on, it was hard to see properly or act fairly. The Evil One laughed until he split his sides, and that tickled him pink.

But outside tiny fragments of glass were still flying about in the air. Now we shall hear!

SECOND TALE:
A LITTLE BOY AND A LITTLE GIRL

In a big city—where there are so many houses and people that there isn't enough room for everyone to have a little garden, and where most of them have to content

themselves with flowers in pots—there were two poor
children, however, who did have a garden somewhat bigger than a flowerpot. They weren't brother and sister, but
they were just as fond of each other as if they had been.
Their parents lived next to each other; they lived in two
garrets; there, where the roof of one house adjoined the
other, and the gutter ran along the eaves, from each house
a tiny window faced the other. One had only to step over
the gutter to go from one window to the other.

Outside, the parents each had a big wooden box, and in
it grew potherbs, which they used, and a little rosebush;
there was one in each box, and they grew so gloriously.
Now, the parents hit upon the idea of placing the boxes
across the gutter in such a way that they almost reached
from one window to the other, and looked just like two
banks of flowers. The pea vines hung down over the
boxes, and the rosebushes put forth long branches, twined
about the windows, and bent over toward each other. It
was almost like a triumphal arch of greenery and flowers.
As the boxes were quite high, and the children knew that
they mustn't climb up there, they were often allowed to
go out to each other and sit on their little stools under the
roses, and here they played quite splendidly.

During the winter, of course, this pleasure was at an
end. The windows were often frozen over completely; but
then they warmed up copper coins on the tiled stove,
placed the hot coin on the frozen pane, and thus there
would be a wonderful peephole as round as could be.
Behind it peeped a lovely, gentle eye, one from each
window. It was the little boy and the little girl. He was
called Kay and she was called Gerda. In summer they
could come to each other at one jump; in winter they first
had to go down the many flights of stairs and then up the
many flights of stairs; outside the snow was drifting.

"The white bees are swarming," said the old grandmother.

"Do they have a queen bee too?" asked the little boy, for he knew that there was one among the real bees.

"So they have!" said the grandmother. "She flies there where the swarm is thickest! She's the biggest of them all, and she never remains still on the earth. She flies up again into the black cloud. Many a winter night she flies through the city streets and looks in at the windows, and then they freeze over so curiously, as if with flowers."

"Yes, I've seen that!" said both the children, and then they knew it was true.

"Can the Snow Queen come in here?" asked the little girl.

"Just let her come," said the boy. "I'll put her on the hot stove and then she'll melt."

But the grandmother smoothed his hair and told other tales.

In the evening, when little Kay was back home and half undressed, he climbed up on the chair by the window and peeped out through the tiny hole. A few snowflakes were falling out there, and one of these, the biggest one of all, remained lying on the edge of one of the flower boxes. The snowflake grew and grew, and at last it turned into a complete woman, clad in the finest white gauze, which seemed to be made up of millions of starlike flakes. She was so beautiful and grand, but of ice—dazzling, gleaming ice—and yet she was alive. Her eyes stared like two clear stars, but there was no peace or rest in them. She nodded to the window and motioned with her hand. The little boy became frightened and jumped down from the chair. Then it seemed as if a huge bird flew past the window.

The next day there was a clear frost—and then a thaw set in—and then came the spring. The sun shone, green sprouts appeared, the swallows built nests, windows were opened, and again the little children sat in their tiny garden way up high in the gutter above all the floors.

The roses bloomed so wonderfully that summer; the

little girl had learned a hymn and there was something
about roses in it, and these roses made her think of her
own; and she sang it to the little boy, and he sang it along
with her:

> "Roses growing in the dale
> Where the Holy Child we hail."

And the children took each other by the hand, kissed the
roses, and gazed into God's bright sunshine and spoke to
it as if the Infant Jesus were there. What glorious summer
days these were, how wonderful it was to be out by the
fresh rosebushes, which never seemed to want to stop
blooming.

Kay and Gerda sat looking at a picture book of animals
and birds. It was then—the clock in the big church tower
had just struck five—that Kay said, "Ow! Something stuck
me in the heart! And now I've got something in my eye!"

The little girl put her arms around his neck; he blinked
his eyes. No, there wasn't a thing to be seen.

"I guess it's gone," he said. But it wasn't gone. It was
one of those fragments of glass that had sprung from the
mirror, the troll mirror. I daresay we remember that
loathsome glass that caused everything big and good that
was reflected in it to grow small and hideous, whereas the
evil and wicked duly stood out, and every flaw in a thing
was noticeable at once. Poor Kay! He had got a particle
right in his heart. Soon it would be just like a lump of ice.
It didn't hurt anymore now, but it was there.

"Why are you crying?" he asked. "You look so ugly!
There's nothing wrong with me after all! Fie!" he suddenly
cried. "That rose there is worm-eaten! And look, that one
there is quite crooked! As a matter of fact, that's a nasty
batch of roses! They look just like the boxes they're standing in!" And then he gave the box quite a hard kick with
his foot and pulled out the two roses.

"Kay! What are you doing!" cried the little girl. And when he saw how horrified she was, he yanked off yet another rose and then ran in through his window away from dear little Gerda.

When she came later with the picture book, he said it was for babies! And if grandmother told stories, he would always come with a "But—" Yes, if he got a chance to, he would walk behind her, put on glasses, and talk just the way she did. It was exactly like her, and he made people laugh. Soon he could copy the voice and gait of everyone on the whole street. Everything queer or not nice about them Kay knew how to imitate, and then people said, "He's certainly got an excellent head on him, that boy!" But it was the glass he had got in his eye, the glass that sat in his heart; and that is why he even teased little Gerda, who loved him with all her heart.

His games were now quite different from what they had been, they were so sensible; one winter's day, as the snowflakes piled up in drifts, he took a big burning glass, and holding out a corner of his blue coat, he let the snowflakes fall on it.

"Now look in the glass, Gerda!" he said. Each snowflake became much bigger and looked like a magnificent flower or a ten-sided star. It was a delight to behold.

"Do you see how funny it is?" said Kay. "That's much more interesting than real flowers! And there isn't a single flaw in them; they're quite accurate as long as they don't melt."

A little later Kay appeared in big gloves and with his sled on his back. He shouted right in Gerda's ear: "I've been allowed to go sledding in the big square where the others are playing." And off he went.

Over in the square the most daring boys often tied their sleds to the farmer's wagon, and then they rode a good distance with it. It was lots of fun. As they were playing there a big sleigh came up. It was painted white, and there was someone sitting in it, swathed in a fleecy white fur and wearing a white fur cap. The sleigh drove twice around the square, and Kay quickly managed to tie his little sled to it, and now he was driving along with it. It went faster and faster, straight into the next street. The driver turned his head and gave Kay a kindly nod; it was just as if they knew each other. Every time Kay wanted to untie his little sled, the person would nod again and Kay remained seated. They drove straight out through the city gate. Then the snow began tumbling down so thickly that the little boy couldn't see a hand in front of him as he rushed along. Then he quickly let go of the rope in order to get loose from the big sleigh, but it was no use. His little vehicle hung fast, and it went like the wind. Then he gave quite a loud cry, but no one heard him; and the snow piled up in drifts and the sleigh rushed on. Now and then it gave quite a jump, as if he were flying over ditches and fences. He was scared stiff; he wanted to say the Lord's Prayer, but the only thing he could remember was the Big Multiplication Table.

The snowflakes grew bigger and bigger; at last they looked like huge white hens; suddenly they sprang aside. The big sleigh stopped, and the one who was driving it stood up—the furs and cap were all of snow. It was a lady, so tall and straight, so shining white. It was the Snow Queen.

"We've made good progress," she said. "But is it freezing? Crawl into my bearskin." And then she seated him in the sleigh with her and wrapped the fur around him; it was as if he were sinking into a snowdrift.

"Are you still freezing?" she asked, and then she kissed him on the forehead. Ugh! That was colder than ice; it went straight to his heart, which of course was half a lump of ice already. He felt as if he were going to die—but only for a moment, then it only did him good; he no longer felt the cold around him.

"My sled! Don't forget my sled!" Only then did he remember it, and it was tied to one of the white hens. And it flew along behind with the sled on its back. The Snow Queen kissed Kay once again, and by then he had forgotten little Gerda and grandmother and all of them at home.

"Now you're not getting any more kisses," she said, "or else I'd kiss you to death!"

Kay looked at her; she was so very beautiful. A wiser, lovelier face he couldn't imagine; and now she didn't seem to be of ice, as she had seemed that time she had sat outside his window and motioned to him. In his eyes she was perfect, nor did he feel afraid at all. He told her that he knew how to do mental arithmetic, and with fractions, at that; and he knew the square mileage of the countries and "how many inhabitants." And she always smiled. Then it occurred to him that what he knew still wasn't enough. And he looked up into the vast expanse of sky. And she flew with him, flew high up on the black cloud; and the storm whistled and roared—it was like singing the old lays. They flew over forests and lakes, over sea and land; down below the icy blast whistled, the wolves howled, the snow sparkled. Over it flew the black screeching crows, but up above the moon shone so big and bright; and Kay looked at it all through the long winter night. By day he slept at the Snow Queen's feet.

THIRD TALE:
THE FLOWER GARDEN OF THE WOMAN
WHO WAS VERSED IN SORCERY

But how did little Gerda get on when Kay didn't come back again? Where was he after all? Nobody knew. Nobody could send word. The boys related only that they had seen him tie his little sled to a beautiful big sleigh,

which drove into the street and out of the city gate. Nobody knew where he was; many tears flowed and little Gerda cried hard and long. Then they said that he was dead, that he had fallen in the river that flowed close by the city. Oh, what truly long dark winter days they were.

Now the spring came and warmer sunshine.

"Kay is dead and gone!" said little Gerda.

"I don't think so!" said the sunshine.

"He's dead and gone!" she said to the swallows.

"I don't think so," they replied, and at last little Gerda didn't think so, either.

"I'm going to put on my new red shoes," she said early one morning, "the ones that Kay has never seen, and then I'll go down to the river and ask it too!"

It was quite early. She kissed the old grandmother, who was sleeping, put on the red shoes, and walked quite alone out of the gate to the river.

"Is it true that you've taken my little playmate? I'll make you a present of my red shoes if you'll give him back to me again!"

And it seemed to her that the billows nodded so strangely. Then she took her red shoes, the dearest things she owned, and threw them both out into the river. But they fell close to the shore, and the little billows carried them back on land to her right away. It was just as if the river didn't want to take the dearest things she owned. Then it didn't have little Kay after all. But now she thought she hadn't thrown the shoes out far enough, and so she climbed into a boat that was lying among the rushes. She went all the way out to the farthest end and threw the shoes, but the boat wasn't tied fast, and her movement made it glide from land. She noticed it and hastened to get out, but before she reached the back of the boat, it was more than an alen out from shore and now it glided faster away.

Then little Gerda became quite frightened and started to cry, but nobody heard her except the sparrows, and they couldn't carry her to land. But they flew along the shore and sang, as if to comfort her: "Here we are! Here we are!" The boat drifted with the stream. Little Gerda sat quite still in just her stockings; her little red shoes floated along behind, but they couldn't catch up with the boat, which gathered greater speed.

It was lovely on both shores, with beautiful flowers, old trees, and slopes with sheep and cows, but not a person was to be seen.

"Maybe the river is carrying me to little Kay," thought Gerda, and this put her in better spirits. She stood up and gazed at the beautiful green shores for many hours. Then she came to a big cherry orchard, where there was a little house with curious red and blue windows and—come to think of it—a thatched roof and two wooden soldiers outside who shouldered arms to those who sailed by.

Gerda shouted to them—she thought they were alive—but naturally they didn't answer; she came close to them, for the boat drifted right in to shore.

Gerda shouted even louder, and then out of the house came an old old woman leaning on a crooked staff. She was wearing a big sun hat, which had the loveliest flowers painted on it.

"You poor little child!" said the old woman. "However did you come out on that great strong stream and drift so far out into the wide world?" And then the old woman went all the way out in the water, hooked the boat with her staff, pulled it to land, and lifted little Gerda out.

And Gerda was glad to be on dry land, but, all the same, a little afraid of the strange old woman.

"Come, now, and tell me who you are and how you came here," she said.

And Gerda told her everything, and the old woman shook her head and said, "Hm! Hm!" And when Gerda had told her everything and asked if she hadn't seen little Kay, the old woman said that he hadn't come by, but he'd

be along, all right; she just shouldn't be grieved, but
should taste her cherries and look at her flowers—they
were prettier than any picture book and each one could
tell a complete story. Then she took Gerda by the hand;
they went into the little house and the old woman locked
the door.

The windows were so high up, and the panes were red,
blue, and yellow. The daylight shone in so strangely there
with all the colors, but on the table stood the loveliest
cherries, and Gerda ate as many as she liked, for this she
dared to do. And while she ate, the old woman combed
her hair with a golden comb, and the yellow hair curled
and shone so delightfully around the lovely little face,
which was so round and looked like a rose.

"I've been really longing for such a sweet little girl!"
said the old woman. "Now you shall see how well we two
are going to get along!" And as she combed little Gerda's
hair Gerda forgot her playmate, little Kay. For the old
woman was versed in sorcery, but she wasn't a wicked
sorceress, she only did a little conjuring for her own
pleasure, and now she so wanted to keep little Gerda. And
so she went out in the garden and held out her crooked
staff at all the rosebushes, and no matter how beautifully
they were blooming, they sank down into the black earth,
and no one could see where they had stood. The old
woman was afraid that when Gerda saw the roses, she
would think of her own and then remember little Kay and
run away.

Now she led Gerda out in the flower garden. My, how
fragrant and lovely it was here! Every conceivable flower,
for every season of the year, stood here blooming magnificently. No picture book could be gayer or lovelier. Gerda
sprang about for joy and played until the sun went down
behind the tall cherry trees. Then she was given a lovely
bed with red silken coverlets; they were stuffed with blue

violets, and she slept there and dreamed as delightfully as any queen on her wedding day.

The next day she could again play with the flowers in the warm sunshine—and so many days passed. Gerda knew every flower, but no matter how many there were, it still seemed to her that one was missing. But which one it was she didn't know. Then one day she was sitting, looking at the old woman's sun hat with the painted flowers on it, and the prettiest one of all was a rose. The old woman had forgotten to take it off the hat when the other flowers had sunk down in the ground. But that's the way it goes when one is absentminded.

"What?" said Gerda. "Aren't there any roses here?" And she ran in among the flower beds, searching and searching; but her hot tears fell on the very spot where a rosebush had sunk, and as the warm tears moistened the ground the tree suddenly shot up as full of blossoms as when it had sunk. And Gerda threw her arms around it, kissed the roses, and thought of the lovely roses at home and of little Kay.

"Oh, how I've been delayed!" said the little girl. "Why, I was going to find Kay! Don't you know where he is?" she asked the roses. "Do you think he's dead and gone?"

"He's not dead," said the roses. "To be sure, we've been in the ground, where all the dead are, but Kay wasn't there."

"Thank you!" said little Gerda, and she went over to the other flowers and looked into their chalices and asked: "Don't you know where little Kay is?"

But each flower was standing in the sunshine and dreaming of its own fairy tale or history; little Gerda was told so very many of these, but no one knew anything about Kay.

And then what did the tiger lily say?

"Do you hear the drum? Boom! Boom! There are only two notes—always 'Boom! Boom!' Listen to the dirge of the women! Listen to the cry of the priests! In her long red kirtle, the Hindu wife stands on the pyre, as the flames leap up about her and her dead husband. But the Hindu wife is thinking of the one still alive here in the ring, the one whose eyes burn hotter than the flames, the one whose burning eyes come closer to her heart than the flames that will soon burn her body to ashes. Can the flames of the heart die in the flames of the pyre?"

"I don't understand that at all!" said little Gerda.

"That's my story!" said the tiger lily.

What does the convolvulus say?

"Overhanging the narrow mountain trail is an old baronial castle; the thick periwinkles grow up around the ancient red walls, leaf for leaf about the balcony, and there stands a lovely girl. She leans out over the balustrade and peers at the road. No rose hangs fresher on its branch than she. No apple blossom borne by the wind from the tree is more graceful than she; how the magnificent kirtle rustles! 'Isn't he coming after all!' "

"Is it Kay you mean?" asked Little Gerda.

"I'm speaking only about my tale, my dream," replied the convolvulus.

What does the little snowdrop say?

"Between the trees the long board is hanging by ropes; it is a swing. Two lovely little girls—their dresses are as white as snow, long green silken ribbons are fluttering from their hats—sit swinging. Their brother, who is bigger than they are, is standing up in the swing. He has his arm around the rope to hold on with, for in one hand he has a little bowl and in the other a clay pipe; he is blowing soap bubbles; the swing is moving and the bubbles are soaring with lovely changing colors. The last one is still hanging to the pipe stem and bobbing in the wind; the swing is moving. The little black dog, as lightly as the bubbles, stands up on its hind legs and wants to get on the swing; it soars, the dog tumbles down with an angry bark, it is teased, the bubbles burst—a swinging board, a picture of flying lather, is my song."

"It may be that what you tell is beautiful, but you tell it so sorrowfully and make no mention of Kay at all. What do the hyacinths say?"

"There were three lovely sisters, so ethereal and fine: one's kirtle was red, the second's was blue, the third's was all white. Hand in hand they danced by the calm lake in the bright moonlight. They were not elfin maidens, but mortal children. There was such a sweet fragrance, and the maidens vanished in the forest. The fragrance grew stronger: three coffins—in them lay the three lovely girls—glided from the forest thicket across the lake. Fireflies flew twinkling about, like tiny hovering candles. Are the dancing maidens asleep or are they dead? The fragrance of the flowers says they are corpses. The evening bell is tolling for the dead!"

"You make me miserable," said little Gerda. "You have such a strong fragrance. It makes me think of the dead maidens. Alas, is little Kay really dead, then? The roses have been down in the ground, and they say no!"

"Dingdong," rang the hyacinth bells. "We're not ringing for little Kay; we don't know him. We're just singing our song, the only one we know!"

And Gerda went over to the buttercup, which shone out among the glistening green leaves. "You're a bright little sun!" said Gerda. "Tell me, if you know, where I shall find my playmate."

And the buttercup shone so prettily and looked back at Gerda. Which song, by chance, could the buttercup sing? That wasn't about Kay, either.

"In a little yard Our Lord's sun was shining so warmly on the first day of spring. The beams glided down along the neighbor's white wall; close by grew the first yellow flowers, shining gold in the warm sunbeams. Old granny was out in her chair; the granddaughter—the poor, beauti-

ful serving maid—was home on a short visit. She kissed
her grandmother. There was gold, a heart of gold in that
blessed kiss. Gold on the lips, gold on the ground, gold in
the morning all around. See, that's my story!" said the
buttercup.

"My poor old grandmother!" sighed Gerda. "Yes, she's
probably grieving for me, just as she did for little Kay. But
I'm coming home again, and then I'll bring little Kay with
me. There's no use my asking the flowers. They know only
their songs; they're not telling me anything." And then
she tucked up her little dress, so as to be able to run
faster, but the narcissus tapped her on the leg as she
jumped over it. Then she stopped, looked at the tall
flower, and asked, "Do you, by any chance, know something?" And she stooped all the way down to it. And what
did it say?

"I can see myself! I can see myself!" said the narcissus.
"Oh! Oh! How I smell! Up in the tiny garret, half dressed,
stands a little dancer. Now she's standing on one leg, now
on two! She kicks out at the whole world. She's only an
optical illusion. She pours water from the teapot onto a
piece of cloth she's holding. It's her corset. Cleanliness is
a good thing. The white dress hanging on the peg has also
been washed in the teapot and dried on the roof; she puts
it on and the saffron-yellow kerchief around her neck.
Then the dress shines even whiter. Leg in the air! See
how she rears up on a stalk! I can see myself! I can see
myself!"

"I don't care at all about that!" said Gerda. "That's not
anything to tell me!" And then she ran to the edge of the
garden.

The gate was locked, but she wiggled the rusty iron
hook, then it came loose and the gate flew open. And then
little Gerda ran barefooted out into the wide world. She
looked back three times, but no one came after her. At
last she couldn't run anymore, and sat down on a big

stone. And when she looked around her, summer was at an end. It was late autumn. You couldn't tell this at all inside the lovely garden, where the sun was always shining and flowers of every season were blooming.

"Heavens! How I've held myself up!" said little Gerda. "Why, it's autumn! I dare not rest!" And she got up to go.

Oh, how sore and tired her little feet were, and on all sides it looked cold and raw. The long willow leaves were quite yellow and dripping wet in the fog: one leaf fell after the other. Only the blackthorn bore fruit, but so sour that it puckered the mouth. Oh, how gray and bleak it was in the wide world!

FOURTH TALE: PRINCE AND PRINCESS

Gerda had to rest again. Then a huge crow hopped on the snow right in front of where she sat. For a long time it had been sitting looking at her and wagging its head. Now it said, "Caw! Caw! Go da! Go da!" It wasn't able to say it any better. But it meant well by the little girl and asked where she was going all alone out in the wide world. Gerda understood the word "alone" very well and felt rightly all that it implied. And so she told the crow the whole story of her life and asked if it hadn't seen Kay.

And the crow nodded quite thoughtfully and said, "Could be! Could be!"

"What? Do you think so?" cried the little girl, and nearly squeezed the crow to death, she kissed it so.

"Sensibly! Sensibly!" said the crow. "I think it could be little Kay. But now he's probably forgotten you for the princess!"

"Is he living with a princess?" asked Gerda.

"Yes, listen!" said the crow. "But it's hard for me to

speak your language. If you understand crow talk, then I can tell it better."

"No, I haven't learned that," said Gerda. "But grandmother could, and she knew Double Dutch too. If only I'd learned it."

"No matter!" said the crow. "I'll tell you as well as I can, but it'll be bad all the same." And then it told what it knew.

"In the kingdom where we are sitting now, there dwells a princess who is exceedingly wise. But then she has read all the newspapers there are in the world and forgotten them—so wise is she. The other day she was sitting on the throne—and that's not so much fun after all, they say. Then she started humming a song, the very one that goes: 'Why shouldn't I wed . . .'

" 'Listen, there's something to that!' she said, and then she wanted to get married. But she wanted a husband who was ready with an answer when he was spoken to. One who didn't just stand there looking aristocratic, because that's so boring. Now she got all her ladies-in-waiting together, and when they heard what she wanted, they were so pleased.

" 'I like that!' they said. 'That's just what I was thinking the other day!' You can believe every word I say is true," said the crow. "I have a tame sweetheart who walks freely about the castle, and she has told me everything!"

Naturally this was a crow too, for birds of a feather flock together, and one crow always picks another.

"The newspapers came out right away with a border of hearts and the princess' monogram. You could read for yourself that any young man who was good-looking was free to come up to the castle and talk to the princess. And the one who talked in such a way that you could hear he was at home there, and talked the best, he was the one the princess would take for a husband! Well, well!" said the crow. "You can believe me, it's as true as I'm sitting

here, people came in swarms. There was a jostling and a
scurrying, but it didn't prove successful, neither on the
first day nor on the second. They could all talk well when
they were out in the street, but when they came in the
castle gate and saw the guards in silver and the lackeys in
gold up along the stairs, and the great illuminated halls,
then they were flabbergasted. And if they stood before the
throne where the princess was sitting, they didn't know of
a thing to say except for the last word she had said, and
she didn't think much of hearing that again. It was just as
if people in there had swallowed snuff and fallen into a
trance until they were back out in the street. Yes, then
they were able to speak. There was a line all the way from
the city gate to the castle. I was inside to look at it
myself!" said the crow. "They became both hungry and
thirsty, but from the castle they didn't get so much as a
glass of lukewarm water. To be sure, some of the smartest
had taken sandwiches with them, but they didn't share
with their neighbor. They thought, 'Only let him look
hungry, then the princess won't take him!' "

"But Kay! Little Kay!" said Gerda. "When did he come?
Was he among the multitude?"

"Give me time! Give me time! Now we're just coming
to him. It was the third day. Then a little person, without
horse or carriage, came marching dauntlessly straight up
to the castle. His eyes shone like yours; he had lovely long
hair, but shabby clothes."

"That was Kay!" Gerda shouted jubilantly. "Oh, then
I've found him!" And she clapped her hands.

"He had a little knapsack on his back!" said the crow.

"No, that was probably his sled," said Gerda, "for he
went away with the sled!"

"That's very likely!" said the crow. "I didn't look at it so
closely! But I do know from my tame sweetheart that
when he came in through the castle gate and saw the
bodyguard in silver and the lackeys in gold up along the

stairs, he didn't lose heart a bit. He nodded and said to them, 'It must be boring to stand on the steps, I'd rather go inside!' There the halls were ablaze with light. Privy councillors and excellencies were walking about barefoot, carrying golden dishes. It was enough to make one solemn. His boots were creaking so terribly loudly, but still he didn't become frightened.''

"That certainly is Kay!" said Gerda. "I know he had new boots. I've heard them creaking in Grandmother's parlor."

"Well, creak they did!" said the crow. "But nothing daunted, he went straight in to the princess, who was sitting on a pearl as big as a spinning wheel. And all the ladies-in-waiting, with their maids and maids' maids, and all the gentlemen-in-waiting, with their menservants and menservants' menservants who kept a page boy, stood lined up on all sides. And indeed the closer they stood to the door, the haughtier they looked. And the menservants' menservants' boy, who always goes about in slippers, is hardly to be looked upon at all, so haughtily does he stand in the door.''

"That must be horrible!" said little Gerda. "And yet Kay has won the princess?"

"If I hadn't been a crow, I'd have taken her—despite the fact that I'm engaged. He's supposed to have spoken just as well as I speak when I speak crow talk. I have that from my tame sweetheart. He was dauntless and charming; he hadn't come to woo at all, only to hear the princess' wisdom; and he found that to be good, and she found him to be good in return.''

"Of course! That was Kay!" said Gerda. "He was wise. He could do Mental Arithmetic with fractions! Oh, won't you take me into the castle?"

"Well, that's easily said," said the crow, "but how are we going to do it? I shall speak to my tame sweetheart about it. I daresay she can advise us, although I must tell you that a little girl like you will never be allowed to come in the proper way."

"Oh, yes, so I will!" said Gerda. "As soon as Kay hears I'm here he'll come right out and fetch me."

"Wait for me by the stile there!" said the crow, wagging its head, and it flew away.

Not until it was late in the evening did the crow come back again. "Rah! Rah!" it said. "She asked me to give you her love! And here's a little loaf for you. She took it from the kitchen, and there's bread enough there, and you're probably hungry. It's impossible for you to come into the castle. Why, you're barefoot. The guard in silver and the lackeys in gold wouldn't allow it, but don't cry. You'll come up there after all. My sweetheart knows of a little back stairway that leads to the royal bedchamber, and she knows where to get hold of the key!"

And they went into the garden, into the great avenue where the leaves fell one after the other; and when the lights were put out in the castle, one after the other, the crow led little Gerda over to a back door that stood ajar.

Oh, how little Gerda's heart was pounding with fear and longing! It was just as if she were going to do something wrong, and yet she only wanted to know whether it was little Kay. Indeed, it had to be him; she could picture vividly to herself his wise eyes, his long hair. She could clearly see the way he smiled, as he did when they sat at home under the roses. Of course he would be glad to see her, and he would want to hear what a long way she had walked for his sake and learn how miserable everyone at home had been when he hadn't come back. Oh, how frightened and glad she was.

Now they were on the stairs; there was a little lamp burning on a cupboard. In the middle of the floor stood the tame crow, turning its head on all sides and regarding Gerda, who curtsied the way her grandmother had taught her.

"My fiancé has spoken so nicely about you, my little miss," said the tame crow. "Your vita, as it is called, is also very touching! If you will take the lamp, then I will lead the way. We go here as the crow flies, so we don't meet anyone!"

"It seems to me that someone is coming right behind me!" said Gerda, and something swished past her; it was just like shadows along the wall, horses with flowing manes and thin legs, grooms, and ladies and gentlemen on horseback.

"It's only the dreams!" said the tame crow. "They come to fetch the royal thoughts out hunting. It's a good thing, for then you can have a better look at them in bed. But if you do come into favor, see to it then that you reveal a grateful heart!"

"Why, that's nothing to talk about!" said the crow from the woods.

Now they entered the first hall. The walls were covered with rose-red satin and artificial flowers. Here the dreams were already sweeping past them, but they went so fast that Gerda didn't catch a glimpse of the royal riders. Each hall was more magnificent than the last—indeed it was enough to made one astonished—and now they were in the bedchamber. The ceiling in here was like an enormous palm tree with leaves of glass, costly glass. And in the middle of the floor, hanging from a stalk of gold, were two beds that looked like lilies. One of them was white and in it lay the princess. The other was red, and it was in this one that Gerda was to look for little Kay. She bent one of the petals aside, and then she saw the nape of a brown neck. Oh, it was Kay! She shouted his name quite loudly and held the lamp up to him. The dreams on horseback rushed into the room again—he awoke, turned his head, and . . . it wasn't little Kay.

Only the prince's nape of the neck resembled little Kay's, but he was young and handsome. And from the white lily bed the princess peeped out and asked what was wrong. Then little Gerda cried and told her whole story and all that the crows had done for her.

"You poor little thing!" said the prince and princess. And they praised the crows and said that they weren't angry at them at all. But still they weren't to do it often. In the meantime they were to be rewarded.

"Do you want to fly away free?" asked the princess. "Or would you rather have permanent posts as Court Crows—with everything that falls off in the kitchen?"

And both the crows curtsied and asked for permanent positions, for they were thinking of their old age, and said, "It's good to have something for a rainy day," as they called it.

And the prince got out of his bed and let Gerda sleep in it, and he could do no more. She folded her little hands and thought, "Indeed, how good people and animals are." And then she closed her eyes and slept so delightfully. All the dreams came flying back in, looking like God's angels, and they pulled a little sled and on it Kay sat and nodded. But they were only reveries, and for that reason they were gone again as soon as she woke up.

The next day she was clad from top to toe in silk and velvet. She was invited to stay at the castle and be in clover, but all she asked for was a little cart with a horse in front, and a pair of tiny boots. And then she wanted to drive out into the wide world and find Kay.

And she was given both boots and a muff. She was dressed so beautifully. And when she was ready to go, a new coach of pure gold was standing at the door. The coat of arms of the prince and princess shone from it like a star, and the coachman, footmen, and outriders—for there were outriders too—sat wearing golden crowns. The prince and princess themselves helped her into the coach and wished her all good fortune. The crow from the woods, who was now married, accompanied her the first twelve miles. It sat beside her, for it couldn't stand to ride backward. The other crow stood in the gate and flapped its wings. It didn't go with them as it suffered from headaches, since it had been given a permanent post and too much to eat. The inside of the coach was lined with sugared pretzels, and in the seat were fruits and gingersnaps.

"Farewell! Farewell!" shouted the prince and princess. And little Gerda cried and the crow cried—thus the first miles passed. Then the crow also said farewell, and that was the hardest leave-taking of all.

It flew up into a tree and flapped its black wings as long as it could see the coach, which shone like the bright sunshine.

FIFTH TALE:
THE LITTLE ROBBER GIRL

They drove through the dark forest, but the coach shone like a flame; it hurt the eyes of the robbers and they couldn't stand that.

"It's gold! It's gold!" they cried, and rushing out, they grabbed hold of the horses, killed the little outriders, the coachman, and the footmen, and then they dragged little Gerda out of the coach.

"She's fat! She's sweet! She's been fattened on nut kernels!" said the old robber crone, who had a long bristly beard and eyebrows that hung down over her eyes. "That's as good as a little fat lamb. Oh, how good she'll taste!" And then she pulled out her burnished knife—and it glittered so horribly.

"Ow!" said the crone at the same moment; she had been bitten in the ear by her own little daughter, who hung on her back and was so wild and naughty that it was a joy to behold. "You nasty brat!" said the mother, and didn't have time to slaughter Gerda.

"She shall play with me!" said the little robber girl. "She shall give me her muff, her pretty dress, and sleep with me in my bed!" And then she bit her again, so the robber crone hopped in the air and whirled around, and all the robbers laughed and said, "See how she's dancing with her young!"

"I want to get in the coach!" said the little robber girl, and she would and must have her own way, for she was so spoiled and so willful. She and Gerda seated themselves inside, and then they drove, over stubble and thickets, deeper into the forest. The little robber girl was the same size as Gerda, but stronger, with broader shoulders and darker skin. Her eyes were quite black, and they looked almost mournful. She put her arm around little Gerda's waist and said, "They're not going to slaughter you as long as I don't get angry with you. I expect you're a princess?"

"No," said little Gerda, and told her everything she had gone through and how fond she was of little Kay.

The robber girl looked at her quite gravely, nodded her head a little, and said, "They're not going to slaughter you even if I do get angry with you—then I'll do it myself." And then she dried little Gerda's eyes and put both her hands in the beautiful muff that was so soft and so warm.

Now the coach came to a standstill. They were in the middle of the courtyard of a robber's castle. It had cracked from top to bottom. Ravens and crows flew out of the open holes, and huge ferocious dogs—each one looking as if it could swallow a man—jumped high in the air. But they didn't bark, for that was forbidden.

In the big old sooty hall a huge fire was burning in the middle of the stone floor. The smoke trailed along under the ceiling and had to see about finding its way out itself. Soup was cooking in an enormous brewing vat, and both hares and rabbits were turning on spits.

"You shall sleep here tonight with me and all my little pets!" said the robber girl. They got something to eat and drink and then went over to a corner, where straw and rugs lay. Overhead nearly a hundred pigeons were sitting on sticks and perches; they all seemed to be sleeping, but still they turned a bit when the little girls came.

"They're all mine," said the little robber girl, and quickly grabbed hold of one of the nearest, held it by the legs, and shook it so it flapped its wings. "Kiss it!" she cried, and beat Gerda in the face with it. "There sit the forest rogues!" she went on, pointing behind a number of bars that had been put up in front of a hole in the wall high above. "They're forest rogues, those two! They fly away at once if you don't lock them up properly. And here stands my old sweetheart, baa!" And she pulled a reindeer by the horns. It had a bright copper ring around its neck and was tied up. "We always have to keep hold of him, or else he'll run away from us! Every single evening I tickle his neck with my sharp knife—he's so afraid of it!" And the little girl drew a long knife out of a crack in the wall and ran it along the reindeer's neck. The poor animal lashed out with its legs, and the robber girl laughed and then pulled Gerda down into the bed with her

"Do you want to take the knife along when you're going to sleep?" asked Gerda, and looked at it a bit uneasily.

"I always sleep with a knife!" said the little robber girl. "One never knows what may happen. But tell me again now, what you told before about little Kay, and why you've gone out into the wide world." And Gerda told from the beginning, and the wood pigeons cooed up there in the cage; the other pigeons were asleep. The little robber girl put her arm around Gerda's neck, held the knife in her other hand, and slept so you could hear it. But Gerda couldn't shut her eyes at all: she didn't know whether she was going to live or die. The robbers sat around the fire, singing and drinking, and the robber crone turned somersaults. Oh, it was quite a horrible sight for the little girl to look upon.

Then the wood pigeons said, "Coo! Coo! We have seen little Kay. A white hen was carrying his sled. He was sitting in the Snow Queen's carriage, which rushed low over the forest when we were in the nest. She blew on us squabs, and all died save the two of us. Coo! Coo!"

"What are you saying up there?" cried Gerda. "Where did the Snow Queen go? Do you know anything about that?"

"As likely as not she journeyed to Lappland. There's always snow and ice there. Just ask the reindeer, who stands tied with the rope."

"That's where the ice and snow are; that's a glorious and a grand place to be," said the reindeer. "That's where you can spring freely about in the great shining valleys. That's where the Snow Queen has her summer tent, but her permanent castle is up near the North Pole on the island they call Spitzbergen!"

"Oh, Kay, little Kay!" sighed Gerda.

"Now you're to lie still!" said the robber girl. "Or else you'll get the knife in your belly!"

In the morning Gerda told her everything that the wood pigeons had said, and the robber girl looked quite grave, but nodded her head and said, "No matter! No matter! Do you know where Lappland is?" she asked the reindeer.

"Who should know that better than I do?" said the animal, and its eyes danced in its head. "That's where I was born and bred; that's where I frolicked on the snowy wastes."

"Listen!" said the robber girl to Gerda. "You see that all our menfolk are away, but Mama's still here, and she's staying. But a little later in the morning she'll have a drink from the big bottle, and afterwards she'll take a little nap upstairs. Then I'm going to do something for you." Now she jumped out of the bed, flung herself on her mother's neck, yanked her moustache, and said, "My own sweet nanny goat, good morning!" And her mother tweaked her nose so it turned both red and blue, but it was all out of pure affection.

Now, when the mother had taken a drink from her bottle and was having a little nap, the robber girl went over to the reindeer and said, "I'd so like to keep on tickling you a lot more with that sharp knife, for then you're so funny. But no matter. I'm going to untie your knot and help you outside so you can run to Lappland. But you're to take to your heels and carry this little girl for me to the Snow Queen's castle, where her little playmate is. I daresay you've heard what she said, for she talked loud enough and you eavesdrop."

The reindeer jumped high for joy. The robber girl lifted little Gerda up and was prudent enough to tie her fast— yes, even give her a little pillow to sit on. "No matter," she said. "There are your fleecy boots, for it's going to be cold. But I'm keeping the muff, it's much too lovely! Still, you won't freeze. Here are my mother's big mittens; they reach up to your elbows. Put them on! Now your hands look just like my nasty mother's!"

And Gerda wept for joy.

"I can't stand your sniveling!" said the little robber girl. "Now you should looked pleased! And here are two loaves and a ham for you so you can't starve." Both were tied to the reindeer's back. The little robber girl opened the door, called in all the big hounds, and then cut through the rope with her knife and said to the reindeer, "Now run! But take good care of the little girl!"

And Gerda stretched out her hands in the big mittens to the robber girl and said farewell, and then the reindeer flew away, over bushes and stubble, through the great forest, over marsh and steppes, as fast as it could. The wolves howled and the ravens screeched. "Sputter! Sputter!" came from the sky. It was just as if it sneezed red.

"They're my old Northern Lights!" said the reindeer. "See how they shine!" And then it ran on even faster, night and day. The loaves were eaten, the ham too, and then they were in Lappland.

SIXTH TALE: THE LAPP WIFE AND THE FINN WIFE

They came to a standstill by a little house; it was so wretched. The roof went down to the ground, and the door was so low that the family had to crawl on their stomachs when they wanted to go out or in. There was nobody home except an old Lapp wife, who stood frying fish over a train-oil lamp. And the reindeer told her Gerda's whole story, but first its own, for it thought that was more important, and Gerda was so chilled that she couldn't speak.

"Alas, you poor wretches!" said the Lapp wife. "You've still got a long way to run! You have to go hundreds of miles into Finnmark, for that's where the Snow Queen stays in the country and burns blue lights every single evening. I'll write a few words on a piece of dried cod—I don't have paper. I'll give it to you to take to the Finn wife up there; she can give you better directions than I can!"

And now, when Gerda had warmed up and had something to eat and drink, the Lapp wife wrote a few words on a piece of dried cod, told Gerda to take good care of it, and tied her onto the reindeer again, and away it sprang. "Sputter! Sputter!" it said up in the sky. All night the loveliest blue Northern Lights were burning—and then they came to Finnmark and knocked on the Finn wife's chimney, for she didn't even have a door.

It was so hot in there that the Finn wife herself went about almost completely naked. She was small and quite swarthy. She loosened little Gerda's clothing at once, took off the mittens and the boots (or else she would have been too hot), put a piece of ice on the reindeer's head, and then read what was written on the dried cod. She read it three times, and then she knew it by heart and put the fish in the food caldron, for it could be eaten and she never wasted anything.

Now the reindeer told first its own story and then little Gerda's. And the Finn wife blinked her wise eyes, but didn't say a thing.

"You're so wise," said the reindeer. "I know that you can bind all the Winds of the World with a sewing thread. When the skipper unties one knot, he gets a good wind; when he unties the second, a keen wind blows; and when he unties the third and fourth, there's such a storm that the forest falls down. Won't you give the little girl a draft so she can gain the strength of twelve men and overpower the Snow Queen?"

"The strength of twelve men!" said the Finn wife. "Indeed, that'll go a long way!" And then she went over to a shelf and took a big, rolled-up hide, and this she unrolled. Curious letters were written on it, and the Finn wife read it until the water poured down her forehead.

But again the reindeer begged so much for little Gerda, and Gerda looked with such beseeching tearful eyes at the Finn wife, that the latter started to blink her eyes again and drew the reindeer over in a corner, where she whispered to it while she put fresh ice on its head.

"Little Kay is with the Snow Queen, to be sure, and finds everything there quite to his liking and believes it's the best place in the world. But that's because he's got a fragment of glass in his heart and a tiny grain of glass in his eye. They have to come out first, or else he'll never become a man and the Snow Queen will keep him in her power."

"But can't you give little Gerda something to take so she can gain power over it all?"

"I can't give her greater power than she already has. Don't you see how great it is? Don't you see how mortals and animals have to serve her, how, in her bare feet, she has come so far in the world? She mustn't be made aware of her power by us. It's in her heart, it's in the fact that she is a sweet, innocent child. If she herself can't come in to the Snow Queen and get the glass out of little Kay, then we can't help! About ten miles from here the garden of the Snow Queen begins. You can carry the little girl there and put her down by the big bush with red berries that's standing in the snow. Don't linger to gossip, but hurry back here!" And then the Finn wife lifted little Gerda up onto the reindeer, which ran with all its might.

"Oh, I didn't get my boots! I didn't get my mittens!" cried little Gerda. She could feel that in the stinging cold, but the reindeer dared not stop. It ran until it came to the big bush with the red berries. There it put little Gerda down and kissed her on the mouth, and big shining tears ran down the animal's cheeks, and then it ran back again with all its might. There stood poor Gerda, without shoes, without gloves, in the middle of the dreadful, ice-cold Finnmark.

She ran forward as fast as she could; then along came a whole regiment of snowflakes. But they didn't fall down from the sky, for it was quite clear and shone with the Northern Lights. The snowflakes ran along the ground, and indeed, the nearer they came, the bigger they grew. Gerda probably remembered how big and queer they had looked that time she had seen the snowflakes through the burning glass. But here, of course, they were much much bigger and more horrible—they were alive. They were the Snow Queen's advance guard. They had the strangest shapes. Some looked like huge loathsome porcupines, others like whole knots of snakes that stuck forth their heads, and others like little fat bears with bristly hair—all shining white, all living snowflakes.

Then little Gerda said the Lord's Prayer, and the cold was so intense that she could see her own breath; it poured out of her mouth like smoke. Her breath grew denser and denser until it took the shape of little bright angels that grew bigger and bigger when they touched the ground. And they all had helmets on their heads and spears and shields in their hands. More and more of them appeared, and when Gerda had finished her prayers there was a whole legion of them. And they hacked at the horrible snowflakes with their spears until they flew into hundreds of pieces, and little Gerda walked on quite safely and fearlessly. The angels patted her feet and hands, and then she didn't feel the cold so much, and walked quickly on toward the Snow Queen's castle.

But now we should first see how Kay is getting along. To be sure, he wasn't thinking of little Gerda, and least of all that she was standing outside the castle.

SEVENTH TALE:
WHAT HAPPENED IN THE SNOW QUEEN'S CASTLE AND WHAT HAPPENED AFTERWARD

The castle walls were of the driven snow, and the windows and doors of the biting winds. There were more than a hundred halls, according to the way the snow drifted; the biggest stretched for many miles, all lit up by the intense Northern Lights; and they were so big, so bare, so icy cold, and so sparkling. Never was there any merriment here, not even so much as a little ball for the bears, where the storm could blow up and the polar bears could walk on their hind legs and put on fancy airs. Never a little game party, with muzzle tag and touch paw; never the least little bit of gossiping over coffee by the white lady-foxes; empty, big, and cold it was in the halls of the Snow Queen. The Northern Lights flared up so punctually that you could figure out by counting when they were at their highest and when they were at their lowest. In the middle of that bare, unending snow hall there was a frozen sea. It had cracked into a thousand fragments, but each fragment was so exactly like the next that it was quite a work of art. And in the middle of it sat the Snow Queen—when she was at home—and then she said that she was sitting on the Mirror of Reason and that it was the best and the only one in this world.

Little Kay was quite blue with cold, yes, almost black; but still he didn't notice it, for after all she had kissed the shivers out of him, and his heart was practically a lump of ice. He went about dragging some sharp, flat fragments of ice, which he arranged in every possible way, for he wanted to get something out of it—just as the rest of us have small pieces of wood and arrange these in patterns, and this is called the "Chinese Puzzle." Kay also made patterns, a most curious one; this was the "Ice Puzzle of Reason." To his eyes the pattern was quite excellent and of the utmost importance. This was due to the grain of glass that was sitting in his eye! He arranged whole figures that made up a written word, but he could never figure out how to arrange the very word he wanted: the word "eternity." And the Snow Queen had said, "If you can arrange that pattern for me, then you shall be your own master, and I shall make you a present of the whole world and a pair of new skates." But he wasn't able to.

"Now I'm rushing off to the warm countries!" said the Snow Queen. "I want to have a look down in the black caldrons!" Those were the volcanoes Etna and Vesuvius, as they are called. "I'm going to whiten them a bit; that's customary; it does good above lemons and wine grapes!" And then the Snow Queen flew off, and Kay sat quite alone in the big bare hall of ice many miles long, and looked at the pieces of ice, and thought and thought until

he creaked. He sat quite stiff and still—you'd have thought
he was frozen to death.

It was then that little Gerda came into the castle through
the huge doors of the biting winds; but she said an evening prayer, and then the winds abated as if they were
going to sleep, and she stepped into the big bare cold hall.
Then she saw Kay. She recognized him, flung her arms
around his neck, held him so tight, and cried, "Kay! Sweet
little Kay! So I've found you, then!"

But he sat quite still, stiff, and cold. Then little Gerda
cried hot tears. They fell on his chest, they soaked into his
heart, they thawed out the lump of ice, and ate away the
little fragment of mirror that was in there. He looked at
her and she sang the hymn:

> "Roses growing in the dale
>   Where the Holy Child we hail."

Then Kay burst into tears. He cried until the grain of the mirror rolled out of his eye. He knew her and shouted jubilantly, "Gerda! Sweet little Gerda! Where have you been all this time? And where have I been?" And he looked about him. "How cold it is here! How empty and big!" And he clung to Gerda, and she laughed and cried for joy. It was so wonderful that even the fragments of ice danced for joy on all sides. And when they were tired and lay down, they arranged themselves in the very letters the Snow Queen had said he was to find, and then he would be his own master and she would give him the whole world and a pair of new skates.

And Gerda kissed his cheeks and they blossomed; she kissed his eyes and they shone like hers; she kissed his hands and feet and he was well and strong. The Snow Queen was welcome to come home if she liked. His release stood written there in shining pieces of ice.

And they took each other by the hand and wandered out of the big castle; they talked about Grandmother and about the roses up on the roof. And wherever they walked, the winds abated and the sun broke through. And when they came to the bush with the red berries, the reindeer was standing there waiting. It had with it another reindeer, whose udder was full, and it gave the little ones its warm milk and kissed them on the mouth. Then they carried Kay and Gerda, first to the Finn wife, where they warmed themselves in the hot room, and were told about the journey home, and then to the Lapp wife, who had sewed new clothes for them and put her sleigh in order.

And the reindeer and the young reindeer sprang alongside and accompanied them all the way to the border of the country, where the first green sprouts were peeping forth. There they took leave of the reindeer and the Lapp wife.

"Farewell!" they all said.

And the first little birds began to twitter; the forest had

green buds; and out of it, riding on a magnificent horse, which Gerda recognized (it had been hitched to the golden coach), came a young girl with a blazing red cap on her head and pistols in front. It was the little robber girl, who had become bored with staying at home and now wanted to go North first and later in another direction if she weren't content.

She recognized Gerda at once, and Gerda recognized her! They were delighted.

"You're a funny one to go traipsing about!" she said to little Kay. "I'd really like to know whether you deserve someone running to the ends of the earth for your sake!"

But Gerda patted her on the cheek and asked about the prince and princess.

"They've gone away to foreign lands," said the robber girl.

"But the crow?" asked little Gerda.

"Well, the crow is dead!" she replied. "The tame sweetheart has become a widow and goes about with a bit of woolen yarn around her leg. She complains pitifully, and it's all rubbish! But tell me now how you've fared and how you got hold of him!"

And Gerda and Kay both told her.

"And snip, snap, snee, go on a spree!" said the robber girl, and taking them both by the hand, she promised that if she ever came through their city, she would come and pay them a visit.

And then she rode out into the wide world. But Kay and Gerda walked hand in hand. It was a lovely spring, with flowers and greenery. The church bells rang, and they recognized the high towers, the big city. It was the one in which they lived, and they went into it and over to Grandmother's door, up the stairs into the room where everything stood in the same spot as before, and the clock said, "Ticktock!" and the hands went around. But as they went through the door they noticed that they had become grown people. The blooming roses from the gutter were coming in through the open window, and there stood the little baby chairs. And Kay and Gerda sat on their own chairs and held each other by the hand. They had forgotten the cold, empty splendor of the Snow Queen's castle like a bad dream. Grandma was sitting in God's clear sunshine and reading aloud from the Bible: "Except ye become as little children, ye shall not enter into the Kingdom of Heaven."

And Kay and Gerda gazed into each other's eyes, and they understood at once the old hymn:

> Roses growing in the dale
> Where the Holy Child we hail.

And they both sat, grown up and yet children—children at heart. And it was summer—the warm, glorious summer.

The Darning Needle

T HERE was once a darning needle who put on such a lot of airs that she fancied she was a sewing needle.

"Now, just mind what you're holding!" said the darning needle to the fingers that took her out. "Don't drop me! If I fall on the floor I'm capable of never being found again, I'm so fine!"

"Well, I wouldn't go so far!" said the fingers, and then they squeezed her around the middle.

"Do you see, here I come with a suite!" said the darning needle, and then she drew a long thread after her—though it didn't have a knot.

The fingers guided the needle straight at the kitchen maid's slipper, where the vamp had been torn and was now going to be sewn together.

"That is degrading work!" said the darning needle. "I'll never go through. I'm breaking! I'm breaking!" And then she broke. "What did I tell you!" said the darning needle. "I'm too fine!"

"Now she's no good for anything," thought the fingers, but still they had to hold her tight. The kitchen maid dripped sealing wax on her, and then stuck her in the front of her kerchief.

"See, now I'm a brooch!" said the darning needle. "I knew very well that I would come into favor. When one is something, one always becomes something." And then she laughed deep down inside, for you can never tell from the outside that a darning needle is laughing. There she sat now, as proud as if she were driving in a carriage, and looked around on all sides.

"May I have the honor of inquiring whether you are of gold?" she asked the pin who was her neighbor. "You're lovely to look at, and you have your very own head. But it is small! You must see to it that it grows out, because not everyone can have sealing wax dripped on his end!" And then the darning needle drew herself up so proudly that she fell out of the kerchief and into the sink just as the kitchen maid was rinsing it out.

"Now we're going on a journey!" said the darning needle. "As long as I don't get lost!" But so she did.

"I'm too fine for this world!" she said as she sat in the gutter. "I'm fully aware of it, and that's always a slight pleasure!" And then the darning needle held herself erect and didn't lose her good spirits.

All sorts of things were sailing over her: sticks, straws, pieces of newspaper. "See how they sail!" said the darning needle. "Little do they know what's behind it all. I'm behind it all! I'm sitting here. See, there goes a stick now. It thinks of nothing but 'sticks,' and it is one itself. There floats a straw—see how it whirls, see how it twirls! Don't think about yourself so much, you'll bump against the paving stones! There floats a newspaper; everything in it is forgotten and still it spreads! I sit patiently and quietly! I know what I am, and this I shall remain."

One day something nearby shone prettily, and so the darning needle thought it was a diamond, but it was a fragment of a broken bottle. And as it was shining, the darning needle spoke to it and presented herself as a brooch. "I daresay you're a diamond, aren't you?" "Well, something like that." And then each one thought the other was quite costly, and so they talked about the arrogance of the world.

"Yes, I lived in a box belonging to a maiden," said the darning needle. "And that maiden was a kitchen maid. On each hand she had five fingers, but I've never known anything as conceited as those five fingers, and yet they existed for the sole purpose of holding me, taking me out of the box, and putting me in the box."

"Did they shine?" asked the bottle fragment.

"Shine? No," said the darning needle. "No. That was arrogance for you! They were five brothers, born 'fingers' all of them. They carried themselves erect, side by side, although they were of different lengths. The outermost one, Thumbkin, was short and fat. He went outside the row, and then he had but one joint in his back and could bow only once. But he said that if he were chopped off of somebody, then the whole of the person was ruined for military duty. Lick Pan made its way into sweet and sour alike, pointed at the sun and moon, and he's the one who squeezed when they wrote. Longman looked over the heads of the others. Ringman wore a golden ring around his belly, and Little Per didn't do a thing and was proud of it. Boast they did and boast they always will, so I went in the sink!"

"And now we're sitting here, glittering!" said the fragment of glass. At the same moment more water came into the gutter; it overflowed, dragging the bottle fragment along with it.

"See, now it has been promoted!" said the darning needle. "I'll stay where I am; I'm too fine, but I'm proud of it, and that is worthy of respect!" And then she held herself erect and thought of many things.

"I'm inclined to believe I was born of a sunbeam, I'm so fine! And then too, the sun always seems to seek me out under the water. Alas, I'm so fine that my own mother can't find me! If only I had my one eye that broke off, I think I could cry—even though I wouldn't do it, crying just isn't done!"

One day some street urchins were poking about in the gutter, where they found old nails, shillings, and the like. It was a messy pastime, but they enjoyed it.

"Ow!" said one, sticking himself on the darning needle. "There's a fellow for you!"

"I'm not a fellow, I'm a miss!" said the darning needle, but nobody heard it. The sealing wax had come off and she had turned black. But black is slimming, and so she thought she was finer than ever.

"Here comes an eggshell sailing along!" said the boys, and then they stuck the darning needle firmly in the shell.

"White walls, and black myself!" said the darning needle. "That's becoming! At least I can be seen! If only I don't become seasick, for then I'll throw up!" But she didn't become seasick, and she didn't throw up.

"It's good for seasickness to have a stomach of steel and to remember that one is a little more than a human being. Now mine has passed over. Indeed, the finer one is, the more one can endure!"

"Crack!" said the eggshell as a loaded cart went over it. "My, how it squeezes!" said the darning needle. "Now I'm going to be seasick all the same! I'm breaking! I'm breaking!" But she didn't break, even though a whole cart load had gone over her. She was lying at full length—and there she can stay!

The Red Shoes

THERE was once a little girl, so delicate and fair; but in summer she always had to go barefoot, because she was poor, and in winter she wore big wooden shoes, so her little insteps turned quite red—and horribly red at that.

In the middle of the village lived old Mother Shoemaker; she sat and sewed, as well as she could, out of strips of old red cloth, a pair of little shoes. They were quite clumsy, but they were well meant, and the little girl was to have them. The little girl was named Karen.

On the very day her mother was buried she was given the red shoes, and had them on for the first time. To be sure, they weren't the sort of thing to mourn in, but she had no others, and so she walked barelegged in them behind the poor straw coffin.

At that very moment a big old carriage came up, and in it sat a big old lady. She looked at the little girl and felt sorry for her, and so she said to the parson, "Listen here, give that little girl to me and I will be good to her!"

And Karen thought it was all because of the red shoes. But the old lady said they were horrid, and they were burnt. But Karen was given clean, neat clothes to wear; she had to learn to read and sew, and people said she was pretty, but the mirror said, "You're much more than pretty, you're lovely!"

Once the queen journeyed through the land, and she took with her, her little daughter, who was a princess. People streamed to the castle, and Karen was there too. And the little princess stood at a window, dressed in white, and showed herself; she wore neither a train nor a golden crown, but she had on lovely red morocco-leather shoes. To be sure, they were prettier by far than the ones old Mother Shoemaker had made for little Karen. After all, there was nothing in the world like red shoes!

Now Karen was old enough to be confirmed. She was given new clothes, and she was to have new shoes too. The rich shoemaker in the city measured her little foot at home in his own parlor, and there stood big glass cases full of lovely shoes and shiny boots. It was a pretty sight, but the old lady couldn't see very well, and so it gave her no pleasure. In the middle of all the shoes stood a pair of red ones, just like the shoes the princess had worn. How beautiful they were! The shoemaker said that they had been made for the daughter of an earl, but they didn't fit.

"I daresay they're of patent leather!" said the old lady. "They shine!"

"Yes, they shine!" said Karen. And they fit and they were bought, but the old lady had no idea that they were red, for she would never have permitted Karen to go to confirmation in red shoes. But that is exactly what she did.

Everybody looked at her feet, and as she walked up the aisle to the chancel it seemed to her that even the old pictures on the tombs—the portraits of parsons and parsons' wives, in stiff ruff collars and long black robes—fixed their eyes on her red shoes. And she thought only of these when the parson laid his hand upon her head and spoke of the holy baptism, of the covenant with God, and said that now she was to be a grown-up Christian. And the organ played so solemnly, and the beautiful voices of children sang, and the old choirmaster sang. But Karen thought only of the red shoes.

By afternoon the old lady had been informed by everyone that the shoes had been red, and she said it was shameful! It wasn't done! And after this, when Karen went to church, she was always to wear black shoes, even if they were old.

Next Sunday was communion, and Karen looked at the black shoes and she looked at the red ones—and then she looked at the red ones again and put the red ones on. It was beautiful sunny weather. Karen and the old lady took the path through the cornfield, and it was a bit dusty there.

By the door of the church stood an old soldier with a crutch and a curious long beard. It was more red than white, for it was red. And he bent all the way down to the ground and asked the old lady if he might wipe off her shoes. And Karen stretched out her little foot too. "See what lovely dancing shoes!" said the soldier. "Stay put when you dance!" And then he struck the soles with his hand.

The old lady gave the soldier a shilling, and then she went into the church with Karen.

And all the people inside looked at Karen's red shoes, and all the portraits looked at them, and when Karen knelt before the altar and lifted the golden chalice to her lips, she thought of nothing but the red shoes; and it seemed to her that they were swimming about in the chalice, and she forgot to sing her hymn, forgot to say the Lord's Prayer.

Now everybody went out of the church, and the old lady climbed into her carriage. Karen lifted her foot to climb in behind her, when the old soldier, who was standing nearby, said: "See what lovely dancing shoes!" And Karen couldn't help it, she had to take a few dancing steps! And once she had started, her feet kept on dancing. 't was just as if the shoes had gained control over them.

She danced around the corner of the church; she couldn't stop! The coachman had to run after her and grab hold of her, and he lifted her up into the carriage. But the feet kept on dancing, giving the old lady some terrible kicks. At last they got the shoes off, and the feet came to rest.

At home the shoes were put up in a cupboard, but Karen couldn't stop looking at them.

Now the old lady was ill in bed. They said she couldn't live. She had to be nursed and taken care of, and Karen was the proper person to do it. But over in the city there was a great ball. Karen had been invited. She looked at the old lady, who wasn't going to live after all, she looked at the red shoes, and she didn't think there was anything sinful in that. She put the red shoes on, too; surely she could do that—but then she went to the ball, and then she started to dance.

But when she wanted to go to the right, the shoes danced to the left, and when she wanted to go up the floor, the shoes danced down the floor, down the stairs, through the street, and out of the city gate. Dance she did and dance she must—straight out into the gloomy forest.

Then something was shining up among the trees, and she thought it was the moon, for it was a face. But it was the old soldier with the red beard. He sat and nodded, and said, "See what lovely dancing shoes!"

Now she became terrified and wanted to throw away the red shoes, but they stayed put; and she ripped off her stockings, but the shoes had grown fast to her feet. And dance she did and dance she must, over field and meadow, in rain and sunshine, by night and by day. But the night-time was the most horrible.

She danced into the graveyard, but the dead there didn't dance; they had something better to do than dance. She wanted to sit down on the pauper's grave where the bitter tansy grew, but there was no peace or rest for her. And when she danced over toward the open door of the church, she saw an angel there in a long white robe, with wings that reached from his shoulders down to the ground. His face was hard and grave, and in his hand he held a sword, so broad and shining.

"Dance you shall!" he said. "Dance in your red shoes until you turn pale and cold! Until your skin shrivels up like a skeleton! Dance you shall from door to door, and where there are proud and vain children, you shall knock so they will hear you and fear you! Dance you shall, dance!"

"Mercy!" cried Karen. But she didn't hear the angel's reply, for the shoes carried her through the gate, out in

the field, over roads, over paths, and she had to keep on
dancing.

One morning she danced past a door she knew well.
The sound of a hymn came from inside, and they carried
out a coffin decorated with flowers. Then she knew that the
old lady was dead, and she felt that she had been abandoned by everyone and cursed by God's angel.

Dance she did and dance she must. Dance in the dark
night. The shoes carried her off through thorns and stubble, and she scratched herself until the blood flowed; she

danced on, over the heath, to a lonely little house. She knew that the executioner lived here, and she knocked on the pane with her finger and said, "Come out! Come out! I can't come in because I'm dancing!"

And the executioner said, "You probably don't know who I am, do you? I chop the heads off wicked people, and I can feel my ax quivering!"

"Don't chop off my head," said Karen, "for then I can't repent my sin! But chop off my feet with the red shoes!"

And then she confessed all her sins, and the executioner chopped off her feet with the red shoes. But the shoes danced away with the tiny feet, over the field and into the deep forest.

And he carved wooden feet and crutches for her and taught her a hymn that sinners always sing; and she kissed the hand that had swung the ax, and went across the heath.

"Now I've suffered enough for the red shoes!" she said. "Now I'm going to church so they can see me!" And she walked fairly quickly toward the church door. But when she got there, the red shoes were dancing in front of her, and she grew terrified and turned back.

All week long she was in agony and cried many heavy tears. But when Sunday came she said: "That's that! Now I've suffered and struggled enough. I daresay I'm just as good as many of those who sit there in church putting on airs!" And then she went bravely enough, but she got no farther than the gate. Then she saw the red shoes dancing ahead of her, and she grew terrified and turned back, and deeply repented her sin.

And she went over to the parsonage and begged to be taken into service there; she would work hard and do anything she could. She didn't care about the wages, only that she might have a roof over her head and stay with good people. And the parson's wife felt sorry for her and took her into her service. And she was diligent and pensive. She sat quietly and listened when the parson read aloud from the Bible in the evening. All the little ones were quite fond of her, but when they talked of finery and dressing up, and of being as lovely as a queen, she would shake her head.

The next Sunday they all went to church, and they asked her if she wanted to come with them. But she looked miserably at her crutches with tears in her eyes, and so they went to hear the word of God while she went in her little chamber alone. It was just big enough for a bed and a chair, and here she sat with her hymn book; and as she was piously reading in it the wind carried the strains of the organ over to her from the church. And with tears in her eyes, she lifted up her face and said, "O God, help me!"

Then the sun shone brightly, and right in front of her stood the angel of God in the white robe, the one she had seen that night in the door of the church. He was no longer holding the sharp sword, but a lovely green branch full of roses. And with it he touched the ceiling, and it rose high; and where he had touched it there shone a golden star. And he touched the walls, and they expanded, and she saw the organ that was playing; she saw the old pictures of the parsons and the parsons' wives. The congregation was sitting in the ornamented pews and singing from the hymn books; for the church itself had come home to the poor girl in the tiny, narrow chamber, or else she had come to it. She was sitting in the pew with the rest of the parson's family, and when they had finished singing the hymn and looked up, they nodded and said, "It was right of you to come, Karen."

"It was by the grace of God!" she said.

And the organ swelled, and the voices of the children in the choir sounded so soft and lovely. The bright sunshine streamed in through the window to the pew where Karen sat. Her heart was so full of sunshine and contentment and happiness that it broke. Her soul flew on the sunshine to God, and there was no one there who asked about the red shoes.

The Jumpers

❖   ❖   ❖

THE flea, the grasshopper, and the skipjack once wanted to see which of them could jump the highest, and so they invited the whole world—and anybody else who wanted to come—to see the fun. And they were three proper jumpers who came together in the room.

"Well, I'm giving my daughter to the one who jumps the highest!" said the king. "For it's poor consolation that those persons should jump for nothing!"

The flea stepped forward first. He had genteel manners and bowed on every side, for he had spinster blood in his veins and was used to associating with people. And that, after all, means a lot.

The grasshopper came next. He, of course, was considerably bigger, but still he had quite good manners. He was wearing a green uniform, which he had been born with. What's more, this personage said that he came of a very old family in the land of Egypt, and that back home he was prized very highly. He had been taken right out of the field and put in a house of cards, three stories high—all face cards, with the colored side turned in. It had both doors and windows that had been cut out of the waist of the Queen of Hearts.

"I sing so well," he said, "that sixteen local crickets, who have been chirping ever since they were small and

have not yet been given a house of cards, were so vexed
that they became even thinner after listening to me sing."

Both of them—the flea and the grasshopper—thus gave
a good accounting of who they were and why they thought
they could indeed wed a princess.

The skipjack said nothing, but it was said that he thought
all the more; and the court hound sniffed at him alone
because he recognized that the skipjack came of a good
family. The old alderman, who had been given three
orders for keeping silent, maintained that the skipjack had
the gift of prophecy: one could tell from his back whether
the winter would be mild or severe, and one can't even
tell that from the back of the man who writes the Almanac.

"Well, I'm not saying a thing," said the old king, "but
then I always did go about this way and keep my thoughts
to myself!"

Now the jumping was to begin. The flea jumped so high

that no one could see him, and so they contended that he
hadn't jumped at all. And this was unfair.

The grasshopper only jumped half as high, but he landed right in the king's face, so the king said that was revolting!

The skipjack stood still and meditated for a long time. At last they thought he couldn't jump at all.

"If only he hasn't become indisposed!" said the court hound, and then he sniffed at him again: SWOOOOOOOSH! The skipjack jumped a tiny, wobbly jump right into the lap of the princess, who was sitting on a low golden stool.

Then the king said, "The highest jump is to jump up to my daughter, for that's the very point! But a head is needed to hit upon such a thing, and the skipjack has shown that he has a head. He has legs in his forehead!"

And so he got the princess.

"Nonetheless I jumped the highest!" said the flea. "But it doesn't matter. Just let her have that contraption of pegs and wax. I jumped the highest! But in this world one needs a body if one is to be seen."

And then the flea went abroad to the wars, where it is said he was killed.

The grasshopper sat down in a ditch and thought over the way of the world as it really is. And then he also said, "What's needed is a body! What's needed is a body!"

And then he sang his own melancholy song, and this is where we have taken the story from. But it could very well be a lie, even if it has appeared in print.

The Shepherdess and
the Chimney Sweep

❖   ❖   ❖

HAVE you ever seen a really old wooden cupboard, quite black with age and carved with scrolls and foliage? Just such a cupboard was standing in a parlor. It had been inherited from a great-grandmother and was carved with roses and tulips from top to bottom. There were the most curious scrolls, and here and there among them tiny stags were sticking out their antler-covered heads. But in the middle of the cupboard had been carved a whole man; just looking at him was enough to make you grin. And grin he did—you couldn't call it laughing. He had the legs of a billy goat, tiny horns in his forehead, and a long beard. The children of the house called him "Billygoatlegs Chiefandsubordinategeneralwarcommandersergeant," for it was a hard name to say, and there aren't many who receive that title. But to have him carved out was also something! Yet there he stood! He was always staring over at the table under the mirror, for there stood a lovely little shepherdess of porcelain. Her shoes were gilded, her dress was daintily tucked up with a red rose, and she had a golden hat and a shepherd's crook. She was delightful! Close by her side stood a little chimney sweep, as black as coal, but of porcelain too, for that matter. He was just as clean and handsome as anybody else—a chimney sweep was only something he was supposed to be. The porcelain-

maker could just as well have made him a prince, it made
no difference.

There he stood so nicely with his ladder, and with a face
as rosy and as fair as a girl's. And this was really a mistake,
for at least he could have been made a little black. He
stood quite close to the shepherdess. They had both been
placed where they were standing, and as they had been
placed like this, they had become engaged. After all, they
were well suited to each other: they were young, they

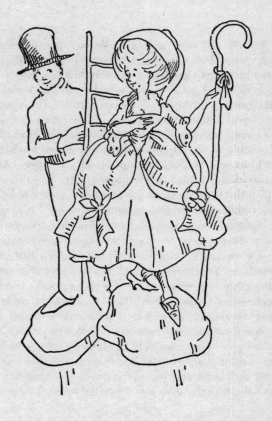

were both made of the same porcelain, and they were equally as fragile.

Close by them stood yet another doll, which was three times as big. This was an old Chinaman who could nod. He was also made of porcelain and said he was the little shepherdess' grandfather. But he certainly couldn't prove it! He insisted that he had authority over her, and this is why he nodded to Billygoatlegs Chiefandsubordinategeneralwarcommandersergeant, who had been courting the little shepherdess.

"You'll be getting a man there!" said the old Chinaman. "A man I'm almost certain is made of mahogany. He can make you 'Mrs. Billygoatlegs Chiefandsubordinategeneralwarcommandersergeant,' and he has the whole cupboard full of silver—in addition to what he has in secret drawers."

"I won't go inside that dark cupboard!" said the little shepherdess. "I've heard it said that he has eleven porcelain wives in there!"

"Then you can be the twelfth!" said the Chinaman. "Tonight, as soon as the old cupboard starts to creak, the wedding will be held—as sure as I'm Chinese." And then he nodded his head and fell asleep.

But the little shepherdess cried and looked at her dearly beloved, the porcelain chimney sweep.

"I do believe I will ask you," she said, "to go out into the wide world with me, for we can't stay here!"

"I'll do anything you wish!" said the little chimney sweep. "Let us go right away; I daresay I can support you by my profession!"

"If only we were safely down off the table!" she said. "I won't be happy until we're out in the wide world!"

And he comforted her and showed her where to place her little foot on the carved edges and the gilded foliage down around the table leg. He also used his ladder, and then they were down on the floor. But when they looked over at the old cupboard, there was quite a commotion!

All the carved deer were thrusting out their heads even farther -and raising their antlers and craning their necks. Billygoatlegs Chiefandsubordinategeneralwarcommander-sergeant hopped high in the air and shouted to the old Chinaman, "There they run! There they run!"

This frightened them a little, and they quickly jumped up into the drawer of the dais. Here lay three or four packs of cards that weren't complete and a little toy theater that had been set up as well as possible. A play was being performed, and all the queens—diamonds and hearts, clubs and spades—were sitting in the first row, fanning themselves with their tulips. And behind them stood all the jacks and showed that they had heads both right side up and upside down, the way playing cards do. The play was about two sweethearts who couldn't have each other, and it made the shepherdess cry, for it was just like her own story.

"I cannot bear it!" she said. "I must get out of the drawer!" But when they were down on the floor and looked up at the table, the old Chinaman was awake and his whole body was rocking—for his lower half was a single lump.

"Now the old Chinaman is coming!" screamed the little shepherdess, and she was so miserable that she fell right down on her procelain knees.

"I've got an idea!" said the chimney sweep. "Let's crawl down in the big potpourri crock that stands in the corner. There we could lie on roses and lavender and throw salt in his eyes when he comes."

"That would never do," she said. "And besides, I know that the old Chinaman and the potpourri crock were once engaged, and there's always a little feeling left when you've been on such terms. No, there's nothing left to do but to go out into the wide world!"

"Do you really have enough courage to go out into the wide world with me?" asked the chimney sweep. "Have you ever thought of how big it is and that we could never come back here again?"

"I have!" she said.

Then the chimney sweep gave her a steady look and said, "My way goes through the chimney. Do you really have enough courage to crawl with me through the tiled stove, through both the drum and the flue? Then we come out in the chimney, and from there I know what to do. We'll climb so high that they can't reach us. And at the very top there is a hole out to the wide world."

And he led her to the door of the tiled stove.

"It looks black!" she said, but still she went with him, through the drum and through the flue, where it was as black as pitch.

"Now we're in the chimney!" he said. "And look! Look! The loveliest star is shining up above!"

And there in the sky was a real star that shone all the way down to them, as if it wanted to show them the way. And they crawled and they crept—it was a terrible way—so high, so high! But he lifted her and he helped her; he held her and pointed out the easiest places for her to put her tiny porcelain feet. Then they came all the way up to the edge of the chimney. And there they sat down, for they were really tired—and so they should be too.

The sky with all its stars was overhead, and the city with all its rooftops lay down below. They could see far around them, so far out into the world. The poor shepherdess had never imagined it was like this. She lay her little head against her chimney sweep, and then she cried so hard that the gold popped off her sash.

"It's much too much!" she said. "I cannot bear it! The world is much too big! If only I were back there again. I have followed you out into the wide, wide world, so now you can just follow me home again if you have any feelings for me!"

And the chimney sweep tried to talk sense into her. He

talked about the old Chinaman, and about Billygoatlegs Chiefandsubordinategeneralwarconmandersergeant. But she sobbed so bitterly, and kissed her little chimney sweep so, that the only thing he could do was to do as she said, even though it was wrong.

And so with considerable difficulty they crawled back down through the chimney, and they crept through the flue and the drum—it wasn't at all pleasant. And then they were standing in the dark stove, eavesdropping behind the door to find out how things stood in the room. It was quite still. They peeked out. Alas! There in the middle of the floor lay the old Chinaman. He had fallen down off the table while trying to go after them, and lay broken in three pieces. His back had come off in one piece, and his head had rolled over in a corner. Billygoatlegs Chiefandsubordinategeneralwarcommandersergeant stood where he always stood, thinking everything over.

"It's gruesome!" said the little shepherdess. "Old grandfather is smashed to bits, and we're to blame! I can never live it down!" And then she wrung her teeny-weeny hands.

"He can still be riveted," said the chimney sweep. "He can be riveted very well. Don't carry on so! After they glue his back and put a good rivet in his neck, he'll be just as good as new and be able to tell us many unpleasantries!"

"Do you think so?" she said. And then they crawled back up on the table where they had stood before.

"See how far we've come!" said the chimney sweep. "We could have spared ourselves all that bother!"

"If only old grandfather were riveted," said the shepherdess. "Can it be too expensive?"

And he was riveted. The family had his back glued, and a good rivet was put in his neck. He was just as good as new, but he couldn't nod.

"You've certainly become high and mighty since you were broken!" said Billygoatlegs Chiefandsubordinategeneralwarcommandersergeant. "Although I don't think that's anything to be so proud of! Am I to have her or am I not?"

And the chimney sweep and the little shepherdess gave the old Chinaman such a piteous look. They were afraid he was going to nod. But he couldn't. And it was unpleasant for him to have to tell a stranger that he would always have a rivet in his neck. So the porcelain people remained together, and they gave grandfather's rivet their blessing and loved each other until they broke into bits.

The Little Match Girl

❖　　　❖　　　❖

IT was so bitterly cold. It was snowing, and the evening was growing dark. It was also the last evening of the year: New Year's Eve. In this cold and in this darkness a poor little girl was walking along the street. Her head was uncovered and her feet were bare. To be sure, she had been wearing slippers when she left home, but what was the good of that? The slippers were quite big; her mother had used them last, they were so big. And the little girl had lost them when she hurried across the street, just as two carriages went rushing past at a frightful speed. One slipper was nowhere to be found, and a boy had run off with the other. He said he could use it for a cradle when he had children of his own.

There walked the little girl now on her tiny bare feet, which were red and blue with the cold. In an old apron she had a lot of matches, and she carried a bunch in her hand. No one had bought any from her the whole day. No one had given her a single shilling. Hungry and frozen, she looked so cowed as she walked along, the poor little thing. The snowflakes fell on her long golden hair, which curled so prettily about her neck. But of course she didn't think about anything as fine as that. The lights were shining out from all the windows, and there in the street was such a delicious odor of roast goose. After all, it was New Year's Eve. Yes, she did think about that.

Over in a corner between two houses—one of them jutted a little farther out in the street than the other—she sat down and huddled. She tucked her tiny legs under her, but she froze even more, and she dared not go home. She hadn't sold any matches, hadn't received a single shilling. Her father would beat her, and then too it was cold at home. They had only the roof above them, and the wind whistled in even though the biggest cracks had been stuffed with straw and rags. Her tiny hands were almost numb with cold. Alas! One little match would do so much good! Did she dare to pull just one out of the bunch, strike it against the wall and warm her fingers? She pulled one out. Scratch! How it spluttered, how it burned! It was a warm clear flame, just like a tiny candle when she held her hand around it. It was a strange light. It seemed to the little girl that she was sitting before a huge iron stove, with shining brass knobs and a brass drum. The fire burned so wonderfully, was so warming. No, what was that? The little girl was already stretching out her feet to warm them too when the flame went out. The stove disappeared. She sat with a little stump of the burnt-out match in her hand.

A new one was struck. It burned, it shone, and where the light fell on the wall it became transparent like gauze. She looked right into the room where the table was set with a gleaming white cloth, fine china, and a splendid, steaming roast goose stuffed with prunes and apples. And what was even more splendid, the goose hopped down from the platter and waddled across the floor with a fork and a knife in its back. Right over to the poor girl it came. Then the match went out, and only the thick cold wall could be seen.

She lit a new match. Now she was sitting under the loveliest Christmas tree. It was even bigger and had more

decorations on it than the one she had seen through the glass door of the rich merchant's house last Christmas. A thousand candles were burning on the green branches, and gaily colored pictures—like the ones that decorate shop windows—looked down at her. The little girl stretched out both hands in the air. Then the match went out; the many Christmas candles went higher and higher; she saw that they were now bright stars. One of them fell and made a long fiery streak in the sky.

"Now someone is dying!" said the little girl, for her old grandmother—the only one who had ever been good to her, but now was dead—had said that when a star falls, a soul goes up to God.

Again she struck a match against the wall. It shone around her, and in the glow stood the old grandmother, so bright and shining, so blessed and mild.

"Grandma!" cried the little one. "Oh, take me with you! I know you'll be gone when the match goes out, gone just like the warm stove, the wonderful roast goose, and the big, heavenly Christmas tree!" And she hastily struck all the rest of the matches in the bunch. She wanted to keep her grandmother with her. And the matches shone with such a radiance that it was brighter than the light of day. Never before had grandmother been so beautiful, so big. She lifted up the little girl in her arms, and in radiance and rejoicing they flew so high, so high. And there was no cold, no hunger, no fear—they were with God.

But in a corner by the house, in the early-morning cold, sat the little girl with rosy cheeks and a smile on her face—dead, frozen to death on the last evening of the old year. The morning of the New Year dawned over the little body sitting with the matches, of which a bunch was almost burned up. She had wanted to warm herself, it was said. No one knew what lovely sight she had seen or in what radiance she had gone with her old grandmother into the happiness of the New Year.

The Drop of Water

❖   ❖   ❖

YOU are familiar, of course, with a magnifying glass, a round spectacle lens that makes everything a hundred times larger than it is. When you hold it up to your eye and look at a drop of water from the pond, you can see more than thousand strange creatures that are otherwise never seen in the water; but they are there and it is real. It looks almost like a saucer full of shrimps frisking about one another, and they are so gluttonous that they tear arms and legs and bottoms and edges off one another—and yet they are happy and contented in their own fashion.

Now, there was once an old man whom everyone called Wiggle-Waggle, for that was his name. He always wanted the best of everything, and when he couldn't get it, he used magic.

One day he was sitting there, holding his magnifying glass to his eye and looking at a drop of water that had been taken from a puddle in the ditch. My, what a wiggling and a waggling there was! All the thousands of tiny creatures were jumping about, stepping on one another and taking bites out of one another.

"Why, how abominable that is!" said old Wiggle-Waggle. "Can't they be made to live in peace and quiet, and each one mind his own business?" And he thought and he thought, but it wouldn't work. And then he had to start conjuring. "I must give them color so they can be seen plainly," he said, and then he poured something resembling a tiny drop of red wine into the drop of water. But it was witch's blood, the very best sort at two shillings. Then all the strange creatures turned a rosy-red all over their bodies. It looked like a whole city of naked wild men.

"What have you there?" asked an old troll who had no name, and that was what was so fine about him.

"Well, if you can guess what it is," said Wiggle-Waggle, "I shall make you a present of it. But it's not so easy to find out as long as you don't know."

And the troll who had no name looked through the

magnifying glass. It really did look like a whole city, where all the people ran about with no clothes on! It was frightful, but it was even more frightful to see how each one shoved and jostled the other, how they nipped and nibbled at one another and dragged one another forth. The ones at the bottom had to be at the top, and the ones at the top had to be at the bottom. "See! See! His leg is longer than mine! Biff! Away with it! There's one who has a tiny pimple behind his ear, a wee little innocent pimple, but it plagues him, and so it shall not plague him anymore!" And they hacked at it and they tugged at him and they ate him for the sake of that tiny pimple. One was sitting there so still, like a little maiden, and desired only peace and quiet, but the maiden had to come forth, and they tugged at her and they pulled at her and they ate her up!

"It's extremely amusing!" said the troll.

"Yes, but what do you think it is?" asked Wiggle-Waggle. "Can you figure it out?"

"Why, that's easy to see," said the other. "It's Copenhagen, of course, or another big city. They all resemble one another, to be sure. A big city it is!"

"It's water from a ditch!" said Wiggle-Waggle.

The Happy Family

❖ ❖ ❖

THE biggest green leaf here in the land is, to be sure, a dock leaf. If you hold it in front of your little tummy, it's just like a whole apron; and if you put it on your head, then in rainy weather it's almost as good as an umbrella, for it's so terribly big. A dock plant never grows alone. No, where one grows, there grow more. It's a great delight, and all that delightfulness is food for snails—those big white snails that fashionable people, in the old days, had made into a fricassee, ate, and said, "Yum! How good it tastes!" because they thought it tasted so delicious. The snails lived on dock leaves, and for that reason the dock plants were sown.

Now there was an old manor house where snails were no longer eaten; they were quite extinct. But the dock plants were not extinct. They grew and grew over all the paths and all the beds. It was no longer possible to cope with them. There was a whole forest of dock plants. Here and there stood an apple tree or a plum tree, otherwise you would never have thought it was a garden. Everything was dock plants, and in there lived the last two exceedingly old snails.

They themselves didn't know how old they were; but they could well remember that there had been many more, that they belonged to a family from foreign parts,

215

and that the entire forest had been planted for them and theirs. They had never been beyond it, but they knew that there was one thing more in the world, called The Manor House. And up there you were cooked and then you turned black and then you were placed on a silver platter. But what happened next no one knew. For that matter they couldn't imagine how it felt to be cooked and lie on a silver platter, but it was supposed to be delightful and particularly distinguished. Neither the cockchafer, the toad, nor the earthworm, whom they asked about it, could give them any information. None of them had ever been cooked or placed on a silver platter.

The old white snails were the most aristocratic in the world, they knew; the forest existed for their sakes, and the manor house existed so that they could be cooked and laid on a silver platter.

They now lived quite happily and secluded, and as they had no children themselves, they had adopted an ordinary little snail, which they reared as their own. But the little one wouldn't grow, for he was ordinary. Yet the old folks, especially Mama—Mama Snail—still thought they could see that he was progressing. And she asked Papa, in case he couldn't see it, to feel the little shell. And so he felt it and found out that Mama was right.

One day there was a heavy downpour.

"Listen to how it rub-a-dub-dubs on the dock leaves!" said Papa Snail.

"Drops are coming in too!" said Mama Snail. "Why, it's running right down the stalks! You'll see how wet it's going to be here! I'm so glad we have our good houses, and the little one has his too! More has certainly been done for us than for any other creatures. It's plain to see that we're the Lords and Masters of the world! We have a house from birth, and the dock forest has been sown for our sakes. I'd so like to know how far it stretches and what is beyond it."

"There's nothing beyond it!" said Papa Snail. "There can be no better place than here where we are, and I have nothing else to wish for!"

"Oh, yes," said Mama. "I'd so like to come up to the manor house and be cooked and laid on a silver platter. All our ancestors have, and you can imagine there's something special about that."

"It's possible the manor house may have fallen down," said Papa Snail. "Or else the dock forest has grown up over it so the people can't come out. There's no need to be in such a hurry, either. But you're always in such a terrible rush, and now the little one is starting too. For three days he's been crawling up that stalk. It gives me a headache when I look up at him!"

"Now, you mustn't fuss!" said Mama Snail. "He's crawling so steadily; he'll be a great joy to us, all right, and we old folks have nothing else to live for! But have you thought of where we're going to find a wife for him? Don't you think that far, far inside the dock forest there might be some of our own kind?"

"I daresay there are plenty of black slugs!" said the old snail. "Black slugs without a house. But that would be such a comedown—and they put on airs! But we could commission the ants to look into it. They scurry back and forth as if they had something to do. They certainly must know of a wife for our little snail!"

"Of course, we know of the loveliest one!" said the ants. "But we're afraid it won't do, for she's a queen!"

"That doesn't matter!" said the old snails. "Does she have a house?"

"She has a castle!" said the ants. "The loveliest ant castle, with seven hundred halls!"

"No, thank you!" said Mama Snail. "Our son is not going into an ant hill! If you haven't got better sense, we'll give the commission to the white gnats. They fly far and wide, in sunshine and in rain. They know the dock forest inside and out."

"We have a wife for him!" said the gnats. "A hundred human paces from here, sitting on a gooseberry bush, is a little snail with a house. She is quite alone and old enough to get married. It's only a hundred human paces."

"Well, let her come to him," said the old snails. "He has a forest of dock plants; she has only a bush!"

And so they fetched the little snail maiden. It took eight days for her to get there, but that was just what was so nice about it—one could tell she belonged to the same species.

And then the wedding was held. Six glow worms shone as well as they could, but otherwise it all proceeded quietly, for the old snails couldn't stand carousing and merry-making. But a lovely speech was made by Mama Snail—Papa couldn't, he was so moved. And then they passed on the entire forest of dock plants to them and said what they had always said: that it was the best forest in the world, and as long as they led honest and unpretentious lives and multiplied, then they and their children would one day come to the manor house, be cooked black, and laid on a silver dish.

And after that speech had been made, the old folks crawled into their houses and never came out again; they had gone to sleep. The young snail couple reigned in the forest and had a huge progeny. But they were never cooked, and they never came onto a silver dish. And from this they concluded that the manor house had fallen down, and that all the people in the world were extinct. And as no one contradicted them, it was true, of course. And the rain beat upon the dock leaves to make music for their sakes, and the sun shone on the dock forest to give color for their sakes. And they were very happy, and the whole family was happy. Indeed it was!

The Collar

❖ ❖ ❖

THERE was once a fashionable cavalier whose entire
inventory consisted of a bootjack and a comb. But he
had the finest collar in the world, and it is about the collar
that we are going to hear a tale.

Now, the collar was so old that he was thinking of
getting married, and then it happened that he was put in
the wash along with a garter.

"My!" said the collar. "I've never seen anyone so slender
and so elegant, so soft and so cuddly! May I ask your name?"

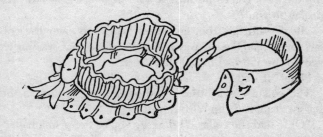

"I'm not saying!" said the garter.

"Where do you belong?" asked the collar.

But the garter was shy and thought this was an odd
question to reply to.

"I daresay you're a waistband!" said the collar. "One of those waistbands that are worn underneath! I can see very well that you're both useful and decorative, little maid!"

"You mustn't talk to me!" said the garter. "I don't think I've given you any occasion to!"

"Oh, yes! When anyone's as lovely as you are," said the collar, "then it's occasion enough!"

"Stop coming so close to me!" said the garter. "You look so masculine!"

"I'm a fashionable cavalier too!" said the collar. "I have a bootjack and a comb!" Now that, of course, wasn't true. It was his master who had them, but he was bragging.

"Don't come near me!" said the garter. "I'm not used to it!"

"Prude!" said the collar, and then he was taken out of the wash. He was starched, hung on a chair in the sunshine, and then placed on an ironing board. Along came the hot iron.

"Madame!" said the collar. "Little widow lady! I'm turning quite warm! I'm becoming quite another! I'm losing my creases! You're burning a hole in me! Ugh—I'm proposing to you!"

"Rag!" said the iron, and went arrogantly over the collar; for it imagined it was a steam engine that was on its way to the railroad to pull carriages.

"Rag!" it said.

The collar was a little frayed at the edges, and so the scissors came to clip off the fuzz.

"Oh!" said the collar. "I daresay you're the prima ballerina! My, how you can stretch your legs! That's the most adorable sight I've ever seen! No human being can ever equal you!"

"I know that!" said the scissors.

"You deserve to be a countess!" said the collar. "All I

have is a fashionable cavalier, a bootjack, and a comb! If only I had an estate!"

"He's proposing!" said the scissors, growing angry. And then it gave him a proper clip, and so he was discarded.

"I daresay I must propose to the comb!" said the collar. "It's incredible the way you keep all your teeth, little miss! Haven't you ever thought of becoming engaged?"

"I'll say I have!" said the comb. "I'm engaged to the bootjack!"

"Engaged!" said the collar. Now there were no more to propose to, and so he scorned proposing.

A long time passed. Then the collar ended up in a box at the paper mill. The rags were having a party, the finer ones for themselves, the rougher ones for themselves— just as it should be. They all had a lot to tell, but the collar had the most—he was a real braggart!

"I've had such a lot of sweethearts!" said the collar. "I was never left in peace! But then I was a fashionable cavalier—with starch! I had both a bootjack and a comb, which I never used! You should have seen me then, seen me when I lay on my side! I'll never forget my first sweetheart! She was a waistband, so fine, so soft, so cuddly! She threw herself into a tub of water on my account! Then there was a widow lady who became red hot, but I let her stand there and turn black! Then there was that prima ballerina, she gave me the scar that I still carry. She was so wild! But my heart bleeds most for the garter—I mean the waistband—who ended up in the tub of water. I have so much on my conscience. It's time I turned into white paper."

And so he was—all the rags turned into white paper. But the collar was made into the very piece of white paper we are looking at here. And that was because he bragged so dreadfully about all the things he had never been. And we should keep this in mind, so that we don't carry on in the same way. For we never can tell if we too won't end up in the rag box and be made into white paper—and have our whole story printed on it, even the most secret, and have to go about and relate it ourselves, just like the collar.

It's Quite True

❖　❖　❖

IT'S a frightful affair!" said a hen, and this was over on the side of town where the business hadn't taken place. "It's a frightful affair in a hen house! I dare not sleep alone tonight! It's a good thing there are a lot of us on the roost together!" And then she went on to tell, and the feathers of the other hens stood on end and the cock dropped his comb! It's quite true!

But we will begin at the beginning, and that was in a hen house on the other side of town. The sun went down and the hens flew up. One of them—she had white feathers and bandy legs—laid her prescribed number of eggs and, as a hen, was respectable in every way. When she came to the roost she preened herself with her beak, and then a tiny feather fell out.

"There it went," she said. "Indeed, the more I preen myself, the more beautiful I become!" Now, it was said in jest, for of all those hens she had the merriest disposition, but otherwise, as has been said, she was quite respectable. And then she went to sleep.

It was dark all around. Hen sat beside hen, and the one who sat next to her did not sleep. She heard and she didn't hear, as indeed you should in this world if you are to have peace of mind. But still she had to tell it to her other neighbor. "Did you hear what was said here? I'm not naming any names, but there's a hen who wants to pluck out all her feathers just to look good. If I were a cock, I'd despise her!"

And right above the hens sat the owl, with owl-husband and owl-children. They had sharp ears in that family. They heard every word the neighbor hen said. And they rolled their eyes, and Mama Owl fanned herself with her wings.

"Just don't pay any attention! But I daresay you heard what was said? I heard it with my own ears, and it'll take a lot before *they* fall off. One of the hens has forgotten what is proper for a hen, to such an extent that she's sitting there plucking out all her feathers and letting the cock look on!"

"*Prenez garde aux enfants!*" said Papa Owl. "That's not for the children!"

"I just want to tell the owl across the way. It's such a worthy owl to associate with." And away Mama flew.

"Whoooo! Hooooo! Whoooo! Hooooo!" they both hooted right down to the doves in the neighboring dovecote.

"Have you heard? Have you heard? Whoooo! Hoooo! There's a hen who's plucked out all her feathers for the cock's sake. She's freezing to death, if she hasn't already! Whoooo! Hoooo!"

"Where? Where?" cooed the doves.

"In the hen yard across the way! I've as good as seen it myself! It's almost an improper story to tell, but it's quite true!"

"Believe! Believe every last word!" said the doves. Then they cooed down to their own hen yard: "There's a hen— yes, some say there are two who have plucked out all their feathers so as not to look like the others, and thus attract the attention of the cock. It's a risky game. You can catch a cold and die of a fever, and they're both dead!"

"Wake up! Wake up!" crowed the cock, and flew up on the fence. Sleep was still in his eyes, but he crowed all the same: "Three hens have died of unrequited love for a cock! They have plucked out all their feathers. It's a dreadful affair! I don't want to keep it! Let it go on!"

"Let it go on!" squeaked the bats. And the hens clucked and the cocks crowed: "Let it go on! Let it go on!" And so the story flew from hen house to hen house, and at last it came back to the spot from which it had originally gone out.

"There are five hens," so it went, "who have all plucked out their feathers to show which of them had grown the shinniest because of an unhappy love affair with the cock! And then they hacked at one another until the blood flowed, and fell down dead, to the shame and disgrace of their families, and a great loss to the owner!"

And the hen who had lost the tiny loose feather naturally did not recognize her own story again. And as she was a respectable hen, she said, "I despise those hens! But there are more of that sort! Such a thing should not be hushed up, and I will do my best to see to it that the story appears in the newspaper. Then it will be known throughout the land. Those hens have deserved it, and their families too!"

And the story did appear in the newspaper; it was printed. And it's quite true: one tiny feather can indeed turn into five hens!

In a Thousand Years

Y ES, in a thousand years they'll come on wings of
steam, through the air and across the ocean! America's young inhabitants will visit old Europe. They will
come to the ancient monuments here and to places falling
to ruin, just as we in our day journey to the smoldering
splendors of southern Asia.

In a thousand years they'll come!

The Thames, the Danube, the Rhine, are rolling still:
Mont Blanc is standing with a snowy cap; the Aurora
Borealis is shining over the lands of the North. But generation after generation has turned to dust, rows of the
mighty of the moment are forgotten, like those who already slumber in the mound, where the prosperous flour
merchant, on whose land it is, makes himself a bench on
which to sit and look out across the flat, rippling fields of
grain.

"To Europe!" is the cry of America's young generation.
"To the land of our fathers, the lovely land of memory and
imagination, Europe!"

The airship comes. It is overcrowded with travelers, for
the speed is faster than by sea. The electromagnetic thread
under the ocean has already telegraphed how large the air
caravan is. Europe is already in sight—it is the coast of
Ireland—but the passengers are still asleep. They are not

to be awakened until they are over England; there they will set foot on European soil in the Land of Shakespeare, as it is called by the sons of the intellect; the Land of Politics or the Land of Machinery is what others call it.

The sojourn here lasts a whole day; so much time the busy generation has for the great England and Scotland.

On they speed through the Channel Tunnel to France, the land of Charlemagne and Napoleon. Molière is mentioned, the learned speak of a Classical and a Romantic school in the far-distant past, and there is jubilation over heroes, bards, and men of science unknown to our time, but who will be born on the crater of Europe: Paris.

The airship flies on, over the land where Columbus sailed forth, where Cortez was born, and where Calderón sang dramas in flowering verse. Lovely dark-eyed women still dwell in the flowering vale, and ancient songs tell of El Cid and the Alhambra.

Through the air, across the sea to Italy, where ancient Eternal Rome once lay; it has been wiped out, the Campagna is a wilderness. Of St. Peter's Church, only the remains of a solitary wall are shown, but its authenticity is doubted.

To Greece, in order to sleep for one night at the luxurious hotel high on the top of Mount Olympus—just to say they've been there. The journey continues to the Bosporus, to get a few hours' rest and see the spot where Byzantium lay. Poor fishermen spread their nets where legend tells of the harem garden in the time of the Turks.

Remains of mighty cities by the foaming Danube, cities our age never knew, are crossed in flight; but here and there—places rich in memory, those still to come, those yet unborn—the air caravan alights only to take off again.

Down there lies Germany, once encircled by the tightest network of railways and canals—the land where Luther spoke and Goethe sang, and where Mozart in his day wielded the scepter of music. Great names shine out in science and art, names unknown to us. A one-day stop for Germany, and one day for Scandinavia, the native lands of Ørsted and Linnaeus, and Norway, the land of the ancient heroes and the young Norwegians. Iceland is taken on the homeward journey; geysers no longer boil, Hekla is extinguished, but, as an eternal monument to the Sagas, the rocky island stands firm in the roaring sea.

"There's a lot to see in Europe!" says the young American. "And we have seen it in eight days. And it can be done, as the great traveler"—the name of a contemporary is mentioned—"has shown in his famous work: *Europe Seen in Eight Days*."

The Nisse at the Sausagemonger's

❖ ❖ ❖

THERE was a real student; he lived in a garret and owned nothing. There was a real sausagemonger; he lived on the ground floor and owned the whole house. And the nisse stuck to him, for here every Christmas Eve he received a dish of porridge with a big lump of butter in it—the sausagemonger could afford it. And the nisse remained in the shop, and that was quite instructive.

One evening the student came in the back door to buy himself candles and cheese. He had no one to send, so he came himself. He got what he ordered and paid for it, and the sausagemonger and the missus nodded "good evening." And that was a woman who could do more than nod: she had the gift of gab! And the student nodded back and then stood there, engrossed in reading the leaf of paper that had been wrapped about the cheese. It was a page torn out of an old book that should not have been torn to pieces, an old book full of poetry.

"There's more of it lying about," said the sausagemonger. "I gave an old woman some coffee beans for it. If you'll give me eight shillings, you can have the rest."

"Thanks," said the student. "Let me have that instead of the cheese! I can eat the bread and butter plain. It would be a sin for the whole book to be torn to shreds and tatters. You're a splendid man, a practical man, but

you don't understand any more about poetry than that tub!"

And that was a rude thing to say, especially about the tub. But the sausagemonger laughed, and the student laughed. It was said, of course, as a kind of joke. But it annoyed the nisse that anyone dared to say such a thing to a sausagemonger who was a landlord and who sold the best butter.

When it was night, and the shop was closed and everyone was in bed except the student, the nisse went in and took the missus' gift of gab. She didn't use it when she was asleep. And no matter which object in the room he put it on, it acquired speech and language; it could express its thoughts and feelings just as well as the missus. But only one could have it at a time, and that was a blessing, for otherwise they would have been speaking all at once.

And the nisse put the gift of gab on the tub in which the old newspapers lay. "Is it really true," he asked, "that you don't know what poetry is?"

"Of course I know," said the tub. "That's the sort of thing that stands at the bottom of the page in the newspaper and is clipped out. I should think I have more of that in me than the student, and I'm only a lowly tub compared to the sausagemonger."

And the nisse put the gift of gab on the coffee grinder. My, how it chattered! And he put it on the butter measure and on the till. They were all of the same opinion as the tub, and what the majority agrees upon must be respected.

"Now the student's going to catch it!" And then the nisse went softly up the backstairs to the garret where the student lived. There was a light inside, and the nisse peeped through the keyhole and saw that the student was reading the tattered book from below. But how bright it was in there! From the book shone a clear ray of light that turned into the trunk of a mighty tree that soared so high and spread its branches far out over the student. Every leaf was so fresh, and each blossom was the head of a lovely maiden—some with eyes so dark and radiant, others with eyes so blue and wondrously clear. Each fruit was a twinkling star, and a wonderfully lovely song rang out.

No, the little nisse had never imagined such splendor, much less seen or experienced it. And so he remained standing on tiptoe, peeping and peeping until the light inside went out. The student probably blew out his lamp and went to bed. But the nisse stood there all the same, for the song could still be heard so softly and sweetly—a lovely lullaby for the student who had lain down to rest.

"How wonderful!" said the little nisse. "I never expected that! I believe I'll stay with the student." And he thought—and thought quite sensibly—and then he sighed: "The student has no porridge!" And so he went—yes, he went back down to the sausagemonger. And it was a good thing he came, for the tub had used up almost all the missus' gift of gab by declaring on one side all the things it contained. And now it was just on the point of turning, in order to repeat the same thing on the other side, when the nisse came and brought the gift of gab back to the missus. But from then on, all the inhabitants of the whole shop, from the till to the kindling wood, were of the same opinion as the tub, and so high was their esteem and so great was their confidence in it that from then on, whenever the sausagemonger read the "Art and Theater Reviews" in his *Times*, the evening one, they believed it came from the tub.

But the little nisse no longer sat quietly and listened to all the wisdom and intelligence down there. No, as soon as the light shone from the chamber in the garret, the rays were like a strong anchor rope that dragged him up there, and he had to go and peep through the keyhole. And a feeling of grandeur engulfed him, such as we feel on the rolling sea when God strides across it in the storm. And he burst into tears. He didn't know himself why he was crying, but there was something so refreshing in those tears. How wonderfully delightful it must be to sit with the student under that tree! But that could never happen. He was happy at the keyhole. He was still standing there on the cold landing when the autumn wind blew down from the trap door in the loft, and it was so cold, so cold. But the little fellow didn't feel it until the light was put out in the garret room and the tones died before the wind. Brrrrr! Then he froze, and he crept back down to his sheltered corner where it was so cozy and warm. And when the Christmas porridge came with the big lump of butter in it, well, then the sausagemonger was master.

But in the middle of the night the nisse was awakened by a terrible commotion at the shutters. People were pounding outside! The night watch was blowing his whistle! There was a big fire; the whole street was ablaze! Was it here in the house or at the neighbor's? Where? It was terrifying! The sausagemonger's missus was so upset that she removed her golden earrings and put them in her pocket, just to have something to save! The sausagemonger ran to get his bonds, and the serving maid ran to get her silk mantilla. And the little nisse ran too. In a couple of bounds he was up the stairs and in the room of the student, who was standing quite calmly at the open window, watching the fire in the house across the way. The little nisse grabbed the wonderful book on the table, put it in his red cap, and held onto it with both hands. The greatest treasure of the house was saved! And then he rushed all the way out on the roof, all the way up to the chimney. And there he sat, lit up by the burning house right in front of him. And with both hands he held onto his red cap with the treasure in it. Now he knew where his heart lay, to whom he really belonged. But then, when the fire had been put out and he had regained his composure—well, "I'll divide myself between them!" he said. "I can't give up the sausagemonger completely for the sake of the porridge!"

And that was quite human! The rest of us also go to the sausagemonger—for the porridge!

Two Virgins

❖ ❖ ❖

HAVE you ever seen a virgin? That is to say, what the street pavers call a virgin: something to pound down the cobblestones with. She is solid wood, broad at the bottom with iron rings all around, and small at the top with a stick for her arms.

Two such virgins stood in the tool yard. They stood among shovels, cordwood measures, and wheelbarrows, and it had been rumored there that the virgin was no longer going to be called a virgin, but a "stamper" instead. And this is the latest and only correct term in the street-paver language for what, in days gone by, we all called a virgin.

Now, among us mortals there exist "emancipated females," among which are included headmistresses of institutions, midwives, dancers (who, by virtue of their office, can stand on one leg), modistes, and night nurses; and behind these ranks of "The Emancipated," the two virgins in the tool yard also ranged themselves. They were Virgins of the Highway Authority, and under no circumstances were they going to give up their good old name and allow themselves to be called stampers!

"Virgin is a human name," they said, "but a stamper is a thing, and we will not allow ourselves to be called a thing. That is the same as being called names."

"My fiancé is capable of breaking up with me," said the youngest, who was engaged to a pile driver, one of those big machines that drives down piles and consequently does on a large scale what the virgin does on a small one. "He will have me as a virgin, but he might not as a stamper, and so I cannot permit them to rechristen me."

"Yes, I'd sooner have my two arms broken off!" said the eldest.

The wheelbarrow, on the other hand, was of another opinion, and the wheelbarrow regarded itself as one-fourth a cart because it went on one wheel.

"I must indeed tell you that to be called a virgin is fairly commonplace, and not nearly as fine as being called a stamper; for in being called by that name one joins the rank of the signets, and think of the Signet of the Law. This is what affixes the judicial seal. In your place I would give up the virgin!"

"Never! I am too old for that!" said the eldest.

"You are certainly not aware of something called 'The European Necessity,'" said the honest old cordwood measure. "One must be kept within bounds, subordinate oneself; one must yield to time and necessity. And if there is a law that the virgin is to be called a stamper, then she must be called a stamper. Everything has a standard by which it is measured."

"Then if worst comes to worst," said the youngest, "I would sooner allow myself to be called 'Miss' instead. Miss smacks a little of virgin."

"But I would rather let myself be chopped into kindling wood!" said the old virgin.

Now they went to work. The virgins were driven; they were put on the wheelbarrow, and that was always fine treatment. But they were called stampers.

"Vir——!" they said as they stamped against the cobblestones. "Vir——!" And they were just about to say the whole word "Virgin"! But they bit the word off short.

They caught themselves in time, for they found that they needn't once bother to answer. But among themselves they always addressed one another by the name virgin and praised The Good Old Days, when everything was called by its right name and one was called a virgin when one *was* a virgin. And virgins they remained—both of them— for the pile driver, the great machine, really *did* break off with the youngest. He would not have anything to do with a stamper!

The Piggy Bank

❖ ❖ ❖

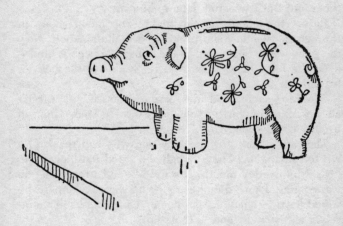

THERE were such a lot of playthings in the nursery; on the top of the cupboard stood the bank. It was made of clay in the shape of a pig. It had a natural crack in its back, and the crack had been made bigger with a knife so that silver dalers could also go in. And two had gone in, in addition to lots of shillings. The piggy bank was stuffed so full that he could no longer rattle, and that is the utmost a piggy bank can do. There he stood now, on top of the shelf, and looked down on all the things in the room.

He knew very well that with what he had in his stomach he could buy it all, and that is what is known as being well aware of oneself.

The others thought about it too, even if they didn't say so. Indeed, there were other things to talk about. The bureau drawer stood halfway open, and a big doll could be seen. She was quite old, and her neck had been riveted. She looked out and said, "Shall we play at being people? At least that's something!"

Now there was a commotion! Even the pictures turned around on the wall to show that there was another side to them too. But it was not done to be contrary.

It was the middle of the night. The moon shone in through the window and provided free illumination. Now the game was to begin, and all the things had been invited— even the baby buggy, who was really one of the heavier playthings.

"There is some good in everyone!" he said. "We can't all be of noble birth. Somebody has to make himself useful, as the saying goes."

The piggy bank was the only one who had received a written invitation. They thought he stood too high up to hear it by word of mouth. Nor did he send a reply that he was coming, for he didn't come. If he was to take part, he would have to enjoy it from home. They could suit themselves accordingly, and so they did.

The little toy theater was immediately set up so he could look right into it. They were going to begin with a play, and then there would be tea and intellectual exercise. But they started with this first. The rocking horse talked about training and thoroughbreds, the baby buggy about railroads and steam power. Indeed, it all had something to do with their professions, which they could talk about. The clock talked about politic-tic-tics! It knew the hour had struck! But it was said that it did not keep the correct time! The rattan cane stood, and was proud of his ferrule and his silver knob, for, indeed, he was capped above and below. On the sofa lay two embroidered pillows—they were beautiful and dumb. And now the play could begin.

They all sat and watched, and they were asked to crack and smack and rumble, all according to how pleased they were. But the riding whip said he never cracked for the aged, only for those who were not engaged.

"I crack for everything!" said the firecracker.

"After all, one has to be somewhere," thought the cuspidor.

Indeed, this was everyone's idea in attending a play. The play was no good, but it was well acted. All the players turned their painted sides out; they could be looked at only from one side—not the wrong side—and they all performed excellently, all the way out in front of the theater. Their strings were too long, but this made them all the more noticeable. The riveted doll was so moved that her rivet came loose; and the piggy bank was so impressed by it, in his fashion, that he decided to do something for one of them: include him in his testament as the one who was to lie buried with him when the time came.

It was such a treat that the tea was abandoned, and they went on with the intellectual exercise. It was called "Playing People." There was no malice intended, for they were only playing; and each one thought of himself and of what the piggy bank was thinking. And the piggy bank thought the most. He, of course, was thinking about the testament and the funeral, and when it was to be held—always before one expects it. CRASH! He fell down from the cupboard and lay on the floor in bits and pieces, and the coins danced and sprang. The smallest spun, the biggest rolled—especially one of the silver dalers. He really wanted to go out into the world, and so he did! And so did every last one of them! And the fragments of the piggy bank ended up in the basket. But the next day, on the cupboard stood a new piggy bank made of clay. There wasn't a shilling in it yet, and so it couldn't rattle, either! In this he resembled the other. It was always a beginning, and with that we shall end.

Cloddy Hans

❖ ❖ ❖

OUT in the country there was an old manor, and in it
lived an old squire who had two sons. They were so
witty that they were too witty by half. They wanted to
propose to the king's daughter, and this they dared to do
because she had proclaimed that she would take for a
husband the one she found who could best speak up for
himself.

Now the two made their preparations for eight days.
This was all the time they had for it, but it was enough.
They had previous learning, and that is useful. One of
them knew the whole Latin dictionary by heart and the
city newspaper for three years—both forward and backward. The other had acquainted himself with all the Guild
Articles and what every alderman should know. So he was
able to discuss Affairs of State, he thought. And what's
more, he also knew how to embroider suspenders, for he
had delicate hands and was clever with his fingers.

"I'm going to win the king's daughter!" they both said,
and so their father gave them each a splendid horse; the
one who knew the dictionary and the newspapers by heart
was given a coal-black horse, and the one who knew about
aldermen and did embroidery got a milk-white steed. And
then they smeared the corners of their mouths with cod-
liver oil to make them more flexible. All the servants were

down in the yard to see them mount their steeds. At the same moment the third brother came up—for there were three of them, but no one counted him as a brother because he didn't have the same kind of learning as the other two, and they only called him "Cloddy Hans"!

"Where are you off to, since you're wearing your Sunday best?" he asked.

"To court to talk the princess into marrying us! Haven't you heard what's being proclaimed throughout the land?" And then they told him.

"My word! Then I've got to come along too!" said Cloddy Hans, but the brothers laughed at him and rode off.

"Father, let me have a horse!" shouted Cloddy Hans. "I'd so like to get married. If she'll take me, she'll take me; and if she won't, I'll take her all the same!"

"That's just twaddle!" said the father. "I'm not giving any horse to you! Why, you don't know how to talk! No, your brothers are real gentlemen."

"Well, if I can't have a horse," said Cloddy Hans, "I'll just take the billy goat! It's mine, and it can carry me very well!" And then he straddled the billy goat, dug his heels into its sides, and rushed off down the highway. Whew! How he flew!

"Here I come!" said Cloddy Hans, and then he sang so the forest rang.

But the brothers rode ahead quite silently. They didn't utter a word. They had to think over all the clever retorts they were going to make, for it had to be so well thought out.

"Hey hallo!" shouted Cloddy Hans. "Here I come! Look what I found on the highway!" And then he showed them a dead crow he had found.

"Clod!" they said. "What do you want with that?"

"I'm going to present it to the king's daughter!"

"Yes, just do it!" they said, and laughed and rode on.

"Hey hallo! Here I come! Look what I found now! You don't find this on the highway every day!"

And the brothers turned around to see what it was. "Clod!" they said. "Why, it's an old wooden shoe that has lost its top. Is the king's daughter going to have that too?"

"Yes, indeed!" said Cloddy Hans. And the brothers laughed and rode until they were way ahead of him.

"Hey hallo! Here I am!" shouted Cloddy Hans. "My! Now it's getting worse and worse! Hey hallo! It can't be beat!"

"What have you found now?" said the brothers.

"Oh," said Cloddy Hans, "it's nothing to speak of! How happy the king's daughter will be!"

"Ugh!" said the brothers. "Why, it's just mud that's been thrown up out of the ditch!"

"Yes, so it is!" said Cloddy Hans. "And it's the finest sort! You can't hold it!" And then he filled his pocket.

But the brothers rode as hard as they could, and they came to the city gates a whole hour ahead of him. There the suitors were given numbers as they arrived and were placed in rows six abreast—so close together that they couldn't move their arms. And it was just as well, for otherwise they would have stabbed one another in the back, just because one was standing in front of the other.

The rest of the populace was standing around the castle, right up to the windows, to see the king's daughter receive the suitors. But just as each one came into the room, his eloquence failed him.

"Won't do!" said the king's daughter. "Scram!"

Now came the brother who knew the dictionary by heart. But while standing in line he had clean forgotten it. And the floor creaked, and the ceiling was of mirrors so he saw himself upside down on his head. And at each window stood three scribes and an alderman, who wrote down everything that was said, so it could go right into the newspaper and be sold for two shillings on the corner. It

was terrible! And then they had made up such a roaring
fire that the stove was red hot.

"It's pretty warm in here!" said the suitor.

"That's because my father's roasting cockerels today!"
said the king's daughter.

Bah! There he stood. He hadn't expected that speech.
He didn't know a word to say, for he had wanted to say
something amusing! Bah!

"Won't do!" said the king's daughter. "Scram!" And
then he had to go. Now the second brother came.

"It's terribly hot here!" he said.

"Yes, we're roasting cockerels today!" said the king's
daughter.

"I beg your . . . I beg! . . ." he said, and all the scribes
wrote: "I beg your. . . . I beg! . . ."

"Won't do!" said the king's daughter. "Scram!"

Now Cloddy Hans came. He rode the billy goat straight
into the hall.

"Well, this is a scorcher!" he said.

"That's because I'm roasting cockerels!" said the king's
daughter.

"Well, now, that is strange!" said Cloddy Hans. "Then
maybe I can roast a crow!"

"Indeed you can, quite well!" said the king's daughter.
"But do you have anything to roast it in? For I have neither
a pot nor a pan!"

"Oh, I have!" said Cloddy Hans. "Here's a cooker with
a tin cramp!" And then he pulled out the old wooden shoe
and put the crow in the middle of it.

"That's enough for a whole meal," said the king's daughter, "but where will we get the drippings from?"

"I've got that in my pocket!" said Cloddy Hans. "I've
got so much that I can dribble some on." And then he
poured a little mud out of his pocket.

"Now you're talking!" said the king's daughter. "Why,
you know how to answer! And you know how to talk!

You're the one I'll have for my husband! But do you know
that every word we're saying and have said is being written down and will appear in the newspaper tomorrow? At
each window you can see three scribes and an old alder-

man. And the alderman is the worst of all because he doesn't understand a thing." Now, she said this just to frighten him. And all the scribes snickered and threw blots of ink on the floor.

"Those are the high and mighty, all right!" said Cloddy Hans. "Then I must give the best to the alderman." And then he turned out his pockets and gave him the mud right in his face!

"That was well done!" said the king's daughter. "I couldn't have done it, but I'm certainly going to learn how!"

And so Cloddy Hans became king and got a wife and a crown and a throne of his own. And we got it straight from the alderman's newspaper—but that's not to be trusted.

Soup from a Sausage Peg

❖   ❖   ❖

"THAT was an excellent dinner yesterday!" said an old she-mouse to one who hadn't been to the banquet. "I sat number twenty-one from the old Mouse King; that's not so bad, after all! Now, shall I tell you the courses? They were put together very well: moldy bread, bacon rind, tallow candles, and sausage, and then the same thing all over again. It was as good as getting two meals. There was a convivial atmosphere and a delightful twaddling, as in a family circle. Not a bit was left except the sausage pegs, and so we talked about them, and then the making of soup from a sausage peg came up. Everybody, of course, had heard about it, but no one had tasted the soup, much less knew how to make it. A charming toast was proposed for the inventor: he deserved to be Purveyor to the Needy! Wasn't that witty? And the old Mouse King stood up and promised that the young mouse who could make the soup in question the tastiest would become his queen. They were to have a year and a day to think it over in."

"That wasn't so bad, considering!" said the other mouse. "But how do you make the soup?"

"Yes, how do you make it?" They asked about that too, all the she-mice young and old. They all wanted to be queen, but they didn't want to take the trouble of going out into the wide world to learn how, and that'll probably be necessary! But, then, it isn't everyone who can leave his family and the old nooks and crannies too. One doesn't go out every day on a cheese rind and the smell of bacon. No, one can end up starving—yes, perhaps be eaten alive by a cat.

I daresay these thoughts also frightened most of them out of sallying forth after knowledge; only four mice—young and pretty, but poor—presented themselves for departure. Each of them wanted to go to one of the four corners of the earth, so it was a question of which one of them Dame Fortune would follow. They each took a sausage peg with them, as a reminder of what they were traveling for; it was to be their pilgrim's staff.

Early in May they set out, and early in May the following year they came back—but only three of them. The fourth one didn't turn up and didn't send any word, and now the day of decision was at hand.

"There always has to be something sad bound up with one's greatest pleasures!" said the Mouse King, but gave orders to invite all the mice for miles around; they were to gather in the kitchen. The three traveling mice stood in a row, by themselves. For the fourth, who was missing, a sausage peg with black crepe around it had been put up. No one dared speak his mind before the three of them had spoken—and the Mouse King had said what more there was to be said.

Now we shall hear!

WHAT THE FIRST LITTLE MOUSE HAD SEEN AND LEARNED ON THE JOURNEY

"When I went out into the wide world," said the little mouse, "I thought, like so many of my age, that I knew everything. But one doesn't; it takes a year and a day before that happens. I went to sea at once; I went with a

ship that was going to the North. I had heard that at sea
the cook has to look after himself, but it's easy to look after
oneself when one has plenty of sides of bacon, barrels of
salt provisions, and flour full of mites. The food is delicious, but one doesn't learn anything that can produce
soup from a sausage peg. We sailed for many days and
nights; we were subjected to a rolling and a drenching.
Then, when we came to where we should, I left the
vessel. That was far up in the North.

"It's strange to come away from home, from your own
nook and cranny, to go by ship—which is also a kind of
nook and cranny—and then suddenly be more than a
hundred miles away and stand in a foreign land! There
were trackless forests of fir and birch! They gave off such a
strong odor! I'm not fond of it! The wild herbs had such a
spicy fragrance that I sneezed; it made me think of sausage! There were big forest lakes; close at hand the water
looked clear, but seen from a distance as black as ink.
White swans were floating there—I took them for foam,
they were lying so still. But I saw them fly and I saw them
walk, and then I recognized them. They belong to the
goose family; you can certainly tell by the gait. No one can
repudiate one's kinship! I kept to my own kind; I attached
myself to the field and meadow mice, who, for that matter, know exceedingly little—especially as far as treating is
concerned. And that, of course, is what I journeyed abroad
for. That soup could be made from a sausage peg was such
an extraordinary thought to them that it spread through
the entire forest at once. But that the problem could be
solved they relegated to the impossible. Least of all did I
think then that here and on that very same night I was to
be initiated in the making of it. It was midsummer, and
that was why the forest gave off such a strong odor, they
said; that was why the herbs were so spicy, the lakes so
clear and yet so dark with the white swans on them. At
the edge of the forest, between three or four houses, a

pole as high as a mainmast had been set up, and from the
top of it hung garlands and ribbons: it was the Maypole.
Lads and lasses were dancing around it and singing to it,
vying with the fiddler's violin. Things got lively at sun-
down and in the moonlight, but I didn't join in. What
business has a little mouse at a forest ball? I sat in the soft
moss and held onto my sausage peg. The moon shone on
one spot in particular where there was a tree, and moss as
fine—yes, I daresay as fine as a Mouse King's hide! But it
was of a green color that was a balm to the eyes. All at
once the loveliest little people, who reached no higher
than my knee, came marching up; they looked like human
beings, but were better proportioned. They called themselves 'elves' and had delicate garments of flower petals,
with fly- and gnat-wing trimmings—not bad at all. Right
away they seemed to be looking for something, I didn't
know what, but then a couple of them came over to me.
The noblest of them pointed to my sausage peg and said,
'That's just the kind we use! It has been carved out, it's
excellent!' And he became more and more delighted as he
looked at my pilgrim's staff.

" 'Borrow, of course, but not keep!' " I said.

" 'Not keep!' they all said. And taking hold of the sausage
peg, which I released, they danced over to the fine mossy
spot and set up the sausage peg right there in the open.
They wanted to have a Maypole too, and it was as if the
one they had now had been carved out for them. Now it
was decorated, yes, then it was a sight to behold.

"Tiny spiders spun threads of gold around it, and hung
up fluttering veils and banners so finely woven and bleached
so snowy white in the moonlight that it dazzled my eyes.
They took colors from the wings of butterflies and sprin-
kled them on the white linen, and flowers and diamonds
were sparkling there. I didn't recognize my sausage peg
anymore. I daresay a Maypole like the one it had turned
into was nowhere to be found in the world. And not until

then did the really great company of elves arrive. They were quite without clothes; it could be no finer. And I was invited to look at the doings—but from a distance, as I was too big for them.

"Now the playing began! It was as if a thousand glass bells were ringing out so loud and strong; I thought it was the swans that were singing. Indeed, it seemed to me that I could also hear the cuckoo and thrush. At last it was as if the entire forest were resounding along with it; there were children's voices, the sound of bells and the song of birds— the sweetest melodies. And all that loveliness rang out from the Maypole of the elves. It was a whole carillon, and it was my sausage peg. Never had I believed that so much could come out of it, but I daresay it depends on whose hands it falls into. I was really quite moved. I cried, as only a little mouse can cry, for pure joy.

"The night was all too short! But, indeed, it isn't any longer up there at that time of the year. At daybreak a breeze sprang up, rippling the mirrored surface of the forest lake; all the delicate, fluttering veils and banners blew away in the air; the swaying gossamer pavilions, suspension bridges, and balustrades—or whatever they're called—that had been erected from leaf to leaf blew away at once. Six elves came and brought me my sausage peg, asking as they did so whether I had any wish they could grant. Then I asked them to tell me how soup from a sausage peg is made.

" 'The way we go about it!' said the noblest of them, and laughed. 'Yes, you saw that just now! I daresay you hardly recognized your sausage peg again!'

" 'You mean in that fashion?' I said, and told outright why I was on a journey and what was expected of it at home. 'Of what advantage is it to the Mouse King, and the whole of our mighty kingdom, that I have seen this magnificence? I can't shake it out of the sausage peg and say:

"See, here's the peg, now comes the soup! Still, it was a course of sorts when one was full!" '

"Then the elf dipped his little finger down in a blue violet and said to me, 'Take care, I'm stroking your pilgrim's staff, and when you come home to the Mouse King's castle, touch your staff at the king's warm breast. Then violets will spring out all over the staff, even in the coldest wintertime. See, there's something for you to take home with you and a little more besides.' "

But before the little mouse said what this little more could be, she touched her staff at the king's breast, and the loveliest bouquet of flowers really did spring out. It had such a strong odor that the Mouse King ordered the mice standing closest to the chimney to stick their tails into the fire right away, in order that there might be a slight smell of something burning, for that odor of violets was unbearable. That wasn't the sort of thing one set store by.

"But what was that 'little more besides' you mentioned?" asked the Mouse King.

"Well," said the little mouse, "I daresay that's what is called 'the effect'!" And then she gave the sausage peg a turn, and then there were no more flowers. She was holding only the bare peg, and she raised it just like a baton.

"Violets are for Sight, Smell, and Touch, the elf told me, but Hearing and Taste still remain!" And then she beat time: there was music, not the way it resounded in the forest during the festivities of the elves, no, but as it can be heard in the kitchen. My, what a to-do! It came suddenly, just as if the wind were whistling through all the flues. Kettles and pots boiled over; the fire shovel pounded on the brass kettle. And then, all at once, it was quiet. You could hear the subdued song of the teapot. So strange, you couldn't tell at all whether it was stopping or starting; and the little pot bubbled and the big pot bubbled; one took no heed of the other. It was as if there wasn't a thought in the pot. And the little mouse swung her baton, wilder and wilder—the pots foamed, bubbled, boiled over; the wind whistled; the chimney squeaked. Hey! Hey! It was so dreadful that the little mouse even dropped the baton.

"That was quite a soup!" said the old Mouse King. "Doesn't the main course come now?"

"That was all!" said the little mouse, and curtsied.

"All! Well, then, let us hear what the next one has to say!" said the Mouse King.

WHAT THE SECOND LITTLE MOUSE RELATED

"I was born in the castle library," said the second mouse. "I, and others of my family there, have never had the good fortune of coming into the dining room, not to mention the larder; only when I journeyed out, and now here today, did I see a kitchen. We often suffered real hunger and privation in the library, but we acquired much knowledge. Up there the rumor reached us about the royal prize that had been offered for making soup from a sausage peg, and it was then that my old grandmother pulled out a manuscript. She couldn't read it, but she had heard it read. On it was written: 'If one is a poet, then one knows how to cook soup from a sausage peg!' She asked me if I were a poet. My conscience was clear, but then she said that I had to go and see about becoming one. But what was needed for that, I asked. For it was just as difficult for me to find that out as it was to make the soup. But Grandma had listened to reading; she said that three main components were needed: 'Intelligence, fantasy, and feeling! If you can go and get those inside you, you're a poet, and then I daresay you'll find that out about the sausage peg!' "

"And so I headed West, out into the wide world to become a poet.

"I knew that in all things intelligence is the most important; the two other components are not held in the same esteem. And accordingly I set out after intelligence. Well, where does it dwell? 'Go to the ant and be wise,' a great king in the Holy Land is supposed to have said. This I knew from the library, and I didn't stop until I came to the first big anthill. There I lay in wait, in order to be wise.

"The ants are quite a respectable race; they are all brain. Everything about them is like a correctly worked problem in arithmetic that comes out right. Working and laying eggs, they say, is the same as living in the present and providing for the future, and that is just what they do. They divide themselves into the clean ants and the dirty ants. Rank consists of a number; the ant queen is number one, and her opinion is the only correct one. She knows everything, and that was essential for me to find out. She said so much that was so wise that I thought it was stupid. She said that their anthill was the tallest thing in the world. But close to the anthill stood a tree. It was taller, much taller; that couldn't be denied and so it wasn't mentioned at all. One evening an ant had strayed over there and crawled up the trunk, not even to the top, and yet higher than any ant had ever been before. And when it had turned around and made its way home, it told in the mound about something taller outside. But all the ants found this to be an insult to the entire society, and so the little ant was sentenced to wear a muzzle, and to everlasting solitude. But shortly afterward another ant came to the tree and made the same journey and discovery, and talked about it, as it is said, with deliberation and articulation. And, as it was an esteemed ant into the bargain—one of the clean ants—they believed it. And when it died, they put up an eggshell to it as a monument to the venerated sciences.

"I saw," said the little mouse, "that the ants perpetually ran about with their eggs on their backs. One of them dropped hers. She did her utmost to get it up again, but without success. Then two others came and helped with all their might, so they very nearly dropped their own eggs. But then they stopped at once, for one has to look after oneself. And concerning this, the ant queen said that both heart and intelligence had been displayed here. 'The two establish us ants as the highest of the rational beings. Intelligence must and should predominate, and I have the most!' And then she stood up on her hind legs; she was so recognizable that I couldn't make a mistake! And I swallowed her. Go to the ant and be wise! Now I had the queen!

"Now I went closer to the big tree in question. It was an oak, it had a tall trunk and a mighty crown, and was very old. I knew that a living creature dwelled here, a woman. She is called a 'dryad' and is born with the tree and dies with it. I had heard about that in the library. Now I was looking at such a tree, looking at such an oak maiden. She let out a terrible shriek when she saw me so close. Like all females, she had a great fear of mice, but then she had more of a reason than the others: for I could gnaw through the tree, and therein, of course, hung her life. I talked to her, kindly and sincerely, and gave her courage, and she picked me up in her delicate hand; and when she found out why I had gone out into the wide world, she promised that, perhaps the same evening, I should obtain one of the two treasures for which I was still looking. She told me that Phantasus was her very good friend, that he was as beautiful as the God of Love, and that many a time he had rested here under the leafy branches of the tree, which rustled even louder above them both. He called her his dryad, she said, the tree his tree. The gnarled, mighty, beautiful oak was just to his liking. The roots spread deeply and firmly down in the ground; the trunk and the crown soared high in the fresh air, and felt the drifting snow and the biting wind the way they should be felt. Yes, this is the way she spoke: 'The birds sing up there and tell about the foreign lands! And on the only dead limb the stork has built a nest; that's a good trimming, and one can hear a little from the land of the pyramids. Phantasus likes it all very well. But even that is not enough for him; I must tell him about life in the forest from the time I was small and the tree was tiny enough to be hidden by a nettle, and up to now, when it has grown so big and mighty. Now, if you just sit over there under the woodruff and pay close attention, when Phantasus comes I daresay I'll have a chance to tweak him in his wing and yank out a little feather. Take it; no poet ever received a better one. Then you'll have enough!'

"And Phantasus came, the feather was yanked out, and I grabbed it," said the little mouse. "I kept it in water until it became soft! It was still quite hard to digest, but I managed to gnaw it up! It's not at all easy to gnaw oneself into a poet, there's so much that has to be taken in. . . . Now I had the two: intelligence and fantasy, and through them I knew now that the third was to be found in the library. For a great man has said and written that there are novels that are produced for the sole purpose of releasing mankind from superfluous tears; that is to say, they are a kind of sponge in which to absorb emotions. I remembered a couple of these books; they had always looked quite appetizing to me—they were so well read, so greasy; they must have absorbed an unending flood.

"I went home to the library, immediately ate practically a whole novel—that is to say, the soft part, the novel proper; the crust, on the other hand, the binding, I left alone. Now, when I had digested that and one more, I was already aware of the way it was stirring inside me. I ate a little of the third, and then I was a poet. I said so to myself, and the others said so along with me. I had a headache, a bellyache—I don't know all the aches I had. Now I thought of the stories that might be connected with sausage pegs, and then so many pegs came to my mind— the ant queen had had exceptional intelligence. I remembered the man who'd been taken down a peg; I thought of old beer with a peg in it; standing on one's pegs; a peg for hanging a claim on; and then the pegs to one's coffin. All my thoughts were wrapped up in pegs! And it should be possible to make up something about them as long as one is a poet. And that's what I am, that's what I've struggled to be. Thus, every day in the week, I'll be able to serve you a peg—a story. Well, that's my soup!"

"Let us hear the third," said the Mouse King.

"Squeak! Squeak!" it said in the kitchen door, and a little mouse—it was the fourth, the one they thought was dead—scurried in. It bowled over the big sausage peg with the band of mourning on it. It had been running night and day; it had gone by rail, on a freight train when the opportunity presented itself, and still had come almost too late. It pushed its way forward, looking disheveled; it had lost its sausage peg but not its voice. It started talking right away, just as if everyone had been waiting for it alone and only wanted to listen to it. Everything else was of no concern to the world. It spoke at once and said what it had to say. It came so unexpectedly that no one had time to take exception to it or to its speech while it was talking. Now we shall hear!

WHAT THE FOURTH MOUSE—
WHO SPOKE BEFORE THE THIRD—HAD TO RELATE

"I went right away to the biggest city," it said. "I don't remember the name. I'm not good at remembering names. I came from the train to the City Hall along with confiscated goods, and there I ran to the jailer. He told about his prisoners, especially about one who had let fall rash words. These words, in turn, had been commented on, and now he'd been given a dressing down. 'The whole business is soup from a sausage peg!' he said. 'But that soup can cost him his neck!' This made me interested in that prisoner," said the little mouse, "and I seized the opportunity and slipped in to him. There's always a mousehole behind locked doors. He looked pale, had a great beard and big flashing eyes. The lamp smoked, and the walls were used to it—they grew no blacker. The prisoner scratched both pictures and verse, white on black. I didn't read them. I think he was bored. I was a welcome guest. He coaxed me with bread crumbs, with whistling, and with kind words. He was so happy because of me; I trusted him, and so we became friends. He shared bread and water with me, gave me cheese and sausage; I was living in great style, but, I must say, it was really the good company in particular that kept me there. He let me run on his hand and arm, all the way up in his sleeve. He let me crawl in his beard, called me his little friend. I grew really fond of him; I daresay that sort of thing is mutual. I forgot my errand out in the wide world, forgot my sausage peg in a crack in the floor; it's lying there still. I wanted to stay where he was; if I went away, the poor prisoner would have no one at all, and that's not enough in this world. I stayed, he didn't. He talked to me so sorrowfully that last time, gave me twice as much bread and cheese rinds, then blew kisses to me; he left and never came back. I don't know his story. 'Soup from a sausage peg!'

the jailer said, and I went to him. But I shouldn't have believed him. To be sure, he picked me up in his hand, but he put me in a cage, on a treadmill. That's dreadful! You run and run, you come no farther, and you only make a fool of yourself.

"The jailer's grandchild was a lovely little thing, with golden curls, the happiest eyes, and a laughing mouth. 'Poor little mouse!' she said, and peered into my nasty cage, and pulled away the iron peg—and I leaped down onto the windowsill and out into the gutter. Free! Free! I thought of that alone, and not of the journey's goal.

"It was dark, night was falling. I took shelter in an old tower. There lived a nightwatch and an owl. I didn't trust either of them, least of all the owl. It looks like a cat, and has the great shortcoming that it eats mice. But one can be mistaken, and I was. This was a respectable, exceedingly well-bred old owl; she knew more than the nightwatch and just as much as I did. The owlets found fault with everything. 'Don't make soup from a sausage peg!' she said. That was the harshest thing she could say here, she was so devoted to her own family. I gained such confidence in her that I said 'Squeak!' from the crack where I was sitting. She found that confidence to her liking and assured me that I would be under her protection. No creature would be allowed to do me harm. She herself would do that in winter, when food became scarce.

"She was wise about each and every thing. She convinced me that the nightwatch couldn't hoot except through a horn that hung loosely at his side. 'He puts on such terrible airs because of that; he thinks he's an owl in the tower! That's supposed to be grand, but it's only a little. Soup from a sausage peg!'

"I asked her for the recipe, and then she explained it to me: 'Soup from a sausage peg is only a human way of talking, and can be interpreted in various ways. And each one thinks that his way is the most correct, but the whole thing is really much ado about nothing!'

" 'Nothing!' I said. It struck me! The truth isn't always pleasant, but the truth is the highest. The old owl said so too. I thought it over and realized that when I brought the highest, then I was bringing much more than soup from a sausage peg. And so I hurried off in order to come back home in time and bring the highest and the best: the truth. The mice are an enlightened race, and the Mouse King is above them all. He is capable of making me queen for the sake of the truth."

"Your truth is a lie!" said the mouse who hadn't yet been allowed to speak. "I can make the soup, and so I shall!"

HOW IT WAS MADE

"I didn't go on a journey," said the fourth mouse. "I remained in the land; that's the proper thing to do. One doesn't need to travel; one can get everything here just as well. I remained. I haven't learned what I did from supernatural beings, or eaten my way to it, or talked with owls. I've thought it out all by myself. Now, if you'll just have the kettle put on and fill it all the way up with water! Make a fire under it! Let it burn; let the water come to a boil—it has to boil furiously! Now throw in the peg! Now if the Mouse King will be so kind as to stick his tail down in the bubbling water and stir. Indeed, the longer he stirs, the stronger the soup will be. It doesn't cost a thing. No additions are needed—just stir!"

"Can't someone else do it?" asked the Mouse King.

"No," said the mouse, "the stock is in the tail of the Mouse King alone!"

And the water bubbled furiously, and the Mouse King took his stand close to it—it was nearly dangerous—and he stuck out his tail the way the mice do in the dairy when they skim the cream from a dish and afterward lick their tails. But he only got it into the hot steam, then he jumped down at once.

"Naturally you are my queen!" he said. "We'll wait with the soup until our Golden Wedding Anniversary. Then the needy in my kingdom will have something to look forward to—and a protracted pleasure!"

And so the wedding was held. But when they came home, several of the mice said, "You couldn't very well

call that 'soup from a sausage peg'; it was more like 'soup from a mouse's tail'!"

They found that one thing or another, of what had been said, had been presented quite well, but the whole thing

could have been different. "Now, *I* would have told it like
this and like that! . . ."

That was the criticism, and that's always so wise—afterward!

And the story went around the world. Opinions about it
were divided, but the story itself remained intact. And
that is what is best—in matters great and small—in soup
from a sausage peg. It's just that one shouldn't expect
thanks for it!

The Girl Who Trod
on the Loaf

❖   ❖   ❖

Y OU'VE probably heard of the girl who trod on the loaf
so as not to soil her shoes, and of how badly she fared. It
has been written down and printed as well.

She was a poor child, vain and overbearing; she had an
ornery disposition, as they say. As quite a little child she
delighted in catching flies and picking off their wings to
make crawling things out of them. She took the cockchafer
and the dung beetle, stuck them each on a pin, and then
held a green leaf or a tiny scrap of paper up to their feet.
The wretched creatures would thereby cling to it, twisting
and turning it, to get off the pin.

"Now the cockchafer's reading!" said little Inger. "See
how it's turning the page!"

As she grew she became worse, if anything, instead of
better. But she was pretty, and that was her undoing, or
else in all likelihood she would have been given a good
many more cuffs than she was.

"It'll take a desperate remedy to cure your ailment!" her
own mother would say. "As a child you've often trod on
my apron. I'm afraid when you're older you'll often come
to tread on my heart."

And that is precisely what she did.

Now she went out in the country to enter the service of
a gentle family. They treated her as if she had been their

very own child and dressed her in the same fashion. She looked good, and her arrogance increased.

She had been out there for a year when her mistress said, "Really, you should pay your parents a visit one day, little Inger!"

She went too, but only to show off. They were to see how grand she had become. But when she came to the village gate and saw the maidens and young lads gossiping by the pond—and her mother was sitting right there, resting with a bundle of twigs that she had gathered in the forest—Inger turned around. She was ashamed that she, who was so finely dressed, should have such a ragamuffin for a mother, who went about gathering sticks. She didn't regret turning back at all, she was merely irritated.

Now another half year passed.

"Really, you should go home for a day and see your old parents, little Inger!" said her mistress. "Here's a big loaf of white bread for you; you can take it to them. They'll be delighted to see you."

And Inger put on her best finery and her new shoes, and she lifted her skirts and walked so carefully in order to keep her feet nice and clean—and she couldn't be blamed for that. But when she came to where the path went over boggy ground, and a long stretch of it was wet and muddy, she tossed the loaf into the mud so as to tread on it and get across dry-shod. But as she was standing with one foot on the bread and lifting the other, the bread sank with her, deeper and deeper, until she had disappeared completely, and only a black, bubbling pool was to be seen.

That's the story.

But where did she come to? She came down to the Marsh Wife, who was brewing. The Marsh Wife is paternal aunt to the elfin maidens—they're well enough known: ballads have been written about them and pictures have been painted of them. But the only thing people know about the Marsh Wife is that when the meadows are

steaming in the summertime, the Marsh Wife is brewing.
It was down into her brewery that Inger sank, and you
can't stand being there for long. The cesspool is a bright,
elegant salon compared with the Marsh Wife's brewery!
The stink from each vat is enough to make people swoon,
and then too the vats are jammed so close together. And if
there is a little opening somewhere through which you
could squeeze, you can't because of all the wet toads and
fat snakes that become matted together here. Down here
sank little Inger; all that loathsome, writhing matting was
so freezing cold that she shivered in every limb; indeed,
she became more and more rigid. She stuck to the loaf,
and it dragged her just as an amber button drags a bit of
straw.

The Marsh Wife was at home. That day the brewery
was being inspected by the Devil and his great-grandma,

and *she's* a most virulent old female, who's never idle. She never goes out unless she has her needlework with her, and she had it along here too. She sewed unrest to put in people's shoes so they couldn't settle down; she embroidered lies and crocheted thoughtless remarks that had fallen to the ground—anything to cause harm and corruption. Oh, yes, great-grandma really knew how to sew, embroider, and crochet!

She saw Inger, held her eyeglass up to her eye, and had another look at her. "That's a girl with aptitude!" she said. "Give her to me as a token of my visit here! She'll be a suitable pedestal in my great-grandchild's anteroom!"

And she got her. And this is how little Inger came to Hell. People don't always rush straight down there, but they can get there by a roundabout way—when they have aptitude!

It was an anteroom that went on forever. It made you dizzy to look ahead and dizzy to look back; and here stood a miserable host waiting for the Door of Mercy to be opened, and they would have a long wait! Big fat waddling spiders spun thousand-year webs over their feet, and these webs clamped like footscrews and held like copper chains. And added to this was an eternal unrest in every soul, a tormenting unrest; there was the miser who had forgotten the key to his moneybox, and he knew it was sitting in the lock. Indeed, it would be too long-winded to rattle off all the various torments and tortures that were endured here. It was a dreadful feeling for Inger to stand as a pedestal; it was as if she had been toggled to the loaf from below.

"That's what you get for wanting to keep your feet clean!" she said to herself. "See how they glower at me!" Indeed, they were all looking at her. Their evil desires flashed from their eyes and spoke without a sound from the corners of their mouths. They were dreadful to behold.

"It must be a pleasure to look at me!" thought little Inger. "I have a pretty face and good clothes." And now she turned her eyes—her neck was too stiff to move. My, how dirty she had gotten in the Marsh Wife's brewery. She hadn't thought of that! It was as if one big blob of slime had been poured over her clothes. A snake had got caught in her hair and was flapping down the back of her neck. And from every fold of her dress a toad was peering out, croaking like a wheezy pug dog. It was quite unpleasant. "But the others down here look just as horrible," she consoled herself.

Worst of all, however, was the dreadful hunger she felt. Couldn't she even bend down and break off a piece of the bread she was standing on? No, her back had stiffened, her arms and hands had stiffened; her entire body was like a pillar of stone. She could turn only her eyes in her head, turn them completely around so they could see backward— and that was a terrible sight, that was. And then the flies came. They crawled over her eyes, back and forth. She blinked her eyes, but the flies didn't fly away—they couldn't. Their wings had been picked off; they had turned into crawling things. That was a torment. And then there was the hunger—at last it seemed to her as if her entrails were devouring themselves, and she became so empty inside, so horribly empty.

"If this keeps up for long, I won't be able to stand it," she said. But she had to stand it, and it did keep up.

Then a burning tear fell on her head; it trickled down her face and breast, straight down to the loaf. Yet another tear fell, and many more. Who was crying over little Inger? Didn't she have a mother up on earth? The tears of grief that a mother sheds over her child always reach it, but they don't redeem it, they burn. They only add to the torment. And now this excruciating hunger, and not being able to reach the loaf she was treading with her foot! At last she had a feeling that everything inside her must have devoured itself. She was like a thin hollow tube that sucked every sound into it. She heard clearly everything up on earth that concerned her, and what she heard was ill-natured and harsh. To be sure, her mother wept deeply and sorrowfully, but she added, "Pride goes before a fall! That was your undoing, Inger! How you have grieved your mother!"

Her mother and everyone else up there knew about her sin: that she had trod on the loaf and sunk down and disappeared. The cowherd had told about it; he had seen it himself from the hillside.

"How you have grieved your mother, Inger!" said the mother. "But then I always thought you would!"

"If only I'd never been born!" thought Inger. "Then I'd have been much better off. My mother's sniveling can't be of any help now."

She heard how her master and mistress, those gentle souls who had been like parents to her, spoke: "She was a sinful child," they said. "She paid no heed to the gifts of the Lord, but trod them under her feet. The Door of Mercy will be hard for her to open."

"They should have minded me better," thought Inger, "cured me of my whims—if I had any!"

She heard that a whole ballad had been written about her: "The arrogant lass who trod on the loaf in order to have pretty shoes!" And it was sung throughout the land.

"Imagine hearing so much about it and suffering so much for it!" thought Inger. "I daresay the others ought to be punished for what they've done too! Yes, then there'd be a lot to punish! Ugh, how tormented I am!"

And her soul grew even harder than her shell.

"One won't grow any better in this company! And I don't want to grow any better! See how they glower!"

And her heart was filled with wrath and spite for everybody.

"Well, now they have something to tell up there! Ugh, how tormented I am!"

And she heard that they told her story to the children,

and the little ones called her "Ungodly Inger." "She was so nasty," they said, "so wicked! She really ought to be tormented!"

There were always hard words against her on the children's lips.

Yet one day, as resentment and anger were gnawing at her hollow shell, and she was hearing her name being mentioned and her story being told to an innocent child, a little girl, she became aware that the little one burst into tears at the story of the arrogant Inger who loved finery.

"But is she never coming up again?" asked the little girl.

And the reply came: "She is never coming up again!"

"But if she were to ask forgiveness and never do it again?"

"But she will never ask forgiveness," they said.

"I'd so like for her to do it!" said the little girl, and was quite inconsolable. "I'll give my doll's wardrobe if only she can come up! It's so gruesome for poor Inger."

And those words reached all the way down to Inger's heart; they seemed to do her good. It was the first time that anyone had said "Poor Inger!" without adding the least little thing about her shortcomings. A tiny innocent child was crying and praying for her. It made her feel so strange; she would have gladly cried, but she couldn't cry. And that was also a torment.

As the years went by there was no change down below; she seldom heard sounds from above, and less was said about her. Then one day she was aware of a sigh: "Inger, Inger, how you have grieved me! But I always said you would!" It was her mother, who had died.

Now and then she heard her name mentioned by her old master and mistress, and the mildest words the housewife said were: "Will I ever see you again, Inger? One never knows where one is going."

But Inger realized very well that her gentle mistress would never be able to come to where she was.

Thus another long and bitter time elapsed.

Then Inger again heard her name being mentioned and saw something shining above her like two bright stars. They were two mild eyes that were closing on earth. So many years had gone by since the time the little girl had cried inconsolably over "poor Inger" that the child had become an old woman whom the Lord now wanted to call up to himself. And at that very moment, when the thoughts from her whole life rose before her, she also remembered how bitterly she had cried as a little girl on hearing the story of Inger. The time and the impression appeared so lifelike to the old woman in the hour of her death that she exclaimed aloud, "Lord, my God, haven't I too, like Inger, often trod on your blessed gifts without a thought? Haven't I too gone with pride in my heart? But you, in your mercy, didn't let me sink. You held me up. Don't desert me in my final hour!"

And the eyes of the old woman closed, and the eyes of her soul opened to what is hidden; and as Inger had been so vivid in her last thoughts, she saw her, saw how far down she had been dragged. And at the sight the pious soul burst into tears. In the Kingdom of Heaven she was standing like a child and crying for poor Inger. Those tears and those prayers rang out like an echo in the hollow, empty shell that encased the imprisoned, tortured soul. It was overwhelmed by all this unthought-of love from above; one of God's angels was crying over her! Why was this being granted to her? It was as if the tortured soul collected in its thoughts every deed it had performed in its earthly life, and it shook with tears such as Inger had never been able to cry. She was filled with anguish for herself; she felt that the Door of Mercy could never be opened for her. But as she acknowledged this with a broken heart, at the same moment a beam of light shone

down into the abyss. The beam was stronger than the
sunbeam that thaws the snowman put up in the yard by
the boys. And then, much faster than the snowflake falling
on the warm mouth of the child melts away to a drop,
Inger's petrified figure faded away. A tiny bird, zigzagging
like lightning, soared up to the world of mortals. But it
was afraid and wary of everything around it; it was ashamed
of itself and ashamed to face all living creatures, and
hurriedly sought shelter in a dark hole it found in the
decayed wall. Here it sat huddled, trembling all over. It
couldn't utter a sound—it had no voice. It sat for a long
while before it was calm enough to look at and be conscious of all the magnificence out there. Yes, it was magnificent: the air was so fresh and mild, the moon shone so
brightly, trees and bushes gave off such a fragrance; and
then too it was so pleasant there where it sat. Its feathered
kirtle was so clean and fine. My, how all creation had been
borne along in love and glory! All the thoughts that were
stirring in the breast of the bird wanted to vent themselves in song, but the bird was unable to do it. It would
gladly have sung like the cuckoo and nightingale in spring.
The Lord, who also hears the worm's silent hymn of
praise, was here aware of the hymn of praise that soared in
chords of thought, the way the Psalm resounded in David's breast before it was given words and music.

For weeks these silent songs grew and swelled in its
thoughts; they had to burst forth at the first flap of the
wings in a good deed; such a deed had to be performed.

Now the holy celebration of Christmas was at hand.
Close to the wall the farmer set up a pole and tied an
unthreshed sheaf of oats to it so the birds of the air could
also have a joyous Christmas and a gratifying meal at this
time of the Savior's.

The sun came up on Christmas morning and shone on
the sheaf of oats, and all the twittering birds flew about
the feeding pole. Then a "cheep-cheep" rang out from the

wall as well! The swelling thoughts had turned into sound; the feeble cheeping was a complete hymn of rejoicing. An idea for a good deed had awakened, and the bird flew out from its shelter. In the Kingdom of Heaven they knew very well what kind of bird this was.

Winter set in with a vengeance, the waters were frozen deep. The birds and animals of the forest had a hard time finding food. The little bird flew along the highway, searching in the tracks of the sleighs, and here and there it found a grain of corn; at the resting places it found a few bread crumbs. Of these it ate only a single one, but called to all the other starving sparrows that they could find food here. It flew to the cities and scouted about, and wherever a loving hand had strewn bread by a window for the birds, it ate but a single crumb itself and gave everything to the others.

In the course of the winter the bird had gathered and given away so many bread crumbs that, altogether, they weighed as much as the whole loaf of bread that little Inger had trod on so as not to soil her shoes. And when the very last bread crumb had been found and given away, the bird's gray wings turned white and spread out wide.

"A tern is flying over the sea!" said the children who saw the white bird. Now it ducked down into the sea, now it soared in the bright sunshine; it shone, it wasn't possible to see what had become of it. They said that it flew straight into the sun.

Pen and Inkwell

❖ ❖ ❖

T HE words were uttered in a poet's chamber as someone was looking at his inkwell, which was standing on
the table: "It's remarkable, all the things that can come
out of that inkwell I wonder what will be next. Yes, it's
remarkable!"

"So it is!" said the inkwell. "It's incomprehensible! That's
what I always say!" it said to the quill pen and to anything
else on the table that could hear it. "It's remarkable, all

the things that can come out of me! Yes, it's almost incredible! And I don't really know myself what will be next, when the human being starts drawing from me. One drop of me is enough for half a page of paper, and what can't appear there? I'm something quite remarkable! All the poet's works emanate from me! These living beings that people think they know, these profound emotions, this good humor, these lovely descriptions of nature. I can't comprehend it myself, because I'm not familiar with nature. But after all it's in me. From me has originated—and does originate—this host of hovering, lovely maidens, gallant knights on snorting chargers! Indeed, I'm not aware of it myself! I assure you, I don't give it a thought!"

"You're right about that!" said the quill pen. "You don't think at all. Because if you did, you'd understand that you merely provide fluid. You provide moisture so that I can express and render visible on the paper what I have in me, what I write down. It's the pen that writes! Not a soul has any doubts about that, and most mortals have as much of an understanding about poetry as an old inkwell!"

"You have only a little experience!" said the inkwell. "You've scarcely been on duty a week, and already you're half worn out. Are you pretending that you're the poet? You're only hired help, and I've had many of that sort before you came—both of the goose family and of English fabrication! I know both the quill pen and the steel pen. I've had many in my employ, and I'll have many more when he, the human being who makes the motions for me, comes and writes down what he gets out of my insides. I wonder what will be the next thing he draws out of me!"

"Inkpot!" said the pen.

Late in the evening the poet came home. He had been to a concert, heard an excellent violinist, and was quite engrossed and entranced by his incomparable playing. He had produced an amazing flood of tones from his instru-

ment; now they sounded like tinkling drops of water, pearl
upon pearl, now like twittering birds in chorus as the
storm raged through a forest of spruces. He seemed to
hear his own heart crying, but in a melody, the way it can
be heard in the lovely voice of a woman. It was as if not
only the strings of the violin rang out but also the bridge,
yes, even the pegs and the sounding board as well—it was
extraordinary; and it had been difficult, but it looked like
play, as if the bow could leap back and forth over the
strings. You would have thought that anyone could imitate
it. The violin rang out by itself, the bow played by itself; it
was these two who did it all. The maestro who guided
them, gave life and soul to them, was forgotten; the maestro was forgotten! But the poet thought of him; he named
him by name and thereby wrote down his thoughts: "How
absurd if the bow and the violin were to put on airs about
their performance! And yet, that is what we mortals do so
often: the poet, the artist, the scientific inventor, the
general. We put on airs ourselves, and yet we are all
merely the instruments upon which the Lord plays. To
him the honor alone! We have nothing to put on airs
about!"

Yes, this is what the poet wrote; he wrote it as a parable
and called it "The Maestro and the Instruments."

"You had it coming to you, madame!" said the pen to
the inkwell when the two were alone again. "I daresay you
heard him read aloud what I wrote down!"

"Yes, what I gave you to write," said the inkwell. "After
all, it was a dig at you because of your arrogance. You
can't even understand when someone is making fun of
you! I've made a dig at you straight from my insides. I
daresay I should know my own malice!"

"Ink holder!" said the pen.

"Writing stick!" said the inkwell.

And they both had the feeling that they had answered
well. And it's a good feeling to know that you've answered

well. You can go to sleep on it, and they did sleep on it. But the poet didn't sleep. The thoughts poured forth like the tones from the violin, rolled like pearls, raged like the storm through the forest. He felt his own heart in there; he was aware of the glimmer from the eternal Master.

To him the honor alone!

The Barnyard Cock and
the Weathercock

❖ ❖ ❖

There were two cocks, one on the dunghill and one on the roof; both of them arrogant; but which one accomplished the most? Tell us your opinion, we'll keep ours all the same.

A plank fence separated the chicken yard from another yard, in which there was a dunghill, and on it grew a huge cucumber that was fully convinced that it was a hothouse plant.

"One is born to that," it said deep down inside. "Not everyone can be born a cucumber. There must be other living species too! The hens, the ducks, and the entire stock of the neighboring farm are also creations. For my part, I look up to the barnyard cock on the fence. To be sure, he is of quite another significance than the weathercock, which has been placed so high. It can't even creak, much less crow! It has neither hens nor chicks. It thinks only of itself and sweats verdigris! The barnyard cock, now, is quite a cock! Look at him strut—that's dancing! Listen to him crow—that's music! No matter where he goes you can hear what a trumpeter is! If he were to come in here, if he were to eat me up—leaves, stalk, and all—if I were to enter his body, what a rapturous death that would be!" said the cucumber.

Later on in the night there was a terrible storm. Hens,

chicks, and even the cock sought shelter. The fence between the yards blew down with a great crash. Tiles fell down from the roof, but the weathercock was firmly fastened and not once did it turn around—it couldn't! And yet it was young, newly cast, but staid and sober-minded; it had been born old, and did not resemble the flighty birds of the air, the sparrows and swallows. It despised them, ". . . those dickybirds, small of size and *ordinaire*." The doves were big, glossy, and shiny, like mother-of-pearl; they resembled a kind of weathercock, but were fat and stupid. Their only thought was to get something in their craws, said the weathercock. They were bores to associate with. The birds of passage had also paid a visit and told of foreign lands and of caravans in the air, and dreadful cock-and-bull stories about birds of prey. It was new and interesting the first time, but later the weathercock knew that they repeated themselves, and it was always the same. And this is tedious. They were bores, and everything was a bore. No one was worth associating with, every last one of them was insipid and vapid!

"The world's no good!" he said. "Drivel, the whole thing!"

The weathercock was what is known as blasé, and this would have made him decidedly interesting to the cucumber had she known. But she looked up only to the barnyard cock, and now he was in the yard with her.

The fence had blown down, but the lightning and thunder were over.

"What do you have to say about that cockcrow?" said the barnyard cock to the hens and chicks. "It was a bit unpolished. The elegance was lacking."

"Garden plant!" he said to the cucumber, and in that one expression all his extensive breeding was revealed to her, and she forgot that he was pecking at her and eating her.

"Rapturous death!"

And the hens came and the chicks came. And when one comes running, the others run too! And they clucked and they "cheeped." And they looked at the cock and were proud of him. He was one of their kind.

"Cock-a-doodle-do!" he crowed. "The chicks turn at once into big hens when I say that in the hen yard of the world."

And hens and chicks clucked and "cheeped" behind him.

And the cock proclaimed great news: "A cock can lay an egg! And do you know what lies in that egg? A basilisk! No one can bear the sight of it. The human beings know that, and now you know it too—know what's inside me, know what a terribly fine barnyard-cock-of-the-walk I am!"

And then the barnyard cock flapped his wings, lifted his comb, and crowed again. All the hens and little chicks shuddered, but they were terribly proud that one of their kind was such a terribly fine barnyard-cock-of-the-walk. They clucked and they "cheeped" until the weathercock

had to hear it, and hear it he did. But he wasn't impressed by it!

"It's all nonsense!" he said to himself. "The barnyard cock will never lay an egg, and I can't be bothered to! If I wanted to, I could certainly lay a wind egg, but the world's not worth a wind egg! It's all nonsense! I can't even be bothered to sit here."

And then the weathercock broke off, but he didn't kill the barnyard cock.

"Even though that's what he counted on doing!" said the hens.

And what does the moral say? "Indeed, it's better to crow than to be blasé and break off!"

The Dung Beetle

❖   ❖   ❖

THE emperor's horse was getting golden shoes, a golden shoe on every single foot.

Why was he getting golden shoes?

He was the loveliest animal, had fine legs, the most intelligent eyes, and a mane that hung about his neck like a silken veil. He had borne his master through clouds of gunpowder and a rain of bullets, heard the bullets sing and whistle; he had bitten, kicked, and fought when the enemy pressed closer; with his emperor he had sprung over the fallen horse of the fiend, saved his emperor's crown of red gold, saved his emperor's life, which was worth more than red gold, and for this reason the emperor's horse was getting golden shoes, a golden shoe on every single foot.

Then the dung beetle crawled out.

"First the big, then the small," it said. "After all, it's not the size that counts." And then it held out its thin legs.

"What do you want?" asked the smith.

"Golden shoes!" replied the dung beetle.

"You're certainly not very bright!" said the smith. "Do you want to have golden shoes too?"

"Golden shoes!" said the dung beetle. "Aren't I just as good as that great beast who is to be waited on, groomed, looked after, and given food and drink? Aren't I a part of the emperor's stables too?"

"But why is the horse getting golden shoes?" asked the smith. "Can't you understand that?"

"Understand? I understand that it's an affront to me!" said the dung beetle. "It's an insult! So now I'm going out into the wide world!"

"Scram!" said the smith.

"Vulgar oaf!" said the dung beetle. And then it went outside and flew a little way, and then it was in a beautiful little flower garden where there was a scent of roses and lavender.

"Isn't it lovely here?" said one of the little ladybugs that flew about with black dots on its red shieldlike wings. "How sweet it smells, and how beautiful it is here!"

"I'm used to better things!" said the dung beetle. "Do you call this beautiful? Why, there isn't even a dunghill here!"

And then on it went, into the shade of a big cabbage. A caterpillar was crawling on it.

"How glorious the world is!" said the caterpillar. "The sun is so warm! Everything is such a delight! And one day, when I go to sleep and die, as they call it, I will wake up a butterfly!"

"Don't give yourself ideas!" said the dung beetle. "Now we're flying about like butterflies! I come from the emperor's stables, but no one there—not even the emperor's favorite horse, who, after all, wears my cast-off golden shoes—has such delusions! Get wings! Fly! Yes, now we'll fly!" And then the dung beetle flew. "I will not be vexed, but it vexes me all the same!"

Then it plumped down on a big plot of grass. Here it lay for a little while, then it fell asleep.

Heavens, how the rain poured down! The dung beetle was awakened by the splashing and wanted to burrow down in the ground at once, but couldn't. It overturned; it swam on its stomach and on its back. Flying was impossible! It would never come away from here alive! It lay where it lay, and there it stayed.

When it had cleared a bit, and the dung beetle had blinked the rain out of its eyes, it caught a glimpse of something white. It was linen spread out to bleach. It went over to it and crawled into a fold of the wet cloth. It certainly wasn't like lying in the warm heap in the stable, but there was nothing better; so here it stayed for a whole day and a whole night, and the rainy weather stayed too. Early in the morning the dung beetle crawled out. It was so vexed by the weather.

Two frogs were sitting on the linen; their bright eyes beamed with pure joy. "What delightful weather!" said the first. "How refreshing it is! And the linen holds the water so wonderfully! My hind legs tickle just as if I were swimming!"

"I wonder," said the other, "if the swallow—who flys so far and wide on its many journeys abroad—has found a better climate than ours: such a drizzle, such humidity! It's just like lying in a wet ditch. If that doesn't make one glad, then one doesn't really love one's country!"

"Then you've never been in the emperor's stables?" asked the dung beetle. "The moisture there is both warm and spicy! That's what I'm accustomed to! That's my kind of climate, but you can't take it with you on your journey. Isn't there any hotbed in the garden where persons of rank, such as myself, can put up and feel at home?"

But the frogs didn't understand him—or else they didn't want to understand him.

"I never ask a second time," said the dung beetle after it had asked three times without receiving an answer.

Then it walked a bit; there lay a fragment of a flowerpot. It shouldn't have lain there, but lying where it did, it provided shelter. Several earwig families were living there; they don't insist upon a lot of room, only company. The

females are especially endowed with maternal love, and for this reason the youngsters of each were the prettiest and the most intelligent.

"Our son has become engaged," said one mother, "the sweet innocent! His highest ambition is to crawl, once, into a clergyman's ear! He's so adorably childish, and the engagement keeps him from running wild! That's so gratifying to a mother."

"Our son," said another mother, "was up to mischief the moment he came out of the egg. He's bubbling over! He's sowing his wild oats! That's a tremendous consolation to a mother! Isn't it, Mr. Dung Beetle!" They recognized the stranger by its figure.

"You're both right," said the dung beetle, and then it was invited inside—as far as it could come under the fragment of pottery.

"Now you're also going to see my little earwig," said a third and a fourth mother. "They're the most lovable children, and so entertaining! They're never naughty—except when they have a pain in their stomachs, but one gets that so easily at their age!"

And then each mother talked about her youngsters, and the youngsters talked along with them and used the little fork they have on their tails to tug at the dung beetle's whiskers.

"They're always up to something, the little rascals!" said the mothers, reeking of motherly love. But the dung beetle was bored, and so it asked if it were far to the hotbed.

"It's a long way out into the world, on the other side of the ditch," said the earwig. "I hope none of my children will ever go that far, for then I would die."

"All the same, I'm going to try to go that far!" said the dung beetle, and left without taking its leave. That's the most polite thing to do.

By the ditch he met several of his kin, all dung beetles.

"Here's where we live!" they said. "It's quite cozy. May we invite you down in the rich dirt? No doubt the journey has worn you out."

"So it has," said the dung beetle. "I've been lying on linen in the rain, and cleanliness in particular takes a lot out of me! I've also got rheumatism in the joint of my wing from standing in a draft under a fragment of pottery. It's really quite refreshing to find oneself among one's own kind."

"Are you by any chance from the hotbed?" asked the oldest.

"Higher up," said the dung beetle. "I come from the emperor's stables, where I was born with golden shoes on. I'm on a secret errand that you mustn't pump me about, as I'm not talking!"

And then the dung beetle crawled down in the rich mud. There sat three young female dung beetles. They snickerered, because they didn't know what to say.

"They're not engaged," said the mother, and then they snickered, because they didn't know what to say.

"I've never seen them prettier in the emperor's stables," said the traveling dung beetle.

"Don't lead my girls astray! And don't speak to them unless your intentions are honorable. But so they are, and I give you my blessing!"

"Hurrah!" said all the others, and then the dung beetle was engaged. First engagement, and then the wedding. After all, there was nothing to wait for.

The next day went quite well, the second dragged along, but on the third day one had to think of food for wife and perhaps tots.

"I've allowed myself to be taken by surprise!" it said. "So now I must take them by surprise in return!"

And it did. Gone it was. Gone the whole day, gone the whole night. And the wife was left a widow. The other dung beetles said they had taken a regular tramp into the family; the wife was now a burden to them.

"Then she can become a maiden again," said the mother, "remain my child. Fie on that dastardly wretch who abandoned her!"

In the meantime it was on its way, having sailed across the ditch on a cabbage leaf. Early in the morning two people came. They saw the dung beetle, picked it up, and twisted and turned it. They were both very learned, especially the boy. "Allah sees the black dung beetle in the black stone in the black mountain! Isn't that the way it's written in the Koran?" he asked. And he translated the dung beetle's name into Latin and gave an account of its genus and nature. The older scholar voted against taking it home with them. The examples they had there were just as good, he said. The dung beetle didn't think this was a polite thing to say, and so it flew out of his hand and flew a good distance—its wings had become dry—and then it reached the hothouse. One of the windows had been pushed up, so it could pop in with the greatest of ease and burrow down in the fresh manure.

"How luscious it is!" it said.

Soon it fell asleep and dreamed that the emperor's horse had fallen and that Mr. Dung Beetle had been given its golden shoes and the promise of two more. That was a pleasure, and when the dung beetle awoke it crawled out and looked up. How magnificent it was in the greenhouse. Enormous fan palms spread out overhead, the sun made them transparent. Beneath them was a luxuriance of greenery, and flowers glowed as red as fire, as golden as amber, and as white as the driven snow.

"What wonderfully magnificent plants! How marvelous it all will taste when it starts to rot!" said the dung beetle. "This is a fine dining room. No doubt some of the family dwells here. I will track them down and see if I can find anyone worth associating with. I have my pride and I'm proud of it!" Then off it went, thinking of its dream about the dead horse and the golden shoes it had won.

All at once a hand grabbed the dung beetle. It was squeezed and turned over and over.

The gardener's little boy was in the hot house with a friend; they had seen the dung beetle and were going to have some fun with it. It was wrapped in a grape leaf and put down in a warm pants pocket. It wriggled and crawled until it received a squeeze from the hand of the boy, who went quickly over to the big lake at the end of the garden. Here the dung beetle was placed in a broken old wooden shoe with the instep missing. A stick was made fast for a mast, and the dung beetle was tied to it with a woolen thread. Now it was a skipper and was going out sailing.

The lake was very large. The dung beetle thought it was the ocean, and it was so astonished that it fell over on its back with its feet kicking in the air.

The wooden shoe sailed, for there was a current in the water; but if the ship went too far out, one of the boys rolled up his pants right away and went out and fetched it. But the next time it drifted, the boys were called—called in earnest—and they hurried away, leaving the wooden shoe a wooden shoe. It floated farther and farther from land. It was terrifying for the dung beetle; it couldn't fly because it was tied fast to the mast.

A fly paid it a visit.

"What glorious weather we're having," said the fly. "Here I can rest and sun myself. You are quite comfortable."

"You're talking as if you were not in possession of your senses! Don't you see I'm tied up?"

"I'm not tied up!" said the fly, and then it flew away.

"Now I know what the world is like," said the dung beetle. "It's an ignoble world! I'm the only respectable soul in it. First I'm refused golden shoes, then I have to lie on wet linen and stand in a draft, and in the end they foist a wife upon me. Then, when I take a quick trip out in the world to see how it is, and how it should be for me, along comes a human whelp and ties me up and puts me in the raging sea! And in the meantime the emperor's horse goes about with golden shoes on! It's enough to make one croak! But one can't expect sympathy in this world. The story of my life is quite interesting, but what's the good of that when no one knows about it? Nor does the world deserve to know about it, otherwise it would have given *me* golden shoes in the emperor's stables when the steed held out its feet and was shod. Had I been given golden shoes, I would have been a credit to the stables. Now it has lost me and the world has lost me. Everything is finished."

But everything wasn't finished yet. A boat came along with some young girls in it.

"A wooden shoe is sailing there," said one.

"A little bug is tied fast to it," said the other.

They were right alongside the wooden shoe. They picked it up, and one of the girls took out a pair of scissors and cut the woolen thread without harming the dung beetle, and when they came ashore she put it in the grass.

"Crawl, crawl! Fly, fly if you can!" she said. "Freedom is a wonderful thing."

And the dung beetle flew right in through the window of a large building and sank exhausted in the fine, soft, long mane of the emperor's charger, who was standing in the stable where he and the dung beetle belonged. It clung fast to the mane and sat for a while to collect its thoughts. "Here I sit on the emperor's charger, sit like a rider. What am I saying? Yes, now it's clear to me! It's a good idea and a correct one at that. Why did the emperor's horse get golden shoes? The smith asked me about that too. Now I see it! The emperor's horse was given golden shoes for my sake!"

And now the dung beetle was in good spirits.

"Travel clears one's head!" it said.

The sun shone on it, shone very beautifully. "The world hasn't gone so mad yet," said the dung beetle. "You just have to know how to take it." The world was lovely: the emperor's charger had been given golden shoes because the dung beetle was to be its rider.

"Now I'm going to climb down and tell the other beetles how much has been done for me. I'll tell of all the pleasures I've indulged in on my journey abroad, and I'll say that now I'm going to remain at home until the horse has worn out its golden shoes!"

What Papa Does
Is Always Right

❖   ❖   ❖

NOW I'm going to tell you a story I heard when I was a boy, and every time I've thought of it since, it struck me as being much nicer, for it's the same with stories as with many people: they grow nicer and nicer with age, and that's so delightful!

Of course you've been out in the country! You've seen a really old farmhouse with a thatched roof. Mosses and herbs are growing on it of their own accord. There's a stork's nest on the ridge—you can't do without the stork. The walls are crooked, the windows low—indeed, there's only one that can be opened. The oven juts out just like a little pot belly, and the elder bush hangs over the fence, where there's a little puddle of water with a duck or ducklings on it, right under the gnarled willow tree. Yes, and then there's a dog on a chain that barks at each and every one.

Just such a farmhouse was out in the country, and in it there lived a couple: a farmer and the farmer's wife. No matter what little they had, there was still one thing they could do without: a horse that grazed in the ditch by the side of the road. Papa rode to town on it, the neighbors borrowed it, and one good turn was repaid by another. But I daresay it was more profitable for them to sell the horse or swap it for something or other

that could be of even more use to them. But what was that
to be?

"You'll be the best judge of that, Papa!" said the wife.
"Now, there's a fair on in town. Ride there and get money
for the horse, or else make a good bargain. Whatever you
do is always right! Ride to the fair!"

And then she tied his neckerchief, for after all she knew
how to do that better than he did; she tied it in a double
bow—it looked so perky—and then she brushed his hat
with the flat of her hand, and she kissed him on his warm
lips. And then he rode off on the horse that was to be sold
or swapped. Yes, Papa was the best judge of that.

The sun blazed down; there wasn't a cloud above. The
dust whirled up from the road, for there were so many
people on their way to the fair—in carts, on horseback,
and on their own two feet. It was sizzling hot, and there
wasn't a bit of shade along the way.

A man was walking along driving a cow; it was as pretty
as a cow can be. "I daresay that cow gives delicious milk!"
thought the farmer. "It could be quite a bargain to get
that!" He said, "Look here, you with the cow! Shouldn't
the two of us have a little chat together? Here's a horse,
which I do believe costs more than a cow, but it doesn't
matter! A cow is of more use to me. Shall we swap?"

"I'll say!" said the man with the cow, and so they
swapped.

Well, that was settled, and now the farmer could have
turned back. After all, he'd done what he'd set out to do.
But as long as he'd made up his mind to go to the fair,
then to the fair he wanted to go, just to have a look at it.
So he went on with his cow. He walked along at a good
clip, and the cow walked along at a good clip, and soon
they were walking alongside a man who was leading a
ewe. It was a fine ewe, with plenty of meat and plenty of
wool.

"I'd like to own that!" thought the farmer. "It'd never

be without something to graze on by the side of our ditch, and in the winter we could bring it into the house with us. As a matter of fact, it would be better for us to keep a ewe than a cow. Shall we swap?"

Well, the man with the ewe was only too willing, and so this swap was made, and the farmer went on down the road with his ewe. There by the stile he saw a man with a big goose under his arm.

"That's a big fellow you've got there!" said the farmer. "It has both feathers and fat. It'd look good tethered by our pond. This is something for Mama to gather peelings for! She's often said, 'If only we had a goose!' Now she can have one—and she shall have one! Do you want to swap? I'll give you the ewe for the goose, and thanks into the bargain!"

Well, the other man was only too willing, and so they swapped. The farmer got the goose. He was close to town; the crowds on the road increased. It was teeming with men and beasts. They walked on the road, and in the ditch, all the way up to the tollman's potato patch, where his hen stood tied, so that she wouldn't run away in her fright and get lost. It was a bobtail hen that blinked with one eye and looked good. "Cluck! Cluck!" it said. What it meant by that I cannot say. But when the farmer saw her, he thought: "She's the prettiest hen I've ever seen. She's prettier than the parson's sitting hen. I'd so like to own her! A hen can always find a grain of corn. She can almost look after herself! I think that would be a good bargain if I got her for the goose." "Shall we swap?" he asked. "Swap?" said the other. "Why, yes, that wasn't such a bad idea!" And so they swapped: the tollman got the goose, the farmer got the hen.

He'd done quite a lot on that journey to town, and it was hot and he was tired. A dram and a bite to eat were what he needed. Now he was by the inn. He wanted to go in, but the innkeeper's hired hand wanted to go out. He met him right in the doorway with a sack heaping full of something.

"What have you got there?" asked the farmer.

"Rotten apples!" answered the fellow. "A whole sackful for the pigs."

"Why, that's an awful lot! I wish Mama could see a sight like that. Last year we had only a single apple on the old tree by the peat shed. That apple had to be kept, and it stood on the chest of drawers until it burst. 'There's always plenty!' said Mama. Here she could really see plenty!"

"Well, what'll you give?" asked the fellow.

"Give? I'll give you my hen in exchange!" And then he gave him the hen for the apples and went into the inn and right over to the bar. He leaned his sack of apples up against the tiled stove. There was a fire in it, but he didn't give that a thought. There were lots of strangers here in the room: horse traders, cattle dealers, and two Englishmen—they're so rich that their pockets are bursting with golden coins, and they love to make wagers!

Now you shall hear.

"Sssssssss! Sssssssss!" What was that noise over by the stove? The apples were beginning to roast.

"What's that?" Well, they soon found out about the whole story—about the horse that had been swapped for the cow, all the way down to the rotten apples.

"Well," said the Englishmen, "you'll be getting a cuff from Mama when you come home! There'll be the devil to pay!"

"I'll get a kiss and not a cuff!" said the farmer. "Our Mama's going to say, 'What Papa does is always right!' "

"Shall we wager?" they said. "A barrelful of gold coins! A hundred pounds to a ship's pound!"

"A bushel is enough," said the farmer. "I can put up only the bushel of apples—and myself and Mama into the bargain! But that's more than a level measure; that's a heaping measure!"

"Heaping! Heaping!" they said, and then the wager was made.

The innkeeper's wagon was brought out, the Englishmen got in, the farmer got in, the rotten apples got in, and then they came to the farmer's house.

"Good evening, Mama!"

"Same to you, Papa!"

"Well, I've made a swap!"

"Yes, you're the best judge of that," said the wife, putting her arm around his waist and forgetting both the sack and the strangers.

"I've swapped the horse for a cow!"

"Heaven be praised for the milk!" said the wife. "Now we can have milk dishes and butter and cheese on the table. That was a lovely swap!"

"Yes, but I swapped the cow for a ewe!"

"That's decidedly better too!" said the wife. "You're always considerate. We've plenty of fodder for a ewe. Now we can have ewe's milk and cheese and woolen stockings—yes, even a woolen nightshirt. The cow doesn't give that. She loses her hair. You're the most considerate man!"

"But I swapped the ewe for a goose!"

"Are we really going to have a goose this year for Martinmas, little Papa? You're always thinking up ways to please me! That was sweet of you. The goose can stand tethered and grow fatter by Martinmas."

"But I swapped the goose for a hen!" said the husband.

"A hen! That was a good swap," said the wife. "The hen lays eggs; it hatches them out—we'll have chickens, we'll have a hen yard! That's just what I've always wanted!"

"Yes, but I swapped the hen for a sack of rotten apples!"

"Now I've got to give you a kiss!" said the wife. "Thank you, my own husband! Now I'm going to tell you something. While you were gone I thought I'd make a really good meal for you—an omelet with chives. I had the eggs, but no chives. So I went over to the schoolmaster's. They have chives there, I know. But the wife is so stingy, that sweet she-ass! I asked if I could borrow! 'Borrow!' she said. 'Nothing grows in our garden, not even a rotten apple! I can't even lend you that!' Now *I* can lend her ten—yes, a whole sackful. What a joke that is, Papa!" And she kissed him squarely on the mouth.

"Now you're talking!" said the Englishmen. "Always down and out, and always without a care! That's certainly worth the money!" And so they paid a ship's pound of golden coins to the farmer, who received a kiss instead of a cuff.

Yes, indeed, it always pays for the wife to realize and

explain that Papa is the wisest, and whatever he does is right.

See, that's a story! I heard it when I was a boy, and now you've heard it too and know that What Papa Does Is Always Right.

The Snowman

I'M fairly creaking inside, it's so delightfully cold!" said
the snowman. "The wind can really bite life into one!
And how that glowerer there can glower!" This was the
sun that he meant; it was just about to go down. "She's not
going to make me blink! I daresay I can hang onto the
fragments!"

He had two big triangular fragments of tile for eyes; the
mouth was a piece of an old rake, and so he had teeth.

He had been born to the cheers of the boys and greeted
by the jangle of bells and the crack of whips from the
sleighs.

The sun went down; the full moon came up, round and
big, bright and lovely in the blue air.

"There she is from another angle," said the snowman.
He thought the sun was showing itself again. "I've made
her stop glowering! Now she can just hang there and shine
so I can have a look at myself. If only I knew what one
does to move! I'd so like to move! If I could, I'd go down
now and slide on the ice, the way I saw the boys doing it!
But I don't understand how to run!"

"Gone! Gone!" barked the old watchdog. He was somewhat hoarse. He'd been that way ever since the time he
was a house dog and had lain under the tiled stove. "The
sun'll soon teach you how to run! I saw it with your

predecessor last year, and with *his* predecessor. Gone! Gone! And they are all gone!"

"I don't understand you, friend!" said the snowman. "Is that one up there going to teach me how to run?" He meant the moon. "Well, of course she can run. She ran before, when I glared at her. Now she's sneaking around from another side."

"You don't know anything!" said the watchdog. "But then you've only just been made! The one you're looking at now is called the moon; the one that left was the sun. She'll be back tomorrow. I daresay she'll teach you how to run down in the moat. We'll soon be getting a change in the weather. I can tell by my hind leg—it's aching. The weather's going to change."

"I don't understand him," said the snowman, "but I've

got a feeling that he's saying something unpleasant. That one who glowered and went down—the one he calls the sun—she's not my friend, either. I can feel it."

"Gone! Gone!" barked the watchdog, turning on his tail three times and lying down in his house to go to sleep.

There really was a change in the weather. Early in the morning a thick, clammy fog settled over the entire countryside. At daybreak the wind started to blow. It was biting cold; the frost really nipped. But what a sight to behold when the sun rose! All the trees and bushes were covered with rime. It was like an entire forest of white coral, as if every branch had been heaped with sparkling white blossoms. The myriads of delicate twigs, which cannot be seen in summer for the many leaves, now came into their own—each and every one. It was like lace, and as shining white as if a radiant white light were streaming from every branch. The weeping birch stirred in the wind; it seemed to be as alive as the trees in summer. It was incomparably lovely; and when the sun shone—my, how it all sparkled! It was as if it had been powdered over with diamond dust, while the big diamonds glittered on the earth's blanket of snow. One might even believe that myriads of tiny candles were burning, whiter than the white snow.

"How incredibly lovely!" said a young girl who came out in the garden with a young man, and stopped close to the snowman to look at the glittering trees. "There's no lovelier sight in summer," she said, and her eyes beamed.

"And there aren't any fellows like this one at all," said the young man, pointing to the snowman. "He's splendid!"

The young girl laughed, nodded to the snowman, and danced on with her friend across the snow, which creaked beneath them as if it were starch.

"Who were those two?" the snowman asked the watchdog. "You've been here in the yard longer than I have. Do you know them?"

"That I do!" said the watchdog. "After all, she has petted me and he has given me a bone. I don't bite them."

"But what are they supposed to be?" asked the snowman.

"Sweeeeeeethearrrrrrrts!" said the watchdog. "They're going to move into a doghouse and gnaw bones together. Gone! Gone!"

"Are those two just as important as you and I?" asked the snowman.

"Why, they belong to the family," said the watchdog. "I must say, there's very little one knows when one was born yesterday. I can tell by the way you act! I have age and knowledge; I know everybody here. And I've known a day when I didn't stand outside chained up in the cold! Gone! Gone!"

"The cold is delightful!" said the snowman. "Tell! Tell! But you mustn't rattle your chain, for it makes me crack inside."

"Gone! Gone!" barked the watchdog. "I was once a puppy—tiny and sweet, they said. Then I lay on a velvet stool inside the house, lay on the lap of the head of the family. I was kissed on the chaps and had my paws wiped with an embroidered handkerchief. I was called "the most delightful" and "cuddly-wuddly." But then I grew too big for them, so they gave me to the housekeeper. I came down to the basement! You can see in there from where you're standing. You can look down into the room where I was lord and master, for that's what I was at the housekeeper's. It was probably a humbler place than above, but it was more comfortable here. And I wasn't mauled and hauled about the way I was by the children upstairs. The food I got was just as good, and there was more of it! I had my own pillow, and then there was a tiled stove—the most wonderful thing in the world at this time of year. I crawled all the way in underneath it until I was out of sight. Oh, I still dream about that tiled stove! Gone! Gone!"

"Does a tiled stove look so lovely?" asked the snowman. "Does it look like me?"

"It's the very opposite of you! It's as black as coal and has a long neck with a brass drum. It eats wood until the flames pour out of its mouth. You have to stay beside it, close up to it, underneath it; it's an infinite pleasure! You must be able to see it through the window from where you're standing!"

And the snowman looked, and he really did see a black highly polished object that had a brass drum. The fire shone out at the bottom. The snowman felt very queer. He had a feeling that he was unable to account for; something had come over him that he had never known before, but which everyone has known who isn't a snowman.

"And why did you leave her?" said the snowman—he felt that it had to be of the female persuasion. "How could you leave such a place?"

"I had to," said the watchdog. "They threw me outside and put me here on a chain. I'd bitten the youngest Junker in the leg for kicking away the bone I was gnawing on. And bone for bone, I thought. But they took exception to this, and I've been chained up out here ever since. And I've lost my clear voice. Listen to how hoarse I am. Gone! Gone! That was the end of that!"

The snowman was no longer listening. He gazed steadily into the housekeeper's basement, down into her parlor, where the stove stood on its four legs and seemed to be as big as the snowman himself.

"I'm creaking so strangely inside," he said. "Will I never come in there? It's a harmless wish, and our harmless wishes ought to be granted. It's my greatest wish, my only wish, and it would almost be unjust if it weren't granted. I must come in there, I must lean up against her, even if I have to break the window."

"You'll never get inside there," said the watchdog. "And if you did get to the tiled stove, you'd be gone! Gone!"

"I'm as good as gone!" said the snowman. "I think I'm breaking in two!"

All day long the snowman stood gazing in through the window. In the twilight the room was even more inviting. From the tiled stove came a gentle glow, as could never come from the moon or the sun; no, it glowed as only a tiled stove can glow when it has something inside it. If the door was opened, the flames shot out as they were in the habit of doing. The snowman's white face turned a scarlet hue, he was red all the way down to his chest.

"I can't stand it," he said. "How it becomes her to stick out her tongue!"

The night was very long, but not for the snowman. He stood deep in his own lovely thoughts, and they froze so they creaked.

In the early-morning hours the basement windows were frozen over; they were covered with the loveliest flowers of ice that any snowman could wish for, but they hid the tiled stove. The panes wouldn't thaw; he couldn't see her. It creaked and it crunched; it was just the sort of frosty weather to satisfy any snowman, but he wasn't satisfied. He could and he should have felt so happy, but he wasn't happy: he had what is known as the "tiled-stove-yearning."

"That's a bad sickness for a snowman to have," said the watchdog. "I've had a little of the same sickness myself, but I've got over it. Gone! Gone! Now we're going to have a change in the weather."

And there was a change in the weather: a thaw set in.

The thaw increased, the snowman decreased. He never said a word, he never complained, and that's a sure sign.

One morning he fell over. Something like the handle of a mop was sticking in the air where he had been standing. This is what the boys had built him around.

"Now I can understand his longing," said the watchdog. "The snowman had a poker inside him. That's what has affected him; now it's over! Gone! Gone!"

And soon the winter was over too.

"Gone! Gone!" barked the watchdog.
But in the yard the little girls sang:

> "Hurry forth woodruff, fresh and fair,
> Willow, hang your woolen tassels there,
> Come cuckoo, lark! Sing, be merry,
> Spring has come in February.
> Cuckoo! Tweet-tweet! I sing too!
> Come, dear sun, the way you often do!"

So no one is thinking about the snowman!

In the Duck Yard

❖   ❖   ❖

A duck came from Portugal, some said from Spain. It makes no difference—she was called "The Portuguese." She laid eggs, was butchered and served for dinner; that's the course of her life. All those who crawled out of her eggs were called "The Portuguese," and that meant something. Now, of the entire stock only one was left in the duck yard—a yard to which the chickens also had access, and where the cock behaved with infinite arrogance.

"That violent crowing of his outrages me!" said The Portuguese. "But he is handsome. That cannot be denied, despite the fact that he is no drake. He should control himself, but controlling oneself is an art. It reveals breeding. That's what the little songbirds up in the linden tree in the neighboring garden possess. How sweetly they sing! There's something so moving in their song. I'd call it *Portugal!* If I had a little songbird like that, I'd be a mother to him, affectionate and good. It's in my blood, in my Portuguese!"

And at the same moment as she was speaking, a little songbird did come. It came headlong down from the roof. The cat was after it, but the bird escaped with a broken wing and fell down in the duck yard.

"That's just like the cat, the scoundrel!" said The Portuguese. "I know him from the time I had ducklings myself! That such a creature is permitted to live and walk about on the rooftops! I don't believe it would happen in Portugal!"

And she took pity on the little songbird, and the other ducks, who weren't Portuguese, took pity on him too.

"The poor little mite," they said, and came one after the other. "It's true that we're not singers ourselves," they said, "but we do have internal sounding boards, or something like that; we feel it even if we don't talk about it."

"Then I want to talk about it," said The Portuguese. "And I want to do something for it, for that is one's duty!" And then she went up to the drinking trough and flapped in the water, so that she almost drowned the little songbird in the deluge he received. But it was well meant. "That's a good deed!" she said. "The others can look at it and follow its example."

"Peep!" said the little bird; one of his wings was broken. It was hard for him to shake himself, but he quite understood that well-meant deluge. "You're so tender-hearted, madame!" he said, but he insisted on nothing more.

"I've never given the tenderness of my heart a thought!" said The Portuguese. "But I do know that I love all my fellow creatures with the exception of the cat. But then no one can ask that of me! I myself am from foreign parts, as you probably can tell by my carriage and my feathered gown. My drake is a native, doesn't have my blood, but I don't put on airs! If you're understood by anybody in here, then I daresay it's by me."

"She was a *portulaca*[1] to the craw," said one ordinary little duckling who was witty, and the other ordinary ducklings thought that *portulaca* was quite splendid—it sounded like Portugal; and they nudged one another and

[1] Purslane.

said, "Quack!" He was so incomparably witty. And then they took up with the little songbird.

"True, The Portuguese has the language at her command," they said. "Our bills are not given to big words, but we participate just as much. If we don't do anything for you, we keep quiet about it, and we find that to be most agreeable."

"You have a sweet voice," said one of the oldest. "It must be delightful to be aware that one gives so much pleasure to so many, the way you do. Of course I don't know anything about that! And so I keep my mouth shut, and that's always better than saying something stupid, the way so many others say to you."

"Don't pester him!" said The Portuguese. "He needs rest and care. Little songbird, shall I splash you again?"

"Oh, no, let me stay dry!" he begged.

"The water cure is the only thing that helps me," said The Portuguese. "Diversion is also quite good! Now the neighboring hens will be coming soon to pay a visit. There are two Chinese hens. They wear pantaloons and have considerable breeding, and they've been imported—which elevates them in my esteem."

And the hens came, and the cock came! He was so polite today that he wasn't rude.

"You're a real songbird," he said, "and with your little voice you do as much as can be done with such a little voice! But something more locomotive is needed for it to be heard that one is of the male sex!"

The two Chinese hens stood enraptured over the sight of the songbird. He looked so disheveled from the deluge he had received that they thought he resembled a Chinese chicken. "He's lovely!" And then they took up with him. They spoke in whispers, and the *p*-sound in proper Chinese.

"Now, we belong to your species. The ducks—even The Portuguese—belong to the web-footed birds, as you no doubt have observed. You don't know us yet, but how many do know us or take the trouble to! No one, not even among the hens, even though we're born to sit on a higher perch than most of the others. Of course it doesn't matter—we go our silent way among the others whose principles are not our own. But we look only at the good qualities and talk only about the good, despite the fact that it's hard to find where none exists. But with the exception of the two of us and the cock, there's no one in the hen house who is gifted. But they are respectable. You can't say this about the occupants of the duck yard. We warn you, little songbird, don't believe the one there with the short tail—she's perfidious! That speckled one there, with the uneven wing bows, she loves to argue and never permits anyone to have the last word. And then she's always wrong! That fat duck talks badly about everybody, and that's contrary to our nature. If you can't say something nice, then you should keep your mouth shut. The Portuguese is the only one who has a little breeding, and with whom one can associate. But she's passionate, and talks too much about Portugal!"

"What a lot the two Chinese have to whisper about!" said a couple of the ducks. "They bore me; I've never talked with them!"

Now the drake came. He thought the songbird was a house sparrow. "Well, I can't tell them apart," he said. "And besides, it makes no difference! He's one of the mechanical musical instruments, and if you've got them, then you've got them."

"Pay no attention to what he says!" whispered The Portuguese. "He's worthy of respect in business, and business is everything! But now I'm going to lie down to rest. One owes it to oneself to be nice and fat until one is ready to be embalmed with apples and prunes."

And then she lay down in the sunshine, blinking one eye. She lay so well, she behaved so well, and then she slept so well. The little songbird pecked at his broken

wing and lay down next to his protectress; the sun shone
warm and delightful; it was a good place to be.

The neighbor hens continued to scrape. As a matter of
fact, they had come there solely for the sake of the food.
The Chinese left first and then the others. The witty
duckling said, about The Portuguese, that the old one
would soon be going into her "Duckage." And then the
other ducks cackled, "Duckage! He's so incomparably witty!"
And then they repeated the first witticism: *"Portulaca!"*
That was very funny. And then they lay down.

They lay there for a while, then all at once some slops
were thrown down in the duck yard. It made such a splash
that the entire sleeping company flew up and flapped their
wings. The Portuguese woke up too and fell over, crushing the little songbird quite dreadfully.

"Peep!" he said. "You tread so hard, madame!"

"Why are you lying in the way?" she said. "You mustn't
be so thin-skinned! I have nerves too, but I've never said
'Peep'!"

"Don't be angry," said the little bird. "That 'Peep' slipped
out of my beak."

The Portuguese paid no attention to this, but flew to the
slops and had her good meal. When it was over and she
had lain down, the little songbird came and wanted to be
pleasant:

> "Twittery-twing!
> About your heart
> I'll always sing,
> Far, far, far on the wing!"

"Now I'm going to rest after the food," she said. "You've
got to learn the house rules in here! Now I'm going to
sleep."

The little songbird was quite taken aback, for he had
meant so well by it. When madame later awoke, he was

standing in front of her with a little grain of corn he had found. He put it in front of her, but she hadn't slept well and of course she was cross.

"You can give that to a chicken!" she said. "Don't stand there and hang over me!"

"But you're angry with me," he said. "What have I done?"

"Done!" said The Portuguese. "That expression is not of the finest sort, I'll have you know!"

"Yesterday there was sunshine here," said the little

bird, "but today it's dark and gray! I'm so deeply grieved."

"You certainly don't know enough about measuring time," said The Portuguese. "The day isn't over yet, so don't stand there and pretend to be so stupid."

"You're looking at me so angrily, the way those two evil eyes looked when I fell down here in the yard."

"Impudence!" said The Portuguese. "Are you comparing me with the cat, that beast of prey? There's not one drop of evil blood in me. I've taken care of you, and I'm going to teach you how to behave!"

And then she bit off the songbird's head. He lay dead.

"Now what's that?" she said. "Couldn't he take it! Well, he certainly wasn't much for this world, then! I've been like a mother to him, that I know, for I do have a heart."

And the neighboring cock stuck his head into the yard and crowed with the power of a locomotive.

"You'll be the death of somebody with that crowing!" she said. "It's all your fault! He lost his head, and I'm about to lose mine!"

"He doesn't take up much room where he lies," said the cock.

"Talk about him with respect!" said The Portuguese. "He had manners and song and good breeding! He was affectionate and softhearted, and that's just as becoming to the animals as to those so-called human beings."

And all the ducks gathered around the little dead songbird. The ducks have strong passions, no matter whether it's envy or compassion. And as there was nothing here for them to be envious of, they were compassionate. And so were the two Chinese hens.

"We'll never have a songbird like that again! He was almost Chinese!" And they cried so they clucked, and all the hens clucked. But the ducks went about with the reddest eyes.

"We have heart," they said. "There's no denying that!"

"Heart!" said The Portuguese. "Yes, that we have—almost just as much as in Portugal."

"Now let's see about getting something in the carcass!" said the drake. "That's more important! If one of the mechanical musical instruments breaks down, we'll still have enough."

The Butterfly

❖ ❖ ❖

THE butterfly wanted to have a sweetheart. Naturally he wanted one of the pretty little flowers. He looked at them; each one was sitting so prim and proper on its stalk, the way a maiden should sit when she is not engaged. But there were so many to choose from that it proved irksome. The butterfly couldn't be bothered, and so he flew to the daisy. The French call her Marguerite. They know that she can foretell the future, and she does it when sweethearts pick petal by petal off her, and with each one they ask a question about the beloved: "Loves me? Loves me not? Loves me a lot? A teeny-weeny bit? Not at all?" Or something like that. Each one asks in his own language. The butterfly also came to ask. He didn't nip off the petals, but kissed each one—it being his opinion that one comes the farthest without resorting to force.

"Sweet Marguerite!" he said. "Of all the flowers, you are the wisest woman! You understand how to foretell the future. Tell me, am I to marry this one or that? When I find it out, I can fly straight over and propose!"

But Marguerite did not reply at all. She could not bear his calling her a woman, for of course she was a maiden, and then one is not a woman. He asked a second time and he asked a third. And when he didn't get a single word out

313

of her, he couldn't be bothered with asking her anymore and flew off to woo without further ado.

It was early spring. There were snowdrops and crocuses in abundance.

"You are quite nice!" said the butterfly. "Lovely, small candidates for confirmation! But a bit green!" Like all other young men, he was looking for older girls. Then he flew to the anemones. They were a little too tart for him, the violets a little too soulful, the tulips too gaudy, the white narcissus too bourgeois, the lime blossoms too small— and they had so many kinfolk. To be sure, the apple blossoms looked like roses, but they stood today and fell off tomorrow—all according to the way the wind blew.

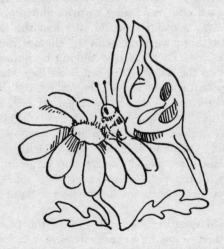

That was too short a marriage, he thought. The sweet pea was the most pleasing: she was white and red, pure and delicate—one of those homey maidens who look good and yet are cut out for the kitchen. He was just going to propose to her when, at the same moment, he saw hanging close by a pea pod with withered flowers on the top.

"Who's that?" he asked.

"That's my sister," said the sweet pea.

"Well, that's the way you're going to look later!" This frightened the butterfly, and so he flew away.

The honeysuckles were hanging over the fence. There were plenty of those maidens—with long faces and sallow complexions. They weren't his type at all.

Well, what was his type? Ask him!

Spring passed. Summer passed, and then it was autumn. He had made just as much headway. And the flowers appeared in the loveliest garments. But what good was that? The fresh, fragrant lightness of heart was lacking. Fragrance is just what the heart needs, and there is not very much fragrance to dahlias and hollyhocks. So the butterfly turned to the mint.

"Now it has no flower at all. But it is all flower, gives off a fragrance from root to top, and has a flower scent in every leaf. She is the one I will take!"

And so he proposed at last.

But the mint stood still and stiff, and at last she said, "Friendship, but no more. I am old and you are old. We could quite well live for each other. But marry? No! Let us not make fools of ourselves at our great age!"

And so the butterfly got no one at all. He had searched too long, and one should not do that. The butterfly became a bachelor, as it is called.

It was late autumn, with rain and drizzle. The wind sent cold shivers down the spines of the old willow trees, making them creak. It was not good flying outside in summer clothes—you'd be in for an unpleasant surprise, as they say. But the butterfly did not fly outside, either. By chance he had come indoors, where there was a fire in the stove. Indeed, it was as warm as summer. He could live.

"But living isn't enough!" he said. "One must have sunshine, freedom, and a little flower!"

He flew against the pane, and was seen, admired, and stuck on a pin in the curio chest. More could not be done for him.

"Now I too am sitting on a stalk, just as the flowers do!" said the butterfly. "But it is not very pleasant. Indeed, it is like being married—one is stuck!" And then he consoled himself with that.

"That is poor consolation," said the potted plants in the parlor.

"But one cannot quite believe the potted plants," thought the butterfly. "They associate too much with people."

The Snail and
the Rosebush

❖   ❖   ❖

AROUND the garden was a hedge of hazelnut bushes, and beyond it were fields and meadows with cows and sheep. But in the middle of the garden stood a flowering rosebush, and under it sat a snail. It contained a lot: it contained itself.

"Wait until my time comes!" it said. "I shall accomplish something more than sending forth roses, bearing nuts, or giving milk, as cows and sheep do."

"I'm expecting a great deal from you," said the rosebush. "May I ask when it's coming?"

"I'm biding my time," said the snail. "You, now, are in such a hurry! It doesn't raise one's expectations."

The next year the snail was lying in just about the same spot in the sunshine, under the rosebush, which was budding and sending forth roses—always fresh, always new. And the snail crawled halfway out, stretched out its horns, and drew them back again.

"Everything looks the way it did last year! There has been no progress. The rosebush keeps on sending forth roses; it makes no further headway."

The summer passed and autumn came. The rosebush kept on sending forth flowers and buds until the snow fell. The weather turned raw and wet. The rosebush bent down to the ground; the snail crawled into the earth.

Now a new year began, and the roses came forth and the snail came forth.

"Now you're an old rose stock!" it said. "You must soon see about dying. You've given the world everything you had in you. Whether it was of any consequence is a question I haven't had time to think over. But still it's clear that you haven't done the slightest thing about your inner development, or else you would have produced something else. Can you justify that? Soon you'll end up as kindling. Can you understand what I'm saying?"

"You frighten me," said the rosebush. "I've never given it a thought."

"No, I daresay you never were much prone to thinking. Have you ever figured out for yourself why you put forth flowers and how the flowering came about? Why this way and not another way?"

"No," said the rosebush. "I flowered for the joy of it. I couldn't help myself. The sun was so warm, the air so invigorating. I drank the clear dew and the strong rain. I breathed, I lived! A force came up in me from the earth and from above; I sensed a joy always new, always great, and for that reason I had to blossom. That was my life—I couldn't help myself."

"You have led a very easy life," said the snail.

"Assuredly! Everything has been handed to me!" said
the rosebush. "But even more has been given to you! You
are one of those thoughtful, profound natures, one of the
highly gifted who wants to astound the world."

"That has never crossed my mind at all," said the snail.
"The world is of no concern to me! What have I to do with
the world? I have enough with myself and enough in
myself."

"But shouldn't each one of us here on earth give the
best we have to others, bring what we can? To be sure, I
have only given roses—but you, you who have received so
much, what have you given to the world? What are you
giving to it?"

"What have I given? What am I giving? I spit at it! It's
no good! It is of no concern to me! You send forth roses.
You can go no further! Let the hazelnut bush bear nuts.
Let cows and sheep give milk. They each have their
public; I have mine in myself! I withdraw into myself, and
there I stay. The world is of no concern to me!"

And then the snail went inside its house and sealed it
up.

"It's so sad," said the rosebush. "As much as I'd like to,
I cannot crawl inside. I must always come out, come out
in roses. The petals fall off; they fly about in the wind.
And yet I saw one of the roses being put in the housewife's hymnbook; one of my roses was placed on the breast
of a lovely young girl; and one was kissed by the lips of a
child in blissful joy. It did me so much good! It was truly a
blessing. This is my reminiscence, my life!"

And the rosebush bloomed in innocence, and the snail
languished in its house. The world was of no concern to
him.

And the years went by.

And the snail was dust in the earth. The rosebush was
dust in the earth; even the keepsake rose in the hymnbook
had withered away. But in the garden new rosebushes

bloomed; in the garden new snails grew; they crawled into their houses and spit—the world was of no concern to them.

Shall we read the story again from the beginning? It will be no different.

The Teapot

❖   ❖   ❖

T HERE was a proud teapot—proud of its porcelain, proud of its long spout, proud of its broad handle. It had something in front and something behind, the spout in front and the handle behind, and it talked about that. But it didn't talk about its lid; that was cracked and had been riveted. It had a flaw, and one is not fond of talking about one's flaws—the others are sure to do that. Cups, cream pitcher, and sugar bowl, the whole tea service, would be sure to remember more the frailty of the lid, and to talk about it, than about the good handle and the excellent spout. And the teapot was aware of this.

"I know them!" it said to itself. "I am also well aware of my flaw, and I acknowledge it. Therein lies my humility, my modesty. We all have flaws, but one also has talents. The cups were given a handle, the sugar bowl a lid. I, of course, was given both, and one thing in front that they will never receive: I was given a spout. That makes me the queen of the tea table. The sugar bowl and the cream pitcher have been granted the privilege of being hand-maidens of palatability. But I am the dispenser, the mistress. I diffuse the blessing among thirsting humanity. In my interior the Chinese leaf is prepared in the boiling, tasteless water."

All this the teapot said in its intrepid youth. It stood on

the ready-laid table. It was lifted by the most delicate hand. But the most delicate hand was clumsy: the teapot fell, the spout broke off, and the handle broke off. The lid is not worth mentioning—enough has been said about that. The teapot lay in a swoon on the floor, the boiling water running out of it. It had received a hard blow. And the hardest blow of all was that they laughed at it, and not at the clumsy hand.

"That memory I will never lose," said the teapot when it later related the course of its life to itself. "I was called an invalid and put over in a corner, and on the following day I was given away to a woman who came begging for drippings. I sank down into destitution, stood speechless, both inside and out. But as I stood there my better life began. You are one thing and turn into quite another. Dirt was put inside me. To a teapot this is the same as being buried, but a flower bulb was put in the dirt. Who put it there, who gave it I do not know. It was given a compensation for the Chinese leaves and the boiling water a compensation for the broken-off handle and spout. And the bulb lay in the dirt, the bulb lay inside me. It became my heart, my living heart. I had never had one like that before. There was life in me, there was vigor and vitality; the pulse beat, the bulb sprouted. It was bursting with thoughts and emotions. It bloomed. I saw it, I bore it, I forgot myself in its loveliness. How blessed it is to forget oneself in others! It did not thank me. It did not think of me: it was admired and praised. I was so happy because of that: how happy it must have been then. One day I heard someone say that it deserved a better pot. I was broken in two. It hurt terribly, but the flower was put in a better pot—and I was thrown out in the yard, to lie there like an old fragment. But I have a memory that I cannot lose."

The Candles

❖   ❖   ❖

THERE was once a big wax candle that was well aware of itself.

"I am born of wax and cast in a mold!" it said. "I shine better and burn longer than any other candle! My place is in a chandelier or a silver candlestick!"

"That must be a delightful existence," said the tallow candle. "I am merely of tallow, only a taper. But I take comfort in the thought that it's always a little more than being a tallow dip! It is dipped only twice, whereas I am dipped eight times to arrive at my proper thickness. I am content! To be sure, it is finer and more fortunate to be born of wax and not of tallow, but after all one doesn't put oneself into this world. They go into the parlor in a crystal chandelier; I remain in the kitchen. But that is a good place too. From there the whole house is fed!"

"But there's something far more important than food!" said the wax candle. "Festivity! To see the radiance and to be radiant oneself! There's going to be a ball here this evening. Soon my whole family and I are going to be fetched!"

The words were scarcely uttered before all the wax candles were fetched. But the tallow candle came along too. The mistress herself picked it up in her delicate hand and carried it out into the kitchen. A little boy was standing there with a basket. It was filled with potatoes, and a few apples had been added. All this the good woman gave to the poor boy.

"Here's a candle for you too, my little friend!" she said. "Your mother sits working far into the night; she can use it!"

The little daughter of the house was standing nearby, and when she heard the words "far into the night," she said with heartfelt joy, "I too am going to stay up until far into the night. We're going to have a ball, and I'm going to wear my big red bows!"

How her face shone! This was happiness! No wax candle can shine like the two eyes of a child!

"What a blessed sight!" thought the tallow candle. "I will never forget it, and I daresay I will never see it again."

And then it was put in the basket under the lid, and the boy left with it.

"Where am I going now?" thought the candle. "I'm going to poor people. Perhaps I won't even be given a brass candlestick, whereas the wax candle is sitting in silver and looking at the most fashionable people. How wonderful it must be to shine for the most fashionable people. After all, it was my fate to be of tallow and not of wax!"

And the candle did come to poor people, a widow with three children in a lowly little cottage right across from the house of the rich family.

"God bless the good mistress for her gift," said the mother. "Why, there's a lovely candle! It can burn until far into the night!"

And the candle was lighted.

"Sputter, phooey!" it said. "What a nasty, smelly match she lit me with! Such a match would hardly have been offered to a wax candle over in the rich family's house!"

There too the candles were being lighted; they shone

out into the street. The rumbling carriages brought the elegantly clad ball guests. The music rang out.

"Now they're beginning over there!" observed the tallow candle, and thought of the little rich girl's radiant face, more radiant than all the wax candles. "I'll never see a sight like that again!"

Then the youngest child of the poor family came, a little girl. She flung her arms around the necks of her brother and sister—she had something very important to tell them and it had to be whispered: "This evening . . . Imagine! . . . This evening we're going to have hot potatoes!"

And her face shone with bliss. The candle shining there saw a joy, a happiness, as great as that it had seen over in the house of the rich family, where the little girl had said, "We're going to have a ball, and I'm going to wear my big red bows!"

"Is having hot potatoes equally as important?" thought the candle. "The children here are just as happy." And then she sneezed; that is to say, she sputtered, a tallow candle can do no more.

The table was set; the potatoes were eaten. Oh, how delicious they tasted! It was quite a feast! And afterward each child received an apple, and the youngest child recited the little verse:

> "Again, dear Lord, my thanks to thee,
> For giving so much food to me! Amen!"

"Wasn't it nice of me to say that, Mother?" the little one now cried.

"You must neither ask nor say such a thing," said the mother. "You should think only of the good Lord, who has given you enough to eat."

The little ones went to bed, received a kiss, and fell asleep right away, and the mother sat sewing until far into the night to earn a livelihood for them and for herself. And

from the house of the rich family, the candles shone and the music rang out. The stars twinkled above all the houses, above those of the rich and those of the poor, just as bright, just as lovely.

"Come to think of it, this was a strange evening," thought the tallow candle. "I wonder if the wax candles were any better off in silver candlesticks. I wish I could find that out before I burn down."

And it thought of the two children—equally as happy—one illuminated by wax candles, the other by a tallow candle!

Yes, that's the whole story!

The Most Incredible Thing

WHOEVER could accomplish the most incredible thing was to have the king's daughter and half the kingdom. The young people—indeed, the old ones too—strained all their thoughts, tendons, and muscles. Two ate themselves to death and one drank himself to death to accomplish the most incredible thing—each according to his own taste—but that wasn't the way in which it was to be done. Little street urchins practiced spitting on their own backs—they considered this to be the most incredible thing.

On a given day each one had to show what he considered to be the most incredible thing. Children from the age of three to people in their nineties had been appointed as judges. There was a whole exhibition of incredible things, but everyone soon agreed that the most incredible thing of all was a huge clock in a case, remarkably contrived inside and out. At each stroke of the clock appeared living pictures that depicted the hour. There were twelve performances in all, with movable figures and with song and speech.

"This was the most incredible thing!" people said.

The clock struck one, and Moses stood on the mount and wrote down the First Commandment on the Tables of the Law: "Thou shalt have no other gods before me."

The clock struck two: now appeared the Garden of Paradise, where Adam and Eve met, both happy without owning so much as a clothes closet, nor did they need one, either.

On the stroke of three, the three Wise Men appeared, one as black as coal—he couldn't help that, the sun had blackened him. They came bearing incense and precious objects.

On the stroke of four came the Seasons: Spring with a cuckoo on a beech branch in full leaf; Summer with a grasshopper on a ripe sheaf of grain; Autumn with an empty stork's nest—the bird had flown away; Winter with an old crow, which could tell stories and old memories in the corner by the tiled stove.

When the clock struck five, the Five Senses appeared: Sight came as an optician, Hearing as a coppersmith, Smell sold violets and woodruff, Taste was a chef, and Touch was an undertaker with mourning crepe down to his heels.

The clock struck six: there sat a gambler casting a die. The highest side turned up and on it stood six.

Then came the Seven Days of the Week or the Seven Deadly Sins—people couldn't agree. After all, they belonged together and weren't easy to tell apart.

Then came a choir singing matins.

On the stroke of nine followed the Nine Muses: one was employed in Astronomy, one at the Historical Archives, and the rest were in the theater.

On the stroke of ten, Moses again appeared with the Tables of the Law. There stood all of God's Commandments, and there were ten of them.

The clock struck again: now little boys and girls were hopping and jumping. They were playing a game, and with it they sang: "Digging, delving, the clock's struck eleven!" And this is the hour it had struck.

Then it struck twelve. Now the nightwatch appeared in

a fur cap and with a spiked mace. He sang the old night-watch cry:

> " 'Twas at the midnight hour
> Our Savior, Lord was born."

And as he sang roses sprang up, and they turned into the heads of cherubs borne by rainbow-hued wings.

It was a delight to hear, it was a joy to behold. The entire clock was such an incomparable work of art—the most incredible thing, all the people said.

The artist was a young man, tenderhearted, fond of children, a loyal friend, and helpful to his poor parents. He deserved the princess and half the kingdom.

The day of decision was at hand, the entire city was decked out, and the princess was sitting on the throne of the land—it had been given a new horsehair stuffing, but this didn't make it any more comfortable or any easier to sit on for that. The judges on all sides stole sly glances at the one who was going to win, and he stood confident and happy—his success was assured: he had accomplished the most incredible thing!

"No! That's what I'm going to do now!" cried a tall, rawboned, strapping fellow at the same moment. "I'm the man to accomplish the most incredible thing!" And then he swung a huge ax at the work of art.

CRASH! SMASH! SHATTER! There it all lay. Wheels and springs flew about. The whole thing was destroyed!

"I was capable of doing that!" said the man. "My deed has surpassed his and overwhelmed you all. I have accomplished the most incredible thing!"

"To destroy such a work of art!" said the judges. "Yes, that was the most incredible thing!"

The entire populace agreed, and so *he* was to have the princess and half the kingdom! For a law is a law, even if it is the most incredible thing.

From the ramparts and from all the city towers it was proclaimed: "The wedding is to be solemnized!" The princess wasn't at all pleased with it, but she looked lovely and she was richly dressed. The church was ablaze with light—it looks its best late in the evening. The noble maidens of the city sang and ushered in the bride. The knights sang and accompanied the bridegroom. He was swaggering as if he could never be brought to his knees.

Now the singing stopped. It grew so quiet that you could have heard a pin drop on the ground. But in the midst of all that silence the church doors flew open with a rumble and a bang, and BOOM! BOOM! The entire timepiece came marching down the middle of the aisle and lined up between the bride and bridegroom. Dead people cannot come back again—we know this very well—but a work of art can come back again. The body had been smashed to bits, but not the spirit. The Art Spirit had returned as a ghost, and this was no joke.

The work of art stood there as lifelike as when it had been whole and untouched. The strokes of the clock rang out, one after the other, all the way to twelve, and the figures swarmed in. First came Moses. Flames seemed to flash from his forehead. He threw the heavy Tables of the Law onto the bridegroom's feet, pinning them to the floor of the church.

"I cannot lift them again!" said Moses. "You have broken off my arms! Remain now as you are!"

Next came Adam and Eve, the Wise Men from the East, and the Four Seasons, and they all told him unpleasant truths: "Be ashamed of yourself!"

But he wasn't ashamed of himself.

All the figures that had been revealed with each stroke of the clock stepped out of the timepiece, and they grew to a terrible size; it was as if there weren't room for the real people. And when the nightwatch stepped out on the stroke of twelve, with fur cap and mace, there was a strange commotion. The nightwatch went straight over to the bridegroom and struck him on the forehead with the mace.

"Lie there!" he said. "One good turn deserves another! We are avenged and the master too! We are disappearing!"

And then the entire work of art vanished. But all the candles around the church turned into huge flowers of light, and from the gilded stars under the roof were shining long bright shafts of light. The organ pealed by itself. All the people said that this was the most incredible thing they had ever experienced.

"Then, will you summon the right one?" said the princess. "The one who constructed the work of art—he is to be my husband and my lord!"

And he was standing in the church. The entire populace was his retinue. Everyone rejoiced, everyone gave him his blessing. There wasn't a soul who was envious.

Indeed, *that* was the most incredible thing!

The Gardener and the Lord and Lady

❖ ❖ ❖

ABOUT four or five miles from the capital stood an old manor house with thick walls and towers and a corbie gable.

Here there lived—but only during the summer—a rich lord and lady who belonged to the high nobility. This manor was the best and finest of all the manors they owned. It looked like new on the outside and was cozy and comfortable on the inside. The family coat of arms had been carved in stone above the gate; beautiful roses twined about the shield and the bay; a whole carpet of grass stretched out in front of the manor; there were red hawthornes and mayflowers; there were rare flowers even outside the greenhouse.

The lord and lady also had a clever gardener. It was a delight to behold the flower garden, the orchard, and the kitchen garden. Adjoining this was what was left of the original old garden of the estate, with several box hedges trimmed to form crowns and pyramids. Behind these stood two enormous old trees. They were almost always bare of leaves, and it was easy to believe that a gale or a waterspout had strewn them with big clumps of dung. But each clump was a bird's nest.

From time immemorial, swarms of shrieking rooks and crows had built their nests here: it was a complete bird

city, and the birds were the aristocrats, the landed propri-
etors, the oldest stock of the family seat, the real lords and
ladies of the estate. None of the human beings down
below was any concern of theirs, but they put up with
these low-flying creatures even though they banged away
with guns now and then, sending chills up the spines of
the birds, so that each one flew up in fright, shrieking:
"Caw! Caw!"

The gardener often spoke to his lord and lady about
having the old trees chopped down; they didn't look good,

and once they were gone, in all likelihood, they would be
rid of those shrieking birds, which would go somewhere
else. But the lord and lady had no desire to be rid of the
trees or the swarm of birds. This was something the estate
couldn't be without; it was something from bygone days,
and that shouldn't be wiped out at all.

"Those trees, after all, are the inheritance of the birds. Let them keep it, my good Larsen!"

The gardener's name was Larsen, but that is of no further consequence here.

"Isn't your sphere of operation big enough, little Larsen? The entire flower garden, the greenhouses, the orchard, and the kitchen garden?"

Those he had; those he tended, looked after, and cultivated with zeal and skill. And the lord and lady admitted this. But they never hesitated to let him know that, while visiting, they had often eaten fruit or seen flowers that surpassed those they had in their own garden; and this distressed the gardener, for he wanted to do the best and he did the best he could. He had a good heart and did a good job.

One day the lord and lady sent for him and told him blandly and superciliously that on the previous day, while visiting distinguished friends, they had been served a species of apples and pears so succulent and tasty that they and all the guests had expressed their admiration. To be sure, the fruits were not domestic, but they ought to be imported, made to thrive here if our climate permitted it. It was known that they had been purchased from the first fruit dealer in the city. The gardener was to ride in and find out where these apples and pears had come from and then write for cuttings. The gardener knew the fruit dealer well. It was to this very dealer that, on behalf of the lord and lady, he sold the surplus of fruit that grew in the garden of the estate.

And the gardener went to the city and asked the fruit dealer where he had gotten these highly praised apples and pears from.

"They're from your own garden!" said the fruit dealer, and showed him both apples and pears, which he recognized.

My, how happy this made the gardener; he hurried

back to the lord and lady and told them that both the apples and the pears had come from their own garden.

The lord and lady couldn't believe this at all. "It's not possible, Larsen! Can you obtain a declaration in writing from the fruit dealer?"

And this he could; he brought back a written attestation.

"How very extraordinary!" said the lord and lady.

Every day now bowls of these magnificent apples and pears from their own garden appeared on the table of the lord and lady. Bushels and barrels of these fruits were sent to friends in the city and beyond, yes, even abroad. It afforded them great pleasure! And yet they had to add that, after all, there had been two remarkably good summers for tree fruit. These had turned out well everywhere in the land.

Some time passed. The nobility dined at the court. On the following day the gardener was summoned to his lord and lady. At the royal table they had been served such luscious, tasty melons from their majesties' greenhouse.

"You must go to the court gardener, my good Larsen, and obtain for us some of the seeds from these priceless melons!"

"But the court gardener has got the seeds from us!" said the gardener, quite pleased.

"Then that man has discovered a way of bringing the fruit to a higher stage of development," replied the lord and lady. "Each melon was excellent."

"Well, then, I can be proud!" said the gardener. "You see, my lady and my lord, this year the court gardener hasn't had any luck with his melons, and when he saw how splendidly ours were standing, and tasted them, he ordered three to be sent up to the castle."

"Larsen! Don't get the idea into your head that they were the melons from our garden!"

"I think so!" said the gardener, and went to the court

gardener and obtained from him written proof that the melons on the royal table had come from the manor.

This was really a surprise to the lord and lady, and they did nothing to keep the story quiet. They showed the attestation; indeed, melon seeds were sent far and wide, just as the cuttings had been sent previously.

They received word that the seeds took and bore quite excellent fruit, and it was named after the lord and lady's family seat, so that this name was now to be read in English, German, and French. This had never occurred to them before.

"As long as the gardener doesn't get too many big notions about himself!" said the lord and lady.

It affected him in another way: now he made every effort to make a name for himself as one of the best gardeners in the land, to try each year to produce something outstanding from every garden variety; and this is what he did. And yet he was often being reminded that the very first fruit he had raised, the apples and the pears, had really been the best; all later varieties were quite inferior. To be sure, the melons had been very good, but after all they were of an entirely different sort. The strawberries could be called excellent, but still they weren't any better than the ones grown on the other estates. And when the radishes failed one year, then only those unsuccessful radishes were mentioned, and not the other good things that had been raised.

It was almost as if the lord and lady found relief in being able to say, "It didn't turn out well this year, my little Larsen!" They were quite happy in being able to say, "It didn't turn out well this year."

Once or twice a week the gardener brought fresh flowers up to the drawing room, always tastefully arranged; it was as if the colors grew stronger by being placed side by side.

"You have taste, Larsen," said the lord and lady. "That is a gift that has come from Our Lord, not from yourself."

One day the gardener brought a big crystal bowl. In it was lying a water lily leaf. On top of this, with its long thick stalk down in the water, had been placed a dazzling blue flower as big as a sunflower.

"Hindustani lotus!" exclaimed the lord and lady.

They had never seen such a flower before, and during the day it was put in the sunshine and in the evening in reflected light. Everyone who looked at it found it to be remarkably lovely and rare; indeed, the highest young lady of the land said so, and she was a princess; she was wise and tenderhearted.

The lord and lady took pride in making her a present of the flower, and it went with the princess up to the castle.

Now the lord and lady went down in the garden themselves to pick a flower just like it if there were any more left. But it was nowhere to be found, so they called the gardener and asked where he had got that blue lotus from.

"We have searched in vain!" they said. "We have been in the greenhouses and all around the flower garden!"

"No, it's not there, all right!" said the gardener. "It's only a lowly flower from the kitchen garden! But how beautiful it is, isn't it! It looks like a blue cactus, and yet it's only the blossom of the artichoke!"

"You should have told us so right away!" said the lord and lady. "We were convinced that it was a rare foreign flower. You have made fools of us in the eyes of the young princess! She saw the flower here and found it to be quite lovely. She didn't recognize it, and she is well versed in botany. But that science has nothing to do with vegetables. What on earth were you thinking of, good Larsen, to put such a flower in the drawing room? It makes us look ridiculous!"

And the magnificent blue flower, which had been taken from the kitchen garden, was thrown out of the lord and

lady's drawing room, where it didn't belong. Yes, the lord
and lady apologized to the princess and told her the flower
was only a vegetable and that the gardener had taken it
into his head to display it. But for that reason he had been
severely reprimanded.

"That was a shame and an injustice!" said the princess.
"Why, he has opened our eyes to a magnificent flower that
we would never have noticed at all. He has shown us
loveliness where it didn't occur to us to look for it! Every
day, as long as the artichokes are in bloom, the castle
gardener shall bring one up to me in my drawing room."

And this was done.

The lord and lady informed the gardener that he again
could bring a fresh artichoke blossom to them.

"As a matter of fact, it is pretty," they said. "Highly
unusual!" And the gardener was praised.

"Larsen likes that!" said the lord and lady. "He's a
pampered child!"

In the autumn there was a dreadful storm. It started
during the night and was so violent that many big trees on
the outskirts of the forest were torn up by the roots. And
to the great sorrow of the lord and lady—sorrow as they
called it, but to the gardener's delight—the two big trees
with all the birds' nests blew down. The shrieking of the
rooks and the crows could be heard above the storm. They
beat on the panes with their wings, said the servants at
the manor.

"Well, you're happy now, aren't you, Larsen!" said the
lord and lady. "The storm has blown down the trees, and
the birds have taken to the forest. Not a vestige remains of
bygone days; every sign and every trace are gone! We are
grieved!"

The gardener didn't say anything, but he was thinking
of what had been on his mind for a long time: the best way
of utilizing the splendid sunny spot, which had not been at

his disposal before. It was going to be the pride of the garden and the joy of the lord and lady.

The huge, blown-down trees had crushed and broken the old box hedges, with all their fancy shapes. Here he raised a thicket of plants, domestic plants from field and forest.

What no other gardener had thought of planting in the garden of an estate he planted here in profusion, in the kind of soil each one was to have, and in shade and in sunshine, as each species required. He tended them with affection, and they grew in splendor.

The juniper bush, from the heath of Jutland, rose, in shape and color like the Italian cypress; the shiny, prickly Christ's-thorn, always green in the cold of winter and in the summer sun, was a beautiful sight. Many different species of ferns were growing in front, some looking like the offspring of palm trees and others as if they were the parents of that delicate, lovely plant that we call Venushair. Here stood the despised burdock, which, in its freshness, is so pretty that it would enhance a bouquet. The burdock grew in dry soil, but farther down in moister earth grew the dock plant—a plant also held in low esteem, and yet, with its height and its enormous leaf, so picturesquely beautiful. Waist-high, with flower upon flower like a mighty many-armed candelabra, soared the great mullein, replanted from the meadow. Here stood woodruffs, primroses, and hellebore, the wild calla lily and the delicate three-leaved wood sorrel. It was a delight to behold.

In front, supported by strings of steel wire, growing in rows, were quite small pear trees from French soil. They received sunshine and good care, and soon bore big, juicy fruits, as in the country from which they had come.

In place of the two leafless trees, a tall flagpole had been erected, from which Dannebrog[1] waved, and nearby

[1] The Danish flag.

yet another pole, around which, in summer and autumn, twined the hop with its fragrant, conelike catkins, but on which in winter—according to ancient custom—was hung a sheaf of oats so that the birds of the air might have their feast in the joyous Yuletide season.

"Our good Larsen is growing sentimental in his old age!" said the lord and lady. "But he is faithful and devoted to us!"

Around the beginning of the New Year, in one of the illustrated periodicals of the capital, a picture of the old manor appeared. One could see the flagpole and the sheaf of oats for the birds in the joyous Yuletide season. And it was referred to, and emphasized, as a lovely thought that such an ancient custom had here been restored to such prominence and veneration, so characteristic of precisely this old family seat.

"Everything Larsen does," said the lord and lady, "they beat a drum for! What a happy man! Why, we should almost be proud to have him!"

But they weren't proud at all. They felt that they were the master and mistress. They could give Larsen notice, but they didn't do it. They were good people. And there are so many good people of their sort, and that is gratifying to every Larsen.

Well, that's the story of "The Gardener and the Lord and Lady."

Now you can think it over!

The Flea and
the Professor

THERE was a balloonist who came to grief. The balloon burst; the man dropped down and was dashed to smithereens. Two minutes earlier he had sent his boy down by parachute. This was the boy's good fortune. He was unharmed and went about with considerable knowledge for becoming a balloonist. But he had no balloon, nor had he any means of acquiring one.

He had to live, and so he went in for legerdemain and talking with his stomach—this is called "being a ventriloquist." He was young and easy on the eyes, and when he had acquired a goatee and put on fashionable clothing, he could be mistaken for the offspring of a count. The ladies found him handsome. Indeed, one maiden was so taken by his good looks and his legerdemain that she accompanied him to foreign lands and cities. There he called himself "professor"; nothing less would do.

His constant thought was to get hold of a balloon and go aloft with his little wife. But they did not yet have the money.

"It will come!" he said.

"If only it would!" she said.

"After all, we're young, and now I am a professor. Crumbs are also bread!"

She helped him faithfully, sat by the door, and sold

tickets to the performance—and this was a chilly pleasure in the wintertime. She also helped him in one of his tricks. He put his wife in the drawer of a table, a huge drawer. There she crawled into the back drawer, and then she could not be seen in the front drawer. It was a kind of optical illusion.

But one evening, when he pulled out the drawer, she had disappeared from him too. She was not in the front drawer, not in the back drawer, not anywhere in the house, nowhere to be seen or heard. This was her legerdemain. She never came back again. She was tired of it all, and he grew tired of it all; he lost his good humor and could not laugh or perform tricks any more, and then no one came. The earnings became poor, the clothes became shabby, and at last the only thing he owned was a big flea—an inheritance from his wife, and for this reason he was quite fond of it. So he trained it, taught it tricks; he taught it to present arms and shoot off a cannon—but a tiny one.

The professor was proud of his flea, and the flea was proud of itself. It had learned something and had human blood in its veins. It had been in the greatest cities, had been seen by princes and princesses and won their highest acclaim—this stood in print in newspapers and on placards. It knew it was a celebrity and could support a professor, indeed, even a whole family.

It was proud and it was famous, and yet, when the flea and the professor traveled by railway, they went fourth class. It arrives just as quickly as first. There was an unspoken promise between them that they would never be parted, never marry. The flea would remain a bachelor and the professor a widower. It all adds up to the same thing.

"One should never revisit the scenes of one's greatest success!" said the professor. He was a judge of human nature, and that too is an art.

At last he had traveled to every land except the land of the Wild Men, and so he wanted to go to the land of the Wild Men. The professor knew, of course, that they ate Christian people there. But he wasn't really a Christian, and the flea wasn't really a person, so he thought they could risk journeying there, for they could make a good profit.

They traveled by steamship and by sailing ship. The flea performed its tricks, and so they had a free passage on the way and came to the land of the Wild Men.

A little princess reigned there. She was only eight years old, but she reigned. She had taken the power away from her father and mother, for she had a will of her own and was so adorably sweet and naughty.

At once, when the flea presented arms and shot off the cannon, she fell so in love with it that she said, "Him or no one!" She became quite wild with love, and indeed, she was already quite wild to begin with.

"Sweet little sensible child," said her father, "if only one could first make a person out of it!"

"You just leave that to me, old boy!" she said, and that wasn't a nice thing for a little princess to say to her father. But she was wild.

She put the flea on her little hand.

"Now you're a human being. You'll rule with me. But you will do as I wish, or else I'll kill you and eat the professor."

The professor was given a big hall to live in. The walls were of sugarcane. He could go and lick them, but he didn't have a sweet tooth. He was given a hammock to sleep in; it was as if he were lying in a balloon—the one he had always wanted and which was his constant thought.

The flea remained with the princess and sat on her little hand and on her delicate throat. She had taken a hair from her own head. The professor had to tie it around the flea's leg, and then she kept the flea tied to the piece of coral she wore in the lobe of her ear.

What a wonderful time for the princess, and for the flea too, she thought. But the professor didn't like it there. He was a traveling man, was fond of going from city to city and reading in the newspapers about his wisdom and patience in teaching human tasks to a flea. Day in and day out he loafed in the hammock and received his good food: fresh birds' eggs, elephant eyes, and roast thigh of giraffe. The cannibals do not live on human flesh alone—that's a delicacy.

"Children's shoulders with piquant sauce," said the princess' mother, "are the tastiest!"

The professor was bored and only too willing to leave the land of the Wild Men, but he had to have the flea with him. It was his prodigy and his livelihood. How was he going to capture it and get hold of it? That was not so easy.

He strained all his powers of concentration, and then he said, "Now I have it! Princess' Papa, permit me to do something! May I train the inhabitants of the land in the art of presentation? This is what, in the biggest countries of the world, is called breeding."

"And what can you teach me?" said the princess' father.

"My greatest skill," said the professor, "is to fire off a cannon so the whole world trembles, and all the most delicious birds of the skies fall down roasted! That's quite a bang!"

"Out with the cannon!" said the princess' father.

But in the whole land there was no cannon except for the one the flea had brought, and it was too small.

"I'll cast a bigger one!" said the professor. "Just give me the means. I must have fine silken cloth, a needle and thread, rope and string, and stomach drops for balloons: they inflate, alleviate, and elevate! They give the bang to the cannon stomach!"

He was given everything he asked for.

The entire population gathered to see the great cannon. The professor didn't send for them before the balloon was all ready to be filled and sent aloft.

The flea sat on the princess' hand and watched. The balloon was filled; it swelled out. It was so uncontrollable that it could hardly be held down.

"I must have it aloft so it can cool off," said the professor, and seated himself in the basket that hung below it.

"I can't possibly manage to steer it alone. I must have an expert companion along to help me. There's no one here who can do it except the flea."

"I'd rather not allow it!" said the princess, but still she handed the flea to the professor, who put it on his hand.

"Let go of the string and the ropes!" he said. "Here goes the balloon!"

They thought he said "the cannon!"

And then the balloon went higher and higher, up above the clouds, away from the land of the Wild Men.

The little princess, her father and mother, the entire population, stood and waited. They are waiting still. And if you don't believe it, just go to the land of the Wild Men. There every child speaks of the flea and the professor and believes they are coming back when the cannon has cooled off. But they are not coming. They are back home with us. They are in their native land, riding on the railroad—first class, not fourth; they earn good money; they have a large balloon. No one asks how they got the balloon or where it came from. They are prosperous folk, esteemed folk—the flea and the professor.

The Gate Key

❖   ❖   ❖

E VERY key has its story, and there are many keys: the chamberlain's key, the watch key, St. Peter's key; we could tell about all the keys, but now we're just going to tell about the Civil Servant's gate key.

It had been made by a locksmith, but it could very well believe it had been a blacksmith, the way the man took hold of it, hammering and filing. It was too big for a pants pocket, so it had to go in a coat pocket. Here it often lay in the dark—but, come to think of it, it did have its fixed place on the wall beside the silhouette of the Civil Servant from his childhood. There he looked like a dumpling in shirt frills.

They say that every human being acquires in his makeup and conduct something of the sign of the Zodiac under which he is born: Taurus, Virgo, Scorpio, as they are called in the Almanac. Madame Civil Servant mentioned none of these. She said that her husband had been born under the "sign of the Wheelbarrow": he always had to be pushed ahead.

His father had pushed him into an office, his mother had pushed him into matrimony, and his wife had pushed him up to the rank of Civil Servant; but she never mentioned the latter. She was a level-headed, good wife, who hauled in the right places, talked and pushed in the right places.

Now he was well on in years, "well proportioned," as he said himself, a well-read, good-natured man, who was as "bright as a key" to boot—something we will be able to understand later on. He was always in good spirits; he liked everybody and was only too fond of talking to them. If he were walking in the town, it was hard to get him home again if Mama wasn't along to give him a push. He had to talk to everyone he knew, and the dinner suffered.

From the window Madame Civil Servant kept watch. "Now he's coming!" she would say to the maid. "Put on the pot! Now he's standing still, talking to somebody, so take off the pot, or else the food will be cooked too much! Now he's coming, so put on the pot again!"

But still he didn't come.

He could stand right under the window of the house and nod up; but then if somebody he knew happened to come by, he couldn't help it, he had to have a few words with him. And if another acquaintance came along while he was talking with this one, then he would hang onto the first by the buttonhole and take the second by the hand while he shouted to a third, who wanted to go by.

It was enough to try the patience of Madame Civil Servant. "Civil Servant! Civil Servant!" she would shout. "Yes, that man is born under the sign of the Wheelbarrow: he can't budge unless he's given a push ahead!"

He was very fond of going to bookshops and browsing in books. He paid his bookseller a tiny fee for permitting him to read the new books at his home, that is to say, for being allowed to cut open the pages of the books lengthwise, but not across the top, for then they couldn't be sold as new. He was a walking newspaper, though an inoffensive one, and knew all about engagements, weddings, and funerals, literary gossip and gossip of the town; indeed, he would let drop mysterious hints that he knew of things that no one else knew. He had got it from the gate key.

Even as newlyweds the Civil Servant and his wife were

living in their own home, and from that time they had had
the same gate key. But they were not aware then of its
remarkable powers; they found out about those later.

It was during the reign of King Frederick the Seventh.
At that time Copenhagen had no gas, it had train-oil
lanterns: it had no Tivoli or Casino, no trolley cars and no
railroads. There were few diversions as compared with
what there are now. On Sunday one went for a walk out of
the city gate to the churchyard, read the inscriptions on
the graves, sat down on the grass, ate from one's lunch
hamper, and drank one's schnapps with it; or else one
went to Frederiksberg, where there was a regimental
band in front of the castle and crowds of people to look at
the royal family rowing about in the tiny narrow canals,
where the old king steered the boat; he and the queen
nodded to everyone without making any distinction in
rank. Well-to-do families went out there from town to
drink their afternoon tea. They could obtain hot water
from a little farmhouse beyond the gardens, but they had
to bring their own samovars with them.

The Civil Servant and his wife took a trip out there one
sunny Sunday afternoon; the maid went ahead with the
samovar and a hamper of provisions and "a drop to wash it
down with."

"Take the gate key," said Madame Civil Servant, "so we
can get in our own gate when we come back. You know
it's locked here at dusk, and the bellpull has been broken
since this morning! We'll be late getting home! After
we've been to Frederiksberg, we're going to Casorti's
Theater at Vesterbro to see the pantomime: 'Harlequin,
Foreman of the Threshers,' where they come down in a
cloud; it costs two marks per person!"

And they went to Frederiksberg, listened to the music,
watched the royal family go bathing with banners waving,
saw the old king and the white swans. After drinking a cup

of good tea, they hurried away, but still they didn't get to the theater on time.

The tightrope walking was over, the stilt walking was over, and the pantomime had begun. As always, they had arrived too late, and for this the Civil Servant was to blame; every moment along the way he had stopped to talk to someone he knew; inside the theater he also met good friends, and when the performance was over, he and his wife had to accompany them to a family on the bridge to have a glass of punch; it was only going to be a ten-minute stop, but this, of course, stretched out to a whole hour. They talked and talked. Especially entertaining was a Swedish baron—or was he German? The Civil Servant didn't remember exactly; but on the other hand, the trick with the key—which the baron taught him—he retained for all time. It was extraordinarily interesting; he could make the key reply to everything it was asked about, even the most secret.

The Civil Servant's gate key was especially suited for this purpose. The bit was heavy, and it had to hang down. The baron let the bow of the key rest on the index finger of his right hand. It hung there loosely and lightly; each beat of the pulse in the tip of the finger could set it in motion, so that it turned—and if it didn't, then the baron knew very well how to make it turn as he wished. Each turning was a letter of the alphabet, from A and as far down in the alphabet as one cared to go. When the first letter had been found, the key turned to the opposite side; in this way one sought the next letter, and thus one arrived at complete words, complete sentences—an answer to the question. It was all a fraud, but always an amusement. And that was precisely what the Civil Servant thought at first, but he didn't stick to it: he became completely wrapped up in the key.

"Husband! Husband!" cried Madame Civil Servant. "The

West Gate closes at twelve o'clock! We won't get in; we have only a quarter of an hour left in which to hurry!"

They had to get a move on; several people, who wanted

to go in the town soon passed them by. At last they reached the outermost guardhouse. Then the clock struck twelve and the gate slammed shut, a large number of people stood locked out, and among them stood the Civil Servant and his wife, with maid, samovar, and empty lunch hamper. Some standing there were thoroughly frightened, others were irritated; each one took it in his own fashion. What was to be done?

Fortunately it had been decided of late that one of the city gates, the North Gate, was not to be locked; here the pedestrians could slip through the guardhouse into the town.

The way was not at all short, but the weather was fine, the sky was clear with stars and shooting stars, the frogs were croaking in ditch and marsh. The party began to sing, one ballad after the other; but the Civil Servant didn't sing, nor did he pay any attention to the stars—no, not even to his own two feet; he fell at full length right by the side of the ditch. One would have thought he'd had too

much to drink, but it wasn't the punch, it was the key that
had gone to his head and was turning there.

At last they reached the guardhouse of the North Bridge;
they went across the bridge and entered the town.

"Now I'm happy again!" said Madame Civil Servant.
"Here's our gate!"

"But where's the gate key?" said the Civil Servant. It
was in neither the back pocket nor the side pocket.

"Good gracious!" cried Madame Civil Servant. "Haven't
you got the key? You've lost it doing those key tricks with
the baron! How are we going to get in now? You know the
bellpull has been broken ever since this morning. The
nightwatch hasn't got a key to the house! Why, this is a
desperate situation!"

The maid began to wail; the Civil Servant was the only
one who maintained his composure.

"We must break one of the windowpanes at the sausagemonger's," he said. "Get him out of bed and come in that
way."

He broke a windowpane; he broke two. "Petersen!" he
shouted, and stuck the handle of his umbrella in through
the opening. Then the daughter of the family in the basement gave a loud shriek. The sausagemonger threw open
the door to the shop, crying, "Nightwatch!" And before
he'd rightly seen the family, recognized them and let
them in, the nightwatch was blowing his whistle, and in
the next street another nightwatch answered and started
blowing. People came to their windows. "Where's the
fire? Where's the riot?" they asked, and were asking still
when the Civil Servant, who was already in his parlor, was
taking off his coat—and in it lay the gate key, not in the
pocket but in the lining. It had fallen down through a hole
that shouldn't have been in the pocket.

From that evening the gate key acquired a singularly
great importance, not only when they went out in the
evening but also when they stayed home and the Civil

Servant showed off his sagacity by letting the gate key provide answers to questions.

He made up the most plausible answer, and then let the gate key supply it. At last he believed in it himself; but not the apothecary, a young man closely related to the Civil Servant's wife.

This apothecary had a good head on his shoulders, a critical head; already as a schoolboy he had written reviews of books and plays, but without his name being mentioned—and that means such a lot. He was what is called a *belesprit*, but he didn't believe in spirits at all—least of all key spirits.

"Of course I believe, I believe," he said. "Blessed Mr. Civil Servant, I believe in the gate key and all the key spirits just as firmly as I believe in the new science that is beginning to make itself known: table-turning, and the spirits in old and new furniture. Have you heard about that? I have! I've had my doubts. You know I'm a skeptic, but I've been converted after reading a frightful story in a quite reputable foreign publication. Mr. Civil Servant! Can you imagine! Yes, I'll tell you the story the way I read it; two bright children have seen their parents arouse the spirit in a big dining table. The little ones were alone, and now they wanted to try to rub life into an old chest of drawers in the same fashion. It came to life; the spirit awoke, but it couldn't tolerate the commands of children. It got up—the chest of drawers creaked—it shot out its drawers—and with its chest-of-drawer legs it put each of the children into a drawer. And then the chest of drawers ran out through the open door with them, down the stairs and out in the street, over to the canal, where it threw itself in and drowned both the children. The tiny bodies were placed in consecrated ground, but the chest of drawers was brought to the town hall, convicted of infanticide, and burned alive in the square! I've read it!" said the apothecary. "Read it in a foreign publication. It's not something I've made up myself; I swear by the key that it's true! Now I swear by all that's holy!"

The Civil Servant found such a tale to be too coarse a jest; the two of them could never talk about the key—the apothecary was "key-stupid."

The Civil Servant made progress in key wisdom; the key was his entertainment and his enlightenment.

One evening, as the Civil Servant was about to go to bed, he was standing half undressed when someone knocked on the door to the entryway. It was the sausagemonger in the basement who had come so late; he too was half undressed; but, he said, a thought had suddenly occurred to him, which he was afraid he couldn't keep overnight.

"It's my daughter, Lotte-Lene, who I must talk about. She's a pretty girl; she has been confirmed and now I want to see her make a good marriage!"

"I'm not yet a widower," said the Civil Servant with a chuckle, "and I have no son that I can offer her!"

"You understand what I mean, Civil Servant!" said the sausagemonger. "She can play the piano and she can sing— you must be able to hear it up here in the house. You have no idea of all the things the girl can do. She can mimic the speech and walk of everyone. She's made for playacting, and that's a good career for pretty girls of good family—they could marry into a family with an estate, although such a thing has never entered my mind or Lotte-Lene's! She can sing and knows how to play the piano! The other day I went up to the Song Academy with her. She sang, but she doesn't have what I call a 'beery-bass voice' in ladies or a canary-bird screech up in the highest registers, which so many songstresses are required to have now. And so they advised her not to choose this career at all. Well, I thought, if she can't be a singer, then she can always be an actress, for a voice is the only thing needed for that. Today I talked about it to the director, as he's called. 'Is she well read?' he asked. 'No,' I said, 'not in the least!' 'Reading is necessary for an artist!' he said. 'She can still acquire that,' I thought, and then I went home. 'She can go to a rental library and read what is there,' I thought. But this evening, while I'm sitting and getting undressed, it occurs to me: why rent books when you can borrow them? The Civil Servant has lots of books; let her read those. There's enough to read there, and she can have it free!"

"Lotte-Lene is a strange girl," said the Civil Servant, "a pretty girl! She shall have books to read! But does she have what is called 'get-up-and-go,' ingenuity, genius? And if she does, what is equally as important, is she lucky?"

"She has won twice in the Merchandise Lottery," said the sausagemonger. "Once she won a wardrobe and once six pairs of sheets! That's what I call luck, and that's what she has!"

"I'll ask the key!" said the Civil Servant.

And then he placed the key on the index finger of his right hand and then on the index finger of the sausagemonger's right hand, and let the key turn and supply letter after letter.

The key said, "Triumph and happiness!" And so Lotte-Lene's future was decided.

The Civil Servant gave her two books to read right away: *Dyveke*[1] and Knigge's *Associating with People*.

From that evening a closer acquaintanceship of sorts grew up between Lotte-Lene and the Civil Servant and his wife. She came often to the family, and the Civil Servant discovered that she was a sensible girl—she believed in him and in the key. Madame Civil Servant found, in the openness with which every moment she revealed her extreme ignorance, something childish and

---

[1] A tragedy by Ole Johan Samsøe.

innocent. The married couple, each in his own fashion, was fond of her, and she was fond of them.

"It smells so delightfully up there!" said Lotte-Lene.

There was an odor, a scent, a fragrance of apples in the hall, where Madame Civil Servant had stored a whole barrel of Gravenstein apples. There was also a smell of rose and lavender incense in all the rooms.

"It produces an atmosphere of quality!" said Lotte-Lene. And then she feasted her eyes upon all the beautiful flowers that Madame Civil Servant always had. Yes, even in midwinter, lilacs and cherry blossoms were blooming here. The cut, leafless branches were placed in water, and in the warm room they soon bore leaves and blossoms.

"You'd think there was no life in those bare branches, but see how they rise up from the dead."

"It has never occurred to me before," said Lotte-Lene. "Why, Nature is lovely!"

And the Civil Servant let her look at his "Key Book," in which had been written down remarkable things said by the key, even about half an apple cake that had disappeared from the pantry on the very evening the maid's sweetheart came calling.

And the Civil Servant asked his key: "Who has eaten the apple cake, the cat or the sweetheart?" And the gate key replied, "The sweetheart." The Civil Servant believed it even before he asked, and the maid confessed—why, that damned key knew everything!

"Yes, isn't it remarkable!" said the Civil Servant. "That key! That key! And it has said 'triumph and happiness' about Lotte-Lene. Now we'll soon see! I'll vouch for that!"

The Civil Servant's wife wasn't so confident, but she didn't express her doubts when her husband was listening. But later she confided to Lotte-Lene that, as a young man, the Civil Servant had been completely addicted to the theater. If someone had given him a push then, he would decidedly have appeared as an actor. But the family dismissed the idea. He wanted to go on the stage, and in order to get there he wrote a play.

"This is a great secret that I'm confiding to you, little Lotte-Lene. The play wasn't bad. It was accepted by the Royal Theater and booed off the stage, so it has never been heard of since, and I'm glad of it. I'm his wife and I know him. Now you want to follow the same career. I wish you well, but I don't think it'll work. I don't believe in the gate key!"

Lotte-Lene believed in it, and in that belief she and the Civil Servant found each other.

Their hearts understood each other in all propriety.

Moreover, the girl had other skills that Madame Civil Servant set store by. Lotte-Lene knew how to make starch from potatoes, sew silk gloves out of old silk stockings, recover her silk dancing slippers—even though she could afford to buy all her clothes new. She had what the sausagemonger called "shillings in the table drawer and bonds in the safe." This was really a wife for the apothecary, thought Madame Civil Servant. But she didn't say so, nor did she let the key say so, either. The apothecary was soon going to settle down and have his own pharmacy in one of the larger provincial towns of the land.

Lotte-Lene was constantly reading *Dyveke* and Knigge's *Associating with People*. She kept these two books for two years, and by then she had learned one of them—*Dyveke* —by heart, all the roles. But she wanted to perform only one of them, that of Dyveke, and not in the capital, where there is so much envy—and where they didn't want her. She wanted to start her artistic career, as the Civil Servant called it, in one of the larger provincial towns. Now it happened, by a strange coincidence, that this was in the very same town in which the young apothecary had settled down as the town's youngest, if not only, apothecary.

The great evening of expectation was at hand: Lotte-Lene was to perform and win triumph and happiness, as

the key had said. The Civil Servant wasn't there; he was
in bed and Madame Civil Servant was taking care of him. He
was to have hot napkins and chamomile tea—the napkins
on his tummy, the tea inside his tummy.

The couple didn't attend the *Dyveke* performance, but
the apothecary was there, and he wrote a letter about it to
his relation, Madame Civil Servant.

"Dyveke's collar was the best!" he wrote. "If the Civil
Servant's gate key had been in my pocket, I would have
taken it out and hissed through it! That's just what she
deserved and just what the key deserved for having lied so
shamefully to her about 'triumph and happiness'!"

The Civil Servant read the letter. It was all spite, he
said, a "key hatred" with that innocent girl as the victim.

As soon as he was out of bed and human again, he sent a
short but venomous letter to the apothecary, who wrote a
reply as if he had interpreted the whole epistle as nothing
more than a high-spirited joke.

He expressed his thanks for this, as well as for every
well-meant contribution in the future to making public the
key's incomparable value and importance. Then he confided to the Civil Servant that, in addition to his profession as apothecary, he was working on a long "key novel,"
in which all the characters were keys and keys alone. The
gate key, of course, was the leading character and had
been patterned after the Civil Servant's gate key—it had
the gift of prophecy; all the other keys had to revolve
around it: the chamberlain's old key, which had known the
pomp and festivity of the court; the watch key, tiny,
elegant, and important, at four shillings from the iron-
monger's; the key to the box pew, which counts itself as
one of the clergy, and which, after sitting all night in a
keyhole in the church, has seen spirits; the keys to the
pantry and to the fuel and wine cellars all make their
appearance, curtsying and circulating around the gate key.
The sunbeams make it shine like silver; the wind—the

spirit of the world—flies into it and makes it float. It is the Key of all Keys, it was the Civil Servant's gate key, and now it is the key to the Pearly Gates, it is a papal key, it is "infallible"!

"Gall!" said the Civil Servant. "Unmitigated gall!"

He and the apothecary never saw each other again. Oh, yes, except at Madame Civil Servant's funeral.

She died first.

She was mourned and missed in the house. Even the cut cherry branches, which sent out fresh shoots and blossoms, grieved and withered away; they stood forgotten, for she no longer took care of them.

The Civil Servant and the apothecary walked behind her coffin, side by side as the two oldest relations.

There was neither the time nor the mood here for bickering.

Lotte-Lene tied a band of mourning around the Civil Servant's hat. She had long since returned to the house, without winning triumph and happiness in an artistic career. But it could come; Lotte-Lene had a future. The key had said so, and the Civil Servant had said so.

She came to see him. They talked about the deceased and they wept—Lotte-Lene was soft; they talked about the arts, and Lotte-Lene was strong.

"The life of the stage is lovely," she said, "but there's so much unpleasantness and envy! I shall go my own way instead. First myself and then the arts!"

Knigge had told the truth in his chapter about actors; she realized this. The key had not told the truth, but she didn't speak of this to the Civil Servant. She loved him.

As a matter of fact, during his entire period of mourning, the gate key had been his consolation and encouragement. He asked it questions and it gave him answers. And when the year was up, and he and Lotte-Lene were sitting together one sentimental evening, he asked the key: "Shall I get married and whom shall I marry?"

There was no one to give him a push, so he gave the key a push and it said: "Lotte-Lene!"

Now it had been said, and Lotte-Lene became Madame Civil Servant.

"Triumph and happiness!"

These words had been said in advance—by the gate key.

Afterword

❖ ❖ ❖

IN the spring of 1835, a tiny booklet entitled *Eventyr Fortalte for Børn*** (literally *Wonder Tales Told for Children*), was published in Denmark. It contained four of the stories that were to make the name of Hans Christian Andersen a household expression, not only in his native land but throughout the world as well. At the time, however, its reception was far from enthusiastic.

Andersen was no newcomer to the Danish literary scene. After successfully passing the university entrance examinations in 1828, he decided not to continue his studies, and devoted himself entirely to writing. He produced a considerable number of poems, travel books, and works for the theater, but few of these attained more than fleeting popularity. Then, in 1833–34, he received a royal grant that enabled him to make his first trip to France and Italy. Instead of a conventional travel book, he was inspired to write his first novel, *The Improvisatore*, which was an unqualified success. It appeared shortly before the *eventyr* and established his reputation as a writer.

The *eventyr*, on the other hand, marked a new trend in Danish literature. At this time a wave of Romanticism was

---

* The word *eventyr* is derived from the Latin *adventura* ("happening"), and has come to mean "a tale about a wondrous happening."

sweeping over Europe. This was more than a revolt against the rigid rules of Neo-Classicism that governed the literature of the day. The old empires were breaking up. Many countries, in the throes of national and social upheaval, were trying to assert themselves as autonomous powers and shake off foreign cultural influence. During this "National Renaissance," as it was called, scholars began discovering a rich native tradition that had previously been virtually neglected.

For centuries the folktales and legends that had been told around the peasant hearths and in the taverns and nurseries had been ignored or held in low esteem by men of letters. They did gain a semblance of official recognition when early Buddhist monks in India and, later, medieval clergymen in France inserted *exempla* into their sermons in order to liven them up while also imparting a moral lesson. Boccaccio delved into the folk tradition, as did Chaucer, Perrault, Voltaire, and Hoffman—to name only a few. These writers exerted a considerable influence on the literature of their day. But it was not until Jacob and Wilhelm Grimm published their *Kinder- und Häusmarchen* (1812–15) that the true value of this native tradition was understood and appreciated, and the attitude of scholars and laymen alike underwent a profound change. At the same time, the Romantic writers were turning to rustic themes for their inspiration, and the "literary folktale" flourished on a grand scale—especially in Germany and Denmark.

Andersen was not the first writer in Denmark to draw his inspiration from the folk tradition, but he was one of the first to break away from the prevailing rigid academic literary style and make use of the vernacular language. He took over the role of the storyteller and faithfully preserved the colloquial speech and style in which the stories had been told to him. He wrote them down, as he said, ". . . just the way I would *tell* them to a child." In the eyes of the critics, however, this was a cardinal sin. At the same time, friends and critics alike expressed the regret that a man of Andersen's stature and promise could stoop to something so childish as writing *eventyr* in the first place. Nor did it help matters that these stories were intended for the *entertainment* of young readers and not for their moral enlightenment. One reviewer was even shocked by the "indecency" of presenting a story for children ("The Tinderbox") in which a sleeping princess was carried on the back of a dog to a soldier—who kissed her! "The Princess on the Pea" was considered indelicate as well as misleading, in that it implied that ladies of rank were extremely thin-skinned. As for "Little Claus and Big Claus," the erotic implications of the story, as well as the author's apparent disregard for human life, made it unsuitable. Andersen was advised not to write any more stories for children.

But one of his closest friends and admirers—H. C. Ørsted, the naturalist and discoverer of electromagnetism—recognized the value of these tales from the very beginning. *"The Improvisatore,"* he said, "will make you famous. The *eventyr* will make you immortal!"

The second volume appeared the same year, and Andersen continued to send out new booklets almost regularly. From 1835 to 1872, he published more than 150 *eventyr*. The earliest of these were based on folktales that he had heard as a child, but which he freely adapted and rewrote in his own fashion. This should be remembered, because Andersen has often been incorrectly classifed with the Grimms as a folklorist. But while the latter were interested in preserving the original structure and content of the folktales and legends, Andersen made any alterations and additions he thought necessary to the improvement of the story. "The Garden of Paradise," for example, was based on a folktale he had heard as a child—one that he liked so much that he wished it were longer: ". . . the four winds ought to be able to relate even more, the Garden revealed in even greater detail. . . ." "The Tinderbox" had been suggested by an old Danish tale called "The Spirit in the Candle," but it also contains features reminiscent of the Aladdin story in *The Arabian Nights*. "Little Claus and Big Claus" and "The Swineherd" were patterned after *skemtehistorier*—the witty, earthy (often coarse) tales that flourished in the taverns and wayside inns. In order to make them suitable for children he toned down or deleted the improper passages.

Later, many of his tales were inspired by literary sources. "The Emperor's New Clothes" had been suggested by a medieval Spanish tale; "The Flying Trunk" was inspired by *The Arabian Nights;* and "The Rose Elf" was taken from Boccaccio's *Decameron*.

From the very beginning, however, Andersen wrote his stories with two audiences in mind. He had discovered that the oral style appealed to adults as well as children. As far as the content was concerned, he said, "I grasp an idea for the grown-ups, and then I recount it to the little ones while remembering that father and mother are listening too, and that they must be given a little food for thought." In other words, the stories had to be simple enough for a child to understand, yet with enough between the lines to appeal to adults as well. But the idea prevailed that these stories were solely for children, and in order to clear up this misunderstanding, as well as to ensure that this phase of his work be taken seriously, he changed the title, in 1843, to *New Wonder Tales*.

Around this time he began developing his own, original themes. In 1837, he had written an original story, "The Little Mermaid," which had received so much acclaim that it sent his imagination soaring and inspired him to create more of his own. Later, as many of the stories began to resemble novellas, the title was changed to *Historier*. Unlike most of the Romantic writers in this genre, however, he never allowed his imagination to run riot. While the Romanticists were attracted to the unusual and the bizarre, Andersen's tales were grounded in realism. He maintained that "the most fantastic *eventyr* spring forth from reality." And the circumstances surrounding his own remarkable life provided him with a far greater range of experiences from which to draw his inspiration than that of any of his contemporaries.

Hans Christian Andersen was born in Odense on April 2, 1805. His parents were married a month or two before he was born. They were very poor, and his father was barely able to eke out a living as a cobbler. He was a restless man, dissatisfied with his work and his marriage, and bitterly disappointed by the fact that he had never received the education he had longed for. He was devoted to the boy, who was his only child, and when he wasn't taking him for walks or making him toys, he would read aloud to him from La Fontaine, Holberg, or *The Arabian Nights*. Once he made him a puppet theater, and this became the boy's most cherished possession.

Andersen's mother was a few years older than her husband. Of doubtful origins herself, she had had a daughter out of wedlock several years before their marriage. Andersen had little or no contact with this half sister, who did not live with her mother, but the idea that she might turn up later in his life caused him considerable anxiety. His mother could only spell out block letters, and never learned to read or write, but she was a good mother to the boy and loved him dearly. She was naïvely orthodox in her religious beliefs, but at the same time she was extremely superstitious. This contrasted greatly with her husband's skeptical attitudes toward life and religion. He was always seeking a rational explanation of the supernatural beliefs of the old people. His wife didn't understand him and was often terrified by his blasphemous remarks about God and the devil: "There is no other devil than the one we have in our own hearts!" he was heard to say. Or: "Christ was a human being like ourselves, but an unusual human being!" These conflicting attitudes made a lasting impression upon the boy. In later years, while preoccupied with the questions of immortality, he was often troubled by religious doubt.

Andersen was a sensitive boy and seldom played with other children. He spent most of his time daydreaming or making up plays and sewing costumes for his puppets. The fact that his grandfather was mentally deranged and sometimes, decorated with flowers and singing at the top of his lungs, would come wandering through the streets of Odense, also caused him to avoid the company of other boys. He lived in constant terror lest he encounter him in the street and run the risk of being teased. And the fear that he might inherit his grandfather's malady haunted him till the day he died.

His grandmother cared for the garden of the hospital for the insane, and he often accompanied her there when she burned rubbish. Sometimes he wandered through the hospital to look at the patients; sometimes he went to the nearby workhouse, where the old women, as they spun and wove, would tell him the old Danish folktales and legends. From an early age he was steeped in native lore. But, as he later wrote in his autobiography, he was often so affected by the stories he heard and the mental patients he saw that he hardly dared venture out of the house when it grew dark.

When Andersen was a boy, Odense was the second largest city in Denmark. It derived its name from Odin, the god who, according to legend, is said to have dwelled there. Situated on the island of Fyn, a province rich in folklore, it was a paradise for a boy with a lively imagination. Many of the old customs that had disappeared from the rest of Denmark still prevailed. The guilds paraded with their colorful signs, a Harlequin running in front. On Shrove Monday the butchers led their fattest oxen, decorated with flowers, through the streets. There were parades and bonfires, fireworks and illuminations. And the fact that Prince Christian Frederick was governor of the province and dwelled in the castle of Odense added luster to the public festivities. These sights, and many more, made a lasting impression upon the boy.

Odense was one of the first cities in Denmark to have its own theater, and young Andersen occasionally accompanied his parents there. The programs varied from plays and operas, in Danish and German, to pantomimes and tightrope acts. The boy's fantasy was kindled, and he was soon making up his own plays, which he presented in his mother's kitchen, performing all the roles himself.

In the meantime his father's restlessness increased, and in 1812—driven as much by dreams of glory as by the hope of improving his economic status—he enlisted in the army and went off to fight on the side of Napoleon. However, he went no farther than Holstein. A treaty of peace had been signed. Two years later he returned home, in poor health and straitened circumstances, and died in 1816, when Andersen was eleven years old. To provide for them, his mother went out to wash and clean for people, and the boy was often left home alone.

From an early age he seems to have had an incredible affinity for coming to the attention of influential people who took an interest in him and wanted to help him. To be sure, he often went out of his way to attract their attention and ask them for help. But it should be remembered that he was born on the lowest rung of the social ladder at a time when social distinctions were much more pronounced than they are now. It was virtually impossible for a poor boy to rise above his social status. At best, he could learn a trade, but a higher education was almost out of the question. Not only did he have to possess unusual talent and ability—as well as considerable willpower—but he also had to be acquainted with well-to-do patrons who were in a position to take upon themselves the financial burden of seeing him through an education.

He became a regular visitor to what he later described as "cultivated homes," where he was permitted to borrow books and where he was often invited to declaim and sing for the assembled guests. At one of these gatherings he met a Colonel Guldberg, who arranged for him to sing and declaim for Prince Christian Frederick in the hope that the latter might award him a grant enabling him to go to school. The prince was willing to help him, but only on the condition that he learn a trade, and so the meeting came to nothing.

But Andersen's mother decided to apprentice him to a tailor. She thought he had ability because of his interest in sewing clothes for his puppets. He did little sewing there, however: when the other apprentices discovered that he could sing, they made him entertain them, while someone else did his share of the work. But after a few days he was teased so much about his voice—which was a beautiful soprano at the time—and treated so roughly, that he fled home and vowed never to return there again.

Two years after his father's death, his mother married again. Her new husband was also a cobbler, but he was considerably younger than she was. He felt that the rearing of the boy was no concern of his, and left him to himself. His family felt that he had married beneath him, and Andersen and his mother were never permitted to visit them. He died after a few years, and they were in worse circumstances than before.

Again his mother felt that the boy should learn a useful trade, but in 1818, a troupe of visiting players from the Royal Theater in Copenhagen came to Odense to perform a number of operas and tragedies. Andersen was hired once or twice to walk onstage as an extra, and his mind was made up. His future lay with the theater. He would go to Copenhagen to become famous. His mother protested violently, but nothing could make him change his mind. At last she took him to a fortune-teller to predict his future.

"Your son is going to be a great man," the woman said. "And one day, in his honor, Odense will be illuminated!" When she heard this, his mother burst into tears, and he was given permission to go.

Equipped with a letter of introduction to the solo dancer at the Royal Theater and a few coins that he had managed to scrape together, the fourteen-year-old lad set out alone. The encounter with the dancer, however, was a failure. The lady did not remember the sender of the letter. And when the gawky youth began to sing and dance for her, using his hat for a tambourine, she thought he had lost his mind and sent him away. Then he went to the manager of the Royal Theater, who told him that they could not hire anyone who had no schooling.

By this time his money had run out, and he decided to apprentice himself at the first place he could find. By chance he discovered a carpenter who needed an apprentice, but he was so roundly teased by the other boys because of his sensitivity to their coarse jokes that he left after a few hours. And again he was without funds or the prospects of earning any.

Then he remembered having read about Giuseppi Siboni, an Italian who was the director of the Royal Conservatory, and he went to see him. Siboni was entertaining friends, but the boy was admitted. After listening to him declaim and sing, the maestro promised to give him singing lessons. Another of the guests took up a collection for him. After six months, however, Andersen's voice started changing, and Siboni advised him to return to Odense and learn a trade!

But now Andersen remembered that in Copenhagen

there lived a poet, Frederik Guldberg, a brother of the colonel in Odense who had given him encouragement. The poet received him kindly and promised to tutor him in Danish and German, as well as to arrange for him to receive lessons in Latin. He was admitted to the Royal Theater's dancing school and even played the part of a troll in the ballet *Armida*. This dancing instruction was short-lived, but by this time his voice had improved, and he was admitted to the theater's chorus. On the other hand his Latin suffered, and when Guldberg discovered this, he refused to give him any more help.

About this time Andersen had written a tragedy entitled *The Robbers of Wissenberg*, which he submitted to the Royal Theater. It was refused with the comment that they had no desire to receive additional plays that revealed such a complete lack of education on the part of the author. Shortly afterward, he was dismissed from the chorus, but the hope was expressed that his friends would look after him and assist him in acquiring the education he so badly needed.

Once again his future looked black. He was in the depths of despair and without funds, but to return to Odense would be to admit failure. Then came the major turning point in his life. He had written a second play, *Alfsol*, which had also been turned down by the theater, but it brought him to the attention of Jonas Collin, a member of the theater's board of directors. Collin, who was a wealthy and prominent civil servant, arranged for him to be admitted to the Slagelse Grammar School and, at the same time, to receive a royal grant that would take care of his living expenses.

In Odense, Andersen's schooling had been scanty. An elderly schoolmistress had taught him the alphabet and the rudiments of reading and spelling. For a while he attended the Charity School, where he was taught religion, writing, and some arithmetic. When he went to

Slagelse, however, he had to start almost from the very beginning.

He arrived there in 1822 and was enrolled in the second class. He was seventeen, and the fact that his classmates were considerably younger did not make life easier for him. The rector of the school, Søren Meisling, seems to have been strict and abusive. He was not above making sarcastic remarks when the work of his pupils did not please him, and Andersen took everything he said literally. As was to be true in his later years, he thrived on praise, but the slightest criticism threw him into the depths of despair. The years at Slagelse were hard. In 1826, he accompanied Meisling when the latter moved the school to Elsinore, but he was miserable. At last he persuaded Collin to allow him to return to Copenhagen, where he was given private tutoring. He passed his matriculation examination in 1828, twenty-three years old.

He had no intention of entering the university, however, and started writing with gusto. He had written a few poems while at Slagelse, but in 1829, his first book, *A Walking Trip from Holmen's Canal to the Eastern Tip of Amager*, appeared. And in the same year his vaudeville, "Love on Nicholas Tower," was performed at the same Royal Theater where he had struggled to gain a foothold several years before. In 1830, he published a volume of poetry. All three works were given a favorable reception by the critics and the public, and he started to earn money.

He spent the summer of 1830 traveling about his native Denmark. In Faaborg he met Riborg Voigt, the sister of a student friend, and fell in love with her. She was already engaged, but he proposed to her and was crushed when she turned him down. About the same time the critics began writing unfavorably about him.

In 1831, to get away from it all, he took his first trip abroad. He went to northern and central Germany, and wrote a book about his travels as soon as he returned. It was well received, but again, he was disappointed in love. This time he had fallen in love with Collin's youngest daughter, Louise, but she became engaged to someone else.

Again he went abroad to forget. This time he received a royal grant that enabled him to go to France, Switzerland, and Italy. A direct outcome of this trip was his first novel, *The Improvisatore*. It was translated into several languages and made him internationally famous. While the setting described the places Andersen had visited, the plot was essentially autobiographical, and the characters were taken from real life.

In 1836, his second novel, *O.T.*, appeared. The initials referred to the main character (Otto Thostrup) as well as to Odense Tugthus (Odense Jail). Again the novel was largely autobiographical. His third novel, *Only a Fiddler*, was published in 1837. These novels were well received and were followed by *The Three Baronesses* (1848), *To Be or Not To Be* (1857) and *Lucky Peer* (1870).

Although Andersen had an undying love for the theater, his dramatic production was never a success. He wrote no less than thirty works for the stage, but of these, only a few attained any measure of popularity. His tragedy, *The Mulatto* (1840), had been widely acclaimed. But the negative reaction of the critics to his dramatic production as a whole was a prime factor in leading Andersen to believe that he was misunderstood and underestimated in his homeland.

Andersen was one of the most widely traveled men of his day. In all, he went abroad some twenty-nine times and visited most of the countries of Europe, as well as North Africa. In 1840, when Louise Collin was to be married, he set out on the longest journey of his lifetime. He visited Germany, Italy, Greece, the Balkans, and Turkey, and did not return until 1841. His impressions of his trip appeared in a *A Poet's Bazaar* (1842). This book, and *In Sweden*, which was the result of a visit to that country in 1849, are regarded as two of his major literary works.

In 1840, he met the third great love of his lifetime, the woman who perhaps exerted the greatest influence over him—Jenny Lind, the "Swedish Nightingale." Three years later they met again, and he proposed to her. But she refused to consider him as more than a brother. He was greatly attracted to her, not only as a woman but as an artist. Her views on life affected him deeply. He said, "Through Jenny Lind I have understood for the first time the sanctity of art. Through her I have learned that one must renounce oneself in the service of something higher. No books, no persons have had a better or more ennobling influence over me as a poet than Jenny Lind." "The Nightingale" was written as a tribute to her.

Andersen never settled down in Copenhagen. Like his father, he had a restless nature, but a contributing factor was also the fact that he never felt at home there. After the years at Slagelse, Jonas Collin had opened his doors to him, and he was regarded as one of the family. But he was never able to free himself of feelings of inferiority as far as the Collin family was concerned. He could never forget his indebtedness to them, or the fact that they had been born to the breeding and culture that he was struggling so hard to acquire. At the same time he was morbidly sensitive, and the slightest criticism or imagined affront was enough to send him packing.

Andersen was lonely too. His mother had died in 1833, while he was in Italy, and his only remaining close relative was the half sister he did not wish to meet. He never married, and the fact is that the few women upon whom he bestowed his affections were already unattainable. Many of his trips abroad were for the purpose of escaping this loneliness. Wherever he went, he carried with him letters of introduction to influential people, and he often went out of his way to get in touch with the outstanding literary celebrities of the day. He duly recorded his social triumphs in his diaries and autobiographies, as well as in his voluminous correspondence with friends and acquaintances back home. To him, this was additional proof that his life was an *eventyr*, but he was often accused of vanity and social climbing, and more than once he found himself caricatured in the literature of the day.

From the 1830's on, as his fame increased, he was a welcome guest in the Danish manor houses, where he often stayed when he wasn't traveling. In 1840, while visting Sweden, he was given his first public ovation by the students at the University of Lund. At Weimar, he was warmly received in circles closely connected with the German court. He stayed with Charles Dickens when he visited England in 1857, and he was lionized by the leading literary salons of the day. In 1867, Andersen was made an honorary citizen of the town of his birth, and just as the fortune-teller had predicted, Odense was illuminated in his honor. After a lingering illness, he died at the home of friends on August 4, 1875.

Throughout his *eventyr* Andersen drew heavily upon his personal experiences. Everything he saw and did made a vivid impression upon him and provided him with inspiration that could remain in his mind for years. "My stories," he said, "lie in my thoughts like a seed that requires no more than a stream, a ray of sunshine, a drop of *malurt* to make it flower."

In "The Ugly Duckling" he presented the bitter struggles and hardships of his early life far more poignantly and artistically than in his official autobiography. An encounter with Riborg Voigt, years after their parting, resulted in "The Sweethearts." A pair of new boots for his confirmation, and the recollection that his thoughts dwelled more upon these than upon the seriousness of the occasion, has its counterpart in "The Red Shoes." In "The Little Match Girl," he drew upon the childhood experiences of his mother when she was sent out to beg. The prince of "The Little Mermaid" is really Louise Collin, and the story portrays Andersen's unrequited love for her. Jenny Lind is "The [Swedish] Nightingale," while "The Swineherd," "The Snowman," and "The Steadfast Tin Soldier" are thinly disguised portraits of Andersen himself.

The settings of the stories range from the fragile porcelain palace of the Emperor of China to a pigsty; from the Gates of Heaven to the Devil's Anteroom; from the Cave of the Winds to the castle of the King of the Sea. We are transported in flying trunks or on the back of the East Wind, in humble wheelbarrows or in airships yet to be invented. But while Andersen's head is in the clouds, his feet are firmly planted in Danish soil. Most of the tales are set in the Denmark of his own time, amid the surroundings he knew and loved so well. His descriptions of the Danish countryside are almost hymns of praise. In the traditional folktale, the scenery remains in the background, but in Andersen's tales it is described in minute detail, thus becoming a part of the story.

The characters range from traditional kings and princesses to earthy farm lads and representatives of the solid middle class; from the Moss Wife and the Nisse (which are more specifically Danish) to mermaids and witches and the devil's own grandmother. We encounter the querulous inhabitants of the duckyard as well as the microscopic creatures to be found in a drop of water. At the same time, the tales abound in a host of inanimate objects that are endowed with the power of speech and movement and permitted to make all manner of ironic observations that Andersen himself did not feel free to utter.

"The whole world," he said, "is a series of marvels, but we're so used to them that we call them *everyday things!*" It is in this everyday world that his strength as an artist lies. Again and again he reminds us that the richness and beauty of life are often to be found in the little things that we ordinarily don't take time to notice. A tiny seed can turn into the most beautiful flower, a kind act can develop into something more significant. The world is a rich gallery of persons and objects, each with his own story to tell, each different. If we keep our eyes open and our minds receptive, we need never be bored.

By adding small, realistic touches, and by treating the supernatural carefully, he manages to make the unreal seem real. In the more traditional tales, the king shuffles around in slippers that are worn down at the heel, the princess reads the newspapers. In the world of flowers, animals, and inanimate objects, human values do not exist. Each one experiences the world from his own limited environment and judges it accordingly. Thus, to a frog, nothing is more delightful than to lie in a wet ditch, while to a wax candle the height of ambition is to stand in a crystal chandelier and shine for the most fashionable people.

There is a striking parallel between the basic ideas inherent in the folk tradition and Andersen's own attitudes toward life. Folktales and legends came into existence at a time when the belief in supernatural powers and their active interference in the daily course of events was much stronger than it is now. The traditional hero, who was good and kind, reached his goal after overcoming seemingly insurmountable obstacles with the help of these forces. Andersen believed in the intervention of a Divine Providence, but his faith in ". . . a loving God who arranges everything for the best" was confirmed by remarkable happenings throughout his lifetime.

The goal he set for himself was fame, but he had no illusions that it was easy to attain. Before setting out for Copenhagen, he had declared to his mother, "First you must go through such a terrible amount of suffering, and then you become famous." Not all of his stories have happy endings, but he had discovered that life could be both good and bad, terrible and happy, tender and brutal—and that friendship was often an empty word. Each tale was written at the moment when one of these moods was particularly strong. But despite the pessimism in many of the stories, there is optimism too: By good deeds, the Little Mermaid will be able to create an immortal soul for herself after three hundred years; by giving away enough crumbs to make up the loaf she scornfully trod in the mire, Inger is able to redeem herself.

Andersen usually tried out his stories on an audience before writing them down. He read them aloud at parties and at the manor houses where he was a frequent guest. Rooted as he was in the oral tradition, he was a born storyteller. Edward Collin once described the way he told his stories to children:

> He told them stories that, in part, had been made up on the spur of the moment, in part, had been taken from well-known sources. But whether he was telling his own or relating another, the narrative style was so exclusively his, and so animated, that the children were enraptured. . . . He gave life to even the driest sentence. He didn't say: "The children got in the carriage and then they drove." Instead: "Then they got in the carriage. Good-bye Papa! Good-bye Mama! The whip cracked: smack! snap! And away they flew! Hey! Do you want to go too!"

The short, coordinating sentences speed the action along. Here and there, like the professional storyteller, he addresses the audience directly by inserting a parenthetical remark, an aside, into the course of events. In some of the tales he can be bitingly satirical, especially when he is making fun of the snobbery and the artificial values of the day. In others he can be highly sentimental. Nonetheless, his effervescent humor is always bubbling beneath the surface, ready to erupt in the form of ironic commentaries and sly allusions.

Shortly before his death, Andersen protested vigorously against plans to erect a statue that would depict him reading his tales to children. Through his *eventyr* he wanted to create a new and universal genre that would appeal to all ages. The universality of his tales is reflected in the fact that they are popular throughout the world, but the misconception still prevails that they are solely for children. Let us hope that this little collection will help to clear up this misunderstanding, as well as to stimulate renewed interest in one of the greatest literary geniuses the world has ever known.

Pat Shaw Iversen
Oslo, 1965

PROTESTANT THEOLOGY AT ⌐⌐⌐ ⌐ADS

Protestant Theology at the Crossroads

*How to Face the Crucial Tasks for Theology
in the Twenty-First Century*

Gerhard Sauter

WILLIAM B. EERDMANS PUBLISHING COMPANY

GRAND RAPIDS, MICHIGAN / CAMBRIDGE, U.K.

Published 2007 by
Wm. B. Eerdmans Publishing Co.
2140 Oak Industrial Drive N.E., Grand Rapids, Michigan 49505 /
P.O. Box 163, Cambridge CB3 9PU U.K.

Printed in the United States of America

12 11 10 09 08 07   7 6 5 4 3 2 1

Library of Congress Cataloging-in-Publication Data

Sauter, Gerhard.
     Protestant theology at the crossroads: how to face the crucial tasks
  for theology in the twenty-first century / Gerhard Sauter.
        p.   cm.
     ISBN 978-0-8028-4034-9 (pbk.: alk. paper)
     1. Theology.   I. Title.

  BT21.3.S38   2007
  230'.044 — dc22

                                                2006039416

www.eerdmans.com

Dedicated to

Princeton Theological Seminary

and

The Divinity School of Duke University

Contents

viii

Foreword

Gerhard Sauter, Emeritus Professor of Systematic and Ecumenical Theology at the University of Bonn, is among the most productive and highly respected theologians of our generation. The present volume contains his Warfield Lectures given at Princeton Theological Seminary in March 2000.

An ordained minister of the Protestant Church of Kurhessen and Waldeck in Germany, Sauter playfully describes himself in these pages as a "mongrel" of German confessionalism. As he explains: on the one hand, he has been a "lifelong" and "intensive" student of the theology of Martin Luther; on the other hand, he has been engaged in "mutually beneficial conversations" with Reformed theologians in a number of countries for many years. Indeed, among Karl Barth scholars, Sauter is well-known as a careful editor of two volumes of the collected works of the great Swiss Reformed theologian. Yet if Sauter by his own admission is a theological "mongrel," it is worth recalling that Barth himself once opined that a theologian steeped in *both* Lutheran *and* Reformed theology has an exceptionally good theological pedigree.

Beginning his graduate studies under the erudite Reformed historian of doctrine Otto Weber, Sauter focused his doctoral dissertation, published in 1962, on the theology of the kingdom of God in the writings of Johann C. and Christoph F. Blumhardt. His *Habilitationsschrift, Zukunft und Verheissung*, published a few years later, highlighted the importance of the themes of promise and future for Christian theology. This work proved to be a seminal contribution to an understanding of the distinctively biblical view of eschatology and how it differs from ways of thinking about the future in much modern theology and philosophy.

In addition to teaching in Bonn from 1973 to 2000, where he occupied the chair of systematic theology formerly held by Barth, Sauter has taught at Oxford, Duke, Princeton Theological Seminary, and other institutions around the world. He has given valuable leadership to the renewal of church life and theological education in Eastern Europe, devastated by the years of the Cold War. On several occasions he has been in residence as a research scholar at the Center of Theological Inquiry in Princeton. Among Sauter's books published in English are *Eschatological Rationality: Theological Issues in Focus* (Baker, 1996); *What Dare We Hope? Reconsidering Eschatology* (Trinity, 1999); and *Gateways to Dogmatics: Reasoning Theologically for the Life of the Church* (Eerdmans, 2003). He has also written a number of major articles in theological encyclopedias and theological journals, and has served as one of the editors of the journals *Verkündigung und Forschung* and *Evangelische Theologie*.

Explorations in eschatology have clearly been at the center of Sauter's theological work. For him an important, even crucial, theological question for our time is, What dare we hope? Christian hope, he contends, is focused on Jesus Christ the crucified and risen Lord. It is expectation of the ever new judgment and grace of God. Christian hope must hold together the seemingly contradictory elements of "reserve and activity," "vigilance and imperturbability," "silence and witness," and "patience and engagement." For Sauter, authentic Christian hope, while focused on God and God's coming reign, in no way disregards our present responsibilities and possibilities. He is fond of quoting a statement often (though mistakenly) attributed to Martin Luther: "If I knew that tomorrow the world would end, I would still plant an apple tree today."

In addition to the themes of promise and hope, Sauter's theological interests include the relationship of theology and science, the history and importance of the doctrines of justification and reconciliation, biblical hermeneutics, the necessity of confession of sins and the experience of forgiveness in Christian life, and the importance of the Jewish-Christian dialogue. In regard to the last, Sauter emphasizes that there is a "shared hope *for* Christians and Jews" based on the free grace of God who "will realize his promises in *his* own and strange way, often in a way contrary to human expectations that might be nourished by these very promises."

According to Sauter's self-description, "I try to do theology in an evangelical way: being faithful to the Scripture . . . involved in the life of the church, and open to the unity of the church." These goals are amply demonstrated in this volume as well as in his other writings. Sauter contends that among the most important tasks of "dogmatics" (don't be afraid of the word, he advises) is the cultivation of the art of reading Scripture. What this means for him is allowing the Bible to speak to us on its own terms rather than compelling it to say what we want to hear or what will not disturb us. A central task of dogmatic theology is helping us learn to read Scripture as witness to the faithfulness of God. As the central content of Scripture, the faithfulness of God is not simply an idea or an abstract principle. It is the living Word of God addressing us and calling forth our faith in ever new times and places. Sauter makes the point this way: "Searching in Scripture is not just looking up references in order to reinforce opinions and prior knowledge, or using it as a book of oracles. Whoever really searches in Scripture hopes that, in the process of searching, God will make himself heard."

Another distinctive mark of Sauter's theology is that it is closely related to the life of the church. A theologian with pastoral experience and a pastoral orientation, he understands his theological research, teaching, and writing as *ministerium verbi divini,* service of the Word of God. In the power of the Spirit, the Word of God calls the church into being, animates its life and worship, and guides its mission. Sauter worries that all too frequently theology and church life have become functions of political parties and special interest groups. That is a danger, of course, not only for Christians who locate themselves at the far ends of the political spectrum but also for those who stand somewhere in the middle.

One of Sauter's innovative suggestions is that theology is best organized around the church year. In celebrating the great acts of God through the church year, we experience a "different reckoning of time." Following the church year provides training in hope. When we attend to the specific narratives of God's acts of surprising grace, we take time to be nourished by the richness of the gospel story. "We cannot rush ahead or miss out on anything. . . . We must rejoice for a time at the crib, but only for a time. We must also tarry for a time at the cross. We cannot leap over the abyss of Holy Saturday. It is fatal to cling too closely to Christmas and to seek to celebrate it forever. And we shall turn into pillars of salt if we look too long at the cross" (*Gateways to Dogmatics*, p. 186).

Sauter's theology also shows an abiding concern for the unity of the church. By church unity he means something far more than the institutional unification of the various Christian denominations. What he has in mind is a rebirth of ecumenical awareness in which the churches rediscover their unity in Christ as attested in Scripture and proclaimed in the rich confessional heritage common to the churches. Sauter's criticisms of what he here calls "contextual theology" may seem rather one-sided to some readers, but the basic question he raises cannot be ignored: "If ecumenical discussion is confined to [particular] experiences, referring only secondarily to the Bible and perhaps, marginally, to confessional doctrinal traditions, how is the theological significance of these experiences to be assessed? How are we to distill from historical experiences theological insights which are important not just to one theologian or group of Christians but to the whole Christian world family?" (*Eschatological Rationality*, p. 57).

As noted earlier, running through all of Sauter's writings is the topic of hope. What can we hope for? That is a question we face today more intensely than ever before, not simply because we find ourselves in the first decade of a new millennium but far more profoundly because terrorist acts and counterterrorist wars have brought the world to the precipice of an abyss. Sauter takes up the question of hope in several of the essays in this volume. His discussion of the religious dimension of American self-understanding and its crisis today should be of special interest to American readers. Coming from a friendly outside observer of American society and history, his critical reflections on the ambiguities and the dangers of the metaphors of America as a "city upon a hill" and a beacon to the rest of the world are insightful. To the question "Where was God on September 11?" Sauter responds by prompting Christians in America and elsewhere to ponder the still deeper question of the very identity of God: "What is God *like* in times of crisis?" and even more pointedly, "*Who* is the God to whom we pray?"

Good theology can always be counted on to raise unsettling questions and to open up new vistas for the living of Christian faith today. Among the virtues of this collection of Professor Sauter's essays is that it serves to remind us of these tasks.

DANIEL L. MIGLIORE
Charles Hodge Professor of
Systematic Theology
Princeton Theological Seminary

INTRODUCTION

Is There Really a Turning Point?

At the beginning of a new century — even after some years of the new millennium — we ask more intensely than at other times, "How will it go on?" And if we wish to carry on, the question arises: "Which direction are we to take? Are there forks in the road that require a decision?" Such decisions have momentous repercussions. Were we to take the wrong turn, we might have to walk back a great distance and consequently lose much precious energy and time — or we may never find the right turn again!

The dialogue between theologians from different countries and traditions offers the opportunity to exchange ideas and communicate experiences of paths that have been trodden. This could help us avoid detours and dead ends.

Along these lines I wish to name several forks in the road, which I have run into and about which I have had discussions with theologians from other European countries, the United States, Korea, and South Africa. These forks in the road represent crucial tasks, which must be faced without delay. Most of them are inherited from the second half of the last century. There was a turning point in doing theology in the 1960s. First, the Second Vatican Council (1962-65) opened up the Roman Catholic Church to other churches and religions, to the reformation of the church service, and to world affairs much more than before. Then, starting with the civil rights movement in the United States and with the so-called student revolution in the United States and all over western Europe, a new sensitivity for the "context" of doing theology arose in Catholic and Protestant theology. It was, and is, directed toward particular cultural heritages, toward race and gender, and toward facing the impact of economic conditions and the structure of social life on Christian theology. In some respects this movement placed social theory and linguistic studies ahead of philosophy as the first and foremost dialogue partner of theology in the academy. At the same time, the interest of North American theologians in having exchanges with their European counterparts that had been shaping theology in the United States for more than two centuries fell away significantly. North American theology became much more self-confident than before. In some respects "contextual theology" has been a product of North American theology and its interest in the interrelation between theology and society. It has enormously influenced biblical studies, historical theology, Christian ethics, and all fields of practical theology, not only in North America but all over the world. It has even promised to restructure systematic theology from top to bottom and, indeed, to provide a new way of doing theology in general.

Today we talk of "globalization," especially of the industrial interchange and the network of the media, but also of global economic challenges, for example, rising poverty, social injustice, many forms of humiliation and exploitation, the ecological crisis, weapons of mass destruction, and most recently, global terrorism. Is there any global response to those challenges? Socialism was purported to promise such a uniting response, yet after the collapse of the Iron Curtain in 1989/90, there was a great awakening of cultural particularity, sometimes labeled "postmodernism." This trend is still alive. However, since September 11, 2001, there have been many debates about another sort of unification. In Europe we are in the midst of the very complex process of uniting part of the Eurasian continent, not only economically but also culturally.

Does this globalizing phenomenon apply also to theology? Many, especially in South America, Africa, and Asia, had, and have, the suspicion that in the past there has been a somewhat monolithic Christian theology deeply rooted in the European tradition, characterized by a fusion of Christian theology with its philosophical heritage fed by Greek philosophy and its followers. Accordingly, many conclude that after the decline of Europe, and even within Europe itself, there must have emerged a plurality of characteristically different theologies, each one rooted in a special context.

Crucial tasks of doing theology, of course, take different forms in different contexts. Yet they are tasks of such a profoundly basic nature that they might nevertheless bring us together. Many contemporaries consider that they are also addressing the task of unifying. Addressing these tasks may lead us toward a coherent and uniting account of doing theology around the world in contrast to the discord we experience today. Such an expectation is surely not just my wishful thinking but one of the great hopes for this new century.

First, we have to ask what dare we hope? In the second half of the twentieth century the expectations of many Christians in different countries were altered dramatically. Forty years ago a grand optimism prevailed. This enthusiasm was promoted by the rapid development in technology, biotechnology, medicine, communications, and other fields as well, and the ongoing socioeconomic progress of Europe and North America. The future seemed to provide the solutions for the abiding social problems of the time.

In contrast to such optimism, during the last two decades many people have developed a skeptical, even resigned, attitude. The economic and environmental crisis, the manifold endangerment of the dignity of humankind, the entanglement of public life, the dependence of politics on economical interests and on the influence of mass media, have made us aware of serious limits and painful breaks. At this point we must remember the appeal to be "accountable to everyone who raises questions about the hope that is in you" (according to 1 Pet. 3:15, my translation). This task is also the central thread of this book. Its chapters are also intertwined in many other ways. For example, there is a recurrent motif of silence — in listening, hopefully watching, and being open to surprising answers, sometimes as speechlessness, as inability to overcome vain theological endeavors, showing the absence of hope. Also, the chapters are connected by the perception of God's acting in different and unexpected ways, by the correlation of promise and fulfillment, by the question of how far theology can immerse itself in culture without being deprived of its own character, and how theology really does shape culture.

To be accountable for hope requires engagement in dialogue with Jewish readers concerning their Scripture and their reasoning with Scripture. I try to introduce this ongoing and promising dialogue in chapter 2, "A Shared Hope for Jews and Christians." Here again the question arises as to what direction we can faithfully take, in mutual respect as well as in facing crucial tasks.

A further fork in the road appears in the shape of the question concerning the relevance of Scripture for theology, for the church, and for our culture. This is a pressing task because the Scripture that nourishes the "hope that is in us" is a lively source rather than a source in the sense of a historical document. The controversy over the authority of the Bible in recent decades has brought forth more confusion than lucidity. On the one hand, it led to a radical contextualization of biblical texts; on the other, there was, and is, a fundamentalist backlash. Both are branches from the same tree that is rooted in rationalism. Scriptural authority is wedged in between fundamentalism and radicalized contextual theology. I oppose both in "The Art of Reading the Bible," chapter 3. To live with the Bible, which accompanies us on the way — indeed, even directs our way — is an art that has to be practiced continuously.

Many contemporaries misinterpret "authority" as "heteronomy" or as sheer dependence on tradition. I do not wish to evade the question of the binding character of the Bible. Instead, I propose to conceive this character as faithfulness to Scripture. For Scripture is a many-voiced witness of God's faithfulness. I explained this character of the Bible in a contribution to a research project of colleagues of Bonn and Oxford from 1995 to 1999 (first published in *Revelation and Story: Narrative Theology and the Centrality of Story*, edited by John Barton and Gerhard Sauter [Aldershot, U.K.: Ashgate, 2000], pp. 7-28), and I extended this chapter substantially in *Gateways to Dogmatics: Reasoning Theologically for the Life of the Church* (Grand Rapids: Eerdmans, 2003).

The faithfulness of Scripture is to be discovered, and in this pursuit we are helped by new tools as they make visible the structure of biblical narratives. These tools — the relation between spirit and letter, law and gospel, promise and fulfillment — enable us to gain surprising insights.

Some theologians in western Europe and in the United States suggest that theology will find its primary context of perception, orientation, and understanding not so much in living with the Bible as in culture. That is even more the case as the church is increasingly cast into the status of a minority. In contrast, the churches in eastern Europe have discovered new opportunities to share responsibility and to fashion the common good in the cultures of their particular nations, after having been suppressed and ghettoized for decades. But the task remains for them to take this into the public sphere, that is, to take up Christian education, for ministers to serve in hospitals, in prisons, and in the military. Christian education especially is a sensitive matter: Should it be limited to Sunday schools, as has been the case under Communist regimes? Or are these nations willing and able to support persons to teach religion in public schools? In most parts of Germany, there is religious education in elementary and high schools, and future teachers are trained in the faculties of theology in the universities.

In other countries, particularly in Asia and Africa, but to some extent also in North and South America, the theological interest in the culture grows as people search for their own roots. This again gives rise to the question of where theology finds its roots and also what it can talk of and what it can communicate to others. I will address this task facing contextual theology and consider the heritage of liberalism in public theology.

Theological communication depends on experiences in thinking incurred in the attempt to account for what theology receives, in communication and communion with the church regardless of all other legitimate interests in communicating in the academy and in public life. The church is based on what God has entrusted to it to say and to do. This source of spirituality is available for the needs of others, because it is no longer enclosed in itself. Theology must not cut itself off from the church, and the church requires theology, because it deals with the grounding of the life and practices of the church. In this respect theology may well be critical of the church while in solidarity with the church. Dogmatics serves this twofold commitment. Therefore I make a plea for having no fear of dogmatics, although I have to wrestle with a widespread traditional aversion to this term, especially in the United States.

During my recent stay in the United States I heard some theologians complaining about a growing trend toward self-interest in relation to churches' concern with their own self-preservation. This may be of serious importance because it supports the "self-enclosure" of church boards that see their function as merely to manage the church instead of to lead it. This tendency endangers the witness of the church and could render it impossible. On the other hand, theology can fulfill its tasks only if it is really rooted in the life and work of the church, that is, if it is faithful to what God has entrusted it to proclaim and to consent to — unconditionally and under all circumstances.

God creates faith; do we consent? This is the question the church must ask itself again and again. The doctrine of justification is a testing ground for the church's essence of being the church. This doctrine presents the church with the task: Are we faithful to what God has entrusted to the church? The new debate on this topic is a hopeful example of ecumenical dialogue. It arose from the Joint Declaration on the Doctrine of Justification signed by representatives of the Lutheran World Federation and the Roman Catholic Church October 31, 1999, in Augsburg, Germany, the place where the Augsburg Confession, one of the most important documents of the Reformation, was presented in 1530. Now we look forward to a renewed perception of God's judging and saving work.

Contextual theology understands and interprets as its context all kinds of circumstances among which theology develops. Contextual theology has accordingly drawn our attention to the empirical preconditions of theological insights, expressions, and all sorts of thought. Yet simultaneously, it has raised the question as to what extent theology is bound to its particular context. Is theology subject to particular political circumstances, especially as theologians are involved in such circumstances? Is theology a function of social constitutions like race, gender, etc.? Theologians in central Europe are particularly sensitive to these questions because they have to look back to very daunting experiences in connection with such a contextual dependence of theology in the last century. Yet again, however, these very experiences can be helpful for other contexts.

Another branch of shaping theology is the interest in the sociopolitical context of doing theology. I address this move in theological reflections on the political changes in Europe in 1989/90. These changes have gained worldwide significance because the geopolitical antagonisms that had predominated collapsed like a house of cards. However, these changes are spiritually significant. They have proved that tracing back historical events to the will of God, or equating the two, deceived many theologians and church leaders. The unexpected and dramatic experiences of 1989/90 destroyed conceptions of history and produced a certain speechlessness, which lasts until today. Therein lies a chance to speak of God's providence anew.

The same is essentially true of September 11, 2001. This momentous event is shaping not only the domestic and foreign politics of the administration of the United States, but also the perception of freedom, of safety, and of its defense. When my German students asked me about the religious dimension of American self-understanding, I often pointed to the biblical metaphor "a city upon a hill" as a symbol of this dimension and its crisis today. Originally it was meant as a marker of God's providential care for people who were called to serve God and the needs of the people in their community. They have to be always aware of God's judgment. Later, this metaphor became a watchword of American civil religion, asserting that the United States is elected to accomplish a divine mission by means of its "manifest destiny."

These two dramatic events are examples of the task: How can we do justice to the situation of doing theology today? This task is explained, for example, in the chapter on contextual theology. The crisis of a supposedly theological justification of the events prior to the political changes in Europe or of September 11, linked with all kinds of self-justification, shows how urgently we need the undistracted perception of the proclamation of justification by faith.

The program "public theology" originated in the United States, but it is also attractive to many theologians in Europe. In Europe one looks back to a long history of amalgamation of Christian values in a shared culture. Therefore, one tends to think that one can gain new benefits from this treasure. Public theology opposes religious privatization and serves as an alternative to a church-bound theology. It accuses any so-called church-bound theology of withdrawing into a self-enclosed internal communication and to a voluntary ghetto. Here, too, we stand at a fork in the road.

The Princeton Theological Seminary invited me to deliver the Warfield Lectures in March 2000. Benjamin Warfield (1851-1921), who donated this series of lectures, was a Princetonian interested in a lively communication with European theologians of his time. I was told that his young wife became seriously ill while they enjoyed their honeymoon in the Black Forest (southern Germany) and that she never really recovered. As Warfield had to take lifelong care of his wife and was not free to travel, he invested much time and energy in his teaching and research at Princeton Theological Seminary. His interest was in promoting theological exchange, especially Reformed theology and, in particular, Presbyterianism. For that reason I included observations on the current state of Reformed theology in my Warfield Lectures. Here I am not interested in traditional and developed Reformed theology's profile on the diffuse theological market, nor am I merely concerned with denominational identity in a theological perspective. Rather, I am looking for the criteria of doing theology in a denominational context — transforming desires to be equally faithful and expectantly open.

At this point you may inquire about my denominational heritage (as has often happened in the United States). In this book you will find many quotations from Martin Luther as well as the concluding chapter on Reformed theology. I was born May 4, 1935, in Kassel in the middle of Germany and baptized as "Hessian Reformed with Lutheran Confession." You may suspect by this that I am a "mongrel" of German confessionalism. Sometimes even I got a bit confused in counting the Ten Commandments because Luther counted them differently than the Reformed theologians (they counted the commandment about the idols separately, while Luther omitted it in his *Small Catechism* and divided the coveting into two commandments). I used to say that I tried to live according to the commandments, but I cannot always name the special commandment to which I am obedient! I am an ordained minister in the Protestant Church of Kurhessen and Waldeck, ordained to the Augsburg Confession (including the ecumenical creeds of the early church), and obliged to the Barmen Declaration of the German Protestant Church (1934). I started to teach theology at Göttingen in a mainly Lutheran faculty; then I was a professor of systematic theology of the Protestant faculties in Mainz (1968-73) and in Bonn (1973-2000). There I served also as director of the Ecumenical Institute. Both faculties are linked with the Evangelical Church of the Union, the church of the former Prussian territory, integrating Lutheran and Reformed confessions. I owe a great deal to my lifelong, intensive study of Martin Luther, but I am grateful for mutual exchange with Reformed theologians of many countries. Like Karl Barth, who taught at Bonn from 1930 to 1935 and whom I succeeded many years later, I try to do theology in an evangelical way: being faithful to the Scripture in an academic framework and committed to the dialogue with colleagues working in other academic fields, involved in the life of the church, and open to the unity of the church — as the Reformers wanted to serve the true catholic church in their time, "catholic" in the sense of the Apostles' Creed: "I believe in the Holy Spirit, the holy catholic church."

While this book is foremost an overall explanation of crucial tasks facing the current state of doing Protestant theology, it contains basic information on the foundation of theology, hermeneutics, biblical theology, church ministry, and Christian ethics, as well as central doctrinal topics, for example, Christology, God the Spirit, church, Scripture (canon), providence, election, justification, the sacraments, and eschatology.

The chapter "What Dare We Hope — at the Beginning of the Third Millennium?" is based on a lecture given October 27, 2000, at Károli Gáspár Reformed University in Budapest. Former versions of the chapter "A Shared Hope for Jews and Christians" were lectures delivered at the Protestant Faculty of Theology of Karl's University in Prague October 16, 2001, and at the University of Virginia in Charlottesville October 20, 2003. I presented a first draft of the chapter "No Fear of Dogmatics!" in 1997 at symposia of the Divinity School of Duke University in Durham, North Carolina, and the Faculty of Protestant Theology in Bonn. Later on I elaborated this paper as a section of my book *Gateways to Dogmatics,* which was mainly written in Princeton, New Jersey. This new version is a response to approving and critical comments on that part. A first draft of the chapter "God Creates Faith — Do We Consent?" was a lecture delivered at Loyola College in Baltimore, January 25, 1998. The chapter "Contextual Theology as a Challenge to Dogmatics" refers to a paper addressed to the first session of an American-European working group at the congress of the American Academy of Religion in Anaheim, California, in November 1989. I presented a revised version, together with "The Theological Grounding for Church Practices" and other topics, as the Dr. Jal Pavry Dasturzada Memorial Lectures in Oxford in May and June 1998. I delivered the lecture "Theological Reflections on the Political Changes in Europe" in Budapest and at several North American universities in the fall of 1993. It was published as "A Certain Speechlessness: Theological Reflections on the Political Changes in Europe," in *Soundings* 78 (1994): 163-77, and with some alterations as "Theological Reflections on the Political Changes in Europe," in *Lutheran Quarterly* 8 (1994): 15-28. A first version of the chapter "The Religious Dimension of American Self-Understanding and Its Crisis Today" was a public lecture delivered on November 13, 2001, as part of the series "America under Attack" by the North American Program of the University of Bonn, Germany. This program provides students of different fields (American studies, political science, law, sociology, geography, history, art history, theology) with an integrated curriculum. In this program I teach "Christianity in the U.S." A first English version was published in *Loving God with Our Minds: The Pastor as Theologian*, Essays in Honor of Wallace M. Alston, edited by Michael Welker and Cynthia A. Jarvis (Grand Rapids: Eerdmans, 2004). A shorter version of the chapter "Observations on the Current State of Reformed Theology" was presented to the ninth Calvin Conference in Davidson, North Carolina, January 30-31, 1998. Chapters 1, 3, 6, 9, and 10 as well as the chapter "Faithfulness to Scripture" of my book *Gateways to Dogmatics* composed my Warfield Lectures at Princeton Theological Seminary.

Steffan Davies (Oxford) helped me translate the chapter "The Art of Reading the Bible," and Professor Arthur Sutherland (Loyola College in Baltimore) the first version of "God Creates Faith — Do We Consent?" and of "The Religious Dimension of American Self-Understanding and Its Crisis Today." As always, my wife Annegrete was very supportive in correcting and improving all chapters. While I was visiting professor of Duke Divinity School in the fall semester of 2003, my upper seminar class discussed all chapters and helped me revise them significantly to make them more accessible to American readers. They noticed many threads that tie together the chapters, and their support enabled me to improve the pattern of my patchwork so that it developed like a quilt. C. Kavin Rowe (Duke Divinity School) improved chapters 3, 4, and 6, Susan and John Patterson (Ballina, Ireland) chapter 4. If not marked otherwise, the translation of German references are mine. The biblical references in most cases are taken from the New Revised Standard Version.

I thank Anne Weston of Duke Divinity School for her excellent redaction of seven chapters and my Princeton colleague Daniel L. Migliore for his understanding foreword. I am very grateful to the president of Princeton Theological Seminary, Professor Thomas W.

Gillespie, and to the dean of Duke Divinity School, Professor Gregory L. Jones, who invited me, and for the warm hospitality that my wife and I enjoyed in Princeton and in Durham. And last but certainly not least, William B. Eerdmans deserves many thanks for his willingness to publish this book.

Bonn, January 27, 2006   GERHARD SAUTER

CHAPTER 1

What Dare We Hope — at the Beginning of the Third Millennium?

Apparently — so it was reported by some in the fall of 1999 — John the Baptist had been brought back to life and was wandering about the desert in Judah, announcing that the end of the world was nigh; the television cameras were soon hard on his heels. Enthusiasts for the apocalypse gathered in Jerusalem, expecting the Messiah to arrive there at the turn of the millennium. "It's always the same!" others probably commented with a tired smile. Troubled spirits made the news as they kept the Israeli security authorities busy. And there were some attempts by radical Palestinians and right-wing Jews to light the fuse of the powder keg in the Middle East with their eccentric, apocalyptic behavior.

The opposite conviction is that history will carry on, without "if's," "and's," or "but's," regardless of groundbreaking changes, far-reaching fault lines, and abrupt cracks across the human landscape. People who hold this belief are inclined to regard any expectation of the end of the world out of the question because it could cloud the image of what is historically possible and historically effective.

Apocalyptic expectations then easily come to be seen as a characteristic of fanatics, agitators, and outsiders of all sorts, cases where faith and delusion are spoken in one breath. Expectations of the end of the world often demonstrate a strained attitude toward the course of history — an attitude that then becomes so overstrained that we distance ourselves from it at once and say, "We don't want anything to do with that!" How can we think our way into such ideas? What does the lifestyle associated with them open up for us? What are the reasons for them? How can all this be described in such a way that something that is of central meaning for those whose lives it has shaped does not strike us as odd or extravagant?

We have lost the sense for various spiritual experiences of ending and new beginning, and therefore the sense for the complexity of true hope. Absent such a sense, we are not able to judge if there is a sound, enriched, and far-reaching hope that can endure disappointments and, more importantly, afflictions. Most of us measure hope only by its effects on our acting, our striving for things to come without transcending what is possible anyway. A well-tempered Christian life seems to call for sobriety in our expectations so that we don't become disillusioned. At least this seems to be true for mainstream Protestantism, which is eager to conform to the course of history so as to contribute its best to that course and not distort it through exaggerated hopes. However, if soberness lacks true, sometimes even ecstatic, hope, it can be converted and perverted into mere repetition. Christian hope is many-layered. For instance, are we still capable of understanding the paradox of "waiting for and hastening the coming of the day of God," as 2 Peter 3:12 tells us? "Waiting for" means being steadfast instead of escaping the place God has given us. "Hastening" includes leaving behind what is really behind through God's judgment, while what enables us to do so is that looking backward no longer restricts us.

In 1999 and 2000, banners hung on the front of many German Protestant churches proclaiming "Every year is a Christ year." Intended as opposition to the spreading millennium fever, the slogan addressed particularly the Roman Catholic proclamation of the new millennium as an important step in salvation history and its intensification of the mission of the church and its propagation. By contrast, the slogan "Every year is a Christ year" avoided any illusion about evident progress in history that could be claimed by the church as significant for faith and hope. But the message implies: "There will be no real difference between last year and next year — relative to Christ they all remain the same!" That notion is correct concerning the presence of Christ in the proclamation of his death until he comes (1 Cor. 11:26), and concerning Christ's hidden presence in people who are in need (Matt. 25:35-45). But are we aware that Jesus Christ, the crucified and resurrected Christ who promises his presence, is the Coming One? Is the prayer of the early Christians in every worship —

Maranatha with the double meaning "Our Lord is coming" and "Our Lord, come!" (1 Cor. 16:22), maybe both in one breath — still vivid in our Sunday services? The slogan "Every year is a Christ year" sounds more like a magic formula for all blessings of Christ, which were, are, and will be present again and again. It evens up all hope and tells us: "Don't exaggerate and don't be presumptuous in expecting Jesus Christ — his saving presence is already here!"

Now that the great millennium spectacles are over, it may be the right time to think about the nature of changing times and times of change. The turn of the millennium, like the turn of every century and every new year, is the artificial product of our measurement of time; it is an arbitrary, or at least conventional, caesura but not a real break in the continuum of time. At most, the attention we paid to the turn of the millennium was an opportunity to pause. It made us look around before we were forced to move along because time inexorably pulls us along at the same pace as itself, even if we would rather stay a little longer and imagine that we can stem the tide of time. Like every notable change of digits, the date that we have been persuaded to take as the beginning of a new millennium provides us with the occasion for a look back and a look ahead. As we looked back, we connected pieces of stored information to what we had experienced, in order to place ourselves at a distance from both: the distance necessary to direct our attention to what is to come. As for the view of the future that had been formed in us, or that may have been just a construct of our imagination, we wanted to be a little clearer about what lies ahead, and we tried to achieve this by weighing up hopes and fears against each other. There was no more than that to what was pretentiously called the "threshold of a new epoch" — we merely thought in greater periods of time than at the usual end of each year.

Despite this, the view could be taken that we are hardly aware of true caesurae in the flow of time and that we very rarely notice how naively we stand at our starting point when part of the past really has come to an end. We are expected to make transitions, but their essence continues to elude us because we don't have the time to take our leave properly. Wasn't this the experience of many, and not just Europeans, when they were surprised by the fall of the Berlin Wall in 1989? That event aroused great hopes, which have since been fulfilled only partly, at best. But the hopes of many were also destroyed, suddenly unmasked as illusions. Their prospects collapsed, leaving only shards behind, shards that either cut other people too or caused old wounds to open and to bleed again and again. All this could and should make us conscious, in an exemplary way, of how basically speechless we are when it comes to articulating a profound change. We are unable to do more than simply discuss this change, unable to express it in such a way that it is clearly distinguished from the very things that did not change, the things that must not change, if history — as is said vaguely — is to "continue."

"Don't expect too much from the end of the world!" a Polish satirist warned a couple of years ago[1] — such paradoxical instructions probably wouldn't occur to a theologian! After all, should we expect any less from the end of the world than a radical change in everything? But the paradox is ambiguous. The satirist is playing a little on the phrase "end of the world," just as the propagandists of the apocalypse played with our expectations as they put out their promises. These include nothing less than a world revolution, for example — this is what the Polish satirist has in mind — which promises to build a new world from scratch on the ruins of the "old" world. That, as he says ironically, will become a painful illusion. Many things will indeed change, some things for the better maybe, but there will not be any really far-reaching changes in such a revolution. Our world will stay in its orbit, as long as we don't destroy the earth. But what can there be that well and truly deserves to be called "new"? Real newness has a different meaning to the prescriptions of time measurement, which distinguish what is later from what is earlier and momentarily establish the "newness" of things that are already old in the next second. We shall have to return to this question.

The deeper meaning of the phrase "the end of the world," however, is "Let us not hold back from expressing our ideas of the end!" Don't let them just lie dormant within us, for they can then slip into our subconscious and play an evil game there. What we really think about the end of the world reveals a great deal about how we see our present time. Our ideas are not mere fantasies that are cast far into an empty future. They shed light on what we see as our present time,

---

1. Stanislaw Jerzy Lec, *Allerletzte unfrisierte Gedanken,* trans. Karl Dedecius (Munich: Hanser, 1996), p. 13.

what elements we would like to keep, and what our dreams are. At the same time, any excessive anticipation of the future can endanger the sensibility for the gift of the present, deforming it to a mere transitional stage. Blaise Pascal (1623-62) has called this into question:

> We never keep to the present. We recall the past; we anticipate the future as if we found it too slow in coming and were trying to hurry it up, or we recall the past as if to stay its too rapid flight. We are so unwise that we wander about in times that do not belong to us, and do not think of the only one that does; so vain that we dream of times that are not and blindly flee the only one that is. The fact is that the present usually hurts. . . .
>
> Let each of us examine his thoughts; he will find them wholly concerned with the past or the future. We almost never think of the present, and if we do think of it, it is only to see what light it throws on our plans for the future. The present is never our end. The past and the present are our means, the future alone our end. Thus we never actually live, but hope to live, and since we are always planning how to be happy, it is inevitable that we should never be so.[2]

Don't we live in the memory of better things or in the hope of better things? *Do we live, or do we only hope to live?* This is a crucial theological task: not to be immersed in the present state of affairs and yet not to escape it!

I would like to outline the significant discernment of hopes within the last century, and I will focus on attempts to restructure the image of Christian life by means of this discernment of hope. This heritage remains important, either because there is a limited number of possible orientations recapitulated again and again or because there are unsolved problems. We will see that the reference to hope and the framing of hopes very often reshaped the whole concept of Christianity, but were later pushed aside by just the contrary valuation. Eschatology often is the field of radical changes in theological orientation.

As the nineteenth century gave way to the twentieth — in German Protestant theology, at least — remarkably little was said of hopes; theologians were generally far too convinced of the progressiveness of

2. Blaise Pascal, *Pensées*, fragment 172, trans. A. J. Krailsheimer (Harmondsworth: Penguin Books, 1966; reprint, 1981), p. 43.

Protestantism and its strength as the religion of an inner experience: of course, this inner experience must grow, but it does not depend on things to be hoped for. Religious self-certainty shaped life conditions in order to enrich human existence. Immeasurably capable of integration, religious experience would be perfectly able to keep up with breathtaking technological developments. Liberal Protestantism represented this outlook at its best in its journal the *Christian World (Die christliche Welt)*. All the more, Protestantism in the United States backed a moral reorganization of society that was completed by technology controlling our lives: the magazine the *Christian Century* was founded during this period. The title proclaimed the idea that "the twentieth century will become the embodiment of the Christian century." Aftereffects of this program are still to be found in current American world policy. The ecumenical movement also began under those hope-saturated conditions. In a world laid waste by wars and divided by religions and churches, hope could be found by joining up to face life together. We could prove our hope by our actions.

In 1946 the legal historian and sociologist Eugen Rosenstock-Huessy published *The Christian Future or the Modern Mind Outrun*.[3] Rosenstock-Huessy had emigrated from Nazi Germany to the United States, and his book spoke to a period in which Germany was busy coming to terms with the immediate present. But in the United States, visions of the future of humanity were blossoming. Rosenstock-Huessy aimed to remind his readers of the Christian hope of salvation, a hope that had become the main thrust of Western history. The hope of salvation set a static social and intellectual order in motion and proved itself to be so intensely alive, time and time again, that it brushed away any cobwebs that had formed. It overcame backward-looking thought and set up a new way of thinking that could help trigger the battle for peace and justice. Theology perceived this way would be a consciousness that is always ahead of its time and demands appropriate action.

In sharp contrast to such a hope interwoven with public life and social history, German theological existentialism, represented by Rudolf Bultmann and Friedrich Gogarten, pleaded in 1954 for a "pure

---

3. Eugen Rosenstock-Huessy, *The Christian Future or the Modern Mind Outrun* (London: Jarrold and Sons, 1947).

hope," an attitude of sheer openness facing a future that could not be construed and planned. The future of Christian hope is not related to any extrapolations of technical knowledge or social utopias. Real hope and those construed futures are incomparable, even in ethical terms. There is no hope outside the very personal openness to an unknown future. In a broadcast discussion entitled "The Christian Hope and the Problem of Demythologization," Bultmann was asked by his disciple Günther Bornkamm what he had to say about the expectation of the cosmos in travail, which (according to Rom. 8:19ff.) longs for the revelation of the children of God. Bultmann calmly replied that this longing did not affect him. He could only say with Luther, "Christian hope knows that it hopes, but it does not know what it hopes for."[4]

As a junior theology student, I was curious about this authoritative reference and looked it up in Luther's works. And I found that Bultmann was wrong — that was my first step into historical-critical research. In fact, Luther says in his *Lectures on Romans* (1515/16): "Thus hope changes the one who hopes into what is hoped for, but what is hoped for does not appear. Therefore hope transfers him into the unknown, the hidden, and the dark shadows [into inward darkness] so that he does not even know what he hopes for, and yet he knows what he does not hope for"[5] — that is, that which you can expect naturally. Luther describes the dramatic process that gives birth to hope created by God's acting, which again we can only conceive, even suffer. We are forged and enabled to "[hope] against hope" (Rom. 4:18) — transferred into hope as spiritual dimension.[6]

In Romans 4:16-25 Paul paraphrases the story of Abraham facing his own inability to pass on the blessings promised to him. He is tempted by the dark, realistic thoughts that he has no reason for hope because he and his wife are much too old to have a son. Abraham has concluded this by himself, now he is hopelessly confined to himself.

4. Günther Bornkamm, Rudolf Bultmann, and Friedrich Karl Schumann, *Die christliche Hoffnung und das Problem der Entmythologisierung* (Stuttgart: Evangelisches Verlagswerk, 1954), p. 47.

5. In *Luther's Works*, vol. 25, ed. Hilton C. Oswald (St. Louis: Concordia, 1972), p. 364.

6. Cf. Gerhard Sauter, "Hope — the Spiritual Dimension of Theological Anthropology," in *Spirituality and Theology: Essays in Honor of Diogenes Allen*, ed. Eric O. Springstedt (Louisville: Westminster John Knox, 1998), pp. 101-11.

But God calls him: "Come out and look!" Abraham is called to see in order to learn to hope. Abraham confronts the impossibility of grasping the heavens and of finding consolation in the uncountable stars. But at the same time, his seeing creates a departure from himself, a looking away from himself, and an emptying of his heart for the sake of something greater, for the sake of God's promise. Abraham's faith grows silent in the face of God (Gen. 15:1-6). In Paul's view, Abraham is already transferred to the cross of Golgotha and to Jesus' tomb on Easter morning. The Christ narrative does not outrun the paradigm of hope — on the contrary, it demonstrates how to talk of God in a new way, and thereby, in the peculiar movement of "hoping against hope," hope is also talked of anew. With the resurrection of Jesus Christ comes revelation of *who God is*, in whom Abraham believed without knowing the significance of hope in maintaining his confidence.

In the 1960s Ernst Bloch's voluminous work *The Principle of Hope* (published in West Germany in 1959) brought us to a different stage.[7] Bloch argued in favor of hope as vigorous, stimulating human energy to imagine possibilities and to anticipate their reality in order to bring them into effect. In 1964 Jürgen Moltmann's *Theology of Hope*, one of the theological best sellers of the last century, adopted this hope — consonant with the widespread readiness for new departures, the overcoming of the status quo, a sociocritical outbreak and breakthrough. In a core section Moltmann states:

> The transforming mission . . . seeks for that which is really, objectively possible in this world, in order to grasp it and realize it in the direction of the promised future of the righteousness, the life and the kingdom of God. Hence it regards the world as an open process in which the salvation and destruction, the righteousness and the annihilation of the world are at stake.
>
> Future as mission shows the relation of today's tasks and decisions to what is really possible, points to open possibilities in the real and to tendencies that have to be grasped in the possible.[8]

---

7. Ernst Bloch, *The Principle of Hope*, trans. Neville Plaice, Stephen Plaice, and Paul Knight, 3 vols. (Cambridge: MIT Press, 1986).

8. Jürgen Moltmann, *Theology of Hope: On the Ground and the Implications of a Christian Eschatology*, trans. James W. Leitch (New York: Harper and Row, 1967), pp. 288-89.

To a great extent, the idea of the world as the *laboratorium possibilis salutis,* a laboratory of salvation to be accomplished, has shaped this face of hope. Its profile was formed by attacks on Christian existentialism and private piety, which decline to get involved in society as its fortunes flow and ebb. Moltmann became one of the most influential critics of Christian inwardness.

But what appeared to be the immeasurably wide scope of human action has narrowed dramatically since then. This scope has been replaced by a new sensibility for the limits of our world, for its givenness, for the limitations of our possibilities, and especially for the linkage of creative possibilities with global life conditions. There is no longer an urgent search for chances to act; otherwise history will collapse. Bloch's title, meanwhile, is quoted even in the mass media but denoting, ironically, a desperate heroism, which is left to the principle of hope because there is no real, promising alternative. Or it is perceived as a sample of illusions, which might be helpful because they bridge a ruthless, dead-end reality.

Let us not forget people who were born in the 1960s and grew up conscious that they were living near the very end of civilization, facing the imminent nuclear self-destruction of humanity. I can never forget the voice of a younger colleague who exclaimed, "I am one of the generation who thought it was the last one on earth."

Without being pessimistic, we can say that the readiness for new departures of the 1960s has disappeared, and the insight into the boundaries of growth has contributed to this sobering. What has remained is the fear that mankind could bring about its own end sooner or later — not only in a nuclear war, but also gradually, by irresponsibly destroying the conditions for life.

Finally, I wish to consider the slogan "the end of history." I don't want to elaborate on the political slants that have been laid on this image. The slogan is widespread among contemporaries who see no cultural space for moving on, especially those social and cultural critics who expected another world order and who now fear a political-economic ice age from which the future must be freed so that it can again become fit for human beings.[9] These critics take issue with the

---

9. For example, Jürgen Moltmann, *The Coming of God: Christian Eschatology,* trans. Margaret Kohl (Minneapolis: Fortress, 1996), pp. 44-46, 199-202, 232-35.

projected "global marketing of all things." And yet the horror might go considerably deeper than that: *an end looms when no other alternative seems to present itself* — a terrifying scenario that freezes historical thought.

On the other hand, the sciences shake our confidence that life will continue — that the world will continue to exist for an unforeseeable length of time.[10] All long-term forecasts speak against hope. Arnold Benz summarizes his book *The Future of the Universe: Chance, Chaos, God?* as follows: "All forecasts of the future, whether they are made for living beings, planets, stars, galaxies or universes, point toward disintegration: the sun will cool down, Earth will be lost in space, and even the matter of the universe will undergo radioactive decay. For this reason there is no scientific basis for hope."[11]

Cosmological explanations lead to the theory that the world will come to an end by cooling down, slowly but surely, or exploding into a ball of flame. The general prognosis of ossification, decay, and decline has a paralyzing effect because it gives us no perspective to which we can actively adapt. This horrifying vision of extinction objects to the ambivalent awareness of life expressed in the commonsense statement "Life goes on!"

Long-standing pillars of hope — such as the feeling of being embedded in a family, a nation, or a far-reaching "mission" — are now crumbling away. Negative cosmological theories destroy the illusion that I am and remain a tiny part of a whole that, in terms of its continuing existence, I can take for granted. As I lose this illusion, I also lose the goal of integrating myself in a wider context. This goal of integration fulfilled the need for both affirming and overcoming myself. Both needs appear pointless when the permanence of the world is denied. Now there is an emptiness that lurks at the border of our daily dealings with life: the emptiness in which humanity is not only off center, but appears to lack any measures, certainly any human measures. It is the emptiness of the Unknown and Inconceivable, of stars, galaxies, and black holes, of unpredictably falling meteors and inevitable catas-

---

10. Cf. John Polkinghorne and Michael Welker, eds., *The End of the World and the Ends of God* (Harrisburg, Pa.: Trinity, 2000).

11. Arnold Benz, *Die Zukunft des Universums: Zufall, Chaos, Gott?* (Düsseldorf: Patmos, 1997), cover.

trophes. The "science fiction" myths of a popular culture seem to be in alliance with the predictions of scientific cosmologies. The question whether there is extraterrestrial life as a contemporary expression of human beings' amazement about themselves may have endangered human existence. By looking for another "existence," people may be hoping for a possibility to confront their own improbability with some measure of certainty.

In this sense, *the state of having been created presents a reason for hope.* God's creation contains a double meaning of "end": creation both keeps the universe from ending and brings it to its end. Creation may be finite — yet it is kept from simply dropping out of existence. The threats and brushes with danger and the nihilistic perspective of a changed cosmology really only mark what was already present in a similar way in the doctrine of the *creatio continua,* of the continuing creation. What humanity experiences as its reality is threatened from all sides. In itself, it is not resistant to the possibility of destruction. When theologians speak of God's preservation of the creation, they reject the tendencies toward Deism: Deism presumes that the activity of the Creator is confined to some distant time at the beginning of the world's history. There is even more to the theological idiom of *conservatio,* "conservation," and *creatio continua.* It is also a statement about the nature of creation and the character of creatures. Both are seen as highly threatened, persistently surrounded by the danger of annihilation. The world as we know it is not in and of itself capable of resisting destruction. It may be ready for radical changes, but it is not ready to be exposed to chaos devoid of any remaining structures.

Modern Protestantism has strongly urged sobriety and has fought against withdrawal from the world. It has denounced the search for consolation in the life after death and turned hope into efforts to improve life before death. The power regarding hope that Protestantism can exert in public — also under the ecumenical banner of "peace, justice, and protecting the creation" — concentrates on averting an unnatural end to all things. It seeks to avoid a global catastrophe that could be caused precisely by the masses expecting too much from the end of the world — expecting a paradise, a heaven on earth — in aid of which we as human beings could alter the creation, converting it to sheer chaos.

This outside view of Protestantism, however, hides some signs of hope that have grown out of the theological work of the past decades. They are not so obviously recognizable as slogans of hope, but they help to discover the character of Christian hope and then to account for the hope that is in us. This, after all, is what 1 Peter 3:15 demands of every Christian.

This hope is the precondition of hopes for theology. But it is not given with our humanity. Ephesians 2:12 states very concisely: we heathen were alienated from the heritage of Israel, "having no hope and without God in the world." Early Christians knew, of course, that there is an ability to hope linked with every sound human condition: a hope that dies last. The trust in "the God of hope" (Rom. 15:13), on the contrary, is the "living hope through the resurrection of Jesus Christ from the dead" (1 Pet. 1:3), brought to life by God's promises; i.e., God is promising God's action, and God is acting in a promising way. This leads us to three crucial aspects of the theological account for hope.

First, the perception of God's promise was much enriched by Old Testament scholars in the fifties, especially by Gerhard von Rad in his *Old Testament Theology*[12] and by my teacher Walther Zimmerli.[13] Zimmerli opened up a new understanding of the *fulfillment of God's promises:* God works on his promises in a surprising way, shaping our expectations, not confirming and closing them. The Old Testament offers no simple scheme of promise and fulfillment that might be understood as prediction of certain events or constellations for the life of the people of God to be realized sometime later in history. Fulfillment does not mean the execution of something predicted by God, something finished at a certain time in such a way that people can assert: "It is done, from now on we ourselves can build up on this ground." In contrast, fulfillment characterizes the very special way and manner God acts to pursue his will. Therefore, fulfillment often shatters expectations based on God's promises; it reshapes them and leads to a renewed hope. The paradigm of this character of fulfillment is the story of the two disciples on their way to Emmaus (Luke 24:13-35). In this narrative the resurrected Christ encounters them and shows

---

12. Gerhard von Rad, *Old Testament Theology,* trans. D. M. G. Stalker (New York: Harper and Row, 1962-65).

13. Walther Zimmerli, *Der Mensch und seine Hoffnung im Alten Testament* (Göttingen: Vandenhoeck & Ruprecht, 1968).

them that the death and resurrection of the Messiah had been promised in the Scriptures. This confrontation with fulfillment is linked to
a renewed reading of the Scripture — an art of reading the Scripture
told by Jesus Christ himself, the Crucified and Resurrected One.

I wonder if this perception of promise and fulfillment transforming expectations might helpfully guide American Christians. In the
United States, there was and remains a strong tendency to perceive
American history as a continuation of some of the Old Testament stories like the exodus, the conquest of the Promised Land, the struggle
to build a new society as a model for other nations, and more recently,
the claim for social justice and liberation. Americans hold firm to divine promises already fulfilled and settled, and others not yet fulfilled
and therefore to be searched for in the present time and in the time to
come. But God's promises are not blueprints for history. They are
given to the people of God in order to create faith in God's acting and
therefore establish hope that is bound to this acting like an anchor —
the symbol of Christian hope. God's promises are heard and understood in the process of perceiving and pointing to God's judging and
saving work. Our explanations of hope are parts of a continuing attempt to articulate this perception.

Paul stated the promise of justice more precisely as the revelation
of the righteousness of God (Rom. 1:17). This new formulation of the
promise of justice is based on the fulfillment of this promise in the
Christ story. Of course, this fulfillment does not at all wipe away our
longing for social justice, but it shapes it critically through the notion
that every attempt to "make" things or relations just is endangered by
human self-righteousness. Justification is and remains God's judging
and saving work. God sustains and enables us to become just, but
only God justifies. We always remain dependent on God's judgment.
God opens us for consent to God's will.[14] So we are called to follow
God's work, even to cooperate with it, in our striving for justice in all
realms of life.

Another example is the promise of peace. Paul speaks of the peace
of God that comes to those who are justified by faith (Rom. 5:1). He
goes on: "We also boast in our sufferings, knowing that suffering produces endurance, and endurance produces character, and character

---

14. See chap. 5, in this volume.

produces hope, and hope does not disappoint us, because God's love has been poured into our hearts through the Holy Spirit that has been given to us" (Rom. 5:3-5).

This is a theological, not a psychic, sequence: it is the chain of fulfillment and promise that creates and sustains hope. Peace is given to us in the unity of the Spirit in the bond of peace (Eph. 4:3). We are called to be faithful to this peace, to keep the bond of peace, to be bound to the promise to become more and more united with God and God's work, to grow in peace. "For we are what he has made us, created in Christ Jesus for good works, which God prepared beforehand to be our way of life" (Eph. 2:10). The promise of peace is also fulfilled in God's work of reconciliation (2 Cor. 5:18-21). God reconciled the world to Godself in Jesus Christ. For this reason Christians are ambassadors for Christ. They beseech and implore people to be reconciled with God. They can be reconciled with each other only if they become reconciled with God because they no longer face each other as enemies or as ones driven by competition. We cannot understand large parts of the New Testament in another way as the witness of struggling with such new formulations of God's promises in the light of the Christ event. The art of reading the Bible in such a way necessarily gives way to hope.

Second, the New Testament as a whole might be read as a document of dramatic endeavors to articulate the *newness* of God's acting on and in Jesus Christ. The critical point of all our images and conceptions of ending and new beginning is the contrast between true newness and mere novelty. What is so new that it will never be old, but everlasting? The witnesses speaking in the New Testament experienced "the end" in the crucifixion of Jesus — and his new life in the resurrection — but in such a way that they were terrified. Despite their traditional understanding of resurrection from the dead, their encounter with a life united forever with the reality of God shook them and rendered them speechless. Many parts of the New Testament wrestle with the language, the elements of which are old and often old-fashioned, but which become apt and even sufficient to bear the newness of God's acting. I propose an art of reading the New Testament from this perspective, as one among others. The notion of newness might help us come to terms with so many claims for newness in our time, especially in a society such as the American, infused with images of newness as ultimate cultural values.

Third, there is the intimate connection between terms that seem to be contradictory or at least inconsistent with one another. In the last century and even earlier, numerous contrarieties defined the Christian hope relative to hopes in the cultural context. For example: transforming, even radically changing activity versus escapism; hope as radical openness to an unknown future against futurology; hope nourished by insights in the course of history — or in opposition to the status quo — versus hope arising from personal inner life withstanding destructive powers from outside. But I have hope that we will discover the spiritual unity of reserve and activity, of vigilance and imperturbability, of silence and witness, of patience and engagement. Hope, which is not self-referential but open to what is hoped for, confidently tackles the needs of today. Those *dialectics shape the momentum of hope.*

What constitutes true Christian hope at the beginning of the third millennium? John Calvin stated in his Geneva Catechism of 1537: "Hope is nothing else than the expectation of the things that faith has believed to be truly promised by God."[15] What can we perceive as this promise, how do we read the figure of its realization, and do these shape our everyday expectations? Will we wait at the same time for the transfiguration of our notion when God "fulfills" his promises in his own, often strange way? Are we open for groundbreaking surprises? The answers to these questions will characterize our hopes at the beginning of the new millennium.

15. John Calvin, *Instruction in Faith* (1537), trans. Paul T. Fuhrmann (Philadelphia: Westminster, 1949), p. 55.

CHAPTER 2

A Shared Hope for Jews and Christians

Remember that you were at that time [before Jesus Christ died and incorporated you in his story] without Christ, being aliens [alienated] from the commonwealth of Israel, and strangers to the covenants of promise, having no hope and without God [*átheoi:* atheists] in the world. But now in Christ Jesus you who once were far off have been brought near by the blood of Christ.

EPHESIANS 2:12-13

For in him [Jesus Christ] every one of God's promises is a "Yes" [they are corroborated] in God. Therefore, through him [Christ] we confirm the Amen ["Yes, it is so!"] to the glory of God.

2 CORINTHIANS 1:20[1]

These two passages are indispensable and decisive for the biblical understanding of a hope that is not "essentially human." Hope in general may play out as a vital longing for a better future, or as the faculty of transcending the present time in order to survive. But no matter how it is manifest, the hope that God creates is given to those God elected. No one can "possess" this hope, which is positive precisely because

---

1. My paraphrase. The NRSV reads: "For in him every one of God's promises is a 'Yes.' For this reason it is through him that we say the 'Amen,' to the glory of God."

God plants and nourishes it. An essentially human hope, on the other hand, is always ambivalent because its goal might be uncertain: that is, a human hope could be corroborated *or* disappointed. That Christians are called to *share* this God-given hope is due to the amazing grace of God who grants them participation in the covenant of promise. God also provides the people of the "commonwealth of Israel" with this hope. As this hope is God-given rather than human, I can refer only to a shared hope *for* Jews and Christians, not to any shared hope *of* Jews and Christians. Some Jews speak and write eloquently about hope (e.g., the philosopher Ernst Bloch), while others are reluctant to talk about any hope that is more than the care for the needs of suffering people (e.g., Holocaust survivor and Nobel laureate Elie Wiesel). The same is true for Christians. This essay attempts to further the conversation from a Christian perspective.

If one argues only historically, comparing Jewish and Christian traditions, one gets the simple but misleading idea that Christians have inherited a Jewish perception of hope and have partly transformed it. Early Christian writings frequently recall expectations found especially in the message of the prophets of Israel and in apocalyptic texts. They repeat some of these expectations (e.g., ultimate justice and peace, the new heaven and earth, the resurrection of the dead), while other expectations, like the promised land (understood as the restoration of living conditions under the reign of David and Solomon), seem to be dismissed. Are expectations such as these "fulfilled" by the death and resurrection of Jesus Christ? Before we can address this question, we must precisely interpret the word "fulfillment." "Fulfillment" means that God will realize his promises in *his* own and strange way, often in a way contrary to human expectations that might be nourished by these very promises. This interpretation has been the proclamation of the prophets of Israel. With this understanding, a renewed listening to the promises of God awakens hope in God. Therefore, fulfillment does not at all mean that God's promises are divine predictions to be fully realized at some point in the future, and that they will be old news after this future has become present and past time. Nor have God's promises been transformed in such a way as to nourish a continuing hope, perhaps in a more idealistic or even utopian way (e.g., to imagine the kingdom of God as a "spiritual unity" of humanity, a perfect universal society), a hermeneutic transformation very common among Christians. And, finally, God's promises are not meant to create an expectant lifestyle of continual looking for breakthroughs in the present, miserable state of affairs, as modern Christian adaptations of idealistic and neo-Marxist theories suggest.

An understanding of these notions of promise, hope, and fulfillment, as I will show, is vital, and even urgent, to the Jewish-Christian dialogue.

It seems to me that the crucial task for Christian theology is to understand rightly how the "fulfillment" of God's promises is based on the expectation of Jesus Christ as the Coming One,[2] who brings God's judging and saving presence to all people. This expectation is shaped by the fervent hope for the coming of Christ.[3] Jesus Christ was, is, and will be the Coming One. According to the Creed of Constantinople (381), the confession that is the most universally accepted of all the formulas of the early church, Jesus Christ, the Crucified and Risen, who "sits on the right hand of the Father, . . . will come again with glory to judge the living and dead."[4] Apart from a small number of "messianic Jews" in Israel and even more in the United States, Jews on the whole do *not* agree with Christians on this expectation. How can we therefore conclude that there is joint hope of Jews and Christians? To the extent that Jews and Christians share the same expectation of the end of the world and of a new creation, we find a joint hope. However, when it comes to the hope of Christ as the Coming One, the hopes of Jews and Christians differ markedly. Most Christians hope that Christ will "come again." Yet, why must he come *again?* Is it so he can complete once and for all the task for which he "came" as Savior two millennia ago? Why should this be necessary? Were his life and death not sufficient? Is "salvation" in its fullest, most realistic, and universal sense still to be expected? Furthermore, for Jews who did not convert to Christianity and who maintain hope for a still-to-come savior, is there another perception of salvation and redemption, or another kind of hope?

2. Cf. Gerhard Sauter, *What Dare We Hope? Reconsidering Eschatology* (Harrisburg, Pa.: Trinity, 1999), pp. 47-50.

3. I would like to avoid the term "the coming again," because it may cause the misleading perception that Christ has disappeared for a while.

4. *Creeds of the Churches: A Reader in Christian Doctrine from the Bible to the Present*, ed. John H. Leith, 3rd ed. (Louisville: John Knox, 1982), p. 33.

This somewhat simplified comparison of Judaism and Christianity has determined the mutual perception of both for a long time. In truth, it is a somewhat subtler view than we have known, particularly from some figurative representations during the Middle Ages and early modern times. Jews have often been concerned about the propagandizing of a false messiah (e.g., Sabbatai Zwi [1626-76])[5] and have fought against misleading expectations in their midst. Such false hopes have usually been focused on an individual who is later unmasked and finally expelled from the community. To Jews, Jesus of Nazareth might have been one of those false messiahs. Among Christians, the "Antichrist" has sometimes been portrayed as a "typical" Jew.[6] Anti-Judaic polemics used the pejorative stereotypes "worldliness" (according to the semibiblical language: "in the way of the flesh")[7] and "visualized future state of affairs" (today we would label it "utopian thinking") as an alternative to our reality. In contrast, Christianity was portrayed as the advocate for "spiritualization" and "otherworldliness" — or, in existentialist terms: *Entweltlichung*, that is, "being taken out of the still existing world"[8] — which, according to Rudolf Bultmann, characterizes salvation as the subject matter of Christian faith and hope. Another point of contrast has been the concept of a twofold Jewish eschatology. On the one hand, there was a *national* hope, "in which the time of salvation to be brought in by God was thought of as the restitution of the idealized ancient kingdom of David."[9] On the other hand, *apocalyptic* texts nourished a hope that

5. Sabbatai Zwi has been portrayed as the crowned messiah as well. Cf. the sympathetic picture in Sharon R. Keller, ed., *Judentum in Literatur und Kunst* (Cologne: Könemann, 1995), p. 137.

6. For example, *Der Antichrist und die fünfzehn Zeichen vor dem Jüngsten Gericht* (Straßburg, 1480), facsimile in *Incunabel der Stadt- und Universitätsbibliothek Frankfurt am Main* Inc. fol. 116 I/II (Hamburg: Wittig, 1979).

7. For example, Saint Jerome in his *Commentary on Isaiah* (Isa. 11:15-16): "We teach that, what Jews or those of us who think in a Jewish way . . . still expect to come in the way of the flesh, has already happened spiritually, so that we . . . are not forced to think in a Jewish way." *Commentarius in Esaiam* IV [407/408], in Corpus Christianorum: Series latina, vol. 73 (Turnhout, Belgium: Brepols, 1963), p. 157.

8. For example, Rudolf Bultmann, *History and Eschatology: The Gifford Lectures* (Edinburgh: University Press, 1957), p. 36.

9. Rudolf Bultmann, *Theology of the New Testament*, trans. Kendrick Grobel, vol. 1 (New York: Charles Scribner's Sons, 1951), p. 4.

awaits salvation "from a cosmic catastrophe, which will do away with all conditions of the present world as it is."[10]

The Contrasting Pattern of "Already–Not Yet"

In recent times another quasi-temporal comparison has become more prominent: Jews only look forward to their salvation, for the ultimate fulfillment of the promises that God has given to them and has intended for them alone, and they therefore always hope for the better. The Christian hope is more complex, even dialectical. At best, Christians exist suspended between memory and hope in a "time between times." Their hope relies on the Christ event as the "already" of salvation — interpreted most often as being released from the binding forces of the world and gifted with liberty through direct unity with God. Add to the "already" the expectation of "not yet," meaning the consummation of the world. But the latter is often understood merely as a perspective of faith — or it is even left out, e.g., with the assumption that the eschatological expectation "was superseded in faith from the very beginning."[11] To the Christian, faith seems to contradict expectancy.

One of the most important biblical references to the idea of the "al-

10. Bultmann, *Theology*, p. 4; cf. Paul Volz, *Jüdische Eschatologie von Daniel bis Akiba* (Leipzig: J. C. B. Mohr [Paul Siebeck], 1903). 2nd ed.: *Die Eschatologie der jüdischen Gemeinde im neutestamentlichen Zeitalter, nach den Quellen der rabbinischen, apokalyptischen und apokryphen Literatur dargestellt* (Tübingen: J. C. B. Mohr [Paul Siebeck], 1934).

You may ask if the idea of this so-called national hope has been mixed up with the notion of Zionism as a movement toward Jewish nationalism. But it would not be fair to label any hope in antiquity as "national" because nations in the strict sense are products of the nineteenth-century political turmoil in Europe introduced by the French Revolution.

It might not be accidental that Gershom Scholem, a Zionist himself, also labels the "ancient prophecies" as "national eschatology" of the "End of the Day": "the reestablishment of the House of David," "the future glory of an Israel returned to God," "everlasting peace and the turning of all nations toward the one God." G. Scholem, "Toward an Understanding of the Messianic Idea in Judaism," trans. Michael A. Meyer, in *The Messianic Idea in Judaism and Other Essays on Jewish Spirituality* (New York: Schocken, 1971), pp. 1-36; quotation is from p. 6.

11. Hans Conzelmann, *An Outline of the Theology of the New Testament*, trans. John Bowden (New York: Harper and Row, 1969), p. 309.

ready" of salvation is the last word of Jesus on the cross, recorded in the Gospel of John: *"teléstai"* (John 19:30). But how is this to be translated: "It is finished" (NRSV) or "It is accomplished"? The cry of the Crucified does not tell us *what* is accomplished or finished, what has happened once and for all, or what it means for the course of history.

The scheme of "already–not yet" strongly influenced the self-understanding of many Christians and, in some ways, of Jews who mirrored themselves opposite to the prevailing Christian self-understanding. This mirroring seems to provide sharply contrasting pictures: Jews and Christians view one another by sketching "the other" as the counterpicture or "negative" of their own self-portrait. From early on this technique of facing each other substituted for seriously listening to each other; understanding came about through caricature rather than dialogue.

The following passages indicate that this pattern persisted in the last century; it persists perhaps even in our own time. The first two are taken from a memorable discussion between Martin Buber, the famous Hasidic philosopher of religion, and Karl Ludwig Schmidt, the New Testament scholar of the Protestant faculty of theology at the University of Bonn. Their attempt to start a dialogue took place in the Jewish teaching house in Stuttgart on January 14, 1933, just seventeen days before Adolf Hitler won the German election and seized absolute power. Some months later Schmidt was expelled from his position at Bonn and was forced to emigrate to Switzerland. Buber describes his picture of the Christian church as follows:

> The church is built on its faith in Christ having arrived [*Gekommensein*] as the salvation that is given to humanity from God. We, Israel, *are not able* to believe that. . . . We *sense* the unredeemed state of the world. The church explains this sense as the consciousness of *our* not being redeemed. But we cannot but understand this sense differently.
>
> Redemption of the world cannot be separated from the completion of creation, and it is unswervingly united with it, with the constitution of a unity that is no longer obstructed in any way, that does not suffer contradiction anymore, that is realized in all the variety of the world, and is one with the fulfilled Kingdom of God. We are not capable of "anticipating" a redemption of the world that has

already been carried out, yet only in part, e.g., a soul that has already been redeemed, though also to us, in our mortal hours, redemption and being redeemed is revealed. We do not notice a caesura in history. We do not know a midpoint, but only one goal, the goal of the way of God who does not stop on his way.[12]

Schmidt replied: "Like the Jews, we, Christians, are also looking toward the end. But we dare do this only for the fact that God has already realized [or: set into motion] the end in Jesus Christ. About the coming of Jesus Christ at the end of days, we speak only of a Second Coming, his coming again."[13]

Here Schmidt confines the comparison to a certain event of time and history: Jesus Christ *is* the end, or at least the turning point, of history. This illustrates a way of speaking that became common in modern Christian theology, that sometimes directly opposed Judaism, or even claimed to supersede the story told in the Old Testament. With this understanding, the question must be asked: How can we speak of the "end of history"? What does it mean to talk about an "end of history" in retrospect, without an overview of the totality of all events? Or could there be a double meaning for the term "history"? Rudolf Bultmann states that the expectations of Jesus and his early followers were shaped by apocalyptic images and not by the nationalistic Jewish hope. He argues along these lines: "The new people of God has no real history, for it is the community of the end-time, an eschatological phenomenon. How could it have a history now when the world-time is finished and the end is imminent! The consciousness of being the eschatological community is at the same time the consciousness of being taken out of the still existing world. . . . Therefore neither the Christian community nor the individuals within it have any responsibility for the present world and its orders, for the tasks of society and the state."[14]

But Bultmann goes on: the followers of Jesus had to deal with the problem that their imminent expectation failed. The radical expectation of the imminent catastrophic end of world history could not last.

12. "Kirche, Staat, Volk, Judentum," in Karl Ludwig Schmidt, *Neues Testament–Judentum–Kirche: Kleine Schriften,* ed. Gerhard Sauter (Munich: Christian Kaiser, 1981), pp. 149-65; quotations are from pp. 158f.

13. "Kirche, Staat, Volk, Judentum," p. 164.

14. Bultmann, *History and Eschatology,* p. 36.

Christ did not come again in the way that the early Christians expected his coming, the parousia. The Christian church was forced to survive at the price of accommodation to the "world" and its history. As a result, the history of the church has been declining since the origin of the Christian faith. Bultmann envisions the Pauline dialectic in this way: "The real historicity of the Christian life becomes apparent . . . from the fact that this life is a continuous being on the way, between the 'no longer' and the 'not yet.'"[15]

Still living in the world but being taken out from its "law" is the signature of the freedom by God's grace. This provides, as Bultmann argues, a new sense for history: Christians have received the Spirit as a token of the new world-time (the "aeon to come"), yet they continue to struggle with their "flesh," a struggle that challenges Christian freedom with the threat of tying a person to his or her past. Therefore, the Christian continues to need the dynamics of God's grace to overcome the power of the past and make possible a future that is not determined by human sin.

In this way, Bultmann suggests as a "solution" that the dialectic of freedom and bondage replace the notion of "time between time," between Christ having arrived and Christ's coming. There is no longer any serious expectation of Christ as the Coming One, as the judge of the living and the dead who will perform the finite redemption of the world. One side effect of this concept is that the portion of the creed cited above stands no longer as a living hope that nourishes and shapes the life of the church; it is reduced to an empty formula only to be recited in Sunday services.

Here I am reminded of a talk with the Jewish philosopher Ernst Bloch, who had published as his main work *The Principle of Hope.*[16] In 1963 he asked me why younger theologians (he mentioned Jürgen Moltmann and Wolfhart Pannenberg) were primarily concerned with an up-to-date explanation of the resurrection of Jesus Christ. Why, he asked, did they try to demonstrate that the Easter event was and is historically evident, at least evident by the history of its effects? Bloch

---

15. Bultmann, *History and Eschatology,* p. 46.

16. Ernst Bloch, *Das Prinzip Hoffnung* (Frankfurt am Main: Suhrkamp, 1959); English trans.: *The Principle of Hope,* trans. Neville Plaice, Stephen Plaice, and Paul Knight, 3 vols. (Cambridge: MIT Press, 1986).

compared their approach with that of prominent Protestant theologians like Adolf von Harnack and Ernst Troeltsch when he was a student at the beginning of the century. Harnack and Troeltsch were not interested in the Easter event at all, but rather in the quest for the historical Jesus. They memorialized the life of this religious hero as revelation of God's presence. Neither endeavor convinced Bloch at all. He argued that only the expectation of Christ as the Coming One could characterize true Christianity. The story of Jesus, from Bloch's perspective, could only be a grand awakening of genuine Jewish messianism. Therefore, Bloch would be much more content with recent movements in Western Christianity, which posit that redemption "is not accomplished yet," against an understanding of Jesus' cry on the cross, "It is accomplished," as a realized eschatology. "It is not accomplished yet" seems to be the signature of the Stations of the Cross, the way of human beings bearing their crosses.[17] Therefore, the last cry of Jesus, according to a now-preferred messianic interpretation, is to be perceived in such a way as to show that the Crucified One stayed the course because he was convinced that his passion opened up an opportunity to resist all powers of sin and death.[18] Compared with the notions of Martin Buber and Karl Ludwig Schmidt on the character of Judaism and Christianity, Bloch moves toward a hope for redemption that seems to unite not only Jews and Christians but all suffering people around the world.

A Revival of Messianism — and Its Crisis

In 1959 Gershom Scholem, the famous Jewish sociologist of religion, presented an essay in Switzerland to an international conference on religious studies. In "Toward an Understanding of the Messianic Idea in Judaism," he states:

> Judaism, in all of its forms and manifestations, has always maintained a concept of redemption as an event which takes place publicly, on the stage of history and within the community. It is an oc-

17. For example, *Es ist noch nicht vollbracht: Werkbuch zum Jugendkreuzweg,* ed. Peter Bleeser, Uwe Seidel, and Hans-Georg Ziebertz (Düsseldorf: Patmos, 1987).

18. For example, Jürgen Moltmann, *The Way of Jesus Christ: Christology in Messianic Dimensions,* trans. Margaret Kohl (San Francisco: HarperCollins, 1990).

currence which takes place in the visible world and which cannot be conceived apart from such a visible appearance. In contrast, Christianity conceives of redemption as an event in the spiritual and unseen realm, an event which is reflected in the soul, in the private world of each individual, and which effects an inner transformation which need not correspond to anything outside.[19]

Is this not a typical example of a self-portrait that is simply the counterpicture of "the other"? To which phenomena does one picture refer to the other? To what extent do the characteristics of the rejected other merely resemble the "negative" of the positive image of the self? Then the reverse might also be possible. Namely, that what is seen as negative of the other, or rather, what one negatively perceives and projects onto the other, in fact becomes attractive and even desirable for a new self-determination.

This reversal seems to be a widespread trend in contemporary Christianity. Many Christians today are reconstructing what was once their reproach, namely, thinking of "privacy" as an individualistic resort, or as something "reflected in the soul," and they are beginning to regret it. In the early 1980s, while revising Luther's translation of the Bible, German theologians and church officials tried to replace "the soul" with "life." They were hindered only by secular specialists in linguistics who argued that "the soul" cannot be erased from Christian anthropology! There was and is a trend to strongly emphasize that all significant elements of Christian faith, hope, and love must, as Scholem said, take "place publicly, on the stage of history and within the community." As a result, many theologians, especially those engaged in the Jewish-Christian dialogue in Germany, try to integrate Christian hope with certain "messianic ideas" so that Christians and Jews might embrace and rely upon a common and relevant religious basis of hope. At the same time, this conversion of thought attempts to liberate Christians from the reproach of retreating into their "life in faith" to escape the challenges of social change and the struggle of overcoming the segregation of races and religions. The historic Christian horror of messianism is suspected of serving as a tool for oppressing Jewish people and even for exterminating them.

19. Scholem, "Toward an Understanding," p. 1.

But now, we must notice and keep in mind that there is a context for the revitalization of messianism that must not be neglected. Only twenty-six years passed between the 1933 Buber-Schmidt dialogue and the remarks of Gershom Scholem, but the point of view changed significantly. In 1959 Scholem looked back on the founding of the state of Israel, while Buber viewed the preconditions of that struggle and the establishment of Israel as a second exodus and as a new conquest of the Promised Land. Now, the scattering of Jewish people, their time of living in the Diaspora, has ended. It is accomplished, not once and for all, but at least as a new beginning, even as a new era. In his *De Profundis* (op. 50b), composed in 1950, Arnold Schoenberg reinterpreted Psalm 130:8. To Schoenberg the psalm no longer meant the divine promise: "Yes, He *will release* Israel from all its sins"[20] (a promise taken up in the announcement of the birth of Jesus in Matt. 1:21). Instead, Schoenberg writes, "He *releases* Israel from all its sins," i.e., from all former bondage. The promise is fulfilled! In the founding of Israel, release has happened, and now it can be sung and heard with sounds of hopeful triumph.

A life based only on a *longing* hope has been transformed into a life that is challenged to preserve a *living* hope. This hope has been granted with conditions no longer dependent on *"a life lived in deferment,"* as Scholem provocatively calls it, "[a life] in which nothing can be done definitively, nothing can be irrevocably accomplished." He continues, "There is something grand about living in hope, but at the same time there is something profoundly unreal about it. It diminishes the singular worth of the individual, and he can never fulfill himself, because the incompleteness of his endeavors eliminates precisely what constitutes its highest value."[21] There is, therefore, "little wonder that overtones of Messianism have accompanied the modern Jewish readiness for irrevocable action in the concrete realm, when it set out on the utopian return to Zion. It is a readiness, which no longer allows itself to be fed on hopes. Born out of the horror and destruction that was Jewish history in our generation, it is bound to history itself and not to meta-history; it has not given itself up totally to Messianism."[22] Now we no longer deal with mere concepts; we strug-

---

20. NRSV: "It is he who will redeem Israel from all its iniquities."
21. Scholem, "Toward an Understanding," p. 35.
22. Scholem, "Toward an Understanding," pp. 35-36.

gle with troublesome, sometimes disturbing experiences that call us to a renewed clarification of our perception of hope and life in hope. Now we can no longer compare the abstract entities "Judaism" and "Christianity"; we must compare unique persons, Jews and Christians and others who are faced with the task of "giving an account of hope," and of being "accountable to everyone who raises questions about the hope that is in you" (1 Pet. 3:15).[23]

In this respect, let me concentrate on one point that is crucial. The scope of the phrase "the hope that is in you" has challenged the Christian churches time and again in relation to the political conditions of their environment. A striking example is the nineteenth-century idea of "the Christian state,"[24] especially of Hegel's philosophy of religion and political philosophy. It is no coincidence that Hegel contrasted Judaism to his perception of reconciliation in the Christ- and Christian-shaped *Geistesgeschichte.* "It was . . . in the Jewish people that God took [the Oriental] principle upon himself as the age-old grief of the world; for here we find the religion of abstract suffering, of the *one* Lord, against whom and despite whom the actuality of life stands its ground as the infinite willfulness of self-consciousness, and all that is abstract is bound together. The age-old curse is undone, it has been met by salvation, in that finitude has for its part validated its claim to be both positivity and *infinite finitude.*"[25]

Hegel concludes that for the Jewish people, relationship to God is troublesome precisely because of the unresolved tension that exists between a transcendent God and a temporal humanity. Therefore, Hegel criticizes Judaism for sticking to the understanding of an "unreconciled" state of the world, for assuming that God remains at a dis-

23. NRSV: "Always be ready to make your defense to anyone who demands from you an accounting for the hope that is in you."

24. Represented by Friedrich Julius Stahl, *Philosophie des Rechts,* 3 vols. (Heidelberg, 1830-37, reprint of the 3rd ed., 1878; Darmstadt: Wissenschaftliche Buchgesellschaft, 1963).

25. Georg Wilhelm Friedrich Hegel, *Lectures on the Philosophy of Religion,* vol. 2, *Determinate Religion,* ed. Peter C. Hodgson, trans. R. F. Brown, P. C. Hodgson, and J. M. Stewart (Berkeley: University of California Press, 1987), p. 231. See also Peter Cornehl, *Die Zukunft der Versöhnung: Eschatologie und Emanzipation in der Aufklärung, bei Hegel und in der Hegelschen Schule* (Göttingen: Vandenhoeck & Ruprecht, 1971), and Jürgen Gebhardt, *Politik und Eschatologie: Studien zur Geschichte der Hegelschen Schule in den Jahren 1830-1840* (Munich: Beck, 1963).

tance from the world, instead of participating in the dialectical process of the reconciliation between God and world in the history of the Spirit.[26] Thus, history becomes the arena of an ongoing fight for the preservation of this reconciliation in all areas of life — religion, art, culture, ethics, politics. We are engaged in an ongoing process of redemption as long as there is a true human history driven by the *Weltgeist* ("spirit of the world"). In his early writings, Hegel sketched the Jewish religion as the stumbling block of historical development because it is fixed on a perverse state of the world by a false, unredeemed consciousness. The young idealist philosopher Johann Gottlieb Fichte proposed a similar idea[27] — a philosophical variation of supersessionist theology.

But what has happened since then? Many Christians, perhaps the majority, lost the self-assurance that Hegel expressed, though he expressed it in a critical way by facing the social and political changes of his time. Today, apathy, or at least a skeptical attitude, often prevails. Many Christians believe that humanity at large is on the wrong track and the world is distorted, even perverse in some respect. How could Jews and others be thought of as subhuman *(Untermenschen)* in the midst of a culture that Hegel and others thought of as shaped by Christianity? That sounds like an empirical objection to the confidence of an ongoing process of reconciliation, and even more, of redemption. Even so, there are some hopeful signs of reconciliation in the political realm, but they are based on an awareness of the unredeemed state of the world.

Often this awareness accompanies a serious shift in the perception of salvation. How realistic is Scholem's profile of the Christian concept of "redemption as an event in the spiritual and unseen realm," or Buber's image of "a soul having already been redeemed," believed by contemporary Christians as a sign of a completed creation? Buber's characterization above of Jewish expectation not only

---

26. Hegel, *Determinate Religion*, p. 230: "this infinite universality of thought, which has no external existence or validity, acquires present actuality; and self-consciousness thus attains to consciousness of the actuality of the universal, it has the universal, the divine, as something that has come into the world as present in the world — God and the world reconciled [cf. 2 Cor. 5:19]."

27. See Hans Joachim Zeller, "Religionsphilosophische Studien zur Kontinuität des Problems der Negativität als geschichtliche Erfahrung" (Ph.D. diss., Cologne, 1975).

sounds convincing in light of the ongoing struggle for peace, justice, and preservation of creation, but sounds much more appropriate: "Redemption of the world cannot be separated from the completion of creation, and it is unswervingly united with it, with the constitution of a unity that is no longer obstructed in any way, that does not suffer contradiction anymore, that is realized in all the variety of the world, and is one with the fulfilled Kingdom of God." If you quoted this rich sentence today without referring to Buber, most Christians would think it a sufficient Christian understanding of redemption and salvation. They would be reminded of the Christ event, to be sure, but mainly as a starting point for the redemption of the world to come. This redemption is now generally thought of as a process in history,[28] perhaps not fully completed in world history, but moved toward fulfillment by the Christ story and by the power of Christ's Spirit. And if you added the following remark of Buber — "though also to us, in our mortal hours, redemption and being redeemed is revealed" — many Christians would understand it as divine encouragement to change the unredeemed state of the world as much as possible.

Is there now a new approach of Jews and Christians united in hope, perhaps even as a conceptual reconciliation? I must ask, however, if a "holistic" understanding of redemption as a historical process really covers the scope and spiritual depth of the perception of being redeemed *both* among Jews *and* Christians. This question seems urgent to me, especially considering some tendencies in recent Christian-Jewish dialogue. Let me touch upon two examples.

Longing for the Completion of the World

On January 10, 1996, the Synod of the Evangelical Church of the Rhineland extended its church order with the sentence: "It [the Evangelical Church of the Rhineland] testifies to God's faithfulness, which clings to his election of his people Israel. With Israel it hopes for new heavens and a new earth."[29]

---

28. Cf. Martin Seils, "Heil und Erlösung IV. Dogmatisch," in *Theologische Realenzyklopädie*, ed. Gerhard Müller, vol. 14 (Berlin: De Gruyter, 1985), pp. 622-37, esp. pp. 634f.

29. *Verhandlungen der 45. ordentlichen rheinischen Landessynode, Tagung vom 7. bis 11. Januar*

This supplement was thought of as a component of the church's confession "to Jesus Christ, the incarnate Word of God, the Lord who was crucified for our sake, resurrected and raised to the right hand [of God], which it [the church] is expecting." But remarkably, this confession did not determine the discussion that was needed to prepare the church to understand the meaning of this doctrinal extension. This confession no longer shaped real Christian hope as it is expressed, e.g., in 2 Peter 3:12-13 — "waiting for and hastening the coming of the day of God. . . . But, in accordance with his promise, we wait for new heavens and a new earth, where righteousness is at home [dwells]." The declaration of the synod would have been much more precise and helpful if it had been formulated like this: "According to the promise read in the Old Testament (Isa. 65:17), and therefore, including the people of Israel, and according to the promise confirmed in the New Testament (2 Pet. 3:13), and therefore, through and with Jesus Christ, the church hopes for new heavens and a new earth in which God's righteousness dwells."[30] But the debate showed that "to hope with Israel" meant moving on together for the sake of the completion of the world. The expectation prevailed that this perspective would unite the hope of Jews and Christians despite different traditional motivations. The debate also revealed that the extension of the church's doctrine was intended as compensation for the failure of Christianity to accomplish a comprehensive perception of redemption, a failure tragically documented in recent history, especially in the Holocaust.

It seems that four prominent North American Jewish historians and theologians, independent of the dialogue going on in Germany, supported this convergence of hope. The last criterion in their remarkable statement on Christians and Christianity, *Dabru Emet* ("Talk the truth!"), published in August 2000, reads:

1996 in Bad Neuenahr, statt Handschrift gedruckt (Düsseldorf: Office of the Synod, 1996), pp. 88-94; reprinted in *Gottes Treue — Hoffnung von Christen und Juden: Die Auseinandersetzung um die Ergänzung des Grundartikels der Kirchenordnung der Evangelischen Kirche im Rheinland*, ed. Katja Kriener and Johann Michael Schmidt (Neukirchen-Vluyn: Neukirchener Verlag, 1998), p. 81.

30. This was the — unsuccessful — proposal of the Protestant faculty of theology of the University of Bonn (in *Gottes Treue*, p. 85).

Jews and Christians must work together for justice and peace. Jews and Christians, each in their own way, recognize the unredeemed state of the world as reflected in the persistence of persecution, poverty, and human degradation and misery. Although justice and peace are finally God's, our joint efforts, together with those of other faith communities, will help bring the kingdom of God for which we hope and long. Separately and together, we must work to bring justice and peace to our world. In this enterprise, we are guided by the vision of the prophets of Israel:

> It shall come to pass in the end of days that the mountain of the Lord's house shall be established at the top of the mountains and be exalted above the hills, and the nations shall flow unto it . . . and many peoples shall go and say, "Come ye and let us go up to the mountain of the Lord to the house of the God of Jacob and He will teach us of His ways and we will walk in His paths." (Isa. 2:2-3).[31]

Thus, the promise of the pilgrimage of all people toward Zion justifies the hope that unites Jews and Christians: specifically that both, "each in their own way," recognize the "unredeemed state of the world" and face the task addressed to them.

Who can ignore the depressing states of oppression in our world — the suppression of human dignity, the segregation, the irreconcilability of peoples, and the failure to acknowledge the lack of basic human needs of millions of people? And who would not agree that we must fight against these scourges of our world today with all the resources that are accessible to us? There's no question about it! But we cannot overlook or try to silence what Jews and Christians recognize "each in their own way" — the unredeemed state of the world. I am convinced that more can and must be said about these different perceptions. But *rather than compare concepts that are mostly the views of our own self-perceptions and the projection of these perceptions onto the other, we must seek to hear and listen to one another.* And our listening must include *how we speak in prayer to and with our Redeemer.* Therefore, the *in-*

---

31. *National Jewish Scholars Project: Dabru Emet. A Jewish Statement on Christians and Christianity* (Baltimore: Institute for Christian and Jewish Studies): www.icjs.org/what/njsp/dabruemet.html.

volvement of liturgy[32] must be more seriously noted in our dialogue. Otherwise, we might pass over the theologically crucial implication of social ethics.

Let us start with just *one* perception of this recognition. Christians are confronted with the last utterance of Jesus on his cross: "It is accomplished." What is accomplished? His passion was his path of obedience to God's will. He let himself be judged by God for all that humans did to him and therefore to God. He exposed himself to the human fault of confusing God's will and God's judgment with one's own justification. Jesus Christ allowed God's will to happen. He suffered God's acting in the midst of the human cruelty he was exposed to. He "became obedient to the point of death — even death on a cross" (Phil. 2:8), the death as a cursed one (Gal. 3:13). "He learned obedience through what he suffered; and having been made perfect, he became the source of eternal salvation for all who obey him" (Heb. 5:8-9). Through his death and resurrection, Jesus let God reveal what God alone has accomplished and what God alone reserves the right to do. Participating in Christ's story, we recognize a redemption that sensitizes us to the state of the world we are part of. We recognize further our existence as reconciled to God but in continuous need of reconciliation with God and with one another (2 Cor. 5:19-20). We believe then, as a catechism of the early church states: "Blessed be the God and Father of our Lord Jesus Christ! By his great mercy he has given us a new birth into a living hope through the resurrection of Jesus Christ from the dead" (1 Pet. 1:3).

This doxology shapes Christian endeavor to protect the creation and to serve and strengthen the fruits of redemption already effective in culture, knowing we are in need of forgiveness and justification.[33] Only if Jews and Christians, "each in their own way," receive and recognize redemption, a shared hope for Jews and Christians is neither a consciousness of being released from all iniquities nor a life lived in deferment. On the contrary, it is the hope that is aware of God's acting here and now, opening us up for the expectation of new heavens and a new earth, where God's righteousness dwells.

32. See, e.g., Peter Ochs, "Israel's Redeemer Is the One to Whom and with Whom She Prays," in *The Redemption: An Interdisciplinary Symposium on Christ as Redeemer*, ed. Stephen T. Davis, Daniel Kendall, and Gerald O'Collins (New York: Oxford University Press, 2004), pp. 121-46.

33. See chap. 9, n. 32, in this volume.

CHAPTER 3

The Art of Reading the Bible

An Art for Everyone?

Often I remind my students what an immensely precious gift it is that we are privileged to read the Scripture of the Jewish community as a part of "our" Bible, of the canon of the Christian church. We are invited to read it, to be involved in the story told there, even to pray the treasure of prayers that it contains. For us as for Jews it is not merely an ancient document of religious literature that may be interesting for comparative religious studies. Here we listen to the living Word of God, full of promises also for us.

My father, a minister and a member of the Confessing Church resisting the Nazi regime, was very concerned about the terrible loss of the Old Testament for the preaching, religious education, and biblical studies of the German church. There were not only anti-Jewish, racist polemics against the Old Testament, but also, since the nineteenth century, theological prejudices that blamed the early church for keeping the Old Testament in the canon. With his small salary, my father bought all the Old Testament studies he could get in the 1930s; we even found in his bookshelves a Jewish prayer book, after his very early death in 1945. Some of his most precious treasures were the recent critical edition of the *Biblica Hebraica* and the Septuagint. During the war, when we had to go in the basement of the house because of the bombing, we always had to take these books with us to keep them from being destroyed. Mostly there was no electric power; we thus had to use candles. Some of these books with their candle stains are now in my study, and whenever I read them I am reminded of a time when it seemed most unlikely that the Old Testament would enrich the German church again.

After World War Two, especially in the 1950s, Old Testament studies were the most vivid and challenging inquiries in German Protestant theology. There was a revival of interest in the story and history told by the Old Testament. But some prejudices remained. In 1965 I delivered my second thesis in theology (*Habilitationsschrift*) and a research lecture to the faculty of theology of the University of Göttingen. One member of the faculty opposed my graduation for teaching theology on the grounds that "He is not a Christian theologian, because he is too much rooted in the Old Testament."

Can we read the Old Testament without prejudice? Again, there is a fork in the road: Do we read the Old Testament only as historical precondition of the Christ event — or do we really listen to it expecting to hear the voice of "the God of Abraham, the God of Isaac, and the God of Jacob" (Mark 12:26), the God who raised Jesus Christ from the dead? There is a story in the New Testament that deals with this exact question.

"Do you understand what you are reading?" With this question Philip, the wandering preacher, greets the Ethiopian treasury official. The official — according to the story in Acts 8:26-39 — is on his way home from Jerusalem. He is reading a passage from the prophet Isaiah about a man who was sacrificed. "Do you understand what you are reading?" This is how Philip interrupts the official, unasked, as he reads out loud; and the official, who is obviously not at all embarrassed, admits that he does not understand: "How can I, unless someone explains it to me?"[1] He needs to be helped on his way — his chariot travels onward but he, the traveler, is unable to move from the spot in his reading. Philip explains the passage, and in such a way that it flows seamlessly into the sermon about Christ. The consequence of this good news is the baptism of the treasurer; having been baptized, he goes on his way rejoicing, having taken this decisive step in his life.

Do *we*, too, understand what we read in this passage? I can only touch upon different interpretations here: Is it the story of a conversion, on the pattern of a surprise attack that even people of high stand-

---

1. NRSV: "How can I, unless someone guides me?"

ing cannot escape?[2] (This interpretation has an additional nice point: that even a secretary of the treasury, of all people, cannot understand what he is reading to himself, even if it is just a devout text!) Or is it an example of early Christian mission, with the particular nuance that it is a God-fearing heathen who is received into the Christian church?[3] Are we given an early instance of the Christian community making use of prophetic texts for its preaching about Christ?[4] Or, to use the same interpretation but in a different and critical way: Are we shown an example of Jews having their holy traditions wrested from them by Christians — what Friedrich Nietzsche denounced as a crying injustice and a conscious misunderstanding of the highest degree? Nietzsche wrote: "[W]hat can be expected from the effects of a religion, which, during the centuries when it was being firmly established, enacted that huge philological farce concerning the Old Testament? I refer to that attempt to tear the Old Testament from the hands of the Jews under the pretext that it contained only Christian doctrines and *belonged* to the Christians as the true people of Israel, while the Jews had merely arrogated it to themselves without authority."[5]

Is the *interpretatio christiana,* the Christian interpretation, a robbery of the suffering servant of God, a new chapter in his suffering?

Yet these interpretations, however convincing and vigorous each one may be in itself, do not fully explore one aspect of the story: that the course of events is structured by the intervention of the Spirit. It is

2. Johann Albrecht Bengel, *Gnomon Novi Testamenti,* 2nd ed. (Tübingen: Johann Heinrich Philipp Schramm, 1759), p. 498: "Mira allocutio ad ignotum eumque magnum hominem. In sancta conversatione sine circuitu agendum de re ipsa" [A peculiar address to an unfamiliar and distinguished man as well. In a spiritual dialogue one must right away and straight come to the matter].

3. Jürgen Roloff, *Die Apostelgeschichte* (Göttingen: Vandenhoeck & Ruprecht, 1981), p. 139.

4. Roloff, *Die Apostelgeschichte,* p. 141, and Rudolf Pesch, *Die Apostelgeschichte* (Zürich: Benziger; Neukirchen-Vluyn: Neukirchener Verlag, 1986), pp. 292-93, draw attention to textual changes in the quotation from Isaiah that facilitate a christological interpretation.

5. Friedrich Nietzsche, "The Philology of Christianity," in *The Dawn of Day,* trans. J. M. Kennedy, in *Works,* vol. 9 (New York: Russell and Russell, 1964), pp. 84-86; quotation is from p. 85. Compare this verdict with Philip's question, which, besides, is formulated as a play on words *("ginoskein — anaginoskein"),* to link "understanding" and "reading." Nietzsche makes use of parody.

the Spirit who sends Philip to the spot, puts the Ethiopian in his path and finally takes him away, leaving the new Christian to go on his way alone, but not lonely. Is this how the main thread of events is formed? Is it not moved forward again and again by a *Spiritus ex machina*, a Spirit who appears like a theatrical effect, and does it thus gain a supernatural character?

Whether this is the case or not is probably decisive in our understanding of what we read. It seems to me that the interventions of the Spirit mark turning points in the narrative and interrupt the plot. We are stopped from simply going further. We have to pause — and to listen. Such interruptions put the question to us even more urgently: Do we really understand what we read there?

The structure of the text, it seems to me, points in this latter direction. Or even more provocatively: the text asks us how we are involved here. Two men come together under God's influence. What one of them tells the other of Christ draws the other into a text with an open meaning. Philip suggests this "way of reading" to the treasury official: he claims that the suffering servant of God stands for Jesus Christ, crucified and resurrected. The official understands this, and moreover, he receives the message of the prophet as a call to be baptized. He transfers himself into the ownership of Jesus Christ and (as is added by v. 37, a textual variant handed down in a part of Western tradition) professes his faith in Christ. Clearly, this is not based on a convincing recalling of the ancient text into the present that could be added to Philip's credentials as an interpreter. Rather, Jesus Christ, the suffering servant of God, meets the reader — first of all the official as he reads, but furthermore everyone who reads the story. Jesus Christ has not left behind some lasting influence that could have proceeded directly from Jesus' life. Jesus Christ established a tradition of proclaiming and receiving his message, his work, and his presence in such a way that he provided that we encounter Christ himself. In the power of the Spirit, through God alone, Jesus Christ brings about faith and creates his body of followers. In this respect the prophetic text is identified. Luke, who composed the Acts of the Apostles, indicates that this happens through the power of God's Spirit — and yet what is crucial is kept *open* precisely by this indication. If I wanted to read this story completely, I would really have to pause, in total silence, every time the Spirit was mentioned, and I would certainly be unable to read past those places. Or — in much the same way — I would have to emphasize the central points of the plot in such a way that my attention was drawn to what remains unsaid.

In his essay "Odysseus' Scar," the literary scholar Erich Auerbach characterizes the difference in style between biblical narrative and Homer's epic poetry. He characterizes Old Testament narratives as follows:

> The externalization of only so much of the phenomena as is necessary for the purpose of the narrative, all else left in obscurity; the decisive points of the narrative alone are emphasized, what lies between is nonexistent; time and place are undefined and call for interpretation; thoughts and feeling remain unexpressed, are only suggested by the silence and the fragmentary speeches; the whole, permeated with the most unrelieved suspense and directed toward a single goal (and to that extent far more of a unity), remains mysterious and "fraught with background."[6]

In the story of the Ethiopian official, too, only a few moments appear in the text: reading and its complications, preaching and baptism. How events move from reading to believing is neither said nor explained at all. This is a gap — and this is where the reader comes into play: the treasury official as a reader, and we, too, the readers of his story.

Perhaps Luke, as a Hellenistic author, is operating on the border between Old Testament storytelling and Greek epic narrative with its clear conclusiveness. Some suspect that his understanding of the Spirit indicates this transition to a hidden rationalization: God's Spirit as the director of salvation history, if not even as the puppet master in the background.[7] And yet the intervention of the Spirit in fact explains nothing, but makes it clear that the story does not develop from

6. Erich Auerbach, "Odysseus' Scar," in *Mimesis: The Representation of Reality in Western Literature,* trans. Willard R. Trask (Princeton: Princeton University Press, 1953), pp. 11-12.

7. Roloff, *Die Apostelgeschichte,* p. 139: "Philippus ist nur ausführendes Organ in einem Geschehen, bei dem der Geist selbst Regie führt" [Philip is only the executive in an event directed by the Spirit]; Ernst Haenchen, *Die Apostelgeschichte,* 7th ed. (Göttingen: Vandenhoeck & Ruprecht, 1977), p. 304, speaks of *"providentia specialissima,"* a very special providence.

within itself, that is, from the motives and opportunities of the people involved in it.

So it is with the question "Do you understand what you are reading?" that the question how understanding is constituted and constructed is first raised. The answer can be seen in the official's wish to be baptized: understanding has the same origin as faith, and the reception of faith is recognized in baptism. They have the same origin: both originate at the same time, they are there together, one does not come after the other, neither can be derived from the other, and even so, a difference is drawn between them. And they refer to each other: the text allows itself to be understood, and the reader comes to believe. The whole story is told in such a way as *to bring the reader into play*, in a still inexplicit way, *when the text is read*.

This notion of "being in the story too" is marked precisely by the fact that any transition from reading to baptism is *not* described. Without faith it would be impossible to read what can be read. Faith does not work like a pair of glasses, however, that allows us to decode the text; glasses can be taken on and off. Faith, on the other hand, is constitutive, like the retina, which makes sight possible in the first place but can only cast an image of what is real!

For the early father Jerome, who translated the Greek Bible into Latin or revised existing translations, this story was the key story for the art of reading the Bible, the *ars scripturarum*.[8] In one of his letters from when he was working on the translation, sent to a certain Paulinus, he writes that we naturally need instruction in all branches of science, arts, and technology. But it is only when reading the Bible that everyone thinks it is possible to get by without a teacher: "It is to the art of interpreting Scripture, and none other, that everybody feels a calling." (In comparison, Jerome attacks poetasters, would-be poets, with a quotation from Horace: "We all occasionally write poetry, whether we can do it or not.")[9] Written around 395, this letter served for centuries as the preface to all editions of the Vulgate, the Latin translation of the Bible.

8. Jerome, "Epistula 53: Ad Paulinum presbyterum" 5f., in Saint Jérôme, *Lettres*, vol. 3, ed. Jérôme Labourt (Paris: Les Belles Lettres, 1953), pp. 14-15.

9. Jerome, "Epistula 53: Ad Paulinum presbyterum" 7: "Sola scripturarum ars est, quam sibi omnes passim vindicent: 'scribimus indocti doctique poemata passim,'" *Lettres*, p. 15.

Now we have to ask about the content of the instruction that the official requests and that is granted to him: the official discovers himself as a part of the text. The reader belongs alongside the suffering servant of God; he is placed at the cross at Golgotha; he is led to the empty grave and he perceives Christ raised from the dead. So the act of reading suddenly turns into preaching about Christ and is fulfilled with the request to be baptized. *The text reads the reader.* And what was right for the official should be true for all following readers of the story. For the official's reading is and remains a highly involved process. And likewise, if you and I as readers of this story want to understand it, then we basically face it with as questioning a stance as the official before the text from Isaiah — even if Luke intended to give a few hints to help us understand it. We "know" the Christ story and are familiar with the Gospel; therefore, we are in fact not in the same position as the Ethiopian. But what do we really know? The Christ story opens us up for reading the Scriptures, the Old Testament as well as the New Testament. Reading the narratives or listening to narrated stories, we experience that we are involved and how we are incorporated. Does the prophetic message tell us the story of Christ calling for faith? This is not at all evident if we stick only to the text. The story embedded in the text does not go out of our sight like the official. It calls us just as the traveler from Ethiopia, even when we were baptized.

The official's reading in no way ends with his being baptized. He "went on his way rejoicing." It is not left to the whims of our imagination to think what further reading lies before him. True enough, our imagination is stimulated by the story, but at the same time it is formed in a particular way — even if it is not set fast. Continuing to tell the story means, at the same time, to perceive how the storyteller and the listener are embraced by it, how they become involved in it, the same as Philip and the Ethiopian. It is not simply a continuation, but rather a penetrative reading.

Therefore, the story does not invite us to go on in our own storytelling. Rather, we perceive ourselves as a part of the story of God acting on and with his people, with humanity, and with the world. We are not encouraged to develop further stories out of it and "read" an abundance of other possible stories "out" of this text, rather "into the text" — including stories in which we seem to be caught up. These kinds of continuations can easily lead to schematic repetitions. Then, segments of the narrative are recited, which are used as clichés for other stories. The characters in the plot are substituted, bringing their story with them, but reducing it in key places to the common denominator, which is already known. Christian devotional literature contains fatal examples. How often pious people claim having experienced the shock of Paul on the road to Damascus understood as a conversion experience that allows continuous glances back at the wrong, "old" life! How often was Luther's reformatory discovery of the justification only by faith and his subsequent resistance against the authority of the oppressive church officials stylized as a model for total independence of the religious subjectivity immediate to God!

To read biblical texts — not only stories, but also prayers, advice, visions, wisdom literature, letters — as parts of an overarching *hidden* story provides the surprise that we discover ourselves as being read in the story. This is one of the advantages of a sound *narrative theology:*[10] a decisive step forward in the manifold and often conflicting ways of using the Scripture.[11] I can only touch this concept and must leave aside its often debated disadvantages. In short, narrative theology may help us to perceive Scripture as a treasure entrusted to us. "Faithful interpretation of Scripture invites and presupposes participation in the community brought into being by God's redemptive action — the church."[12] In listening to Scripture while "interpreting," the reader discovers himself or herself as being opened to the message of Scripture. It does not at all contradict, but fruitfully contrasts, the many attempts to open the text, that is, to fill or at least to bridge the enormous temporal and cultural gap between the time when the text was conceived and the time of the reader — our time. Especially that has

10. Cf. Garrett Green, ed., *Scriptural Authority and Narrative Interpretation* (Philadelphia: Fortress, 1987); John Barton and Gerhard Sauter, eds., *Revelation and Story: Narrative Theology and the Centrality of Story* (Aldershot, U.K.: Ashgate, 2000).

11. See David A. Kelsey, *The Uses of Scripture in Recent Theology* (Philadelphia: Fortress, 1975).

12. Thesis 6, "Nine Theses on the Interpretation of Scripture," in *The Art of Reading Scripture*, ed. Ellen F. Davis and Richard B. Hays (Grand Rapids: Eerdmans, 2003), p. 3. Cf. as an instructive collection of essays of pastor-theologians: William H. Lazareth, ed., *Reading the Bible in Faith: Theological Voices from the Pastorate* (Grand Rapids: Eerdmans, 2001).

been elaborated by hermeneutics, which operates with the correlation of past and present time to translate, rather to transfer, the text into the present. It was a long and difficult way from the defense of the infallibility of all biblical texts and of their sufficiency for all knowledge in the "Princeton Theology"[13] or in the rigid conservative Lutheran "System" that Richard Lischer portrays so impressively,[14] toward *the perception of the biblical canon as the story of the triune God acting on and with humanity and on the world — involving us into his story*. When the early church consented to the canon, it understood in a new way what it means to be the church: perceiving the Scripture as a dramatic whole that tells the story of the triune God, the story of creation, salvation, and consummation.[15]

Today we ask and are asked: Why do we search in the Scriptures? Why do we read the Bible at all? Indeed, why do we not just turn to it now and then, when we need some information, or perhaps even instruction, to put pressure on those who are not of our own "Bible-believing" persuasion?

Searching in Scripture is not just looking up references to reinforce opinions and prior knowledge, or using it as a book of oracles. Whoever really searches in Scripture hopes that, in the process of searching, God will make himself heard. Therefore "you search the scriptures because you think that in them you have eternal life; and it is they that testify on my behalf," says Jesus (John 5:39).

When I served in the ministry, I got to know an engaged couple. They wanted their wedding text to be, "Do justice and fear no one." Unquestionably, that is an appealing proverb, but it does not occur anywhere in the Bible. Was it out of the question then to use it for the

---

13. Cf. Mark A. Noll, ed., *The Princeton Theology, 1821-1921: Scripture, Science, and Theological Method from Archibald Alexander to Benjamin Breckinridge Warfield* (Grand Rapids: Baker, 1983); Mark A. Noll, ed., *The Princeton Defense of Plenary Verbal Inspiration* (New York: Garland, 1988).

14. Richard Lischer, *Open Secrets: A Memoir of Faith and Discovery* (New York: Broadway Books, 2002), pp. 25-26.

15. I suggest that we would value the Bible much more if we remember what a tough and troublesome process it was to form the canon. To give just a hint how costly this treasure is: in Poland after the Counter-Reformation, Protestants had a very difficult time and often could meet for worship only in the woods. As a rule, the oldest son of a farmer inherited the farm and the next oldest the family Bible: the farm and the Bible were considered to be of nearly the same value.

wedding ceremony? I could have found a way out by suggesting a Bible verse that sounds similar, something like Deuteronomy 6:18, "Do what is right and good in the sight of the LORD, so that it may go well with you." Yet when I asked why they chose that particular saying, it soon became clear that the betrothed wanted to hear a wise rule of life — this motto of sincerity — endorsed just once in a solemn setting. They wanted to use this rule to bind their relationship with each other. They wanted to promise each other that neither would do anything that would have to be hidden from the other.

What can be said against that? Nothing, except the kind of confidence that would have to be placed in such a promise! This couple was trying to base their confidence on their constancy, each on its own and on that of the other. This is what they hoped for, continually to remain true to each other. On the contrary, the Old Testament commandment, however much it wants to impress similar behavior upon us, places what is right and good under the direction and promise of God. What people promise each other as a result rests on God's promise of faithfulness. In God's promise, human promises of faithfulness find their support, and in this alone their future is rooted.

The couple might have chosen the Old Testament verse "Do what is right and good in the sight of the LORD" instead of their slogan for a confident lifestyle, "Do justice and fear no one." But they may still have understood the biblical verse in just the same way: as a rule of life.

Those who seem to "choose" God's Word profess that they are addressed by it in an incomparable way. With this profession they may wish to confirm what they have already heard in other ways and therefore "know," but now they let it be promised to them anew. In this way they place themselves under the Bible. In contrast with much selective listening — not to mention selective exhortation — one must be prepared for surprises, even disturbing experiences, if one appeals to the Bible.

Every Reader an Artist?

This puts us only a small distance away from reception theory (*Rezeptionsästhetik*) — similar to the reader/response criticism that started in the United States. This flourishing branch of contemporary literary studies steers our understanding of texts, their reception and circulation, in a different direction: it is not only the "message" of the text that counts, or even just the intention of the author that has to be deduced by many different means of reconstruction. Rather, the recipients expose themselves to the structure of the text, and that is how the text is read to the full, with a long-lasting effect. Poetic texts in particular, read as works of art, lead themselves naturally to the "art of reading." The reader becomes involved in what he makes out to be the text, in accordance with the Swiss proverb: "The good spectator joins in with the work" [Ein guter Zuschauer schafft mit]. Above all, it is the vacancies and broken strands in the text that awaken the reader's imagination and tempt him to continue the story himself and to find himself within it.

So far I am referring essentially to Wolfgang Iser's essay *The Act of Reading*[16] and to his observations of the perception of texts.[17] According to Iser, vacancies *(Leerstellen)* or missing links are "a condition of communicating the text." They mark out "the collision of textual patterns, by omitting these patterns' connectability."[18] The thing to do is precisely not to fill these vacancies but to leave them open, so that the pattern of the text as such is visible. And this comes about if we take their essentially perspectival nature into account: "A literary text is a perspectival connection to objectivity. . . . In narrative literature, a perspectival connection arises from a series of changing and interwoven perspectives. . . . Now, in the reading process, the reader will

16. Wolfgang Iser, *The Act of Reading: A Theory of Aesthetic Response* (Baltimore: Johns Hopkins University Press, 1978).

17. Wolfgang Iser, "Die Appellstruktur der Texte: Unbestimmtheit als Wirkungsbedingung literarischer Prosa" (The appellative structure of texts: Inexactness as a condition of effect in literary prose), in *Rezeptionsästhetik, Theorie und Praxis*, ed. R. Warning, 2nd ed. (Munich, 1979), pp. 228-52; Wolfgang Iser, "Im Lichte der Kritik," in *Rezeptionsästhetik*, pp. 325-42. Umberto Eco notes observations in a similar direction in his critical review of the interpretation of his essay "Das offene Kunstwerk" (Frankfurt am Main: Suhrkamp, 1977) in *Lector in fabula* (Munich: Fink, 1990). For much of the following, I am grateful to Dr. Rainer Fischer, who wrote his thesis on *Die Kunst des Bibellesens* (The art of reading the Bible): *Theologische Ästhetik am Beispiel des Schriftverständnisses*, Beiträge zur theologischen Urteilsbildung, vol. 1 (Frankfurt am Main: Peter Lang, 1996).

18. Iser, "Im Lichte der Kritik," p. 326.

never stay in all these perspectives at the same time, but will always glance over from one to the other, and will change perspective several times during the process of reading. From these changes of perspective, the imaginary object is constructed as an idea in the reception-consciousness."[19]

Thus the reader does not meet an original meaning that must be determined by all the means known to philological archaeology or empathy to be communicated to the present day. There is no meaning, assumed to be contained within the text, that must be "found out," salvaged and decoded. (In contrast to the assumption of hermeneutics, too, such a meaning cannot be decoded by a fictitious dialogue between the reader and the author through a text, where both communicate on their self-understanding or another basic point of view and probe the question more and more deeply.) Iser writes in "Die Appellstruktur der Texte":

> If it really were the case, as the "Art of Interpretation" would have us believe, that the meaning is hidden in the text itself, then the question is why texts play hide-and-seek with interpreters in such a way; and even more, why meanings, once they are found, change again, although the letters, words and sentences of the text stay the same. Doesn't a method of interpretation which looks for the deeper meaning of texts begin, at that point, to mystify them, and thus cancel out its own declared aim, to clarify and illuminate the texts?[20]

Everybody who is acquainted with the history of biblical interpretation — even sketchily — knows plenty of such charades played by texts that clearly elude their interpreters as they, in turn, try to grasp and hold on to their meaning. Why?

To pursue that I confine myself to discussing *the vacancies that reception theory judges to be a constitutive element of the art of reading.* These vacancies are similar to the cuts of a film: the more drastic they are, the greater the demands they make on our imagination. Our involvement in the action is indispensable, for it is not meant just to be played out in front of us, as if we could simply shake it off after watch-

19. Iser, "Im Lichte der Kritik," p. 327.
20. Iser, "Die Appellstruktur der Texte," p. 229.

ing it. A form of interaction takes place between the picture and the viewer, comparable to the interaction between the text and the reader.

Theologians have also taken up the motif of the vacancy, though in a way that misuses the insights of reception theory. In his article "The Art of Reading the Bible Today," the practical theologian Rainer Volp refers to Iser's definition of vacancies. Iser wrote: "Whenever a segment becomes a theme, the previous one must lose its thematic relevance and be turned into a marginal, thematically vacant position, which can be and usually is occupied by the reader, so that he may focus on the new thematic segment."[21]

Volp reads this as if these vacancies, if not filled, should still be put into use, by means of free combinatorial analysis and creative associations. "These vacancies are something like the joint between the changing perspectives when we read."[22] According to Volp, it is a matter of keeping these joints movable, and therefore not stiffening them with dogmatic prescripts or basic theological subjects. On the contrary, Iser separates exactly this arbitrary choice of a projected "experience from life" from the perspective envisaged in the structure of texts.[23] This perspective opens us up to the *aesthetic quality* of the text — a quality that does not want to be observed but that attracts us, inviting us to be really at home here, enriched and "informed," even transformed by its trustworthy beauty, even if this quality is often subtle, sometimes very dramatic and therefore often first disturbing or even frightening.[24]

If the reader — or in the case of a sermon, the listener[25] — is supposed to have a part in deciding what a text has to say, reception theory becomes a vehicle for emancipation: for liberation from everything

21. Iser, *The Act of Reading*, p. 198.
22. Rainer Volp, "Die Kunst, heute die Bibel zu lesen: Zum Umgang mit der Bibel in einem nachliterarischen Zeitalter," *Pastoraltheologie* 74 (1985): 294-311; quotation is from p. 300 n. 17.
23. Iser, "Im Lichte der Kritik," p. 327.
24. For the Old Testament, see Meir Sternberg, *The Poetics of Biblical Narrative: Ideological Literature and the Drama of Reading* (Bloomington: Indiana University Press, 1985).
25. See, for example, Albrecht Beutel, "Offene Predigt: Homiletische Bemerkungen zu Sprache und Sache," *Pastoraltheologie* 77 (1988): 518-37, esp. p. 524: "Der Rezipient entscheidet darüber, was das Rezipierte für ihn ist" [The recipient decides what has been received], that is, what he or she thinks discloses meaning for him or her.

that has been thought or said before, for the examination of heteronomy, for freeing oneself from the prejudices of the texts, and for a call to participate in the business of reading. Here the only question may be whether it is at least a matter of an equal participation, arranged between the author, the text, and the reader. But can we honestly still speak of "art" in this case? In music, for example, such participation would be regarded as ridiculous. It cannot be negotiated between the score, the artist, and the listener. Of course, the score is not in itself the music, the interpreters do re-create the sound at the moment they play, and therefore they intensely participate in it. Even the listeners take a certain part in forming what they hear, in their own and often different ways. This participation does not dominate, but rather serves and receives; its concern is to be shaped rather than to form; otherwise the work of art would be deformed or even destroyed. The same is true for the art of reading.

Volp confuses the impact of the reader with the process of receiving. His method of reading does not exhaust the possibilities for dialogue with reception theory. His understanding leads to the demand on all readers to become artists (according to the maxim "every reader is an artist"). It would be far more fruitful theologically to learn from structural observations, so as to invite the reader to be drawn into the events of the text. Declaring the reader to be an artist, who participates in creating the work of art to which he subjects himself, demands too much — even if, as is surely true, much more creative potential does lie dormant in us, undiscovered.

Concern about overexertion of this kind may have been the essential element in the "reading barrier" or "reading fence" (*Lesezaun*) the church erected around the Bible for a long time. The question behind the ban on "laypeople" reading the Bible can be formulated in this way today: "Can someone who has no knowledge of literature perform so difficult a reading task as constructing an old text by reading?"[26] Luther translated the Bible into German not for the people as recognition of their vernacular language (which did not even exist then as a standardized language), but as a form of instruction for pastors and heads of families. In no way did he want to withhold the Bible from

---

26. Walter Magaß, "11 Thesen zum Bibellesen — und zum 'Suchen' in der Schrift (John 5:39)," *Linguistica Biblica* 47 (1980): 5-20, quotation is from p. 11.

the "laity," but he would never have wanted to put it in their hands without instructions, that is, without preaching and catechism.

To return to the comparison of textual vacancies with film sequences: we are also familiar with cuts that are simply meant to interrupt a film, in order to fit in a commercial break. Something crucial is just beginning to emerge, and we are whisked off to the day-to-day problems of dog food, types of coffee, and detergent that washes whiter than white. What a treacherous murder of aesthetics! If the "vacancies" in the text are to be used as opportunities to switch from one perspective of reality to another, then art falls by the wayside. People fall with it, in the long term, as too much is asked of their constitution and, overstrained, they fall prey to control from outside. This is what can happen when vacancies are to be "allocated" and "reallocated" by the readers and their changing perspectives rather than by an external authority. Today, the attraction of reception theory rests for many on this misunderstanding. Such a reception of reception theory demands the question, "Do you also read what you think you have understood?"

Illuminating Scripture through Scripture — the True Art[27]

To read the Bible right is an art, much more than a skillful reciting. It is "a creative discipline that requires engagement and imagination."[28] This art is applied to biblical texts as canonical writings and at the same time to theological tools, which prepare the reader to leave

27. See M. Luther, *Auf das überchristlich, übergeistlich und überkünstlich Buch Bock Emsers zu Leipzig Antwort* (*Dr. Martin Luther's Answer to the Superchristian, Superspiritual, and Superlearned Book of Goat Emser of Leipzig*) (1521): "schrifft mit schrifft erleuchten und außlegen" [to illuminate and interpret Scripture through Scripture], in *Martin Luthers Werke*, Kritische Gesamtausgabe, vol. 7, ed. Paul Pietsch (Weimar: Böhlau, 1897), p. 639, "und das ist auch die rechte kunst, das man die schrifft recht und wol zusamen trage" [and this is also the proper art of rightly and adequately bringing together Scripture], that is, to correlate different parts of Scripture to achieve a consistent understanding, p. 639. A. Steimle translates: "interpret and explain Scripture by Scripture" and "and this is the true method of interpretation which puts Scripture alongside of Scripture in a right and proper way" (in *Works of Martin Luther*, vol. 3 [Philadelphia: Holman and Castle: 1930], p. 334).

28. Davis and Hays, *Art of Reading Scripture*, p. xv.

space for God to speak his own word, rather than hinder the hearing of this word.

This is so broad a topic that I can only outline it here. In our context, "canonical" means *to know something about the Bible that we cannot manage on our own authority — and to learn to read with this aporia*. Theological aporias are distinct descriptions of what we need to know as the contours of the "secrets of faith," for example, "mysteries" in the language of the apostle Paul (Rom. 11:25; 1 Cor. 15:51) or the christological definition of Chalcedon about the unity of God and humanity in Jesus Christ (451). They are "disclosures" for faith and hope, but only in a way that we are called to receive their promise and to follow this promise, even in our thinking experiences, and therefore they remain tasks for our rationality.[29] The secret of understanding consists in reading the Bible as the form of address and the self-announcement of God. This is an art, which does not claim and make demands on the "creative," and does not simply exhaust itself in a variety performance of associations. It is not an art that has to do with human skill and ability. Rather, art in our sense has to do with a certain, limited form of knowledge. It is not the same as *ars* in the classical sense, a rule-bound and practiced skill, but it does not stand in stark contrast to it either.

Faithfulness to Scripture takes account of the fact that the church confirmed, in the process of canon formation, what had been impressed upon it — God's faithfulness, disclosed in a *wide variety of perspectives of expectation* in the Scriptures. These perspectives cannot be traced back to one another; nor can they be modeled after one another. They engage with each other in such a way that perception never comes to an end.[30] The textual level contains several vanishing points, which draw attention to themselves in such a way that the view is repeatedly directed anew toward other texts, yet without losing the unity of the whole. Consistency and openness are not mutually exclusive here; the perception is neither arbitrary nor fully traced out. For example, Hans Urs von Balthasar inquires in view of the

---

29. See Gerhard Sauter, *Wissenschaftstheoretische Kritik der Theologie: Die Theologie und die neuere wissenschaftstheoretische Diskussion* (Munich: Christian Kaiser, 1973), p. 355.

30. Rowan Williams, "The Discipline of Scripture," in *On Christian Theology: Challenges in Contemporary Theology* (Oxford: Blackwell, 2000), pp. 44-59.

"four-fold form of the Gospel" whether the "unique, divine plasticity of the living, incarnate Word" could be otherwise attested "than through this system of perspectives which, although it cannot be further synthesized, compensates for this by offering a stereoscopic vista."[31] Therefore, to see the Bible right *as Scripture,* i.e., as a complex whole with all its dimensions, we need a comprehensive *art of reading* the Scripture.

Experiences in perceiving the variety of perspectives of expectation are based on three elementary distinctions that arise out of the canon taken as a whole, but that have, at the same time, proved themselves to be "instructions for readers," perspectives of their own kind, which are clasped together but cannot be confused with each other or brought down to a common denominator. Precisely in this way, these distinctions summarize the aporia I have described. The distinctions are: spirit and letter, law and gospel, promise and fulfillment. These are distinctions, formed under the influence of theology, that build a perception structure for the form of reception called "faith." They do not seek to prescribe any conclusions drawn from interpretation. Rather they seek, as the reader works on the metalevel of the text and tries to grasp its meaning, to act as support for an art of reading that unlocks the reader, making the reader open to the structure and perspectives of the text. These distinctions can never lead to a higher insight that would read the texts in a different way, more deeply or more logically than the distinctions like to provide. On the contrary, their "depth" unlocks us in order to draw us out of our self-enclosed existence.

Theological Rules of Bible Reading

The art of reading Scripture is dependent on a combination of consistency and openness that emerges from biblical texts. Therefore there is a need for reliable aids, such as are provided by Scripture itself. These are rules, bound up with fundamental distinctions that will en-

---

31. Hans Urs von Balthasar, *The Glory of the Lord*, vol. 1, *Seeing the Form*, trans. Erasmo Leiva-Herikakis, ed. Joseph Fessio and John Riches (San Francisco: Ignatius, 1982), p. 32.

able us to perceive each biblical text as it was intended to be heard, and not only heard but listened to. These rules help us not to cut the texts short, not to "harmonize" them arbitrarily, and so to use them appropriately. The theological distinctions "spirit and letter," "law and gospel," and "promise and fulfillment" form a nexus of perceptions for the faithfulness to Scripture; they build a structure for perception of biblical texts. They must not be regarded as expository findings. They rely on experiences in scriptural reasoning that provide basic theological knowledge intertwined with the art of reading. They are rules for dialogue that assist toward a reading that opens the reader for the structure and perspectives of the text. These distinctions cannot encourage an interpretation that is supposedly greater than that which the text itself freely offers, and by which one might read the text any differently, any more deeply or with any greater consequence than what the text provides.

The term "literal sense" indicates that the stories that are being told, and the conflicts and irritations to which the biblical texts direct our attention, draw us into the very questions and answers that are at stake in them. We have to comprehend their argumentation and not merely reflect upon or even repeat them. Thus today's readers of the Bible are introduced to the different voices that come to speech in Scripture.

The first distinction, *spirit and letter,* is the oldest in the history of biblical understanding in the Christian church, and it has a really extravagant story. Origen took two ideas from it. In the first place, and above all, the art of Bible reading is a spiritual perception[32] requiring prayer.[33] His second idea was fraught with implications for the history of biblical interpretation and had consequences that were highly problematic: "spirit" was conceived as a human capacity, as a divinely imparted intellectual/spiritual sense that is open to the "upper world" as this has entered the world through Jesus Christ and now fills it. This anthropological allocation is problematic because it gives the appearance that the "spirit" does not belong to all Christians, but only to the

32. Origen, *De principiis* 1.1.9; 4.4.10; *On First Principles,* trans. G. W. Butterworth (New York: Harper and Row, 1966), pp. 13, 327-28.

33. *Epistula ad Gregorium Thaumaturgum* 3; *Patrologia Graeca* 11:92A; *A Letter from Origen to Gregory,* in *The Ante-Nicene Fathers,* ed. Alexander Roberts and James Donaldson, 4:394.

elect, especially the monks. This leads the church to make a spiritual and sociological demarcation of the "spiritually gifted" from all others. Despite this misleading, special doctrine of Origen, the distinction between spirit and letter helped the early church to read the Holy Scriptures of the Jews as a Christian book. God's Spirit had preceded the law, which shaped Jewish history; it is the Spirit that reveals the logical and temporal first sense of each text.

This distinction refers to a passage from 2 Corinthians 3. Paul stresses its point in 4:5: "For we do not proclaim ourselves; we proclaim Jesus Christ as Lord." This is then worked out in a very condensed and tangled discussion about the Torah and its reception among the devout Jews. The key sentence reads, "For the letter (*gramma*) kills, but the Spirit gives life" (3:6).

But this translation of *gramma* is misleading. It does not mean, as is so often understood, a "dead letter" in contrast to a "living spirit": that would be something written down in which life has been deposited, in which meaning — so to speak — lies buried until our spiritual or intellectual capacity can raise it up. This is not at all what Paul meant with *gramma*. Rather, to put it more precisely: "it is (only written), lacking the power to effect the obedience that it demands. Since it has no power to transform the readers, it can only stand as a witness to their condemnation."[34]

Augustine makes something different clear in his essay *De spiritu et littera* (4.6–5.8). Here "letter" means the will of God expressed in the law of Sinai. People hide behind this law. In the presence of God they pull back to themselves, paradoxically in their very attempt to penetrate the law. Quite different is Christ, the Spirit, who makes alive and liberates, whom we face standing upright: "Now the Lord is the Spirit, and where the Spirit of the Lord is, there is freedom" (2 Cor. 3:17). He is the living form of the will of God, its gestalt. In him God encounters us in divine freedom — in such a direct way that we need not hide. "Thus, the Christian tradition's reading of the letter-spirit dichotomy as an antithesis between the outward and the inward, the manifest and the latent, the body and the soul, turns out to be a dramatic misreading, indeed a complete inversion," because Paul points to the

34. Richard B. Hays, *Echoes of Scripture in the Letters of Paul* (New Haven: Yale University Press, 1989), p. 131.

community of the new covenant where the Spirit makes "Christ's message visible to all. The script, however, remains abstract and dead because it is not embodied."[35]

The distinction between letter and spirit refers to God's freedom in his judgment. God will not refuse, of course, what God has spoken. On the contrary, God communicates the divine freedom to us and breaks open the walls we have built around ourselves, opening us up to listen to God's own self. In this respect the distinction between letter and spirit should guide every reading of the Bible. It should draw attention to the fact that we hear and interpret rightly only when we hope that God will break us open for God's own self.

The second distinction, *law and gospel*, connects with the first and seeks in a particular respect to make it more precise without either superseding or completely replacing it. As a theological (not literary-critical) distinction, it does not seek to separate two sorts of texts from each other, i.e., regulations and words of comfort. It implies rather that every biblical word can encounter us as either law or gospel. In this sense Martin Luther repeatedly called the distinction between law and gospel an art — and it is worth noting in what way he deemed this art to be both indispensable and impossible to achieve.

In a sermon on Galatians 3:23-29 dated January 1, 1532, Luther calls this distinction "the highest art in Christendom, an art with which we should be acquainted."[36] "Therefore advance whoever is really good at this art and call him Doctor of Holy Scripture, for without the Holy Spirit this distinction cannot be discerned. I experience in myself and observe daily in others how difficult it is. The Holy Spirit belongs to this distinction."[37]

No one can have the authority to state that one text is God's word of judgment and another is God's word of grace. Law is God's sentence of judgment and gospel is God's sentence of salvation. Both may come upon us with the same word, for one person this way, for another person another way, or for the same person in one way one moment and in another way the next. We can neither determine nor codetermine how or when a text will be law or gospel. What we can "know," however, is

---

35. Hays, *Echoes of Scripture*, p. 131.
36. In *M. Luthers Werke*, vol. 36, ed. Karl Drescher (Weimar: Böhlau, 1909), p. 25.
37. *M. Luthers Werke*, p. 29.

that God is judge *and* savior. Those who know the difference between God's judging and saving action — and how else can they know it but through the Bible! — will be able to hear the demand of the law where the sound of the gospel prevails, if God so chooses. Or they will be able to hear the message of the gospel and proclaim it when God places demands on them and others. They will understand the one or the other in its time and place and accept it for themselves. As judge and savior God is one and the same, or, to be exact, it is possible that we perceive the same word of God at different times differently, but always as the assurance of God's sovereign faithfulness.

The intent of this distinction is to prepare all who are ready to hear the word of the Bible as God's sentence to expose themselves to the complex action of God and to entrust themselves to this action. They should be ready for this dialectics, no more and no less.

Both of the theological distinctions identified above prepare us to answer the question, Who is the God about whom we read in the Bible? God meets us as personal in God's freedom (spirit and letter) and in God's sentencing (law and gospel).

The third distinction, *promise and fulfillment*, already has been sketched in the first two chapters of this book. It deals with the fact that God promises future action, along with God's future, and even God's own self. Who but God could do that? "The Word of the Lord is truthful, and what he promises he certainly keeps" (Ps. 33:4 in Luther's translation). "For HIS speech is upright, all he does is in faithfulness" (Martin Buber). In speaking, God opens up a stretch of space and time in which God acts.

However, the time-space conception of history is especially susceptible to schematization. In an effort to review contexts of events and categorize them for historical understanding, persons place themselves in time. They do this by distinguishing everything they can already look back on from what is yet to come.

The theological, not historical, interrelation of promise and fulfillment points to God's speaking and acting, which cannot be separated clearly from each other. By fulfilling what God has promised, God displays his promise. Promise and fulfillment form a unity, and this is why we cannot disassemble them. God does not wait for what God says to come true. "It is a characteristic of God always to reserve further action for himself in the future, but to 'throw forward' some part of that future action into the present *as a promise.*[38] The contour of promise invites us to sense the consummation of God's ongoing work.

God acts in his own way to fulfill what God promises. Therefore "fulfillment" does not mean the filling of a void, but the penetration of all things by the uncreated fullness of God. God keeps what God promises — in just the way that *God* promises. Often God fulfills his promise in a different way than we expect. Fulfillment does not mean that God checks something off (perhaps a segment of history) and leaves it behind with the stamp of "finished" on it. Promise continues to endure as God's pledge for fulfillment. It does not subsist as a kind of remainder, which is still unsettled.

The Christ story is the quintessential paradigm for the richly diverse unity of promise and fulfillment. In Jesus Christ, God confirms the divine promise in such a way that people, in communion with Christ, may hope in God, may expect God anew, and may expect something new from God. We can only believe as those who hope. To read a biblical text as promise means, therefore, to hear it as God's promise of faithfulness. Thus we become aware that God's faithfulness is not a check to be paid in the future. God has already spoken the divine Yes here and now, therefore we can cling to that Yes. In this regard the third distinction to be observed in reading the Bible carries the reading of Scripture to a special level, without canceling out the other two. Kept in mutual movement, they work together, increasingly opening up new and surprising, often disturbing, perspectives and proving to be signs of faithfulness to Scripture.

38. Geoffrey Wainwright, *Eucharist and Eschatology,* 3rd ed. (Akron, Ohio: OSL Publications, 2002), p. 19, summarizing my second thesis, *Zukunft und Verheissung: Das Problem der Zukunft in der gegenwärtigen philosophischen und theologischen Diskussion* (The problem of the future in the contemporary philosophical and theological discussion) (Zürich: Zwingli, 1965).

CHAPTER 4

No Fear of Dogmatics!

A Lack of Clarity and Commitment

The art of reading the Bible does not restrict biblical interpretation to an inner circle of experts or, according to Origen, to specially gifted Christians. But it does imply that serious dialogue cannot occur, including dissenting interpretations, unless it is rooted in the community of people who search in the Scriptures. Without such rootedness there may be — at best — an ideal communication on a very abstract level.

To be rooted means at the same time to engage in further participation with others, even with others who seem to be completely different or are seen as such. Therefore, it is a sign of hope that conversations of Jews with Christians are no longer confined to mere comparisons of shared traditions, obstacles to mutual understanding, and joint moral responsibilities. Started by American Jews, the society of "textual reasoners" now gathers a working group of Jews, Christians, and Muslims in a mutual reading of their Scriptures and ways of interpreting them. The practice of the Jewish members of this group is grounded in the insight "that rabbinic hermeneutics should not be colonized by some particular academic science *and* that its intrinsic rationality *cannot* be deemed 'impenetrable' to 'outsiders,' or comprehensible only to some traditional elite."[1]

1. Peter Ochs, introduction to *Textual Reasonings: Jewish Philosophy and Text Study at the End of the Twentieth Century*, ed. Peter Ochs and Nancy Levene (Grand Rapids: Eerdmans, 2002), p. 5.

The community of Bible readers is not an enclosed society. Indeed, it is open to communication with "diverse others to whom we need to listen and from whom we need to learn. This includes critics who charge us with ideological captivity rather than fidelity to God."[2] But even this habit of openness is eventually not as decisive or indispensable as it might be. Nevertheless, this community, by keeping its mind open as to how to love God, enables us to become aware in turn of how we are in the presence of that which is not within our reach, and here we are fully exposed to and addressed by God's diverse actions.

What does this mean concerning the reach and radius of theological communication and the actual doing of theology? It opposes the striking alternatives of "public theology" on the one hand and "church-bound theology" on the other. Arguably, church-bound theology entails playing a language game within the confines of the church that is liable to generate stable, mostly conservative, attitudes of pious people. The exercise of theological rediscovery may also be done to clarify and reinforce commitment, and this is not confined to the same set of people. By contrast, public theology aims to do theology in public in dialogue with culture at large. This program can be carried out both within the church and external to the life of the church. Conceiving of it as an academic framework of religious consciousness shaped by culture and shaping culture is a misleading alternative (and one I shall deal with in the chapter on public theology). But it must still be asked: Does the distinction between the internal communication of piety and the external exchange of those religious motifs thought to be Christian really help clarify the momentum that drives theology forward? Certainly, distinguishing sociologically between insiders and outsiders shows how theology depends on cultural conditions. That is, theological inquiry inevitably reflects the circumstances of its practice; but these are never in themselves a sufficient condition for theological rationality.

Theology as a discipline of reasoning is characterized by an *intrinsic rationality* that obtains whether or not its communication is internal or external. While theologians try to make themselves understandable to those who do not assent to what they argue, they cannot submit the ra-

2. Thesis 8, "Nine Theses on the Interpretation of Scripture," in *The Art of Reading Scripture*, ed. Ellen F. Davis and Richard B. Hays (Grand Rapids: Eerdmans, 2003), pp. 4-5.

tionality of their argument to any vague universality. Yet if theology is subordinated to extrinsic criteria, as, for example, a sort of sociological "stocktaking" of valuable religious experiences and of systematized religious orientations, theology will be subsumed by religious culture as a sociological category within Western civilization. Then, Christian doctrine becomes a collection of topics to be arranged and rearranged, often to be reduced to a principle or subjected to selectivity to concentrate on motifs that seem to be up-to-date, thus promoting a free-floating exchange of religious ideas and values claiming to be independent of any institutional and faith-communitarian prerequisites. Often this corresponds with a growing distance from the life of the church as the natural place for theological reasoning and communication. Here again, then, is a challenging fork confronting us on the theological road.

Many Western Christians, especially theologians, today suffer from a "ghetto syndrome," as I would like to call it. Some of us associate a ghetto with a secluded place where Jews were forced to live together — for example, a *stetl* in eastern Europe, a little town within a town or at its fringes — where the gateways were closed in the evening to hinder communication and trade with non-Jews. Often we recall the terrible pictures of the ghetto in Warsaw and other Polish cities where Jews were herded in by the Nazis and totally cut off from the outside world. In this case "ghetto" becomes synonymous with a maximum security prison, or perhaps even with death row. But if you come to the old city of Worms, a town rich in German and Jewish history, you will find that the gates of the ghetto were very similar to the doors of the cathedral. Jewish people often appreciated their ghetto because it provided a space in which to live together undisturbed, to build up strong neighborhoods, and to protect their religious as well as their cultural traditions. To live together in this way often helped strengthen Jews for their encounters and interactions with other people. In no way do I intend to whitewash either the threat or the danger of such temporary seclusion. But I do want to challenge us to overcome our fashionable Christian ghetto syndrome that confuses our notion of being deeply rooted in the community of Christian faith with a deliberately chosen self-isolation.

This may be illustrated by an anecdote. Hans von Soden (born in 1881), a disciple of the leading liberal church historian Adolf von

Harnack, later a colleague and friend of Rudolf Bultmann at Marburg, used to say to his students now and then: "During the week I am so much involved in the history of the church that I need at least one day off: on Sundays, I enjoy my cultural and other interests." Of course, he never neglected his church affiliation. But the Sunday service did not seem to contribute anything valuable to his doing theology, which he understood as a historical-critical representation of different church traditions. In 1933 he found himself in the midst of the church's struggle against a regime starting to show signs of developing totalitarian interference, and commensurate with this occurred a deeply rooted disagreement concerning the task of the church. He thus felt called to reason theologically for the life of the church; it was the dogmas of the early church — one of his preferred fields of research and teaching — that provided him with the ground for making his theological judgment and arriving at his Christian commitment. In 1937 he wrote: "In the final analysis theological decisions are dogmatic decisions."[3] The old-fashioned confrontation of conservatives and liberals collapsed, and a new attention to the basis of consensus started: first of all in consenting to God's outspoken will, and second, but only in relation to this consent, in agreeing with others. Hans von Soden's story illustrates how a serious crisis of the church may lead to insights into a commitment that is able to comprehend very different situations. These situations, while specific in their criticality, do not themselves shape the church's reasoning.

Perhaps, one might say, that may be true for a critical situation, one threatening the life of the church, but it does not apply in "normal" circumstances where church and theology are embedded in a democratic, tolerant, and gradually developing culture. But does one really know if, and how far, a "normal" situation obtains, especially as

3. Cf. Erich Dinkler and Erika Dinkler-von Schubert, eds., *Theologie und Kirche im Wirken Hans von Sodens: Briefe und Dokumente aus der Zeit des Kirchenkampfes 1933-1945*, 2nd ed., Arbeiten zur Kirchlichen Zeitgeschichte series A, vol. 2 (Göttingen: Vandenhoeck & Ruprecht, 1986), p. 235. Von Soden became a leading member of the Confessing Church in Hesse, and after the war he helped the Protestant Church of Kurhessen-Waldeck (the church where I was ordained) obtain a new constitution and church order. He was in mind for the position of first chairman of the Rat der Evangelischen Kirche in Deutschland, the board of leaders of the Evangelical (Protestant) Church in Germany, but he died of a heart attack on Oct. 2, 1945.

an apparent normality can be very dangerous because it hinders us from being prepared for unrevealed crises, hidden intolerance, and temptations only implicit in the unrecognized conflicts that accompany and confront the Christian life again and again? Without dramatizing current trends following an apocalyptic point of view, it might be said that theology is always a preparation for emergency, at least in some respects — and we miss this at our peril.

If one looks at theological education and research today, the relationship between theology and the church appears to be problematic, at least in Europe and in the United States. There is a lack of commitment, and theologians who are very committed to social and political activities often mistrust theology as being merely abstract and valueless. This corresponds to, and presents itself as, uncertainty about the task and character of theology. Students of theology frequently make statements such as: "This is what I believe, but I can speak only for myself." They do not want to be aggressive; neither do they expect anybody else to believe as they do. In their perspective it seems to be right not to say anything in matters of faith without the concluding qualification: "What I said applies only to myself. Its validity may be confined to myself. Others are very welcome to share my convictions, but they cannot be expected to do so, for their convictions are of the same value as mine." They may be ready to share convictions, but they hesitate to question what is true and credible. This reveals their troubled relationship to the church, even when they are willing to serve in the ministry.

Such attitudes express a caution that may be seen as alignment with a fundamental skepticism against otherwise binding theological statements. One feels that in these statements a claim is being made that crosses the boundaries of personal opinion or conviction. This claim is disturbing because it is obviously not marked by the same modesty that is considered appropriate to modern or postmodern discourse about matters of faith. It is disturbing because it does not fit into the progressively more accepted rules of that discourse — a discourse in which people are persuaded by the force of convictions and the expressiveness with which these convictions are uttered. This preformed exchange of convictions, however, is marked by a loss of theological language and judgment; the participants of such a discourse are no longer willing or ready to be straightforward about the grounding of Christian existence. They may mistake this for arrogance or an offense against other people's independence and liberty to form their own convictions. And who wants to make theological statements, if doing so means appearing arrogant or offensive? Should not the church, as a social structure sui generis, lead the way in allowing people to express their innermost beliefs and convictions without fear of censorship?

But the church is not to be equated with a social structure concerned with mutual exchange of religious worldviews and moral values. It is the creature of God's Word and God's Spirit as a decisive element of God's ongoing action in, and with, humanity and the world. As God's promises create and constitute the church,[4] the church is called to specific practices in order that it clearly and distinctively points to its creative origin and lively constitution, as formed, proved, and nourished by God's Spirit. Theology — and especially dogmatics — serves this clarity and distinctiveness. With this help (and only with this help), the practices of the church become and remain unmistakable and free from false, misleading considerations. Accordingly, dogmatics is neither a collection of religious ideas nor an executable program of an ideal society; neither is it a collected tradition to be watched over and preserved. Rather, it is a movement in thinking that is being addressed by God's immense, tireless, and often disturbing actions and blessed with the abundance of God's promises. It can serve the commitment of the church only insofar as it is itself exposed to God's speaking and acting. Dogmatics participates in the "wound of knowledge" that marks Christian spirituality, the perception of the "intractable *strangeness* of the ground of belief."[5] It "is born out of struggle as men and women come face to face with the paradox of God's purpose made flesh in a dead and condemned man."[6] Part of the ongoing task of dogmatics is to give an account of its being questioned by the inner tension of its "object" — "an experience of pro-

4. Martin Luther, *The Babylonian Captivity of the Church* (1520), trans. A. T. W. Steinhäuser, rev. Frederick S. Ahrens and Abdel Ross Wentz, in *Luther's Works*, vol. 36 (Philadelphia: Fortress, 1959), p. 107: "For the church was born by the word of promise through faith, and by this same word is nourished and preserved."

5. Rowan Williams, *The Wound of Knowledge: Christian Spirituality from the New Testament to St. John of the Cross*, 2nd ed. (London: Darton, Longman and Todd, 1990), p. 1.

6. Williams, *The Wound of Knowledge*, p. 3.

found contradictoriness."[7] Dogmatics is driven forward through such an experience in thought.

Dogmatics as Gymnastics

But there is a widespread mistrust of dogmatics we must deal with. Today "dogma" and "dogmatics" arguably have only negative associations for most Christians. Sadly, the most positive association these terms may have is probably in relation to *Dogma*, the irreverently funny Kevin Smith movie, in which the practice of dogmatics is the butt of the film's ongoing joke. In our culture of relativism, any claim to truth that is not subject to the "proof" of scrutiny of evidence is seen as arrogance, and the concept of authority is seen as oppressive. The idea of dogma is at best irrelevant and at worst politically and ecclesially incorrect. Even in the church the term "dogma" seems outdated, something from a time of weaker minds and less rational thought. Dogma is related to something that restrains and hinders our freedom. It smacks of a barrier between us and Christ, a placing of something or someone in a position of undeserved authority to tell us what to think and how to act if we really want to know Jesus. Thus the "freedom of a Christian" and "dogmatics" are regarded as contradictory. Dogmatics seems to close all discourse, not to open it.

Usually "dogma" is understood as "something held as an established opinion," or as "a point of view or opinion set forth as authoritative without adequate grounds." Therefore, dogma as "doctrine or body of doctrines concerning faith and morals laid down by a church" seems indistinguishable from mere opinion.[8] Dogma is associated with arbitrariness,[9] "dogmatic" with "asserted without proof,"[10] and dogmatics is assumed to be dictated by the church as a means to regulate the convictions of its members.

What a distorted picture! Let me mention just some examples to

7. Williams, *The Wound of Knowledge*, p. 1.

8. *Websters's New Encyclopedic Dictionary*, rev. ed. (New York: Black Dog and Leventhal, 1995), p. 297.

9. For example, in *Webster's Revised Unabridged Dictionary* (1913).

10. *Webster's New World Dictionary*, ed. Victoria Neufeldt (New York: Simon and Schuster, 1990), p. 177.

prove the opposite. The art of reading the Bible relies on fundamental distinctions. These distinctions are based on experiences of scriptural reasoning, and they require dogmatic unfolding. If the need for the assistance of dogmatics is ignored, biblicism or even fundamentalism is the likely result. Here, one ignores the fact that reading the Bible itself promotes questions to be dealt with by dogmatics. Both need each other: dogmatics cannot dictate or anticipate what is to be perceived by reading the Bible; on the other hand, biblical texts cannot prove the statements of dogmatics. Their dialectical interrelation induces a merry-go-round of questions and answers, opening up our trust in God and raising our expectation of God's presence. In addition, dogmatics provides us with tools for being self-critical and making ongoing corrections, thereby encouraging dialogue instead of closing it. It requires us to reimmerse ourselves in our reflected experiences, again and again, thereby enriching them and helping us to state them more precisely and also to clarify them as regards their grounding.

However, dogmatics may give rise to very divergent experiences. For example, the South African theologian John de Gruchy reports how disappointed he was to find theological doctrines inadequate in dealing with an extremely difficult task of pastoral care; as a consequence, he decided to move to Bible studies straightaway to "work through the problem" and to do justice to "praxis."[11] By contrast, a young German minister thought she would have been helpless when confronted with immense suffering — and with desperate attempts to make sense of it — had she not been sufficiently trained in dogmatics. She had been taught to move within the space that dogmatics provides instead of "translating" and applying to the situation the collected concepts of Christian faith. Of course, dogmatics ought not to be preached: one cannot "use" it immediately in pastoral care, not even in Christian education or parish study groups. But the serious study of dogmatics helps us to become acquainted with the framework of theological interconnections, and it affords us with numerous perspectives from which to perceive the ambiguities of human life as well as showing us their limits of applicability. Here I can only outline a few examples.

11. "The Nature, Necessity and Task of Theology," in *Doing Theology in Context: South African Perspectives*, ed. John W. de Gruchy and Charles Villa-Vicencio (Maryknoll, N.Y.: Orbis; Cape Town and Johannesburg: David Philip, 1994), p. 2.

It is stimulating to observe how dogmas can be traced back to elementary questions with many ramifications. The questions "Who is God?" and "What is the name of God (Exod. 3:13) that allows us to invoke God?" led to the doctrine of the triune identity, which posited, after a very complicated and troublesome process of specification, that God is one in three persons. The persons are different; but while one cannot be derived from the other, at the same time the persons are inseparably related to each other. The works of the triune God are, in relation to us, indivisible. That is, from our point of view, we are unable to attribute the particular works of the triune God — creation, preservation, judgment, salvation, reconciliation, and consummation — to the trinitarian persons. However, intense Bible reading has helped our understanding of the character of the divine persons and led us to see the term "person" as meaning "facing each other." The definition of the Council of Chalcedon (451) of the mystery of Jesus Christ's being true God and true human answers the question "Who is Jesus Christ?" in a way that significantly differs from the sorts of answers that would follow upon the quest for the historical Jesus: "Who was Jesus of Nazareth?" The very complex answer is: "Jesus Christ is true God and true human being." It tells us to distinguish God and humanity in Jesus Christ, but not to separate them.[12] This direction very helpfully clarifies how the relationship of God's acting to human activity connects with the unity of humanity and communion with God in Jesus Christ. If one does not distinguish between them, one risks equating human actions, especially the actions of the church, with God's own and sovereign action. But if one separates them, one is under enormous pressure to show, and even to demonstrate and to prove, whether the action is in accordance with God's intention and whether such action is indeed the appropriate answer to God's intention. Complete fusion and complete separation of God and humanity in Jesus Christ would be equally dangerous and misleading.

Dogmatics is not limited to the formulations that church councils have explicitly defined as "dogmas." Most of its topics evolve from an ongoing struggle to perceive the enormous reach of God's action into every realm of human life, connected with the inexhaustible complex-

---

12. *Creeds of the Churches: A Reader in Christian Doctrine from the Bible to the Present,* ed. John H. Leith, 3rd ed. (Louisville: John Knox, 1982), pp. 35f.

ity of what God has given in creation and salvation and what God has held in reserve to transform and complete. There is always a productive tension between the "given" and the promise included in it. Consider, for example, the elementary question in the invocation: "What are human beings that you are mindful of them, / mortals that you care for them?" (Ps. 8:4). The answer is "given" in the contingent fact of our creatureliness being dignified by promises to be fulfilled in diverse, often hidden ways in life and death. There again, how do human beings discover themselves as incorporated in God's acting, as created, as blessed in many ways, as sinner and justified, in communion with God, therefore saved and vulnerable, claiming the hope that their life that is "hidden with Christ in God" (Col. 3:3) will be revealed? Thus the doctrine of justification answers the question of how we are called to God, how God views us, and how we can know ourselves before God.[13]

In this way the practice of dogmatics involves discovering how to start with the right questions, questions that are to be answered by reasoning theologically. It enables us to contend with questions that seem irresistible and to evaluate them in the right context. Dogmatics is accordingly gymnastics: it helps us to be agile-minded, to be watchful, open to surprises, amazed. And it protects us against spiritual stiffness and a pious know-all manner — against exactly what many suspect it causes!

Dogmatic statements assert who God is, what God has done, and what God has promised to accomplish, and insofar as these are based on the freedom of faith and hope, they are outspoken about what has been *entrusted* to us. This requires responsible reflection on what needs to be said under all circumstances, in a way that does not neglect the empirical context while not being determined by it either.[14]

The elementary questions and answers of dogmatics are intertwined with church practices, especially with proclamation, with the administration of sacraments, and with liturgy, prayers, blessings, pastoral care, and education. The questions and answers of dogmatics are not confined to these practices, but their vitality will be renewed by such practices and symbolic acts that *point to God* in a striking and

13. See chap. 5, in this volume.
14. Cf. chap. 6, in this volume.

(if carried out appropriately) distinctive way. Here reflection leads one to the intrinsic *rationality* that *grounds* the church and its various practices. Dogmatic theology endeavors to base the context of comprehensive, coherent, and consistent argument on this intrinsic rationality. It does not settle the questions posed by church practices but deals with them and keeps them open for both the present and coming generations. Therefore, dogmatics serves the vital memory of the church.

Beyond the interior life of the church there is the question of its place with respect to contemporary events and problems; and every once in a while there is also the question of whether the church even still has a place and, if so, for what. Yet, when the relevance of the church is being challenged and some action on its part is urgently required, reference to external reasons such as tradition and cultural obligations is not sufficient. We need to be more precise: What enables the church to act as it does, and not in another fashion and in a different direction? Or still more precisely: What is required to make the church and its practices recognizable? It is only if the church answers these questions that it can confidently state why it is still there: this is because it has something to say that would otherwise be lost, in which case Christians would lose not only their common profile but also their grounding.

Reflection on the grounding of the life and practices of the church directs us away from the practices of the church and toward what is really external to it: God's promises and his outspoken will, which may often oppose the church's self-understanding. "Oppose" is a harsh word, for it implies criticism and conflict of the kind we experience in human affairs. The church is confronted with the source of its preaching, and this confrontation may be a terrifying one, wounding the church's own understanding of itself in order to heal its practice. For there is always something external to the church, facing it and holding it responsible for the assumptions that underpin its practices. Dogmatics speaks up for this responsibility. In this way it awakens the church and keeps it receptive to the greater extension of God's truth that transcends the church. This opposition may be a confrontation, but it is more than that and perhaps even the primary reason that we can be encouraged to speak confidently and freely of what we truly believe — not because it is our favorite conviction, but because it is the truth that liberates us. This is exactly what needs to be formulated.

Martin Luther often asked for the "true old church," in contrast to church traditions that continue historical developments by the force of those traditions. The true old church is by no means an artifact purported to be the starting point of Christianity. "Old," according to the language of the Reformers, is not the opposite of something new, developed, or progressive. For the Reformers "old" meant genuine, reliable, trustworthy, and independent of age. Therefore, Luther speaks of the true old church as "the *hidden* church,"[15] hidden by means of God's acting, God's own and often strange work (Isa. 45:15: "Truly, you are a God who hides himself, / O God of Israel, the Savior"). The hidden church is not at all an invisible or mere ideal society, but its characteristics are the features formed and engraved by the specific actions of God toward humanity. They mark the physiognomy of the church, and they tell something about the story of the church. The existence of the church is grounded in God's acting. Accordingly, the church's own words and deeds point to God's work. They draw attention to the fact that the church does not speak by and for itself, that is, that it can produce neither itself nor the aims of its practices. These hints of the church's hiddenness are signs: they are the *notae ecclesiae*, the marks of what it means to be the church.

To communicate the being of the church means to argue in faith, hope, and love. This applies to the real church, which is characterized by marks that not only tell where the church exists — as in comparison to other social organizations — but also identify the church *as* the church. These marks consist in proclamation of the gospel, the sacraments, liturgy, teaching, and ecclesial guidance, social welfare work, and the Christian life shaped by the church year. Luther added the cross and suffering,[16] acknowledgment of marriage and well-established political order, the suffering of the church in the world, and the abandonment of retaliation.[17] These signs are not all on the same level. Neither do they result in a closed checklist by which we

15. M. Luther, *The Bondage of the Will* (1525), trans. and ed. Philip S. Watson, in *Luther's Works*, vol. 33 (Philadelphia: Fortress, 1972), p. 89.

16. M. Luther, *On the Councils and the Church* (1539), trans. Charles M. Jacobs, in *Luther's Works*, vol. 41, ed. Eric W. Gritsch (Philadelphia: Fortress, 1966), pp. 148, 151-54, 164-65.

17. M. Luther, *Against Hanswurst* (1541), trans. Eric W. Gritsch, in *Luther's Works*, 41:194-98.

can move from one issue to another to see whether the church is or is not in existence. Put together, these signs do not show us something like the outer appearance of the church as it may be visible for everybody — as opposed to some inner essence of the church that can be grasped by and communicated to only those who belong to it. The signs of the church are interrelated because they point to the origin of the church: to what the church owes its life and to what it is entrusted to say and to do. This is the character and meaning of every single sign of the church — each of them participates in this character and meaning at its particular place and in its own manner, and they are all thereby interrelated to one another. Thus, for example, marriage needs the proclamation of God's promise and commandment, and suffering can lead to confession and prayer.

These signs and symbolic acts point resolutely to the intrinsic rationality and grounding of the church. They can make sense only if they signify the tight connection between the actual church and that which the church cannot hold onto nor present, but can only draw attention to. The signs repeatedly point to new things to say and to do, and they do this precisely so that they can identify themselves without directing attention to themselves. They signify the optimal certainty of the church as they point away from and above themselves. This special ecclesial discernment should be enabled and held open to allow the actual being (Da-sein) of the church, its existence, to pose the question "What should the church be (not ideally, nor in part, but really)?"

For example, Luther emphasized in his series of sermons on 1 Corinthians 15 (1532-33) that the evangelical sermon, that is, one true to the gospel, is not meant to teach a more successful way of life, or better management of one's life, or more responsibility for others. Reasonable people can find these things, important as they are, on their own. For such things no preaching is really needed.[18] These days

---

18. ". . . non erecta praedicatio propter presentam vitam, vivit, ut haushaltest und land und leut regirst, hoc noverunt gentiles etc. et ratio docuit et necessitas . . . ," in *M. Luthers Werke*, vol. 36, ed. Karl Drescher (Weimar: Böhlau, 1909), p. 534; cf. (abridged) in the translation of Martin H. Bertram: "Commentary on 1 Corinthians 15," in *Luther's Works*, vol. 28, ed. Hilton C. Oswald (St. Louis: Concordia, 1973), p. 101; "For we are not baptized and called, and we do not hear the Gospel, to discover how to become rich, how to acquire and retain goods and honor. That the jurists must teach and deal with" (p. 107).

they can be found in other places. Indeed, they are often much better found through communication with experts in special fields than in a service where the minister is bound by limited life experiences and the particularities of social training. Luther goes on to argue that preaching is urgently needed because it leads us "somehow" out of the "vale of tears" — the realm of afflictions (because we have fallen in misery) — and forward into the future life.[19] If this does not happen, then preaching is wasted time and a useless or even damaging enterprise. Accordingly, if the preacher is theologically responsible in this preaching, he or she sometimes can open the eyes and ears of the congregation to also seeing and listening to everyday tasks in a new, surprising way. Listeners may receive wisdom by connecting the proclaimed Word with their experiences and open questions, by asking God for his providential way. Then, there may be an intertwinement of hope and experience.

This intrinsic rationality moves within the realm in which the church transcends any actual existing congregation. At the same time, it is only within this realm that the church is both the old and true church and is renewed by God's acting through God's Word and Spirit. In this respect dogmatics is neither a mere reflection on church practices nor a theory of church activities, but is itself a genuine part of the practice of the church.[20] As such, dogmatics maintains the freedom of the church and its language, even with respect to the Bible.

Dogmatics as Building Up Consensus

"Doing theology," as a process rooted in and responsible for the teaching of the church, is not at all contrary to being open to dialogue in the academy or, for that matter, in public life. Of course, theology shares many academic tools and indeed has in turn contributed them. But

---

19. "Sed si baptizatus, ut incipiam aliam vitam, et ista praedicatio ist nicht gericht ad praesentem vitam, sed quomodo ex isto jamertal in futuram," in *M. Luthers Werke*, vol. 36, p. 534, cf. *Luther's Works*, vol. 28, p. 101; "No, we hear the Gospel that we may direct our hearts to another life and existence, which is not yet present and yet will surely appear" (p. 108).

20. Cf. Reinhard Hütter, *Suffering Divine Things: Theology as Church Practice* (Grand Rapids: Eerdmans, 2000).

this contribution to the academy depends on what theology has to say, and this statement cannot be made in isolation from the church. The voice of the church must be clear, unmistakable, and undistracted in order to witness to the being and the work of the triune God. Therefore theology, in participating in this task, unconditionally states, in its own way, what it has to say. In this respect only is it able to demonstrate that it is an independent discipline of reasoning, with the ability to develop and communicate its experiences in thought — and not only to "insiders."

Mutual understanding might also imply some kind of participation in the religious practices of others, at least between Christians, without this involving reductive assimilation where rites are regarded as interchangeable, let alone any syncretistic or pluralistic attitudes. As Geoffrey Wainwright notes in his systematic theology, "Practical participation in the worship of the other confessions, as fully as respective disciplines and consciences allow, had been proved in the experience of recent times to draw Christians and churches closer together."[21]

Accordingly, practicing dogmatics means to be on the way with the wandering people of God, to perceive that "God is greater than our hearts, and he knows everything" (1 John 3:20). The kingdom of God is much more far-reaching than the boundaries of the church. But that does not permit us to desert the church in order to reach freedom. Instead, it opens us up to the horizon of an expectant church, which is not self-enclosed or self-referential. Here, as always, processes of clarification are risky but necessary purifications, in order to preserve distinctiveness.

The most crucial theological statements — the basic dogmas — were developed to clarify or correct theologically church practices that had become distorted. Often under an enormous state of neglect, tension, and deep-rooted disagreement, there was urgent need to reach consent over *why* we do *what* we do in the church — and, for that matter, what we are *not* able to do. An instructive example is prayer for other people. The apostle (or one of his disciples) writes in 1 Timothy 2:1: "First of all, then, I urge that supplications, prayers, intercessions, and thanksgivings be made for everyone." Why is it necessary to pray

---

21. Geoffrey Wainwright, *Doxology* (New York: Oxford University Press, 1984), p. 289.

for everyone? Why can we not simply pray for those who are close to us, or only for those who have special need of an interceding prayer? And how do we discern the limits of such a need? In 1 Timothy 2:3-4 we read the explanation and justification: "This is right and is acceptable in the sight of God our Savior, who desires everyone to be saved and to come to the knowledge of the truth." Again, this leads us to other questions: for example, How are our prayers connected with this help? And when it is said that they will come to the knowledge of truth, does this not require much more than just prayers? Prayers, after all, are generally not even heard by those for whom they are said.

There is a sufficient answer to this question in the doctrine of God's grace. Since God extends his grace beyond human abilities and understanding, the church is obliged to pray not only for its members but also for all of humanity. The relationship between petitionary prayer (intercession) and the doctrine of grace is not merely of historical interest. Augustine has shown that there are compelling theological reasons for connecting the doctrine of grace with the practice of prayer. One dogmatic statement keeps the question alive that undergirds the practice of our prayers for everyone. We point to God's grace, to his merciful will toward all human beings.[22] This interrelation needs to be explained to show what prayer does and says and where its limits are.

One may ask: Is it sufficient for the practices of the church to point to God's acting? Are the characteristics of ecclesial being mere marks, signs that point to God's hiddenness? Do these signs only represent God's presence, or is God present here, binding himself to the practices of the church? The Second Helvetic Confession (1566) states that the preaching of the Word of God *is* the Word of God.[23] Truly, God identifies the preaching of his Word — if it is truly the proclamation of his Word! — as his own Word by the power of the Spirit. Therefore, the "is" in the statement cited remains in *statu promissionis*, in the "state of promise" of God's identification. The preacher trusts this promise. But the preacher is never allowed to identify his or her words with God's Word. The preacher's words are at best approaches

---

22. Cf. Gerhard Sauter, *Gateways to Dogmatics: Reasoning Theologically for the Life of the Church* (Grand Rapids: Eerdmans, 2003), pp. 139-42.

23. *Creeds of the Churches*, p. 133.

to consenting to God's Word, approaches that imply an opening of the perception of the congregation to God's speaking to them, to his acting on and with them, to fulfill his providential will through them.

An altar painting in the old church at the marketplace in Wittenberg, where Luther used to preach, shows the Reformer in the pulpit and the congregation listening to him. But in the midst, between both, stands the cross of Jesus Christ. Luther points to this *Deus crucifixus* so that his listeners look at Christ as the essence of proclamation.

If the church claims to be inseparably united with Jesus Christ, it can do so only by referring to Christ's promise that he is the head of the church, his church. It would be a terrible mistake if the church were to claim for itself that it *is always* in Christ and Christ himself *is* in the church, or, to put it another way, that Christ and the church "constitute a single 'whole Christ.'"[24]

Very often, the basic theological statements that led to dogmatics were formulated when the church was facing deep conflict, distortion, and far-reaching dissent within itself. Accordingly, dogmatics is concerned with what needs to be disputed among Christians when crucial matters of faith are at stake. We need to find consensus in the face of the alternative of faith or disbelief — whether to follow Jesus Christ or deny him — whether to count the hope that is in us or conceal it. In all these struggles the being and survival of the church *as* the church are in danger.

Among the matters that need to be questioned are some that seem to be taken for granted by many in the church. Today, for example, the church needs to reclarify what it means by proclamation: how this differs from instructing people to motivate them for their greater well-being, to improve their morality, or to indoctrinate them with a religious worldview. Another question for consideration is whether the practice of infant baptism today really does reflect the meaning of baptism. For example, I have been told that some parents who were themselves baptized but presently feel grave reservations regarding

---

24. Identical with the Catholic Church, as stated for example in the declaration *"Dominus Iesus": On the Unicity and Salvific Universality of Jesus Christ and the Church* (Rome: Congregation of the Doctrine of Faith, Aug. 6, 2000), "IV: Unicity and Unity of the Church."

the church, to the point of understanding themselves as "unbelievers," have asked whether their children could be baptized later so that
they could make their own decisions. These parents will not promise
to communicate their faith. But is it possible at all to communicate
one's faith to someone else, in the sense of handing it on? I should say
it is not, but what we *can* do is to provide the constellation that makes
talk of, and expression of, faith possible. Here, dogmatics is urgently
needed to explain what Christian education teaches about baptism.
What kind of Christian education and preparation for baptism would
be appropriate here? And what do we actually celebrate in the Lord's
Supper? How does our sense of church community, and of its grounding in the memory of Christ's death and the expectation of his coming, arise from participation in this practice? Today the Lord's Supper
is often celebrated as the gathering of a community that rejoices solely
in its own communal spirit. This attitude supersedes the remembrance of the crucified Christ and the eager expectation of his coming
to judge the living and the dead. The Lord's Supper reminds us that
the church is the community of justified sinners, bound together by
the forgiveness of sins and by the shared hope incorporated in the
death and life of Jesus Christ. Dogmatics is not just helpful, but indispensable, for the church to practice these basic performances of its life
"correctly," i.e., according to the message entrusted to it. Protestant
theology can be confident that a vital dogmatics will provide sufficient
energy for self-correction if it is faithful to its task. It does not need a
magisterium to order and discipline its teaching. Yet this makes it all
the more important that dogmatics joins with the church and with
theology in mutual engagement and support.

In Germany, in the first half of the twentieth century, dogmatics
was clearly seen and explicitly perceived as a "function of the church."
This does not mean that dogmatics is a function of church officials.
Dogmatics is not responsible for keeping the church functioning like
clockwork. On the contrary, dogmatics contributes to church leadership, by both helping those in charge to avoid false considerations and
in building up a true consensus about the source of church practices,
while being sometimes critical of their current performance and intentions. In this respect there has been a rare consensus among leading
theologians. Dietrich Bonhoeffer has stated, "Theology is a function
of the church. For there is no church without preaching, nor any

preaching without remembrance. But theology is the memory of the church."[25] One may be surprised to learn that even Paul Tillich, the advocate of a theology embedded in the culture, in art, and in public affairs, shared the conviction that theology is a function of the church.[26] But the late Paul Lehmann, who was Bonhoeffer's close friend and who taught at Princeton, Harvard, and Union Theological Seminary in New York, told me this story: "After a convocation speech at Harvard, Tillich approached me and said: 'Paul, I essentially agree with your talk. The main intention of my doing theology, even of my *Systematic Theology,* is to explain the Nicene Creed [Nicaea 325 and Constantinople 381], the basic Creed of the Christian church. Maybe my theological language does not clearly show this intention. That might be a difference between you and me: I am not reading the Bible so intensely as you do.'" Dogmatics is the reminder of the church's origin — and therefore also a sign of the church's hope. Dogmatics helps the church to consent to God's agency and thereby encourages the agreement of those who want to believe, helping them to stay within the community of faith. It is certain that dogmatics cannot exist without the church; yet sometimes the church can be wrong to such an extent that dogmatics itself becomes a sign of the church and the place at which the church can be found.[27]

Without dogmatics the church runs the risk of losing itself in ideological confrontations or in the plurality of religious opinions. Dogmatics can be expected to preserve the church's freedom to say and do what has been entrusted to it as its proper proclamation and practice. Being institutionally independent of theological research and education may be part of that freedom, provided dogmatics, when practiced in the academic situation, is able to resist the pressure of public opinion about what it is appropriate to discuss. On the other hand, the capacity to resist the pressure of public opinion concerning what is or is not worthy of discussion does not give dogmat-

25. Dietrich Bonhoeffer, *Act and Being,* in *Dietrich Bonhoeffer Works,* vol. 2, trans. H. Martin Rumscheidt (Minneapolis: Fortress, 1996), p. 130.

26. Paul Tillich, *Systematic Theology,* vol. 1 (Chicago: University of Chicago Press, 1951), p. 3.

27. To some extent, that was the case with the first volume of Karl Barth's *Church Dogmatics,* vol. I/1, trans. Geoffrey E. Bromiley (Edinburgh: T. & T. Clark, 1975; German ed., 1932), during the German church struggle in the years 1933-34.

ics license to develop the habit of confrontation. It is sufficient for dogmatics "to say its distinct thing," so to speak, and to give an account of it.

This sufficiency and independence of theological arguments are embedded in their relationship to the church. Nevertheless, their truth is not confined to the church because they refer to the triune God who is the creator of the universe and of all humanity and "who desires everyone to be saved and to come to the knowledge of the truth" (1 Tim. 2:4). The early fathers were right to distinguish without separation the kingdom of God and the church; God's kingdom is the eschatological reality in the church, but it is not identical with the church. It shines through the church whenever the church witnesses to the power of the kingdom of God. The reach of God's kingdom is promised to exceed the boundaries of the church, but it is misleading if any church claims itself as the realized kingdom of God, or if God's kingdom is interpreted as a cultural goal promoted by the church.

Since the Enlightenment at least, there has been confusion and distortion about how to interpret and embody the universal truth of the Christian faith. This confusion has its roots in the split between the Roman "Catholic" Church and Protestant churches and in the ensuing conflicts in the seventeenth century. The philosophers of religion and some theologians of the Enlightenment envisioned private piety in contrast to public religion[28] (in the United States: civil or civic religion). Particular churches and denominations were seen as congregations where persons could share their private piety. If a church represents well-established and far-reaching values and if it can argue on common grounds, it is able to influence public affairs. But truth claims — so the argument goes — are universal by definition. If Christians want to share in this universality, faith must defer to reason as a general human faculty. Otherwise it becomes confined to particular convictions and motivations, even if it is the "faith of a church."

Against this background we can understand why the Roman Catholic Church at the First Vatican Council (1870-71), in claiming the universality of the Christian faith, identified faith and reason as

---

28. Cf. Trutz Rendtorff, *Church and Theology: The Systematic Function of the Church Concept in Modern Theology*, trans. Reginald H. Fuller (Philadelphia: Westminster, 1971).

foundational.[29] However, this claim can mutate to an apologetic imperialism. Cultural Protestantism of the nineteenth and twentieth centuries tried to demonstrate the fusion of Christianity and European/North American culture in critical philosophies such as German idealism, especially in relation to the radical Christian principles such as liberty and true subjectivity rediscovered by the Reformers.[30] Following this line directed theology more and more toward the academy and away from the church. In former times, doing theology primarily was the task of bishops in order to educate clergy. When theology entered the European university, its main purpose was to enable theologians to account for their hope and faith in response to those who would raise questions about their words and deeds. For example, when Anselm of Canterbury made a case for theology as "faith seeking understanding," he addressed not only Christians but also Jews, perhaps even Muslims. Today we urgently need to maintain the balance between responsibility for the life of the church and the exchange of grounds, views, and methods in the academy, a balance that always will be delicate, just as the position of the church in society will always be delicate.

There is no doubt that there are many actual and potential interchanges between Christianity and its different cultural contexts. To this end there is, and hopefully will be, a continuing process of giving and receiving. Yet it would amount to a blend of discourses if the proof of theological statements were linked with their evident universality — even if this universality were understood in respect to the independence of religion as a self-sufficient realm of subjectivity, as for example Friedrich Schleiermacher has convincingly argued.

Operating in terms of an alleged absence of universality and unity, today's so-called postmodernist worldview seems to enable social identities to live, to act, and to reason in relatively independent modes. Yet this fragmentation simply amounts to another distortion: the

---

29. Elaborated and more differentiated in the encyclical of Pope John Paul II *Fides et Ratio: To the Bishops of the Catholic Church on Relationship between Faith and Reason* (Aug. 14, 1998).

30. Cf., for example, Ernst Troeltsch, *The Social Teachings of the Christian Churches*, trans. Olive Wyon (Chicago: University of Chicago Press, 1981); Ernst Troeltsch, *The Absoluteness of Christianity and the History of Religions*, trans. David Reid (Richmond: John Knox, 1971).

search for truth demands that which is not only interpersonal but also transpersonal and therefore constitutes openness and caring for one another. Without this sense there would be no mutual understanding and no sound discourse at length. Earlier I quoted students of theology who were afraid to talk about the faith beyond "what I believe." This attitude may be a symptom of religious pluralism, but it is not true tolerance because it denies the real encounter with questions concerning life and death that cannot be reduced to private affairs. It denies to us the opportunity to be exposed to the very existence of "the other" person. And it misses the adventure of practicing dogmatics.

CHAPTER 5

God Creates Faith — Do We Consent?

Why Are We Protestants?

Some years ago my wife was asked to start a religious education program in a school for disabled children. Religion is, as you may know, a regular subject in German public schools. But these children and young people between six and twenty years of age had never had any religious education in school or from their families, the majority of whom had no strong church affiliation. They had been so confined by their peculiar situations that they lacked any idea of their relation to a community beyond the school. Most of the children were unable to walk and unable to communicate properly, and they were incapable of attending Sunday services in the local churches or of exchanging religious views or criticism with others of the same age. Because religion has to be taught according to the church affiliation of the children's families, Catholic teachers taught religion to Catholic children and Protestant teachers taught Protestant children. Most of the children in my wife's class were confronted for the very first time with the fact that they were Protestants. The first question they asked my wife was, "Why are they Catholics and we're Protestants?"

What is the real difference between Protestants and Catholics? How would *you* answer this simple question? Could you clarify this with an explanation that is easy to understand? Could you do it without relying on characteristics of worship, different religious practices, and obviously different forms of religious common life?

My unfortunate wife couldn't find any satisfactory answer at the moment — and I am sure I would have been unable to support her properly had I been there. Then a boy put up his hand and said, "Well, Catholics are born on odd-numbered days of the month and Protestants are born on even-numbered days of the month." A persuasive response, isn't it? And it nicely shows the conviction, customary to all confessional self-explanations: "We are right — and you are wrong. You may have your reasons, but we have ours, and ours are better."

Why are we called Protestants — why are others called Catholics? What is the *crucial* difference between Protestantism and Catholicism beyond the fact that there are different churches, cultural traditions, and religious habits that most of us were either born into or inherited and have just carried on? What is the essence of being Catholic or Protestant? I doubt if any of my students in Bonn could answer this question with any depth if they were educated only with a traditional Protestant self-understanding. Of course, as theology majors they would be ready to refer to Martin Luther or to John Calvin and maybe to other reformers. But is recalling the authority of those religious heroes any more convincing or better than appealing to the pope and his teaching authority?

A more substantial answer might refer to doctrinal differences, for instance to the doctrine of justification, because this doctrine has been the historically contentious issue between Rome and the churches that emerged from the Reformation after the sixteenth century.[1] It has often been taught that Protestants are justified by faith alone (and some add tacitly: justified by *their* own faith), but that Catholics will be justified by faith supported by their good deeds — that is, their moral righteousness. Some go further and conclude that Catholics are able to contribute something to their salvation. Because their sinful attitude has been changed through baptism, they may deserve salvation due to their efforts to do right, to obey all the commandments of God, and to follow the moral and spiritual advice of their priests. Protestants, on the contrary, seem to get into trouble because they neglect to strive for righteousness since they find righteousness exclusively through their faith in God. In this respect they stand confronted directly with God; they are bound by their own con-

---

1. For further details, see my article "God Creating Faith: The Doctrine of Justification from the Reformation to the Present," *Lutheran Quarterly* 11 (1997): 17-102.

science and are independent from authorities, even from the teaching of the church. But at the same time, they have such a low opinion of themselves as sinners that they cannot imagine struggling with their weakness, overcoming step-by-step something alien to God's righteousness, and making some religious progress by doing better. This is what many say and believe.

But what a terrible caricature this picture is! It is unfair for two reasons. *First,* this view reflects a superficial connection between church doctrines and moral consequences, which are supposed to mirror these doctrinal elements. But if we look closer, the divisive picture portrays even more clearly the contrast between liberal and conservative attitudes. Liberalism is so strong that it supersedes confessional heritage, especially its claim for the independent moral self and its responsibility. On the other hand, many Protestant denominations besides the mainline churches are poisoned with a morality that is cultivated by traditionalistic Catholicism as well.

Second, and much more important, is the oversimplification of deeply rooted doctrinal differences. The "split" of the Western Church goes back to the pope's exercise of his authority. His criticism primarily addressed not Luther's theology but Luther's bad behavior: Luther did not submit to the advice that he received from Rome. The indulgence controversy, the internal destruction of confession, and the doctrine of grace were only indications of, perhaps even only symptoms of, the split, and not the cause of it.

Martin Luther's "Rediscovery" of God's Judging and Saving Action

Martin Luther asked for the "true old church" to be faithful to its origin in God's Word and Spirit, and he called the church's authorities to account for their reasons for fundamental changes in administering the sacraments, especially the confessional. He asked: Are these reasons faithful to the Bible? Do they account for genuine Christian hope? The pope and his advisers in the sixteenth century judged these questions to be attempts to disturb both the order of the church and the delicate balance between church and state. Therefore they decided that the Reformers and their followers had to be dealt with firmly. As if this were not enough, because the Reformers' message of the freedom of the Christian found such strong acceptance in the population of central Europe, Rome attempted to draw the line against the doctrine of the Reformers by condemning it. In so doing, they expelled all so-called Protestants from the Catholic Church and refused to recognize the Lutheran and Reformed churches as legitimate. This breach happened at the Council of Trent (1545-63), starting the Counter-Reformation. The council's article on the doctrine of justification, declared in 1547, states that justification is a transformation of the sinner by divine grace that enables the sinner to cooperate with God's initiative and to save himself through membership in the church. By this definition God acts like a transmission that provides divine power for human activity, or both are connected like gears. Or, to use another image: God's grace works like an infusion (*gratia infusa*) that gives a sick person medication or new blood to gain new energy. On the one hand, this was a condemnation of the Reformation doctrine that sinners are justified by faith alone, exclusively by the righteousness of Jesus Christ that is attributed to them by divine grace. On the other hand, it marked progress in understanding the doctrine of divine grace — but was not as radical as the Reformers' perception: the proclamation of God's grace guides all doctrines because it deals with God's sovereign action toward humanity. However, the council's condemnation served to cut off conversation between the two groups when several attempts to compare and settle the contested doctrines of justification had already been made. Why? The main reason was that justification was not the only doctrine in dispute. The authoritative Catholic interpretation, as it became the standard for doctrine in Trent, was bound up with an idea of a gradual *transformation* of human beings who are infused with divine grace. According to the council, grace seems to be a supernatural causation that brings to effect another, better life that throws a light on the union of divine and human activity. That causation of the renewed human will is represented to some extent by the spiritual power of the pope and the clergy to give advice on matters of daily life and to grant absolution to the obedient of the church. A theological image of true humanness (Christian anthropology), a sophisticated concept of the combination of divine and human action, and the structure of the church and its authority are closely linked.

The Reformers denied all three of these elements. Luther defines the subject of theology in his meditation on Psalm 51. That psalm — one of the major prayers of penitence in Luther's time — reads in part:

> I know my transgressions,
>   and my sin is ever before me.
> Against you, you alone, have I sinned,
>   and done what is evil in your sight,
> so that you are justified in your sentence
>   and blameless when you pass judgment. . . .
> Purge me with hyssop, and I shall be clean;
>   wash me, and I shall be whiter than snow. . . .
> Hide your face from my sins,
>   and blot out all my iniquities.
> Create in me a clean heart, O God,
>   and put a new and right spirit within me.

Luther interpreted this psalm as a paradigmatic prayer of repentance, as a confession of a guilty person, a sinner before God. He explains: "The proper subject of theology is man guilty of sin and condemned, and God the Justifier and Savior of man the sinner."[2] According to Luther, theology has to speak of *God's acting toward persons,* reshaping their whole existence by placing them in the realm of God's holiness, justice, and life. God creates faith and hope by addressing us with God's promises: the promise of eternal life in accordance with God. God creates faith, hope, and love by placing us in the new creation, in the community with Jesus Christ. This creative act is not at all limited to a certain date or starting point in our life, which might be surpassed and replaced by our efforts to walk in accordance with God's will. To live a life of Christian freedom means that we begin every moment of our life by coming back from our obstinate selves because we are called back by God to our baptism — to God's acting on humanity and on the world. This coming back is not a looking back but a looking forward, based upon God's promise.

2. *Commentary on Psalm 51* (1532) in *Luther's Works,* vol. 12, trans. Jaroslav Pelikan (St. Louis: Concordia, 1955), p. 311; my paraphrase: "The characteristic subject matter of theology is humanity that is guilty of sin and condemned, and God who justifies and saves sinful humanity."

The church witnesses to this justifying and saving action of God. Divine grace frees humans from their past rebellion against the living will of God, now spoken in the gospel of unearned grace. We are called to admit that God is right in his judgment over us, a judgment that justifies us and saves us at the same time. Following God's will means to live and act, to hope, and to love in view of this judgment by God. Therefore, Luther concluded: preaching the gospel as God's Word of unmerited forgiveness and its reality in baptism, the Lord's Supper, and binding and loosing in the name of Christ are marks of the true old church.

The doctrinal difference regarding justification therefore did not cause church division but reflects major differences in the life of the church. Furthermore, any understanding of *only* the doctrine of justification does not by itself promise more today than it did yesterday. Real progress in dialogue could be achieved only by seriously considering the questions: Are we faithful to what God has entrusted the church? And how can this faithfulness become unmistakably convincing, not merely expressed as another dry fact? Such a self-examination allows only a clarification of doctrines linked with a theological critique of the life and the practices of the church.

Mutual understanding presupposes that representatives of the churches suffering from the missing unity of the church seek to speak to each other openly, i.e., to be open to each other in order to learn from each other and to find out how much further they have to go to meet. Neither a sophisticated comparison of theological traditions nor a strategy of seeking the least common denominator can help to find common ground.

But there seems to be another impediment to moving further toward a mutual understanding of justification — an impediment that seems at the same time to make any further dialogue on this doctrine unnecessary and even pointless. This is the suspicion that the doctrine of justification covers only the pious concerns of the particularly self-focused religiosity of the late Middle Ages — a time five hundred years ago when people were full of the fear of God and the last judgment, when people were anxious to stand on the right side of God. It was a time when people were preoccupied with heaven and hell, when dying people, crowded in a large hospital room and surrounded nightly by the screams of the suffering, were confronted with pictures of the last judgment on the walls asking them: "Will you be saved? Or will you be condemned?" It was in this context that Martin Luther was and often still is portrayed as a person burdened with the question, How can I find a gracious God? The story goes that eventually he was able to find the answer to lift his soul: God has already saved me through the crucified Christ — and now I do not need to be afraid of his scrutiny in examining what I have done and what I have left undone. I am already safe! And, it was told, because Luther shared his question, How can I find a gracious God? with most of his contemporaries, his answer was very well received and became the consensus of more and more people, clergy, monks and nuns, laymen and laywomen. This, it is said, explains the success of the Reformation. If that were true, the Reformation was only mass psychosis.

This religious success story is just a fairy tale. Let me refer to Luther himself. He called the question, How can I find a gracious God? a misleading question that seduces one to run on a treadmill. In the 1534 sermon "On Sacred Baptism" Luther said, "I have been a faithful monk for fifteen years, eager to follow all instructions to reach the goal of saving my life, to make God gracious and merciful to me. In going this way, I never found any consolation in the promissory event that I had been baptized and therefore I was exposed to the proclamation of Jesus Christ and his baptism. That means the baptism God himself had given from heaven and the opportunity to act in it."[3]

Luther wanted to confirm that salvation is not a goal to be reached from some God-given starting point. It means exposure to God's acting and being opened to the various ways of God's acting through justification. The salvation of our lives is bound to the crucified and risen Christ who comes to us with the creative power of the Holy Spirit and becomes the real center of our lives — according to the unique statement of the apostle Paul: "I have been crucified with Christ; and it is no longer I who live, but it is Christ who lives in me. And the life I now live . . . I live by faith in the Son of God, who loved me and gave himself for me" (Gal. 2:19b-20). Faith is rooted in the perception of the placement of my "I" into the presence of Christ. Only in Christ am I "able" to stand and not to fall, to walk and not to circle around myself.

3. In *Martin Luthers Werke*, Kritische Gesamtausgabe, vol. 37, ed. Karl Drescher (Weimar: Böhlau, 1910), p. 661, my paraphrase.

Therefore, Luther did *not* ask, "How can I find a gracious God?" On the contrary, he corrected this question by quite radically confronting us with the question, "Where do we stand when we ask that question?" To perceive the faith that God creates implies that we are able and willing to ask our questions in the right way and that we can look for answers that really show us our way.

The Doctrine of Justification according to John Calvin

John Calvin's conception of justification is, like Luther's, influenced by intense consideration of Paul's epistle to the Romans, on which he wrote a commentary. In the first edition of the *Institutes of the Christian Religion* (1536),[4] Calvin does not dedicate a specific section to the doctrine of justification. Rather, following Luther, he discusses the doctrine in different contexts. In the second edition (1539), he gives it a separate chapter and subordinates it to the theme "rebirth." He maintains this sequence in the final edition (1559) as well, and lengthens it by making his own position distinct, particularly with his argument that justification is participation in God's justice by virtue of Christ's death and resurrection;[5] it depends on Christ's presence in the power of the Spirit. In addition, he accuses the Council of Trent's doctrine of justification of a relapse into synergism. Calvin combines his reception of Luther with influences from Augustine and the Greek Fathers (concerning "sanctification").

Calvin explains the theological connection of justification, regeneration, repentance, and sanctification to emphasize the formation of the new life.[6] The doctrine of justification marks the beginning, like a primal scream. By this systematic placement, Calvin forever shaped the theology and piety of Reformed Protestantism. By subordinating the doctrine of predestination to the doctrine of justification, Calvin wanted to show that justification makes election clear.[7] Sanctification is interlocked with justification. Through the Holy Spirit, it expresses

4. John Calvin, *Institutes of the Christian Religion*, translated and annotated by Ford Lewis Battles (Atlanta: John Knox, 1975).

5. Calvin, *Institutes of the Christian Religion* (Philadelphia: Westminster, 1960), 3.11.8.

6. Calvin, *Institutes* (1960), 3.3ff.

7. Calvin, *Institutes* (1960), 3.21ff.

the eschatological character of the regeneration of the justified. Calvin stresses the weakness of mere faith more emphatically than Luther does. However, he does this to avoid the idea that faith may be a work and that humans could cooperate in attaining sanctification. He anchors this resistance to synergism (going back to Bernard of Clairvaux) specifically to the idea of *unio cum Christo*. United with Christ in the Spirit, justification and sanctification are related to each other and do not come apart because their unity is found in Christ alone. One does not happen without the other.

In response to anti-Reformation criticism that the doctrine of justification is a cheap grace asking too little of human readiness to do the right thing, Calvin's conception emphasizes the necessity of good works that cannot achieve salvation but will still be counted in the last judgment. The justifying God deals with humanity in such a way that the individual grows into sanctification. The righteousness of faith is experienced as a new creation. To present this idea, Calvin speaks of the justification of the godless and the justification of the believer whose works are judged and acknowledged as "fruits of faith."[8] He strongly rejects all works righteousness. However, with the demand to prove righteousness, an understanding of righteousness creeps in that tends to expose, for the sake of ethical guidelines, that the very character of God's judgment can be demonstrated by means of human life.

Calvin regarded rebirth and justification as equal in value. The second does not follow the first as another condition. Rebirth is, of course, the side of justification that cannot be demonstrated. However, in just this way it provides the answer to the question how the Christian life begins. It owes its existence to God's acting. At the same time, it serves as the beginning of a development that the believer can rely on in order to gauge his progress toward the completion of life.

Later on Calvin's explanation became the leading understanding in other Protestant churches, for example, in Methodism. Justification and sanctification were regarded as a sequence like steps on a path. It was didactic information, a kind of checklist of the main markers of Christian life — like prevenient grace, repentance, justification, assurance, regeneration, sanctification, Christian perfection, final salvation

---

8. Calvin, *Institutes* (1960), 3.17.4-10. Justification is referenced with the *tertius usus legis*, the third, ethical use of God's law.

— that you had to learn and follow to be on the right track. Good works "follow after justification."[9] This temporal scheme dominates the whole explanation. In a conversation on June 26, 1744, John Wesley asserted that "as faith increases, holiness increases, till we are created anew." He asserted further that there are some reliable proofs of salvation, for example, if "those who are thus saved" "gave a distinct account of the time and manner wherein they were saved from sin, and from the circumstances thereof," and "if, upon a strict inquiry afterward from time to time, it appeared that all their tempers, and words, and actions, were holy and unreprovable."[10] This is a noticeable change of the Reformer's doctrine of justification. However, there are hymns that correct that change or at least modify it. Consider, for example, Edward Mote's hymn "My hope is built on nothing less / than Jesus' blood and righteousness" (1834), especially the fourth stanza that refers to 2 Corinthians 5:2:

> When he [Jesus Christ] shall come with trumpet sound,
> O may I then in him be found!
> Dressed in his righteousness alone,
> faultless to stand before the throne![11]

One of the crucial tasks for theology today is to properly teach the doctrine of justification in order to prepare for the proclamation of God's judging and saving work and to clarify that justification and sanctification remain God's acting alone. It is misleading to attribute justification to God and then to ask for experiential proof of it — and then, for consistency's sake, to understand sanctification as just a goal to be reached by a true Christian life. Of course, a "cheap justification" would not be a misunderstanding, but rather a denial of God's justice that heals us and enables us to consent to God's will. Therefore, the Barmen Declaration (1934) repudiated in its second article

9. "The Articles of Religion" (1784), art. X, in *Creeds of the Churches: A Reader in Christian Doctrine from the Bible to the Present*, ed. John H. Leith, 3rd ed. (Louisville: John Knox, 1982), p. 356. There is also "sin after justification" that needs repentance granted by God's grace (art. XII, p. 357).

10. *Creeds of the Churches*, p. 377.

11. Hymn 368 in *The United Methodist Hymnal: Book of United Methodist Worship* (Nashville: United Methodist Publishing House, 1989).

"the false teaching that there are areas of our life in which we belong not to Christ but another lord, areas in which we do not need justification and sanctification through him."[12]

How to Proclaim and Teach Justification Today

Now, let us consider the present ecumenical situation. During recent decades there has been a strange consensus that avoids the outlined verification of the elementary questions concerning faith and hope in God. This consensus claims that the proclamation of God's justice and justification by faith alone can no longer be understood. It says that the doctrine of justification is old-fashioned and has to be interpreted in quite a new way. This was the message of the assembly of the Lutheran World Federation in 1963 in Helsinki, Finland, a meeting of representatives of the Lutheran churches, almost comparable to a council of the Catholic Church. The Lutheran assembly in Helsinki attempted to make the meaning of justification more understandable. There were some contributions based on the Lutheran tradition, but they seemed to repeat categories of the sixteenth and seventeenth centuries decorated with personalistic attributes. A majority of delegates advanced the opinion that the doctrine of justification is part of an outdated theology and has long since been replaced by a new set of questions. Accordingly, they said, we cannot reach an agreement about the doctrine among ourselves because it no longer has anything to say to us. It neither tells what is distinctive about God's acting on us, nor does it enrich what we can say about being a Christian today when we face the enormous challenges of being authentic.

Therefore the Helsinki assembly stated: "The Man of today no longer asks, 'How can I find a gracious God?' His question is more radical, more elementary: he asks about God *per se*, 'Where is God?' He suffers not from God's wrath, but from the impression of His absence; not from sin, but from the meaninglessness of his existence; he asks not about a gracious God, but whether God really exists."[13]

---

12. *Creeds of the Churches,* p. 520.

13. Document 98, "Message of the Assembly," in *Offizieller Bericht der Vierten Vollversammlung des Lutherischen Weltbundes* (Proceedings of the fourth assembly of the

Here the potency of justification is reduced to the challenges of morality under the conditions and circumstances of our everyday life. The traditional religious elements are much less valuable than in the past. Today — it was said again and again — we have to face quite different challenges, even in our religious orientation.

I refer to this explanation of the essence of justification and its recent dismissal in order to check our understanding of the very basic questions about being Christian today. In 1957 the Swiss Catholic theologian Hans Küng, now retired as professor of ecumenical theology at the University of Tübingen, published a provocative study comparing the conception of the doctrine of justification according to the *Church Dogmatics* of Karl Barth with the conception according to the Council of Trent. Amazingly, he concludes that there are no real differences.[14] In 1974 he went even further in his well-known book *On Being a Christian*, claiming that we have to seek another ecumenical agreement faithful to today's basic questions. Küng's understanding is quite similar to the vision of Helsinki. He compares average Christians in the sixteenth century and our contemporaries:

> It is not surprising that people in all Churches today talk, not about "Christian justification," but about "social justice." . . .
>
> If we set out schematically the old and the new statement of the problem, it looks like this:
>
> Formerly the question was asked in great cosmic and spiritual anguish: how do I get a gracious God? But now the question is asked with no less cosmic and existential anguish: "How does my life acquire a meaning?" Formerly this God was seen as God the judge who acquits man from his sin and declares him just. Now he is seen as partner who calls man to freedom and to responsibility for world and history.
>
> Formerly it was a question of individual justification and of "saving our souls" in a purely personal sense. Now it is the question of the social dimension of salvation and of all-round care of our

Lutheran World Federation), July 30–Aug. 11, 1963, Helsinki, Finland (Berlin: Lutherisches Verlagshaus, 1965), p. 426.

14. Hans Küng, *Justification: The Doctrine of Karl Barth and a Catholic Reflection*, trans. Thomas Collins, Edmund E. Tolk, and David Granskou (Philadelphia: Westminster, 1981).

fellow men. Formerly people were concerned in a spiritual sense with salvation hereafter and peace with God. Now they are concerned wholly and entirely with social conditions and the reform or even revolution of structures. Formerly man was constrained to justify his life before God. Now he is constrained to justify his life to himself and his fellow men.[15]

However, we should ask: Are these the really urgent questions for us today? Are they the questions of those who cry about social justice as well as of those who have a troubled conscience afflicted by hopeless attempts to accuse, to defend, and to judge themselves? Are these the questions of the suffering, of the aged, and of the dying who are confronted with the questions: Who am I now? What shall I be and become? We must face these questions not by referring to polls and charts of religious opinions but by questioning ourselves — this task is ours. Here I must restrict myself to the proposal that the doctrine of justification has been the answer to the question, How can I find a gracious God? and that this question is no longer valid, and must be replaced by an answer to the questions that really address people today. If that were true, the doctrine of justification might be religious garbage to be put on the curb or, if possible, recycled and infused with energy to answer the challenges of our situation today in the midst of global tasks. If even that recycling is not possible, the doctrine of justification may be a relic of former Christian convictions, to be displayed in a museum of religious artifacts and curiosities.

Although both Protestants and Catholics frequently advance it, this picture is a distorted image of the doctrine of justification. One might even state that this image represents a consensus between many Catholics and Protestants: "The issue of justification has passed into history, so therefore there is no real difference between us anymore! Let's start again with today's real challenges, with the cry for justice and the endeavor for peacemaking, mirroring God's liberating and redeeming power!" But let us remind ourselves that it was against precisely this point of view that Luther argued that the question, How can I *find* a gracious God? was a denial of the grace of baptism. Luther

---

15. Hans Küng, *On Being a Christian*, trans. Edward Quinn (Garden City, N.Y.: Doubleday, 1976), p. 582.

preached the recognition *(Wahrnehmung)* of the grace-filled action of God: God proclaims us justified. Luther's real question was, Who is God really, and who am I before this God?

That question was the reason for the forensic perception of the doctrine of justification: God and humanity stand opposite each other in a judgment scene as judge and accused. One is called before God to give an answer, but finds in this forum that he or she is incapable of proving himself or herself and is given no other place to stand. The forensic language indicates that the accused person has been indicted and faces charges that cannot be evaded. "Woe is me! I am lost," cried Isaiah when he noticed God, even only a corner of God's robe (Isa. 6:5).

But Jesus Christ steps between, so to speak, the holiness of the judging God and the one who is lost before God. Earlier the image of humanity was fixed on the comparison between what one should be and must become and what one really is. Now the "stepping between" of Christ ransoms one from this condition. God and humanity become recognizable to each other because God sees humanity in Jesus Christ, the one who died for humanity. From this point of view, humanity no longer stands in the position of perishing before God. Instead, humanity comes to stand in the place of Christ, proclaimed justified by God through the crucified and resurrected One. The one lost before God *becomes* God's righteousness because Christ takes the place of the perishing, and the sinner is moved into the place of Christ (cf. 2 Cor. 5:21). In the event of justification, humanity is given a new place to stand before God. This "standing before God" acquires a completely different redemptive meaning.

In this situation God judges humanity by this new created relationship. The saving judgment of God is not the reckoning of what one has done or has omitted, nor is it the generous offer of a second chance that can make up for omissions and squandering. The Creator, who separates being from nonbeing, speaks judgment on life and death: on the life of the creature with God and on death that ruins life. God has revealed this judgment in Jesus Christ and therefore it remains bound to him. It is inseparable from him who died in God-abandonment and arose from it. Therefore, humanity perceives God's judgment while looking at Jesus Christ and receives God's righteousness as it is incorporated in Christ's story.

Where God sees Jesus Christ, whose death God has turned to salvation and whom God has raised from death, God pronounces his justifying judgment, the promise of life with God. The promise of life gives one all the certainty that one needs in life and death. Such certainty *(certitudo)* throws itself on God's promise. Insofar as it relies on God's faithfulness, it separates itself from every feeling of self-security. It is expressed in a *self-renunciation* that is the reverse of a highly vigilant awareness of the righteousness of God. One learns the right time to be silent and by doing so praises and honors God alone. Thus justification accomplishes the death of the old way of being.

The doctrine of justification explains how God and humanity become joined through God's acting on humans for their sake. What the Reformers intended to present in the doctrine of justification was that the revelation of God's righteousness in the death of Jesus Christ fulfilled what had been demanded in the promise-filled first commandment, that is, to admit that God is right; to agree *with* God's will, not only to agree *to* it.

Ironically — or I may say true to God's providence (and that is sometimes the same as a very strange coincidence) — the Second Vatican Council, which started in the early 1960s, ran parallel to the assembly in Helsinki. The council did not deal with the doctrine of justification but opened the way for an ecumenical dialogue by stating that there is indeed only one Catholic Church, but there are other communities of faith that are not excluded from God's revelation and acting.

One of the far-reaching effects of Vatican II was a new listening to the Bible. A renewed listening had begun in Continental Protestantism in the first half of the century and led, because of the threat of Fascism, to closer ecclesial relationships and to further doctrinal clarification. This new and expectant listening to the Bible by Protestants and Catholics caused their churches and theologians to begin to think in the following way:

First, the whole church is addressed by God's promise. Therefore, faith and hope are not properties of one church or another, and doctrines need to be formulated to expect God's judgment on believers' speaking and acting in all churches.[16]

---

16. See *Joint Declaration on the Doctrine of Justification / The Lutheran World Federation and the Roman Catholic Church* (Grand Rapids: Eerdmans, 2000), pt. 1, no. 8: "Our com-

Second, consensus is in the first place not an agreement about religious convictions, but assenting to God's will, consenting to his acting. It means to hear the words of Paul, "For if while we were enemies, we were reconciled to God through the death of his Son, much more surely, having been reconciled, will we be saved by his life" (Rom. 5:10). Consensus is therefore not an overlap in various conceptions that then are highlighted to converge in a compromise.

Third, this consensus is not only to be stated, it is to be participated in: through conceding that God's judgment is right, that it destroys all our self-justification, and that it creates space for atonement and reconciliation. There cannot be true reconciliation without justification, and vice versa. This causes a revolution of our questions inside ourselves — in our moral and responsible selves — and a revolutionary impact on the challenges brought to us in the tasks of our world today. This revolution would result in asking about the way of life that justification gives witness to and of the ways of thinking that allow us to appropriately argue about this event.

These three aspects characterize the *Joint Declaration on the Doctrine of Justification* of the Lutheran World Federation and the Roman Catholic Church, proposed in January 1997 and accepted by Lutheran bishops worldwide in 1998.[17] After an intensive and sometimes heated debate, especially among German theologians, and after some irritating reservations were overcome, it was confirmed also by the Vatican in May 1999, and signed by representatives from both groups in a joint worship service in Augsburg, Germany, October 31, 1999. The declaration states that justification as a dynamic and decisive action of the triune God, the judge and savior, liberates the sinner from the power

---

mon way of listening to the word of God in Scripture has led to such new insights" (p. 11). Pt. 3, no. 17: "We also share the conviction that the message of justification directs us in a special way toward the heart of the New Testament witness to God's saving action in Christ: it tells us that because we are sinners our new life is solely due to the forgiving and renewing mercy that God imparts as a gift and we receive in faith, and never can merit in any way" (p. 16). Pt. 3, no. 18: "Therefore the doctrine of justification . . . is an indispensable criterion that constantly serves to orient all the teaching and practice of our churches to Christ" (p. 16).

17. *Joint Declaration on the Doctrine of Justification.* As an example for further revisions of other traditions, see Geoffrey Wainwright, "The Lutheran–Roman Catholic Agreement on Justification: Its Ecumenical Significance and Scope from a Methodist Point of View," *Journal of Ecumenical Studies* 38 (2001): 20-42.

of the hostility against God's creative will, and at the same time unites the justified person with Christ.[18] This unification with Christ reminds us of Calvin's conception of the *unio cum Christo.*

Therefore, *the doctrine of justification implies above all the task of the truthful performances of the church, of what it says, performs, and has been entrusted with* in its repentance from misdeeds and, thereby, from the mistakes it makes in arguing. Thus, the doctrine of justification remains a proof stone or a testing ground for the ecclesial essence of the church. Are we indeed the church, which God through his Word and his Spirit has called into life? To what extent do we either stand within the faithful treatment of God's justification or obscure it by what we say and do?

While the result of this high-level negotiation is of tremendous interest to theologians, Martin Luther was realistic about the attention the proclamation of justification might attract on the local level. One day in a lunch conversation he said: "It is really telling that if one preaches the doctrine of justification the people sleep and cough, but when one tells stories and moral paradigms they sit up, take notice, and listen carefully [attentively]."[19]

That God justified the sinner — the quintessence of the proclamation of justification — not only sounds odd, but is obviously rather difficult to make plausible. At best, it would be conceivable that God declares the sinner justified so that he or she no longer remains a sinner. The oddity of the proclamation of justification and of its doctrinal explanation is seemingly removed by the slogan "Of course we are imperfect and often failing people, but God poses God's 'nevertheless' against it and therefore we may feel fully accepted by God." This seduces one to the cheap saying, "Everyone is accepted by God, just as he or she is," which is currently a widespread surrogate for justification. It means that God moves to fight against every achievement principle because God values — it is said — the person more highly than he or she manages to do. Thus God is declared to be the opponent of Western achievement-oriented soci-

18. "We confess together that God forgives sin by grace and at the same time frees human beings from sin's enslaving power and imparts the gift of new life in Christ." *Joint Declaration* 4.2, no. 22; p. 18.

19. In *M. Luthers Werke: Tischreden* (Table talks), no. 2408b, vol. 2, ed. Karl Drescher (Weimar: Böhlau, 1913), p. 455.

ety, the negative consequences of civilization, and its dehumanizing way of working and living.

Even this, however, reveals an attempt to demonstrate God's justifying action, though precisely this is eventually impossible. That God's justifying action cannot be demonstrated positively means that "I" am taken away from "myself" because God placed me into the undepictable nature of God's reconciliation in Christ. Therefore, justification of the sinner and righteousness of faith are dialectically correlated: one cannot be said without the other. This character of the doctrine of justification creates productive unrest, again and again, for the church and for theology.

CHAPTER 6

Contextual Theology as a Challenge to Dogmatics

Contextual Theology as an Intricate and Multifaceted Phenomenon

Recently, I was invited to lecture on the topic of justification by faith to Catholic students from African and Asian countries. At first they repudiated the topic altogether. They argued: justification is a typical regional problem of the Western theological tradition that has been concerned with forensic and religious legalistic matters such as, for example, personal guilt before God as the lawgiver and judge. Justification by faith thus seemed to them to be enclosed in private religiosity. Alternatively, they wanted to understand theology as focused on the cry for justice in a broader, even holistic sense, combined with efforts in peacemaking, renewal of social relations — the relation to God included — and personal growth in accordance with a humane communal life. It took much effort and serious dialogue to awaken their attention to the proclamation of justification as God's judging and saving action for a people called to be witnesses to the abundant will, providence, and promise of the triune God. Eventually, we discovered that this proclamation, and it alone, provides the unity of theology despite all possible regional differences and cultural diversities. It is the theologically constructive response to the challenge of globalization, without being merely a reaction to that challenge.

This leads us into the midst of the often-heated debate on a worldwide movement in Christian theology that claims to be a new, up-to-date, and ecumenically relevant type of theology. It is the program of seriously "doing theology" in contrast — as the provocative saying goes — to merely "theological thinking and talking." This movement claims to do justice to the *context of theology:* here, "context" is mostly understood as the entirety of conditions and circumstances that mold theology. "Contextual theologians" argue: all people — theologians included — find themselves in a certain time and space, in a situation or position due to their origin, their gender, their education, their social and cultural relationships; therefore, they should be able to diagnose how much they are influenced by the situation of the world in which they are living together with other people, whether in agreement or in discrepancy or protest. Finally, they must interact with this situation in order to cope well with it and to fulfill their assignment and mission.

Contextual theology will provide the adequate methodical tools — even the only sufficient ones — for such a diagnosis and therapy. "Contextual" refers to the situation from which theology *emerges.* This means that Christian theology may rely on the gospel of Jesus Christ, but the tradition of the gospel is always mediated by culture, and the message of the gospel corresponds with God who is already effective in the situation, that is, in the subject who reflects on his or her situation. God is present in one way or the other, and the task of theology is to find the claim of God's presence. In this respect contextual theology compels us to fully and radically recognize the social, political, and anthropological conditions that shape or form today the development of churches and theologians, regardless of whether they were or are in agreement or in disagreement with their contemporary life conditions. On that score, the primary question contextual theologians normally ask is, "How can theology be done?" That is, how can it be done to sufficiently respond to its context? The question, What must be said theologically, and what is its content? is subordinated to the primary task. For its content can only be a *function* of doing theology adequately. And this depends to a great extent upon the sensitivity of the theologian concerning his or her context.

So far I have outlined contextual theology as a programmatic challenge. But what matters most is that the very nature of this program demands that you become personally engaged in the account of doing theology. In fact, it demands the rigorous account of the source and the grounding of theology that justify, direct, and form the boundary of theology by your doing theology. This account must be ethically relevant, a doing as praxis that corresponds to the given context. I will sketch this concept by three preliminary remarks, based on experiences in discussions and confrontations concerning contextual theology.

First, if you approach contextual theology in any of its contemporary variations — for instance, indigenous theology, liberation theology, feminist theology — you will be asked about your own *contextuality*. It would not be satisfactory to tell only who you are, where you are from, and how you are conscious of your actual situation. You must take into account the decisive connection of your reasoning theologically. Yet, already here is a fork in the road! In contextual theology today, this connection is mostly thought of as an overall cultural one, particularly as some kind of involvement in public affairs meant as essential for doing theology. But when Paul Lehmann introduced the term "context" in Christian ethics, he asked, "What am I, as a believer in Jesus Christ and as a member of his church, to do?"[1] Every faithful answer requires the perception of God's work in its whole scope; therefore, for Lehmann it presupposes dogmatics. I would add: dogmatics as the comprehensive account of the inner grounding of the whole range of church practices that characterize the witness of the church. If that is the real meaning of the context of theology, your contextuality will be at best a participation in this context given by God's grace, providence, and outspoken will in his promise and fulfillment. Therefore, you cannot grasp your contextuality by an exhaustive self-reflection on all noticeable circumstances of your life, on your activity in a local church or in a Christian movement, or on your Christian background that is behind your engagement. In contrast, as a baptized Christian you are integrated in the *theological context* of God's acting on you within the story of the triune God. This context of your very being and acting is prior to all your observations, reflections, and intentions. As a rule, you will best encounter and discover your contextuality if you are confronted with it by others who view, think, and argue differently and claim this as being related to their context in contrast to yours. Then you must find

1. Paul Lehmann, *Ethics in a Christian Context* (New York: Harper and Row, 1963), p. 25.

if these differences are concerned with the substance of arguing theologically or about different perspectives related to different situations, that is, different ways of coping with situations, or, most complicated, about the interrelation of both. My arguments are due to such experiences in ecumenical dialogue.

Second, my own theological contextuality relies, at least in part, on the vivid memory of the church struggle in Germany from 1934 to 1945: the controversy concerning the so-called German Christian theology that claimed to derive theology from German history, culture, and race — understood and practiced as the theology of Germans addressed to Germans about Germans. These "German Christians" especially criticized theology as done by Karl Barth and his companions as too "abstract" because it would neglect God's incarnation in history, i.e., God's presence in the course of history. Therefore they suspected Barth's theology of being not only countercultural but even acultural.

"The Theological Explanation of the Confessional Synod of the German Evangelical [Protestant] Church," the Barmen Declaration, on May 31, 1934, opposed the German Christians and stated (thesis 1):

> Jesus Christ, as he is testified to us in the Holy Scripture, is the one Word of God, whom we are to hear, whom we are to trust and obey in life and in death.
>
> We repudiate the false teaching that the church can and must recognize yet other happenings and powers, images and truths as divine revelation alongside this one Word of God, as source of her preaching.[2]

Can or even must this controversy be understood as a "contextual" event only that is limited to the German Christians who mostly were nationalistic, extremely conservative, in part even racist? That would be much too simple, and if it had been the case, the Barmen Declaration would have been outdated long since. But it was not at all a partisan document of church politics. Many of its signers were just as concerned as their opponents with the urgent economic and political needs of the day such as unemployment, depression, and unrest that bordered on civil war. However, whereas the German Christians

2. *Creeds of the Churches: A Reader in Christian Doctrine from the Bible to the Present,* ed. John H. Leith, 3rd ed. (Louisville: John Knox, 1982), p. 520.

were looking for a strong political leadership that promised to build up national unity solving these problems, the declaration pointed to Jesus Christ as the true shepherd leading his flock on the way of truth, justice, and peace. The signers were engaged in listening to the living Word of God instead of to a soliloquy of people. The result of the struggle with the German Christians and the political power that supported them yielded a theological insight into a permanent task for the proclamation of the church and for doing theology. Therefore, the Barmen Declaration became and remains a document of high dogmatic quality that itself unmasks a kind of distorted contextual theology, which operates with a misleading doctrine of incarnation and tries to equate the course of history with the will of God. The declaration shows *how to argue theologically pointing to distinctions necessary for faith,* for example, political "happenings and powers" and cultural "images and truths" versus the Word of God as source of the preaching of the church.

Of course, I am not simply equating the German Christian pseudotheology with the various concepts of contemporary contextual theology. But the "challenge" of an overarching, even totalitarian reference to a context remains a very sensitive topic, not only for interpreting the history of the church, of church doctrine, and of theology in general but above all for the distinctions necessary for faith.[3] You cannot seriously *derive* theology from any contextual factors, or at least you must realize that such derivation would define theology from outside its genuine grounding. Its function, for instance the commitment for true humane life conditions based on liberty, justice, and peace — as demanding as they are to all Christians concerned with the common good! — would mold what the church is entrusted to say and to perform under all circumstances.

Third, Korean graduate students who wanted to study with me were troubled with the task of being "indigenous" — intertwined with their culture — and at the same time being serious Christian theologians called by a proclamation that was brought to their country by foreign missionaries. The gospel was and remains *essentially* "strange" to their people not because of cultural differences but because it is an

---

3. Cf. Gerhard Sauter, *Gateways to Dogmatics: Reasoning Theologically for the Life of the Church* (Grand Rapids: Eerdmans, 2003), pp. 44-50.

"unrequested" message: a message that does not spring from "flesh and blood" (1 Cor. 15:50) and even not from deep-rooted spiritual sources but is created by the surprising and often deeply shaking Spirit of God, the externality that God creates.

These young Korean theologians — and the same is true for other Asian and African theologians — are longing for their true *authenticity*. At the same time, they ask for reasoning theologically in the context of Christianity and its true source. We must take seriously both: being authentic as indigenous Christians and reasoning theologically within the context of Christianity, and neither identify nor confuse them. My Korean students were already familiar with the conviction, very common among contextual theologians, that there is an enormous gap between "Western" theology linked with Western culture and theologies in other parts of the world, especially in economically underprivileged and politically struggling ones. Western theology is criticized for being individualistic, to a great extent secularized, mainly intellectualistic, and far too little concerned with the everyday needs of ordinary people, particularly of marginalized ones.

As justifiable and necessary as such criticism might be, it tends to lead our primary concern of reasoning theologically to a dead end. Indeed, after only one or two generations of Asian and African theologians' attempts to establish an indigenous theology often in opposition to Western theology, many younger theologians have noticed various traps within the enterprise itself. The methodical tools of criticizing Western theology mostly are a blend of political sciences, sociology, philosophy of culture, cultural anthropology, social psychology, hermeneutics, and linguistics — those methods are likewise "imported" from the West. How can they serve indigenous theologians better as Western theology? Such Western university methods may be helpful in some ways, but they cannot substitute genuine theological reasoning for the life of the church. In fact, most of these methods mirror or reflect ideological clashes within Western academies. They are, therefore, quite contextual indeed, and they must be regarded as such. If you study various methods or models of contextual theology, you are very often reminded of good old-fashioned typical "Western" — mostly "liberal" — concepts of theology. For instance, there is an "anthropological model" primarily concerned with "the establishment or preservation of cultural identity by a person of

Christian faith,"[4] or a "transcendental model" concerned "with one's own religious experience and one's own experience of oneself"[5] that puts emphasis "on the authenticity of the subject who is trying to express his or her experience as a person of faith and a person of a particular context."[6] Or there is a rigorous social criticism that looks something like a counterestablishment attitude mixed up with an immediate reference to the Bible. All these approaches can be debated, but if we regard that reasoning theologically is not equal with sheer intellectualism but is an unavoidable task of the Christian faith, such approaches do not provide a sufficient answer to the questions of what is the source of the proclamation of the church, what are the inner groundings of church practices, and how we can take account of these groundings.

You will discover the character of this reasoning by studying dogmatics seriously. Dogmatics consists of experiences in thinking.[7] They might be provoked sometimes by certain circumstances, but they are constituted as the consensus of the church looking for God's acting in the power of God's Spirit. These experiences in reasoning produced theological tools of "differentiating without separating" God and world, God and humanity, the history of God's acting in the world and the history of humanity. These tools are rooted in the Bible, and most of them were explained by the early church, for example in the Formula of Chalcedon (451) on the unity of God and humanity in Jesus Christ. This formula has itself been a productive result of overcoming contextually rooted controversies in Christology (Antioch and Alexandria). I argue that we have an urgent need for remembering and studying such experiences in thinking that nourished theology and church for centuries. I am convinced that they will be true and enormously helpful for dealing with contemporary tasks.

Studying dogmatics as reasoning theologically, you will also notice that there is mostly a creative *tension* between theological perceptions and critical insights of historical, cultural conditions. There are not only contextual "challenges" and theological "answers" — that

---

4. Stephen B. Bevans, *Models of Contextual Theology*, revised and expanded ed. (Maryknoll, N.Y.: Orbis, 2002), p. 54.
5. Bevans, *Models of Contextual Theology*, p. 104.
6. Bevans, *Models of Contextual Theology*, p. 106.
7. Cf. chap. 4, in this volume.

would be not only much too simple but also reactionary — but theological tasks that shape and renew misleading practices, intellectual and religious habits included. Korean theology, for instance, must struggle with the veneration for the ancestors. It must learn to differentiate between due respect for ancestors and respect for the cultural heritage and the obsession that the dead remain in power over the living. A similar struggle faces animism in Asia and in Africa, or wherever the existence of a spiritual world is taken as an obvious fact. Here, the confession might be at stake that Jesus Christ the Crucified and Risen One is "God's mighty claim in our whole life; in him we encounter a joyous liberation from the godless claims of this world to free and thankful service to his creatures" (Barmen Declaration, thesis 2).[8] Both Western theology and theology in other parts of the world were and are confronted with this task, though not always in the same way, but nevertheless unavoidably on the way of theology in history and among various cultures. "Western" theology can support "Eastern" and other theologians in coping with their own tasks by communicating to them its thinking experiences in regard to similar situations.

The Redefinition of Theology by the Aspirations of Contextual Theology

Now, we need to analyze more closely the term "context." In the way it is used in "contextual theology," it is relatively young. It emerged in the controversies of the late sixties and early seventies of the last century. Initially it evolved among various trends in the United States of America. It then became more and more popular among South American, African, and Asian theologians who attacked what was considered the burdensome legacy of European and, in part, North American colonialism even in theology. Originally "context" meant the verbalized connection of a text, or metaphorically "a web," a "word-web": the syntactical interrelationships of a text. For a long time "context" was spoken about in these linguistic and hermeneutical categories. They refer to the association of signs with other signs. But concurrent

8. *Creeds of the Churches*, p. 520.

with the expansion of semiotics into a full-fledged theory of signs and symbols, the meaning of "context" was enlarged. As research in linguistics and sociology of speech has shown, signs and symbols can also be prespeech and beyond-speech. Now, "context" means the whole structure into which a formulated text is woven: the conditions under which we exist, under which we also act, think, and speak. Those who know these conditions know also what in one way or the other can be said, can be meant, or can happen. The *context is thus the world*, first of all a particular environment, often called "situation," but then more inclusively the world as a whole. It is the basis for everything that subsequently develops. We affect these interrelationships whether they are of act, speech, or thought in order. In turn, we understand ourselves in relationship to them. In short, "context" includes the totality of all reciprocal relationships in which something, not only a text, exists or happens.

The comprehensive meaning of "context" can be understood and used in what we might call a "soft" and a "hard" manner. In the first, literal sense, it leads to the careful and thorough recognition of the various interrelations of a text by establishing the linguistic shape of its surrounding area. For instance, if you struggle with a difficult sentence in Paul's letter to the Romans, you must read the whole letter, and maybe other Pauline texts, too. So far the primary interest applies to the text, that is, to what it says. It is helpful, often even necessary, to know further interrelations of a text to discover how it developed, how it was perceived when it was formed, and how it can be valued today. Then, you rely no longer only on the text but more and more on assumptions about its conditions. Yet, if your reconstruction of the context defines the function of a theological text as dependent on all situational circumstances that you regard as decisive, the result would be a "hard" contextual theology: an exclusive shape of theology because it claims to include all factors that can be demonstrated as being relevant to theology and how it can be relevant for us today. In the following, I will talk of this hard understanding of context in theology as *Contextual Theology*. It claims that "context" is the quintessence of the interrelationships of life and activity that *illuminate and determine* all sorts of texts. Knowing the context becomes even a new *authority:* what must be known *beforehand* that allows the text — or a speech preserved as a text — to be interpreted.

To illustrate these two manners of understanding "context," let us take as example Martin Luther's treatise *The Freedom of a Christian* (1520).[9] It was written in the midst of a torrent of demands for political liberty. In this situation Luther emphasized the freedom for which "Christ has set us free" (Gal. 5:1): it is the underivable freedom granted by the free will of God, given to us by faith that is true under *any* circumstances, even in prison. We are set free to trust and to obey God. Insofar as the Christian is not subject to anybody or to any situation, no emperor and no pope can take this freedom from us because they cannot provide it. At the same time, this freedom directs our care for the need of our neighbors because it is faithful to God's ongoing work and God's will in God's creation. On that score, Christians are subject to everyone; they are even slaves who have to do what is demanded from them unconditionally.

To what degree are we concerned at this point with the "context" of Luther's essay on Christian freedom that is the freedom of faith? I prefer to be concerned with the context only insofar as the historical interrelations that surround Luther's statement enable its profile to become distinct. The historian investigates these interrelations and thereby assists in the recognition of the historical profile. This, in turn, provides the interpretation of the work with a much greater historical depth than would otherwise be the case.

However, regarding how the term "context" is used in Contextual Theology, another preunderstanding appropriates the exclusive role, a preunderstanding that can cause a methodological prejudice. According to this program, Luther's treatise must be regarded in relation to the cry for liberty in all realms of life. It will be judged by the impact on liberating life conditions and patterns of thought. Luther is asked for his contribution to this movement that was in some way originally supported or even caused by his resistance against the church authorities. Yet, during the peasants' revolt in 1525 Luther opposed revolutionary intentions. He harshly criticized all tendencies toward destroying or radically changing laws and orders. Therefore, Luther will be judged to have taken a first step toward liberty, social justice, and human rights but failed to take the second, decisive step. He is even

---

9. In *Luther's Works*, vol. 31, *Career of the Reformer I*, trans. W. A. Lambert, rev. and ed. Harold J. Grimm (Philadelphia: Fortress, 1957), pp. 333-77.

regarded as becoming a traitor to poor people who understood Christian freedom as an encouragement for liberation from all sorts of oppression. He moved back, supported the political authorities, and captivated Christian freedom within a self-sufficient inner life.

If Luther's text is reconstructed in this "contextualized" manner, it remains relevant only in a way confined to the relation of theology to political progress measured by the norms determined by the later cultural development or by wished-for goals that are regarded as normative. Luther's text is judged by this function. Then, Luther's witness will easily be ignored. It is no longer noticed that Luther tried to clarify the undeserved gift of the freedom of faith in a really dialectical way: this unconditioned gift must not be exchanged with the liberty we may long for. By no means does Luther restrict Christian freedom to an inner independence from threatening life conditions. But he shows that we might be tempted to give away the God-given freedom if we submit ourselves to any ultimate goal of being independent and becoming completely and perfectly liberated by our own efforts.

Sometimes a thoroughly contextual reconstruction paints a grotesque picture. For example, the book of Ecclesiastes — this wonderful example of faithful wisdom, asking for understanding of the order of nature, political life, and individual destiny, full of sober skepticism that opens up again and again to deep gratitude for the created life and its measure! — is often "interpreted" today as an expression of the disappointment of a high official depressed by his inability to master the political life and to make sense of the obvious disorder in an overaged, declining, and individualistic culture. It seems to me that such a terrible misinterpretation rather mirrors the occupational disease of the interpreter and projects contemporary academic dilemmas onto the text. It shows that we suffer from serious difficulties in perceiving and realizing the ways in which former generations have dealt with basic questions of faith facing their often extremely difficult and complicated life conditions.

If the *literary relationship of text and context* is carried over into the *relationship of text and situation,* the text becomes the *expression* of the situation — that is to say, the productive confrontation with the surrounding circumstances — and this endeavor explains the text functionally: now it is not what the text says that really counts, but rather what it can mean under certain conditions, what it intends and achieves. This *outlook on the function* is a *unifying element* in Contextual Theology; this common interest is important because Contextual Theology honors *diversity* so much. The unifying element is crucial because there is a broad variety of ways in which outspoken Contextual Theologians understand both the meaning of context and the manner in which they relate to and how they use the term "context." Just to sketch a few examples: North American evangelical theologians interested in Christian mission use extensively a cultural anthropology often within a functionalist understanding.[10] Latin liberation theologians, on the other hand, often rely on Marxist-oriented sociology. But there are more differences. Many Contextual Theologians argue that the context provides the "form" of theology but the "content" is derived from the gospel as witnessed in the New Testament. But, for example, the South African Catholic theologian Albert Nolan argues just the opposite: the gospel provides the form or shape of theology and the context provides or shapes its content.[11]

Another common denominator is the emphasis of a majority of Contextual Theologians on social, economic, and political concerns, in short, on the involvement in public affairs. They claim that these are the most urgent conditions "under which theology is done" and within which it has a very specific, relevant function. This follows the definition of Contextual Theology according to the representative *Ökumene-Lexikon* that states:

First, one does theology. *Theology is a reflection on social reality and an activity of productive thinking,* under specific conditions that it must adopt to really be productive. "Doing theology" means to engage in ongoing social, economic, and cultural processes, to *respond to challenges* in this realm. To this I would add that this engagement often is linked with spirituality and a new awareness of community and communication.

Second, theology always has a function; it can and should be explained by its functionality. It allows itself to be identified only in relation to public processes, mainly the urgent need of suffering people. For Contextual Theology, the leading expectation is the liberation of humanity

10. Cf. Charles H. Kraft, *Christianity in Culture: A Study in Dynamic Biblical Theologizing in Cross-Cultural Perspective* (Maryknoll, N.Y.: Orbis, 1979); Charles H. Kraft, *Anthropology for Christian Witness* (Maryknoll, N.Y.: Orbis, 1996).

11. A. Nolan, *God in South Africa: The Challenge of the Gospel* (Grand Rapids: Eerdmans, 1988).

from oppression that results from their actual living conditions, conditions that do not allow them to reach the point where they can live adequately as human beings.

Third, theology is measured by its relevance. It will be judged and justified by what it achieves. Contextual Theologians argue that theology has to struggle for truly humane human life because God's salvation is not to be separated from the welfare of humanity.[12]

I want to illustrate my explanation of this threefold objective — as defined by the *Ökumene-Lexikon* — with an example from liberation theology. John de Gruchy, a prominent South African theologian, writes: "Hermeneutics is a circular task, or more correctly, there is a *hermeneutical spiral* involved in this way of doing theology. This means that doing theology begins with the witness of the church in the world, then proceeds to reflect critically on that witness both through reflection on the Scriptures and through an analysis of what is happening in the world, and finally it seeks to inform Christian witness so that it may be more faithful to the gospel and more relevant to the needs of the world."[13]

This sounds appealing indeed. But it seems like a shortcut, because the witness of the church is reflected only by referring to the Bible mediated by the analysis of the given situation. Theology as service for interpreting Scripture, dogmatics as champion for the art of reading the Bible and for faithfulness to Scripture are left out. As a consequence there is no sufficient theological "safety device" that secures the witness of the church. This witness as entrusted by God is not a mere reflection of an analysis of the situation — even if such an analysis might be in conjunction with biblical motifs. For example, when Luther's proclamation of Christian freedom is interpreted as support of a widespread demand for political liberty. Or today, God's justice is often equated with social justice. And there are further serious reductions. Theology is reduced to soteriology, and what is worse, soteriology itself is being treated in a deficient way: the doctrine that

---

12. Paul Löffler, "Kontextuelle Theologie," in *Ökumene-Lexikon: Kirchen–Religionen–Bewegungen*, ed. Hanfried Krüger, Werner Löser, and Walter Müller-Römheld (Frankfurt am Main: Lembeck/Knecht, 1983), pp. 714-15.

13. "The Nature, Necessity and Task of Theology," in *Doing Theology in Context: South African Perspectives*, ed. John W. de Gruchy and Charles Villa-Vicencio (Maryknoll, N.Y.: Orbis; Cape Town: David Philip, 1994), p. 10.

God reconciles the world with God, creating anew a totally destroyed relationship by God's sovereign acting, is replaced by the proposal that God merely "repairs" damaged relations. A process of peacemaking and overcoming of guilt replaces the gift of atonement and the gift of forgiveness of sin. God's mercy and compassion are no longer accompanied by God's judgment and by the "cultic" sphere of God's communication with humanity. This kind of reduction does not strengthen the moral responsibility of Christians but weakens their ethical discernment.

In spite of much diversity among liberation theologians, there is an overarching convergence in many respects. Their leading question is, What is God doing to address the social and economic realities that cause oppression — in order to radically change them? They argue that the answer can be perceived only in solidarity with the basic sensitivities of humanity, and that implies that we must intercede on behalf of all who are subjugated in any form. For whom would it not be desirable to be liberated from obedience to alien institutions, from subjection to the purposes of others, and from the alienation of one's own being? This longing is hidden in the heart of every person. It is an inextinguishable memory of our common destiny as human beings. It lights our way as a torch at the head of a procession toward a new world order. We get enlightened like that: this is God's acting in favor of all.

In addition, liberation theology wants to expose human bondage as a collective obliviousness of God. People live and have lived in sin or have been thrust into separation from God. Many liberation theologians would put this more strongly: human bondage is a rejection of God and an attack on God. To cause a human being to suffer is to cause God to suffer. This reality, so the argument goes, must be illustrated by the conditions in which people live, such as the loss of political rights and social oppression. Theology has a crucial function in this regard. It contributes to the resistance against cruel, unjust structures. This is the first step toward liberation. The political and socioeconomic realities are subject to critique and change.

The second and decisive step is change. The change cannot be extensive enough. Above all, change must be a continual process if one is serious about overcoming human obliviousness to God. Nonetheless, communion with God is not a utopian yearning for the eschaton. On the contrary, it is to be found in solidarity with those who suffer, with those with whom God has identified, and with those for whose cause God has intervened. Every time one experiences liberation from the various forms of material, intellectual, and spiritual affliction and misery, one experiences God and one experiences also a common bond with humanity — even if these moments are transient.

This is merely *one* floodlight that provides a closer look at liberation theology in its various colors. One should say much more in this regard. One should answer the questions: How does it raise consciousness against injustice? How does it struggle against indifference that is placidly accepted and ignored? Liberation theologians in Western Europe and in the United States might tend to respond to this challenge by reclaiming human liberty as one of the foremost universal values to be realized in a secular world based on universal human rights. At the same time, many of them do not share an anxiety about talking of God and of God's acting in history, an anxiety that is widespread in the West, inherited by the Enlightenment and its criticism of the perception of God's acting. Liberation theologians view this anxiety as linked with a society that is concentrated only upon itself in such a way that it is blind to the abyss that opens before it. In contrast, liberation theologians in the so-called Third World live, work, and reflect in a social-cultural context where talk of God and of God's actions in history is unproblematic and could even be identified with overcoming injustice, oppression, and humiliation. But here we need to argue: every true theological reluctance to identify God's acting with the change *or* the justification of life conditions is not inherited from the skepticism of the Enlightenment only. Rather, it stems originally from the Jewish and Christian differentiation between God's acting and the course of history. This differentiation does not mean separation. However, the people of Israel and Christians had to learn in a very difficult and demanding way to ask for God's will *in the midst* of their suffering and healing experiences in order to expect God as sovereign of life and death. God reveals Godself in history, but the course of events is not the revelation of God: this was the message of the prophets of Israel as well as the proclamation of Augustine in his *City of God* and of other theologians and spiritual leaders.

"Contextual Theology" is an umbrella term like "situation ethics" because it appears to be realistic, flexible, and responsive. Both sound attractive. Yet they are not very distinctive. The umbrella term "con-

text" seems to provide protection against traditions regarded as oppressive, especially against dogmatics suspected of being "abstract"
and unrealistic, alienated from vital tasks. Even a reasoning that is
faithful to the grounding of theology — mediated by the consensus of
the church truly kept in dogmatics — seems to be a sort of oppression.
This criticism reminds us that dogmatics needs indeed a self-critical
reflection to avoid deterioration into a mere administration of theological traditions and their observance. Precisely in this way, Contextual Theology is a productive challenge to dogmatics. Of course, dogmatics is *situation-related*. So are all biblical texts and all human speech
because they occur in the medium of language. However, dogmatics
ought not be *situation-dominated* by the derivation from conditions that
can be mastered by reflection on that situation, by its analysis, and by
coping with its problems. Here again is a fork in the road. Though theology always relates in different ways to different situations and living
conditions in which theologians in solidarity with other people find
themselves, it nevertheless cannot be induced from these situations.
They are not its source. Dogmatics will neither be nourished by it nor
appear as its product. In this respect, it is actually dogmatics that
guards truly the faithful independence of theology.

In light of our analysis of Contextual Theology, we should now explain the crucial task introduced in chapter 4: What must be said in
faith, hope, and love, unconditionally under all circumstances? How is
it related to factors that shape our circumstances — for we always believe, trust, and act among certain living conditions? This twofold
question is primary, elementary, and unavoidable for every act of reasoning theologically. It gives theology its momentum.

The Grounding of Theology in Jesus Christ
as the Means of the Cohesion of Various Contexts

In 1972-74 I participated in three representative consultations of the
Ecumenical Institute in Bossey, Switzerland, on doing theology today.[14] After a very aggressive paper delivered by the Afro-American

14. Documented in part in *Doing Theology Today*, ed. Choan-Seng Song (Madras, India: Christian Literature Society, 1976).

liberation theologian James H. Cone (Union Theological Seminary, New York), all "white Western" theologians were silenced. Cone told us that Jesus Christ had deserted our churches and found a new home in the hearts of other people and in another new time of history destined for liberation. No further dialogue seemed to be possible. Then an Indian bishop stood up. He did not portray another Christ, an indigenous one. Instead, he said:

> Brother, Western missionaries brought a Christ to us who was marked by the history of the European and North American churches with all their quarrels, their splits, their involvements in politics, the burdens of their cultures. We needed a very long time until we were able to view the authentic face of Jesus Christ who is encountering us. Please, do not introduce a new Jesus Christ, *your* particular image of the suffering and liberating Jesus Christ! Let us look together to Christ who is looking to us, who is our Lord, and whom we expect as the Coming One.

Indeed, all images of Christ are contextual, as Christian art shows. Most pictures of Christ are meant as visualizations of the presence of Christ in the situation of the artist and in his "context" (with the possible exception of Byzantine, Greek, and Russian icons, which try to be windows to eternity and means of contemplation). So far, images of Christ — the images produced by the quest for the "historical Jesus" included! — are unavoidably contextual. At the same time, they are subject to human longing for the Messiah, the Savior, and to the prejudices of all-too-human yearning.

Images of Christ perceive him "according to the flesh" (2 Cor. 5:16),[15] in correlation to our self-understanding and its expectations. The prejudices of such perceptions caused Jesus of Nazareth to suffer and to die, and the Easter narratives show how difficult it was even for the disciples to expose themselves to the risen Christ, to recognize the Crucified One in his gestalt and vice versa the glory of the Transformed One in his wounds. Christology cannot be an endeavor to depict Jesus Christ, even in another way, for example, in a literal one. Regarding this impossibility, we are reminded of the essentially a posteriori character of all talk of God and about God. This is recounted in

15. NRSV: "from a human point of view."

the story of God's appearance according to Exodus 33:18-23: God promises to bring God's divine presence into the presence of Moses. God even proclaims God's name before him. However, Moses has to shield himself from the fullness of God's power and brilliance so that when God passes him God shows only God's back. No one is allowed to see God directly. We can speak of God only after God has confronted us. Therefore theology is able to speak of God only post hoc, that is, afterward. Christian theology can perceive the crucified and risen Christ only a posteriori, in hindsight, not a priori, in advance. This is crucial for the *theologia crucis,* the theology of the cross. Nobody is able to say that God reveals Godself if God had not acted in this moment and in God's own strange way. It is impossible to say beforehand where God is to be experienced and how God is to be found. It is because God has already established God's communication with us through the suffering and death of Jesus Christ that it would be misleading to search for God anywhere else than in the contingent act in which God has shown and will disclose Godself to us: God's revelation on the cross of Jesus Christ.

In this respect Christian theology, in comparison to one of the function-oriented disciplines — like cultural anthropology, political science, sociology, and social psychology — is less than defined, or "underdetermined" *(unterbestimmt).* The crucial point here is that the pattern of judgment relevant to theology is quite different from that which is applicable to forms of knowledge in the function-oriented disciplines.[16] From its beginning to its end, theology is the basis on which people place themselves under God's judgment with regard to both their activity and lack of activity in counterdistinction to scrutinizing themselves in a process of self-justification. Persons are called to God so that they follow God's promise and outspoken will despite the interference of other perspectives and other considerations. This means listening to God's Word and assuredly trusting what God has previously conveyed in word and deed, as well as moving toward what God is bringing near to us. In this way persons *are* liberated from self-

16. I explained this qualitative difference methodically as the distinction between the (theological) "context of justification" (or "context of validation") and the (contextual) "context(s) of discovery" in *Eschatological Rationality: Theological Issues in Focus* (Grand Rapids: Baker, 1996), pp. 179-89, and in *Gateways to Dogmatics,* pp. 257-59.

centered speech and endless discourse. To *judge theologically* means to have experienced the distinction between a posteriori and a priori in regard to the question of how to begin to talk of and about God.

This is truly different from the challenge posted by Contextual Theology. Its program relates theology to and even identifies it with actions for the reestablishment of the world as it ought to be. In addition, many Contextual Theologians claim to understand dogmatics only as a component part of the Western academic community that tried to form a world unity by understanding the world itself as representative of divine unity. Instead of referring to this world unity, which has been expressed in and imposed through a unified theological thought structure having authoritative and even imperial claims, Contextual Theology relies first on a plurality, developed from different expressions of faith, but then it searches for processes unifying humanity. The key problem is its obligation to deep-rooted human affections, speech, and thought in contrast to the rationality of Christian faith that must not be mistaken for intellectualism. Contextual Theology intends to transform the concept of oneness of faith into that of global unity: the world in the process of unification as established by continuing interaction for the sake of rescuing true humane existence. This is the contextual "world formula." Contextual Theology operates with the utopian assumption that the one world will materialize when all people are able to live under humane conditions. The unity of this perception is called for in view of the one reality that, though not yet accomplished, is the goal that guides us on our way because it is the basis of living together.

In contrast, the theological grounding to which the church of Jesus Christ must witness is not to be extracted from each particular context, even though there are a number of different situations that theology must take into account. It is certainly true that the grounding of theology is always found within a particular context. However, this grounding must be identified unambiguously and clearly even if the same words are not used in all contexts. The nonderivability of the theological grounding is related to the faithfulness in the one God, in the one Lord Jesus Christ, and in the one unifying Spirit, based on the hope "that God may be all in all" (1 Cor. 15:28). Under various circumstances this nonderivable theological grounding will bring forth cohesion between various contexts. The unity of faith, hope, and love will not grow out of just any particular theology that claims to be universal. Theology that is aware of its context can be done only a posteriori to this acknowledgment. Nevertheless, contextual diversity may lead to a many-voiced doxology praising the unifying work of the triune God.

The following chapters might serve in part as examples for the impact of the political and cultural circumstances, the "situation," that influence theology, especially in times of crisis. They will show in more detail how theology often is in danger of being shaped rather by its particular context than it is capable to give account of and point to God's promises and acting accordingly. Lacking dogmatics, theology runs the risk of becoming a mere reflection of its context. In this way theology without dogmatics only mirrors its context instead of reflecting upon the situation and carefully considering it in a way that is theologically responsible. Insofar as dogmatics allows us to avoid such a pitfall, it is not oppressive but indeed is a precious gift that needs to be treasured and cared for.

CHAPTER 7

Theological Reflections on the Political Changes in Europe

A Certain Speechlessness

On November 9, 1989, the day the Berlin Wall collapsed, I was in Princeton as a guest lecturer. In the late afternoon, by chance I switched on the television set. To my surprise I saw people cheering and waving flags while standing on the wall. I assumed it was a new American movie and admired the excellent scenery in what I took to be a play. Then other guests of the house entered the room, embraced me, and congratulated Germany on this miraculous event. I felt as if I was dreaming. Throughout the weeks before, I had been afraid of political unrest and bloodshed. After all, there had been brutal repression in China some months earlier. I had visited friends in East Germany in October, and they were very concerned, particularly about the reaction of the government to the protest demonstrations and to the refugees trying to escape to West Germany via Czechoslovakia, Hungary, and even Poland.

Now the wall had broken down; the Iron Curtain — the symbol of the Cold War — had been removed. Some days later at the meeting of the American Academy of Religion, I heard an American theologian remark that he had had his doubts about the second coming of Jesus Christ, but not anymore. Because after the collapse of the Berlin Wall, he considered all things to be possible.

Was this a theologically appropriate conclusion to draw from this event? As an event, it was no doubt contingent and basically inexplicable. Of course, later there were many attempts to explain the causes of what had happened. But I do not know of any serious politician, political expert, or journalist who can honestly claim that he or she had foreknown or predicted this incident. After all, one might reasonably think there would have been an omen of some sort. And to be sure, the end of the Cold War did not come down from heaven. A great many people played parts in very different and divergent ways, often unsuspectingly or even contrary to their own intentions and plans. Many had only reacted to developments that seemed unavoidable; afterward they saw that events had happened in a way quite different from what they had intended.

The dominant impression I remember from that time was a peculiar speechlessness, a silence with respect to theological affirmations or even the posing of such questions. The heart of the events seemed to be unspeakable. There were of course many comments and explanations, but what they tried to grasp remains unutterable. Excuses and self-justification have shattered the silence about theological affirmations on the one hand, as have self-righteous declarations (especially by people from the former West Germany) on the other.

Pastors and parishioners in East Germany were reluctant to explain — even incapable of explaining — the events they saw. They were overwhelmed by the end of an era during which they had suffered so much. They had searched for declarations and actions to open up their closed society and thereby had contributed something to the changes that eventually took place. They had asked for a bit of political liberty, at least for some involvement in government decisions, freedom of speech, and — very important for most of the people — the chance to travel to foreign countries for a while and to escape the feeling that they were in a prison. Their demands in recent years were made in the hope of achieving peace and of overcoming tensions within the socialist society. But the final event was quite different from the political alternative they had sought "within" the existing society. How was this new situation to be understood? As a new political alternative only? Or, viewed theologically, was it to be seen as an altogether different situation and challenge?

But in East Germany there was only the silence. This was even more pronounced in West Germany. An example: On October 3, 1990, the unification of Germany was realized. Germany was one nation again. The German government tried to make the celebration as magnificent and solemn as possible. Church bells should ring out thanksgiving, as they had in former times for victories and peace. But most representatives of the churches in the western part were very reluctant to accommodate the government's request. They voiced their disagreement, recalling that in recent German history, during the nineteenth century and the first half of the twentieth century, churches quite often were too affirming of government actions, too ready to bless them. Now church authorities wanted to avoid the mistake of confusing religion and politics. They refused to start a civil religion. But unwittingly, they contributed to the intricate relationship between church and state that had previously existed in the eastern part of the country. They were prepared to be critical not so much of political matters as of actions conducive to the well-being of the state. By contrast, many church people in former East Germany had tried very hard to be constructive in affairs of state and to engage themselves in matters of common interest, respecting the state at least to the extent that it provided a framework of living and working together for the public welfare. Some church officials, professors of theology, and church members went so far as to cooperate with the Secret Service or to be involved in activities of the government, often interested in a gradual reform of the socialist system; others had contributed to the very limited public life by criticizing the loss of human rights and oppressive structures without claiming a radical change of the political order; many hoped in a "third way" between socialism and capitalism (or Western-oriented market economy) to be realized in a unified Germany. Therefore, the mood was very mixed.

Finally many parishes decided to ring the bells as an invitation to a special service — although some people would not have known how to distinguish this from heralding other ceremonies. It was a good chance to have an ecumenical service, to celebrate unity in Christ as a focus of national unity. I wonder what was said in these evening services. Some sermons were published later or documented in other ways, and an article dealing with the main topics of these sermons has appeared.[1] For the most part, these sermons expressed thankfulness for the surprising

---

1. Martin Dutzmann, "Gottesdienst am Nationalfeiertag?" in *In der Schar derer, die da feiern: Feste als Gegenstand praktisch-theologischer Reflexion*, ed. Peter Cornehl, Martin Dutzmann, and Andreas Strauch (Göttingen: Vandenhoeck & Ruprecht, 1993), pp. 200-211.

political solutions. They also reflected a spontaneous gratitude to God, who was seen as having done a good job by ending all troubles and bringing about peace, a peace often understood as a chance to achieve a more equitable economic life. Often it was said that reunification was a gift. On a number of occasions the German chancellor Helmut Kohl said it was a gift of history. This sounds as if history amounts to Santa Claus punishing bad children and rewarding good children. What does it mean that unity is a gift? What does the givenness of the gift tell us about what was said, thought, and done four decades earlier? And how could the givenness of the event point to a future where what was previously unthinkable now seemed possible?

I risk a suggestion that I will try to explain later: the emphasis on being grateful only for surprisingly positive events shows a strange fear of speaking of God's action in history, and is in sharp contrast to emphasizing God's ongoing will. That is the first point I want to make.

During the previous decades, many had appealed to God's will — not in the sense of God's purposes, but in the sense of declaring what God demands of us. They asked: What does God want us to do to ensure that there is not another historic catastrophe akin to the terrible last world war, which *must* be the last, for God's sake! What are we obliged to do when it seems that God did not intervene at the concentration camp of Auschwitz; nor at Coventry, the English city bombed by the Germans; nor at Stalingrad, the Russian city totally destroyed by the Germans, where there is a mass grave of German and of Russian soldiers; nor at Dresden, the German city burned to the ground by the British air force just weeks before the end of the war — to mention only some symbolic places? God seemed to remain silent. Perhaps he fell silent in the face of the terrible things human beings were and are able to achieve, or perhaps he even "died away." Some theologians did in fact declare the death of the god who rules the world in the magnificent way our ancestors told us. Such a god is dead. He bequeathed the responsibility for our world, for better or for worse, into our hands.

Was the collapse of the Berlin Wall a sign for an opposing idea of a god who works seemingly by accident, taking us by surprise with such positive events? Or does the decisive point of post–world war history provoke us to question our understanding of history, especially our concepts of the agency of history? The challenge may arise from the observation that in 1989 most leading people did more reacting than acting.

How Can We Refer to God's Will?

The peculiar speechlessness — the silence regarding theological affirmations, so widespread today — stands in strange and sharp contrast to the overflowing eloquence we experienced during the previous four decades: a readiness to refer to God's will, to make him correspond to the course of the world, or — better — a readiness to instruct the church to respond to the predictable course of events. Most often this course was commended to the will of God in an attempt to avoid what was threatening to happen. This is the second point I would like to emphasize.

Let me give you an example of a crucial experience for my understanding of the complications of theological criteria in matters of politics. In 1956, when the uprising in Hungary broke out, I was a student at Göttingen University. With others, I helped to prepare shelters for Hungarian refugees. From the refugees we learned about the outburst of hate and vindictiveness that they had suffered. But also some of the women told us that they now expected to get furs and to be able to afford other expensive items. They had heard that these goods would be part of the standard of living in the "West" and that everybody would have the right to such things. To what propaganda had they listened? Would they now see themselves in an economic trap? We students felt very uneasy about it. How could we prevent their inappropriate expectations from distorting reality, while realizing our good intentions of helping them cope with their true situation and showing our solidarity?

Some days later — after the Russian army had marched in and put down the uprising with terrible bloodshed — I heard one of my respected theology teachers remark on the Hungarian uprising. He concluded that the Russian invasion might be understandable and even reasonable from the Russian point of view. Anyone who heard this theologian would suspect that what he meant was: "Don't allow yourself to be seduced by your Western self-justification! Think about the political situation in Europe and the danger of a new confrontation that can spontaneously convert the Cold War into a deadly hot conflict that might spread all over the world. Don't forget for even a moment that the Iron Curtain is the result of World War Two, which has to be the last big war by all reasonable means. Otherwise Europe will ruin itself!"

Such a warning, and the "calming down" it called for, seemed to be thoroughly appropriate. It revealed the difficult situation: foreign policy and its possible development should determine our judgment. Whatever was said in the West had to be examined for its implications for the East-West conflict. That is, domestic politics and even moral values were to be determined by considerations of foreign policy, and especially by the calculated reactions of "the other side." It seemed impossible to see an event in its singularity, because it was assumed that anything that could happen could be explained from the beginning only by the geopolitical constellation of the postwar period. This was another trap. Could one be fair to suffering people (i.e., not taking the point of view of their oppressors) and at the same time be fair to them according to the political environment? A dualistic structure of views and options reflecting the antagonism of the world powers prevailed in that period. Now there is an absence of such dual options, an absence that makes many of our contemporaries feel uneasy and even lost.

Unfortunately, there were many voices in the church and in theology that strengthened the dualistic worldview, not only regarding the opposition of Russia and the United States, the contradictory values of the East and the West, but also echoing the differing patterns of ethical orientation. The antagonism of East and West was matched by a moralistic dualism of good and evil, often combined with the distinction between regression to the past and emergence to the future.

God's Acting on and in History

Some years after the Hungarian uprising, a theologian from Budapest reported that the revolt had been undertaken by shady and sinister reactionary powers intending to reestablish fascist conditions. Obviously he could not imagine any other possibilities for designing economic and social life other than fascism and socialism. He was a victim of totalitarian thinking. But did we not all share this totalitarian dualism in one or another way?

This Hungarian colleague tried to identify reactionary attitudes with lack of faith.[2] The other side of the coin would be progress, marching in step with the forces of history as a demonstration of faith and hope!

We must try to understand this inclination to reduce political decisions to an either/or response to God's promises. Political decisions are not viewed as actions undertaken merely in response to historical circumstances. They are immediately imagined to be matters of faith. Theologians who prefer one political option in this way are inclined to blame others who go another way as unfaithful, even as people who resist God's will found in the course of history. They confuse groundings of faith, hope, and love with political options. Here we must ask: Can political decisions be matters of faith in another respect than in the sense that we are questioned about the grounding of faith and hope on which we rely when we risk political judgments? I am convinced that we cannot directly derive political judgments from spiritual insights. The connections here are complex and cannot be reduced to a simple either/or under normal circumstances. I concede that the reduction of moral options to sharp contrasts may be helpful in very difficult and confusing situations. In decisive cases there might even be a convergence between the confession of faith and a specific political decision. But in the Cold War period there was a nearly totalitarian tendency among theologians toward an overjustification of responses and habits with the aid of theological terms or biblical statements. The reference to faith and lack of faith, to obedience and disobedience, was often misused in mapping the realm of decision making. This is the third problem we have to face.

The key for understanding the tendency to identify lack of faith with a reactionary attitude is to be found in the endeavor to avoid a twofold mistake. On the one hand, there was the danger of the church being tied to conservative political concepts. On the other hand, there

2. The same identification was expressed by Bishop Tibor Bartha in an address to the faculty of the Reformed Theological Academy at Debrecen in 1958. See István Szabó, "Einige Informationen zum Verständnis der Lage des ungarischen Protestantismus und seiner Theologie im 20. Jahrhundert," *Verkündigung und Forschung* 38, no. 2 (1993): 76-77.

was the danger of the separation of faith and politics. According to the neo-Lutheran doctrine of the two kingdoms, there was the danger of the separation of an inward faith from involvement in the cultural and political process, as was common also within Continental liberalism. This was seen as the most urgent task for the church. It might be illustrated by the example of Germany after World War One. The constitution of the Weimar Republic at that time called for a separation of church and state. But many Protestants held on to a national conservative ideology. Called the "German national" movement, this was seen as the only position appropriate to the Protestant tradition, and it had been renewed in the founding of the German nation in the nineteenth century. This political view did not, however, prevent National Socialism, the Nazi movement, from rising up. Many prominent Protestants saw Hitler and his party as the only political power of the 1930s able to solve the urgent economic crisis and to save Germany from political chaos. In the beginning, Pastor Martin Niemöller (who for his eventual opposition to the Nazi movement was imprisoned in a concentration camp as a personal prisoner of Hitler) thought this way. Only when the religious followers of Hitler, the so-called German Christians, tried to force the Protestant church to become a mere functionary of the state did Niemöller and others turn away from German nationalism. They started the Confessing Church, claiming the necessity of freely proclaiming the free grace of God without any conditions and making this claim for the well-being of all members of society. We need to keep in mind this decisive point: this radical change whereby political thinking and ecclesial thinking are both felt and thought of as a conversion.

This was the case even more so after World War Two. Many church officials, ministers, and church members — especially those influenced by Karl Barth, the Swiss theologian whose theology had an important impact on German Protestantism — had learned the lesson: German national ideology had been one of the causes of the catastrophe leading directly to German imperialism, to war, and to the Holocaust. Because of this lesson, these members of the Confessing Church resisted any kind of conservative ideology in nationalistic terms. There was, however, an alternative just around the corner. The socialist experiment seemed to be one at least worth trying, not to be rejected out of hand. The only question seemed to be: Was the socialism shaped by Soviet Communism a valid alternative to German National Socialism, the Nazi movement?

But, according to the argument of these German Protestants (most of them leading members of the Confessing Church), after the war that question was only a theoretical one. The real issue was: What should be our attitude to the actual political situation in which East Germany is strongly attached to the Soviet Union? Here again foreign politics was the crucial point. It was assumed that simply rejecting the pattern of socialism shaped by Soviet Communism in Germany would necessarily mean endangering the very delicate situation of all Germans placed between East and West.

There is no doubt that the experiences of the Nazi totalitarian state led to a wide range of reservations and to reflections in relative terms about the workability of the socialism operating in East Germany. But the relative yes to a particular kind of socialism as a realistic solution amounted to showing readiness to accept the burden of the past. This was a political option — or for many people sometimes merely an inevitability — combined with their conversion in thinking and judging. This combination of conversion and "the other way" is the matter we now address.[3]

May I give another example? In May 1947, two years after the end of the war and two years before the Federal Republic of Germany was founded, in Darmstadt, West Germany, the board of the Confessing Church agreed on a memorandum called "To the Political Way of Our People." The memorandum was initiated by Karl Barth and Hans Joachim Iwand, a theologian close to Barth. It had two main topics: first, the task of the church to proclaim the message of reconciliation given in Jesus Christ for the world, and second, the political consequences of that proclamation as readiness to make way for peace, and as denial of former errors and tortuous paths. The message of the reconciliation of the world with God (2 Cor. 5:18) was now interpreted as a demand to achieve particular attitudes in affirming certain political claims.

3. This conversion often was understood as the only way toward the reunification of Germany — of a new Germany as mediator between the West and the East, but linked more to the East than to the U.S.-dominated West. Martin Lotz, *Evangelische Kirche 1945-1952: Die Deutschlandfrage — Tendenzen und Positionen* (Stuttgart: Radius, 1992).

The third paragraph of the Darmstadt memorandum reads: "We have been misled by the attempt to establish a 'Christian front' against reorderings needed in the social life of the people. The alliance of the church with the political powers, which preserved the old and traditional ways, avenged itself upon us heavily. We have betrayed the Christian liberty that enables us and commands us to change the structures of life where living together demands such a change. We have denied the right to revolution, but approved the development leading to an absolute dictatorship."[4]

Though this is in part an accurate expression of some attitudes characteristic of some of the authors (as well as many other people), now these same people attempted to disassociate themselves from their past actions, for many of them actions fifteen years in the past. They no longer associated with others who were unready or unwilling to go in the other, new direction. But is this really a confession of sins? Can we confess our sins without confessing that we remain sinners, and remain in community with other sinners?[5]

Thus conversion identical with the new and other way is identified with progressive political insights, with readiness for radical change, or at least with knowing the right direction for going further. Looking back to former errors and tortuous paths is an attempt to express and confess guilt more concretely. But at the same time, the claim is made that going the new way — just the opposite of the former way — will prevent one from becoming guilty again. But is not Christian life again and again a step toward a confession of guilt? Of

4. "Wir sind in die Irre gegangen, als wir begannen, eine 'christliche Front' aufzurichten gegenüber notwendig gewordenen Neuordnungen im gesellschaftlichen Leben der Menschen. Das Bündnis der Kirche mit den das Alte und Herkömmliche konservierenden Mächten hat sich schwer an uns gerächt. Wir haben die christliche Freiheit verraten, die uns erlaubt und gebietet, Lebensformen abzuändern, wo das Zusammenleben der Menschen solche Wandlung erfordert. Wir haben das Recht zur Revolution verneint, aber die Entwicklung zur absoluten Diktatur geduldet und gutgeheißen." Martin Greschat, ed., *Im Zeichen der Schuld* (Neukirchen-Vluyn: Neukirchener Verlag, 1985), p. 85.

5. Cf. Gerhard Sauter, "'Vergib uns unsere Schuld.' Eine theologische Besinnung auf das Stuttgarter Schuldbekenntnis," in Gerhard Besier and Gerhard Sauter, *Wie Christen ihre Schuld bekennen: Die Stuttgarter Erklärung 1945* (Göttingen: Vandenhoeck & Ruprecht, 1985), pp. 63-128. See also G. Sauter, "Bekannte Schuld," *Evangelische Theologie* 50 (1990): 498-511.

course, we try to avoid former errors as much as possible. But the confession of guilt and repentance are speech acts of another dimension, and we can only hope that these acts will lead us toward a more complex perception of reality, hopefully even toward new possibilities we did not see before — or away from temptations we did not detect as such. That might be the difference between theology and moralism.

It is only a small step from this view of repentance, going just the opposite way, to ascribing divine responsibility for outstanding events of history. This leads in turn to the simple course of understanding history as evidence of God's goals being equivalent to those of humanity. This identification of God and history — the fourth point of my reflections — was common especially in the Hungarian church during the fifties and sixties.[6]

I quote from a memorandum of Ervin Vályi-Nagy, "God or History: On the Premises of the Governing Body of the Reformed Church of Hungary Today,"[7] which was written in 1955 for the World Council of Churches but disappeared in the files of the ecumenical bureaucracy in Geneva:

> You talk of God who continually creates new situations in history, and in reality you mean the ongoing history in its inner dialectic order, and following the concept of man. The God to whom the governing body of the church refers is often synonymous with the Marxist concept of history. They ask the obedience of faith in this creating God, but the concrete content of his work the obedient has

6. It led to the ideological concept of the so-called Theology of Service: Christian stewardship understood as service to the people, in fact a support of the policy of the state. Cf. István Szabó, "A Long Period of Inner Bleeding: The Theology of Service as the Reflection of the Miseries of the Reformed Church in Hungary," *Zeitschrift für kirchliche Zeitgeschichte* 2 (1989): 190-98. In East Germany, Dietrich Bonhoeffer's phrase "Church for other [people]" was used by many theologians and clergy to interpret "Church within Socialism." Cf. chap. 9, n. 28, in this volume.

7. In 1955 Ervin Vályi-Nagy served as a minister in a village on the border of Hungary and Yugoslavia. At the beginning of the uprising he was elected mayor; after the uprising he was in prison. His paper "Gott oder Geschichte? Von den Prämissen der heutigen reformierten Kirchenführung in Ungarn" was published in *Verkündigung und Forschung* 38, no. 2 (1993): 3-14. Later he taught theology at the Reformed Seminary (now Károli Gáspár Reformed University) in Budapest, but retired early because of political suppression. He died Dec. 4, 1993.

to refer to is always the current phase of history. God's will is to be approved without reservation, but that means history only in its present factuality and in its next step. It is this creating God that is history itself that saves humankind.[8]

Is the need of the moment the command of God? Can history be seen as a manifestation of God's will? Do political crises, or social problems, lead us to the recognition of God's will, as implied by Paul in Romans 12:2: "Do not be conformed to this world, but be transformed by the renewal of your mind, that you may prove what is the will of God, what is good and acceptable and perfect"?[9] In response let me invoke the opening statement of the Barmen Declaration, the document that, since 1934, the Confessing Church in Germany has used to discern theological criteria for spiritual knowledge and decisions in political matters: "Jesus Christ . . . is the one Word of God, whom we are to hear, whom we are to trust and obey in life and in death. We repudiate the false teaching that the church can and must recognize yet other happenings and powers, images and truths as divine revelation alongside this one Word of God, as source of her preaching."[10]

This statement refuses a theology of history that identifies God's actions with historical events. It distinguishes between Jesus Christ as the one and finite Word of God and various historical happenings, powers, images (patterns), and truths. This will help us to ask after God's will, not attempting to discern God's will by confusing the living Word of God with the voice of people, whether the voice of the ruling powers or the voice of the manipulated and oppressed.

Precisely the identification of God's will with the goals of the socialist government, as claimed by the clergy of the Hungarian Reformed Church in the fifties and sixties, prevented drawing attention to the needs and troubles of individuals and groups within that society: for example, the farmers who became economic targets of socialist experiments. These oppressed and distressed people were made

---

8. Vályi-Nagy, "Gott oder Geschichte?" p. 4.

9. NRSV: ". . . by the renewing of your minds, so that you may discern what is the will of God. . . ."

10. *Creeds of the Churches: A Reader in Christian Doctrine from the Bible to the Present*, ed. John H. Leith, 3rd ed. (Louisville: John Knox, 1982), p. 520.

the object of major social goals in such a way as to justify their trouble as but a temporary expedient.

Confidence in God's Providence

Behind this ascription of history to God lies a crisis of confidence in God's providence. This is my last point and final task for theological reflection on these events. Divine providence is not a blueprint of fortunate developments but a main criterion for faithfulness to and confidence in God's purposes. The Christian doctrine of God's providence provides neither a map of divine goals for history nor assurance regarding God's foresight of all possible events, including the human involvement in them.[11] The doctrine of providence is primarily an explanation of the promise that, as Paul writes in his letter to the Romans, "in everything God works for good with those who love him, who are called according to his purpose" (8:28).[12] Later he assures us that neither "things present, nor things to come . . . will be able to separate us from the love of God in Christ Jesus our Lord" (8:38-39). Note that he does not mention the past; the past is already under the forgiveness that can change things we do not have to handle anymore.

In European history the term "providence" has acquired some notoriety. Adolf Hitler, for example, invoked providence to justify his own political goals. This pseudoreligious element of National Socialism has been something that those proclaiming God's free and universal grace have had to work against. The crisis of the doctrine of divine providence in the postwar period was not very evident. One is, how-

---

11. This misunderstanding has been promoted by the Latin *pro* and *videre*, "to see ahead," but it also means "to look after": Georgia Harkness, *The Providence of God* (New York: Abingdon, 1960), p. 17. For a long time Christian theology ascribed an exhaustible foreknowledge to God's character; see, e.g., John Sanders, *The God Who Risks: A Theology of Providence* (Downers Grove, Ill.: InterVarsity, 1998), p. 12. But that contradicts the biblical understanding of God's (fore)knowledge; cf. James D. G. Dunn, *Romans*, World Bible Commentary, vol. 38 (Dallas: Word, 1988), p. 482: God's knowing as "involving a relationship experienced and acknowleged"; p. 699: "(fore)knowledge of his own." For a more elaborate systematic evaluation of this topic, see Michael J. Langford, *Providence* (London: SCM, 1981).

12. NRSV: "We know that all things work together for good. . . ."

ever, able to detect it in the ethical mobilization that often shaped preaching, church statements, and some theological concepts of the era. This mobilization had as its own driving and guiding motif the view that "only we are responsible! We have to keep guard and be ready to act, otherwise we shall be responsible for catastrophes to come!" How often theological reflection became restricted to the claim: "Each of us is fully responsible and has to act in a farsighted perspective, for God's sake!"

I want to venture a suggestion that could easily be misunderstood. But I cannot avoid it if we are to take up the challenge of determining which theological criteria were used for decision making by the churches in the East-West conflict. We have to question the relationship of the peace movement of the church to the events of 1989. I do not want to question this movement as such, but we must ask about the theological expectation that lay behind it and pushed it forward. Numerous committed Christians in the East as well as in the West worked for reconciliation and peace. For them, these tasks were essential to Christian belief in the saving will of God. Therefore they uncompromisingly opposed every kind of rearmament. Did their attitude contribute to the end of the Cold War in the sense that the powers that gained the upper hand had not placed their trust in confrontation? Or, contrarily, is it a perverse thought to allow that nuclear armament carried too far led finally to disarmament? Did the security-driven politics of NATO with the economic superiority that stood behind it put the Soviet Union into a state of economic crisis that President Gorbachev cleverly enough did not risk trying to overcome?

I do not mean to imply that these conflicting hypotheses support in any way the so-called judgment of history, which agrees with the one who succeeds. Rather, the question is, could anybody be totally right here? It would be wrong to credit either side in the debate with sole responsibility for the outcome of history. We may never be able to understand completely how history managed to avoid the outcome anticipated in the well-known slogan *Nach Rüstung kommt Krieg* (a German play on words, literally translated "after the armament comes the war"). Rather, in the end we should say, "Thanks be to God!" However, we cannot expand the doxology with an after-the-fact reading of objectives. That is, we cannot conclude, on a pragmatic reading, that God gave preference to the system of the West, that God applauded and supported democracy and market economy. Nor can we conclude that God stands against a communist-planned economy that made impossible nearly all acts of personal initiative and that denied people's right to have an independent opinion that might contradict the official stand of the government on a particular issue. Nor does a faithful "Thanks be to God!" allow us to look for new crises or catastrophes to come that may confirm our critical attitude to the Western way of life. This seems to be a real danger now. Of course, there are enormous economic problems, increased by the claim for comprehensive social security of the kind people were used to. People in the East demand the same living standard as has been enjoyed in the West. Many people in the West fear the prospect of compromising their standard of living. They are reluctant to share their prosperity. Indeed, there are many who would now like to undo the whole process. We have to be prepared to consider that it might be a self-fulfilling prophecy that democracy and market economy will be unable to immediately replace a planned economy and guarantee social justice. If there is no real hope, confidence, and preparedness to endure, we will very soon get into serious political trouble.

May we be forcefully reminded that God has the generosity and the sense of humor to know what to do with our doing, even with our wrongdoing. He knows as well what to do with our best intentions that often have the opposite effect of what we intend. Do we not have grounds to be surprised that we are still here, despite our doing? In recent years I have often been reminded of Lamentations 3:21-23: "But this I call to mind, / and therefore I have hope: / The steadfast love of the LORD never ceases [Martin Luther's translation is even stronger: 'The loving kindness of God keeps us from being totally extinguished'], / his mercies never come to an end; / they are new every morning; / great is your faithfulness." The reflection turns into a prayer, "your faithfulness." All this is a part of a struggle with both retrospective criticism and attempts to justify one's own predictions after the fact. But God can make use of us if we are faithful and confident. But what limits our understanding of what constitutes achievement?

Dietrich Bonhoeffer wrote in his prison cell in 1943:

I believe that God both can and will bring good out of evil, even out of the greatest evil. For that purpose he needs men who make the best use of everything. I believe God will give us all the power we need to resist in all time of distress. But he never gives it in advance, lest we should rely upon ourselves and not on him alone. A faith as strong as this should allay all our fears for the future. I believe that even our errors and shortcomings are turned to good account and that it is no harder for God to deal with them than with our supposedly good deeds. I believe God is not just timeless fate, but that he waits for and answers sincere prayer and responsible action.[13]

This is no less true fifty, sixty years later. The doctrine of God's providence does not fill the void of that silence God has created for us. But it can prepare us to listen and to search for new criteria. Here the reflection ends, and here it may start again.

13. Dietrich Bonhoeffer, *Prisoner for God: Letters and Papers from Prison*, ed. Eberhard Bethge, trans. Reginald H. Fuller et al., enlarged ed. (London: SCM Press, 1971), p. 11.

CHAPTER 8

The Religious Dimension of American Self-Understanding and Its Crisis Today

No Speechlessness after September 11, 2001?

On September 11, 2001, I was staying at the Bossey Ecumenical Institute in Switzerland studying eschatological issues along with American ministers serving congregations in Europe and the Near East. Many of the pastors had relatives and friends living in New York, some of whom had jobs in or near the World Trade Center. When the shock of seeing the disturbing images on TV began to wear off, a period of self-critical reflection began.

One topic emerging from this reflection focused on America's new vulnerability. The American pastors commented that the Civil War brought destruction, but that it was a war fought among fellow citizens. The events of September 11 no longer permit Americans to think of themselves as inviolable in their own country. The destruction of the illusion of inviolability may lead to actions that can be extremely dangerous. Moreover, Americans now experience a vulnerability already familiar to Europeans and persons living in Israel, in Palestine, and in other places of our endangered world. The pastors observed that the trusted government security measures formerly in place had been invalidated and the current administration's "Star Wars Program" rendered senseless by these events. Americans will now have to learn to live with vulnerability in a way that other countries have had to learn and have never been able to forget. Insecurity has become the key signature of the world, and the United States is no exception.

These comments pointed to a peculiar religious dimension of America's self-understanding. *Americans are convinced that they are a chosen people with a unique destiny, that they enjoy the special protection of God's providence or of the other national god called "Liberty."* Many Americans who live abroad for an extended period of time and do not flutter as tourists from blossom to blossom like butterflies but look critically at the history of their environment, perceive their country and its politics from a different perspective when they return, a perspective much different from that of the majority of their compatriots. For them a demythologizing of the American dream of exclusiveness takes place. They view September 11 in this regard, without easing the shock that was caused by this event. One of the pastors asked me, after having seen the first pictures of the ruins and the people fleeing in bewilderment: "Does that remind you of what took place in World War Two?" I answered, "Yes, but there was no television."

A few days later, at the National Cathedral in Washington, D.C., the country's political elite proclaimed its deep emotional shock and assured itself of its hope. Representatives of different religious groups, including a chief rabbi, led in prayer. Billy Graham, the Baptist evangelist, who from time to time is regarded as the senior pastor of the American nation, beseeched God's help for this crisis just as God had rescued America and granted it safety in earlier times. The notion that this might have been an affliction from God was totally out of the question. Then the president spoke and promised retaliation. Was that — so one would like to ask with all the caution that is due to a foreigner — really the voice of America?

The "Battle Hymn of the Republic" was sung. The National Cathedral actually is an Episcopal church, but it is also a symbol of American *civil religion*, the oddity that results from concurring with the constitutional separation of church and state.[1] I will say more about this later.

---

1. The term "civil religion" was introduced by Robert N. Bellah. See William G. McLoughlin and Robert N. Bellah, eds., *Religion in America* (Boston: Houghton Mifflin, 1968); Robert N. Bellah, *The Broken Covenant: American Civil Religion in a Time of Trial* (New York: Seabury Press, 1975); Robert N. Bellah and Phillip E. Hammond, *Varieties of Civil Religion* (San Francisco: Harper and Row, 1980); Gail Gehrig, *American Civil Religion: An Assessment* (Storrs, Conn.: Society for the Scientific Study of Religion, 1981); Leroy S. Rouner, ed., *Civil Religion and Political Theology* (Notre Dame, Ind.: University of Notre

In any case, in this solemn ceremony one thing became clear: God, as called on at this occasion by some people, was the God of America, not the God of the world, Lord of all people. God was seen as the guarantor of American identity and the one who also ensures that this nation remains unharmed. Other nations, particularly Germany, were cured of a religious guarantee of identity like this through the bitter experiences of the last century. Is that now in store for the United States? The answer to the question would not be found in the purification of the national consciousness from some religious remnant, nor would it be about a total secularization of political life. Rather the question is: *Can one talk of God* in regard to revolutionary political events concerning the way of the world and to events that result in so much loss of life? Many Christians in the United States raise this question, and many sermons are devoted to it.

Was the solemn event in Washington really a worship service? Or was it a rite that sought to symbolize the cohesion of the American nation? Are the two supposed to be separate in civil religion? Some of my American friends watched the commemoration on TV with quite mixed feelings. It was noted that George W. Bush said God would be present in the suffering of the people, but by that he meant the "innocent victims" in New York and Washington, not the potential and also innocent victims of American retaliation. There was and is no bumper sticker "God bless the people of Afghanistan." During the spontaneous worship of prayer in the chapel at Bossey, only a few hours after the attack, God had been called on as the Reconciler of the World. Can we speak of God in a way other than as the Reconciler of the World?

Another problematic sign was the inclination to regard hesitation as a sign of weakness. The Anglican Rowan Williams, who was near the World Trade Center on September 11, admonishes not only the United States of America but all of us to be "very wary of doing something so that it looks as if something is getting done."[2] Because President Bush acted the opposite way, his readiness to declare war was praised as evidence of "leadership." It seemed that he was able to

---

Dame Press, 1986); Martin E. Marty, ed., *Civil Religion, Church and State* (Munich and New York: K. G. Saur, 1992).

2. Rowan Williams, *Writing in the Dust: After September 11* (Grand Rapids: Eerdmans, 2002), p. 23.

unite the American people and to strengthen their patriotism by this and other gestures. In his State of the Union Address on January 29, 2002, the president assured: "We've come to know truths that we will never question: evil is real, and it must be opposed. Beyond all differences of race or creed, we are one country, mourning together and facing danger together. Deep in the American character, there is honor, and it is stronger than cynicism. And many have discovered again that even in tragedy — especially in tragedy — God is near."[3]

But — "near" in what a sense? I think Rowan Williams, very much a political theologian himself and at the same time a theologian deeply rooted in spirituality, recalls a fork in the road:

> In that time, there is no possibility of thinking, of explanations, resolutions. I can't remember much sense of panic, much feeling about the agony going on a couple of hundred yards away, let alone much desire for justice or vengeance. It was an empty space. I don't want to forget that, as feeling returns in various ways. We don't fully know what goes on when, in the middle of terror or pain, this emptiness and anesthesia set in (it happens in many contexts). But somehow the emptiness "resources" us. Not to run too fast to explore the feelings and recover the words seems important.[4]

But at the ceremony at Washington Cathedral President Bush asserted: "Just three days removed from these events, Americans do not yet have the distance of history, but our responsibility to history is already clear to answer these attacks and rid the world of evil."[5]

Here is a motif that not only accompanies many military and domestic actions of American policy but is deeply implanted in the American religious conscience from the very beginning: *to do God's work*. It can support humane responsibility and readiness to help where urgent help is needed, but it becomes very dangerous if connected with the moralistic distinction between "good" and "evil" as judged by humans. So often in history the zeal for doing absolutely and being right leads to dangerous, even fatal and self-destroying, activity.

---

3. www.whitehouse.gov/news/releases/2002/01/20020129-11.html.

4. Williams, *Writing in the Dust*, p. 10.

5. Lee Griffith, *The War on Terrorism and the Terror of God* (Grand Rapids: Eerdmans, 2002), p. 272.

In late October 2001, on a flight from Frankfurt to Newark, I read in a newspaper (*USA Today*, if I remember it correctly) that President Bush keeps a Bible on his desk, from which he often reads, particularly during these days, in order to get directives for his decisions. Is that just part of a conservative American president's image that he puts on for a segment of his constituency? How does he read the Bible? What does he gather from it? He prays — that is not just a show. But does he pray "Your will be done, on earth as it is in heaven. . . . Forgive us our trespasses, as we forgive those who have trespassed against us" (Matt. 6:10, 12)?[6] Would he conceive forgiveness differently? How does it relate to his maxim that first evil has to be wiped out and then we can proceed to making peace? Or would he argue that politics and spirituality are two totally different realms? Then it would be only consequent if he would not further use biblical images as justification for his political rhetoric.

As I approached Newark I saw an eerie gap in the skyline of New York City. It lacked the two bright silver towers. The whole view was different. The city had another face: the nose was missing. The taxi driver told me, "I see that every day, but even now I cannot get used to it. The gap that has been torn there only allows us to take every day as it comes." The blaze of lights in Manhattan, weaker than before, reminded me of what an old American friend of mine who has seen a lot of the world once told me: "The power consumption of Manhattan approximately corresponds to that of the whole African continent, perhaps excluding South Africa." There I was immediately facing the economic power of the United States compared to that of other countries. Was the discrepancy between the two the target of the terrorists' attacks? Or did they attack an open society and its liberality?

These impressions offer a picture of the complexity of the emotions and thoughts that followed the World Trade Center bombing. Let us try to understand what is going on here. Even more complex is the political rhetoric that invokes and uses terms that arouse religious associations without really being rooted in the religious traditions of the country. One of these mistakes was, for example, when George Bush talked about the "crusade" the free world had to wage against terrorism. This term is used in the United States for evangelism; it

6. NRSV: ". . . Forgive us our debts, / as we also have forgiven our debtors."

means to win people over to the Christian message. It could have been this context from which the president spoke. But he did not take into consideration the fact that the term "crusade" had to bring back the worst memories for Muslims. Others quickly talked him out of using this language as well as his thoughtless talk about *infinite justice* as the title for the operation in Afghanistan. There was severe protest in America against this type of rhetorical faux pas, and I was also told that even the president's father exercised his parental authority against this type of demagogy. But even if one avoids these types of rhetorical mistakes, a certain pattern of thinking can remain obscured and unchallenged. I would like to uncover what I call the religious dimension of the American self-consciousness and to try to understand it. I want neither to theologically justify nor to condemn it, but I try to make clear why this is an important ingredient of American behavior and thinking. We have to take it into account if we want to comprehend fairly what has been going on — not in any mood of criticizing the United States of America from an outsider's view, but asking for the theological task that is embedded here.

"A City upon a Hill"

To understand this we have to go far back in the history of North America, to some of its first settlers. They understood themselves to be the "chosen people" who, like the people of Israel, were destined to set off for the promised land and to create there a new community, even a "new Adam" and a new world, out of the wilderness. Therefore they were convinced to trust in divine providence.

John Winthrop, an English lawyer and first governor of the Massachusetts Bay Colony, preached in 1630, while crossing to the colony on the *Arbella*, the flagship of a little fleet of boats of immigrants, a lay sermon that is often regarded as pathbreaking. In this speech, "A Model of Christian Charity," the biblical metaphor first turned up that would henceforth accompany American history: *a city upon a hill*. This metaphor, like the term "manifest destiny" — the destination, even the obligation of the American people to extend their territory and, furthermore, to bring their constitutional values (and often much more than that!) to all other countries — has become the mark of the religious dimension of America's self-understanding.[7] It was and is linked with the comparison of the exodus of the enslaved Israelites from Egypt with the foundation of the American nation after the revolution. When you go to Savannah and visit the synagogue there, you will see a letter written by President George Washington to the Jewish community, asserting that God who liberated the people of Israel is the same God who installed the American nation with unfading liberty. This conviction is the birth of American *civil religion*.

Civil religion is a network of religious symbols, metaphors, and values accepted by the public and, especially, used by politicians to claim an overarching orientation of society. The use of religious symbols to build up a national unity seems especially similar to some trends of European politics in the nineteenth and twentieth centuries. Although there has not been such a strict separation of church and state as in the United States — in Scandinavia the Protestant (Lutheran) church even remains a kind of "state church" — there was and is much more "ideological" independence of church from state and vice versa. The United States lacks the criticism of this kind of use that has been vital in Europe most the time except under totalitarian regimes.

But there was much more to say about the divine American mission. In 1900 Senator Albert Beveridge of Indiana stated:

God has not been preparing the English-speaking and Teutonic peoples for a thousand years for nothing but vain and idle self-contemplation and self-admiration. No! He has made us the master organizers of the world to establish a system where chaos reigns. He has given us the spirit of progress to overwhelm the forces of reaction throughout the earth. He has made us adept in government that we may administer government among savage and senile peoples. Were it not for such a force as this the world would relapse

---

7. E.g., John Quincy Adams to John Adams, Aug. 31, 1811: "The whole continent of North America appears to be destined by Divine Providence to be peopled by one *nation*, speaking one language, professing one general system of religious and political principles, and accustomed to one general tenor of social usages and customs. For the common happiness of them all, for their peace and prosperity, I believe it indispensable that they should be associated in one federal Union." *The Writings of John Quincy Adams*, ed. Worthington C. Ford (New York: Macmillan, 1913-17), 4:209.

into barbarism and night. And of all our race He has marked the American people as His chosen nation to finally lead in the regeneration of the world. This is the divine mission of America, and it holds for us all the profit, all the glory, all the happiness, possible to man. We are trustees of the world's progress, guardians of its righteous peace.[8]

In 1846 the ideology of *manifest destiny* was formulated by the journalist William Gilpin and soon afterward read to the U.S. Senate:

The *untransacted* destiny of the American people is to subdue the continent — to rush over this vast field to the Pacific Ocean — to animate the many hundred millions of its people, and to cheer them upward . . . to reach old nations a new civilization — to conform the destiny of the human race. . . .

Divine task! Immortal mission! Let us tread fast and joyfully the open trail before us! Let every American heart open wide for patriotism to glow undimmed, and confide with religious faith in the sublime and prodigious destiny of his well-loved country.[9]

But what was the context into which Winthrop had put the metaphor *a city upon a hill?*

Now the only way . . . to provide for our posterity is to follow the counsel of Micah: to do justly, to love mercy, to walk humbly with our God. For this end, we must be knit together in this work as one man. We must entertain each other in brotherly affection; we must be willing to abridge ourselves of our superfluities, for the supply of others' necessities; we must uphold a familiar commerce together in all meekness, gentleness, patience and liberality. We must delight in each other, make others' conditions our own, rejoice together, mourn together, labor and suffer together: always having before our eyes our commission and community in the work, our community as members of the same body. So shall we keep the unity of the spirit in the bond of peace, the Lord will be our God and

8. Charles D. Ameringer, *U.S. Foreign Intelligence: The Secret Side of American History* (Lexington, Mass.: Lexington Books, 1990), p. 71.

9. Robert Hughes, *American Visions: The Epic History of Art in America* (New York: Knopf, 1997), pp. 189-90.

delight to dwell among us, as His own people, and will command a blessing upon us in all our ways, so that we shall see much more of His wisdom, power, goodness, and truth than formerly we have been acquainted with. We shall find that the God of Israel is among us, when ten of us shall be able to resist a thousand of our enemies, when He shall make us a praise and glory, that men shall say of succeeding plantations: "The Lord make it like that of New England." For we must consider that we shall be as a city upon a hill, the eyes of all people are upon us. So that if we shall deal falsely with our God in this work we have undertaken, and so cause Him to withdraw His present help from us, we shall be made a story and a byword through the world: we shall open the mouths of enemies to speak evil of the ways of God and all professors for God's sake; we shall shame the faces of many of God's worthy servants, and cause their prayers to be turned into curses upon us, till we be consumed out of the good land whither we are going.[10]

Here again the art of reading the Bible and the task of telling the overarching biblical story properly are at stake.

Winthrop alludes to Jesus' Sermon on the Mount, "You are the light of the world. A city built on [upon] a hill cannot be hid" (Matt. 5:14). A person who has been to the Sea of Galilee might think of Safed, the little town above the lake whose white houses sparkle in the sunlight. This city on the hill later became the center of the Kabbalah, a Jewish mystical renewal of the perception of the mysteries of God, the world, and humanity. The city upon a hill can be seen from far away, but it shines only if lighted. It is not a shining light by itself. If its houses sparkle because they are clean and painted white, it may intensify the light from above. But it cannot illuminate itself.

Winthrop's speech also refers to other biblical motifs, metaphors, and stories, as well as to prophetic proclamations that outline the overall picture; it is interspersed with biblical allusions. The repetition of the exhortation of the Old Testament prophet Micah (6:8) emphasizes the self-understanding of the settlers. They considered themselves the descendants of the people of Israel; they, too, were on their

10. John Winthrop, "A Model of Christian Charity," in *The American Puritans: Their Prose and Poetry*, ed. Perry Miller (Garden City, N.Y.: Doubleday, 1956), pp. 79-84; quotation is from p. 83.

way to the "promised land." They are allowed to take the land, and the instructions of God make the social order obligatory. Their numerical inferiority reminds one of the story of Gideon, the spirited fighter for God. With ten other men he pulled down the idolatrous altars of his father, who had come to terms with the country's customary religion (Judg. 6:25). And then, with three hundred men, he utterly destroyed an enormous army that lay "along the valley as thick as locusts; and their camels were without number, countless as the sand on the sea-shore" (7:12). The colonialists are elected to form a unity and are called to be united. They owe this unity to the Holy Spirit, who is the bond of peace (Eph. 4:3). This means they are one Christian commu-nity, members of one body, of the body of Christ (1 Cor. 12:12). And to this community already is granted what in the Revelation of John, the last book of the Bible, is promised only for the last days: in the new world God will dwell among humanity, "they will be his peoples, / and God himself will be with them" (21:3b).

For Winthrop the city upon a hill symbolizes the responsibility of a people's community and its accountability to God. That is why this community places itself under God's judgment right from the begin-ning. Winthrop could have pointed to 1 Peter 4:17: God's judgment be-gins with the house of God, not with its enemies. The "world" forms the audience of what is going on in the city of God and on behalf of it. The city of God is the stage of God's action toward humanity. Only in regard to this is it an exemplary community.

Yet, what remained of Winthrop's speech in the collective mem-ory of the United States is the metaphor "a city upon a hill." The same is true also for academic publications where this metaphor is men-tioned.[11] Often the phrase is trimmed to "America shall be the shining example." For example, on January 9, 1961, John F. Kennedy put it that way when he wanted to denounce political corruption before the Su-preme Court of Massachusetts.[12]

The second part of Winthrop's sermon concerning God's judg-

---

11. Even Sidney E. Ahlstrom in his standard survey *A Religious History of the Ameri-can People*, vol. 1 (Garden City, N.Y.: Doubleday, 1975), p. 193, quotes only excerpts of Winthrop's speech in a way that creates the impression that the city upon a hill is a communal task that has to be fulfilled.

12. Samuel Eliot Morison, *The Oxford History of the American People* (New York: Ox-ford University Press, 1965), p. 65 n. 1.

ment was repressed and therefore the meaning of the metaphor was changed: the city upon a hill with its constitution, with its rules, norms, and customs, became the *ideal society* instead of a community that can exist only under God's judging and saving action. This shift of meaning could take place only through amputation. The "jeremiads" that had accompanied American sermons on the city upon a hill throughout two centuries fell into oblivion. Jeremiads are sermons that call people to repentance and that seek to remind them of the lamentations, attributed to the prophet Jeremiah, in the Old Testament. Under no circumstances are they whiny lamentations about bad times and increasing immorality. Here speaks the confidence that after every affliction one may experience the grace of God again (e.g., Lam. 3:22-23) — but not assuring that anytime "God is near," "especially in tragedy," as President Bush said in his State of the Union Address on January 29, 2002.

The amputation of the metaphor "a city upon a hill" seems to me much more pernicious than some influence of the understanding of repentance by the book of Deuteronomy, especially Deuteronomy 28:1: "If you will only obey the LORD your God, by diligently observing all his commandments that I am commanding you today, the LORD your God will set you high above all the nations of the earth." It might be true that for the religious-infiltrated American history "repentance is seen as a turning backward to recover former values; and the call to return is accompanied by glowing promises of the elimination of defeat and humiliation. This form of repentance, in contrast to the radical kind of self-examination and sharpened moral responsibility demanded by the great prophets, lends itself nicely to political rhetoric."[13]

For others like Jonathan Edwards (1703-58), it was crystal clear: one can rightly speak of the city of God only in regard to the judging and saving action of God. But even he was positive of the "analogy" of the settlers from England and the people of Israel conquering the Promised Land.[14] However, by the beginning of the twentieth century, at the latest, the reference to God's complex acting, so vital to Ed-

13. Robert Jewett and John Shelton Lawrence, *Captain America and the Crusade against Evil: The Dilemma of Zealous Nationalism* (Grand Rapids: Eerdmans, 2003), p. 282.
14. Griffith, *War on Terrorism*, p. 141.

wards, fell into oblivion. Only the metaphor "a city upon a hill" remained. Moreover, it was now said with a different meaning: America is the light and it shines into a dark world; everybody else is located in the shadow, if not in black darkness altogether. The visibility of God's city — not to be ignored because of what happens on behalf of it — is interchanged with its brightness, its function as an example, and its identification with the good, the just, with what is well pleasing to God. Thus, America is subject to a rigorous moral demand and at the same time understands itself to be founded on grounds that are sounder than those of other peoples. The American nation is seen as a shining example for all other nations.

The crucial point of the dilemma facing America's religious self-understanding can be traced to this interchange of meaning, this metaphor torn in half. The dilemma is not new; it is rather over a hundred years old. But now it breaks out again, and many, too many, try to cover it up, disguise it, or at least gloss over it.

The jeremiads, even when they denounced a morally deplorable state of affairs, were not fixed on it but viewed it in a larger perspective, as Winthrop did with his reminder to turn to each other, to be devoted to one another, to care for each other, to take one another seriously in every distress and to help, to carry the burden together, to share joy, and to understand themselves as *community*, as *members of the same body*. They stressed a communitarian characteristic, which remained alive in the United States at least in smaller neighborhoods, and which has recently gained a renewed attention.

Jeremiads do not have anything in common with the sorts of moralistic lectures that are given with pleasure in the United States when they are addressed to others. On a television show Pat Robertson declared that the destruction of September 11 was a divine judgment upon the immorality of modern America, because of its abortion laws and the acceptance of homosexuality. Neither economic nor social policy was the topic, let alone the entanglements of America in world politics. Franklin Graham, son of Billy Graham, charged Islam as the "archenemy" of Christianity. But as this did not seem to go well with *political correctness*, Graham Jr. was brought back into line.

Providence as Sentence and Promise of God

On September 11, 2001, this trust of being chosen and sustained by God in a special way, which had provided the security of the United States to be inviolable, was shaken to its roots. How does this affect the quest for God's action in history and for the manifestation of divine providence? Even though American society is secularized, it still holds religious convictions to be vital. It will be critical for America, in light of this dilemma, to recall and reestablish the intrinsic profoundness of talk about God: God should be addressed as the One who promised to judge and to save in reconciling the world with God.

John Winthrop's sermon, one of the outstanding religious documents of the American Puritans, is indeed far away from that sort of moralism that seeks to divide the "world" into good and evil and, by claiming God for the renewal of broken conditions, seeks to eradicate evil in order to realize the ideal society. Winthrop and all the others who followed him in thinking, speaking, and acting in the same spirit, conceived America as being under the sentence of God, not on God's side. This became apparent in other ways. One sees this, for example, in President Abraham Lincoln's last public speech on April 11, 1865, one day after the surrender of General Robert E. Lee. Lincoln felt that after the end of the American Civil War, with its devastating consequences for the South but also many wounds for the North, one should not speak of either victor or defeated.[15] As Lincoln had said earlier in his Second Inaugural Address on March 4, 1865, slavery was a sin against God's providence. Because of this the outcome of the war was some sort of trial by ordeal. It was not the partisanship of the living God on behalf of one of the fighting parties, each of which had called on God for victory. Both were placed under God's judgment: "The judgments of the Lord are true and righteous altogether." Lincoln quoted this from either Revelation 16:7 or 19:2 (the contexts speak about shed blood of the holy and the prophets!) and continued: "with malice toward none; with charity for all; with firmness in the right, as God gives us to see the right, let us strive on to finish the work we are in."[16]

---

15. Morison, *Oxford History*, p. 703: "For Lincoln did not consider himself a conqueror."

16. Edwin S. Gaustad and Mark A. Noll, eds., *A Documentary History of Religion in*

That was spoken in a spirit of reconciliation that presupposed that none of the participants was innocent. That is why assignments of guilt did not occur: charge and revenge are out of place. A political scientist might read Lincoln's message as a document of unprecedented wisdom or maybe as a clever tactical turn. In my opinion, it is rather a symptom of American *civil religion,* the transfer of religious symbols into the national self-understanding. Lincoln's bond with the church was — in contrast to that of his wife — rather loose, but as one well versed in the Bible, he was convinced that the nations were tools of the *Almighty* and that this went especially for the United States as *the chosen people.*[17] What could slap this "chosenness" harder in the face than this people's rupture? Lincoln might have asked himself secretly how a reconciliation that amounts to more than just repairing a disturbed social relationship could be possible, hoping nevertheless to get a positive response from the majority of his compatriots. This would have been an understanding that itself presupposed a prior experience with reconciliation.

Since Lincoln's assassination many have regarded his understanding of reconciliation as a bequest for the arduous way toward national unity of the United States.

Maybe Lincoln's addresses remain exceptions in the political history of the United States; after all, they were directed to domestic affairs, not to foreign politics. For the latter, as mentioned before, it was the splitting of Winthrop's metaphor "a city upon a hill" that resulted in one model for society and another for the "world" of geopolitical concerns. This split image could eventually lead to an imperialism fed by religious roots and lived out in moralistic dualism. The desire to set the world in order might ultimately result in the subjugation of all who do not want to submit to the example of the shining city.

We might take the *just war theory* as an example of something that has become real after September 11. This theory has a long and tangled

---

America, vol. 2 (since 1877), 3rd ed. (Grand Rapids: Eerdmans, 2003), p. 575; cf. also James M. McPherson, *Battle Cry of Freedom: The Civil War Era,* Oxford History of the United States, vol. 6 (New York: Oxford University Press, 1988), pp. 843-44. For a detailed analysis of Lincoln's address and its context, see Ronald C. White, Jr., *Lincoln's Greatest Speech: The Second Inaugural* (New York: Simon and Schuster, 2002).

17. Ahlstrom, *A Religious History,* 2:136-37; William J. Wolf, *The Almost Chosen People: A Study of Abraham Lincoln* (Garden City, N.Y.: Doubleday, 1959).

story within secular philosophy and Christian theology.[18] The limitations on what justifies war and on how far wars may be pursued were gradually increased in the era after the Enlightenment. Legitimate wars were made to face the test of justice. Wars of conquest were banned, and martial law was put under the control of specified norms. But American voices of the twentieth century advocated military campaigns against "the evil" in the world. These campaigns were considered "just" when they were directed against unrestrained oppression, injustice, and the intention to exterminate. Under these ideas the United States considered itself the trustee of humanity and acted on behalf of all humankind. The American nation must — and can — prove "just cause" in intervening in world events. The turn to legitimacy is discernible with President Woodrow Wilson, a dyed-in-the-wool Presbyterian, when he asked the American Congress on April 2, 1917, to consent to the declaration of war against Germany[19] and to his "Fourteen Points" of the Peace Conference of Paris (January 8, 1918). Here he outlined that reconciliation between nations meant fighting for peace, relentlessly and until victory, just because one has to eradicate the reasons of war root and branch.[20] Harry S. Truman was not self-critical either when he claimed international standing for the moral values of the American nation after the victory over fascism. Here, too, just war means *to place oneself as justified in world society and in world history.*

Even the general condemnation of wars that was urged especially by the Americans in the ecumenical movement after the end of World War Two shows ambiguous characteristics. The statement "War is not according to God's will" issued by the first assembly of the World Council of Churches in Amsterdam (1948) "formulates not so much a consensus as the already achieved possibility of legitimizing future wars as just wars."[21]

This moralistic, nonpolitical, pragmatic gulf between the inten-

18. Heinz-Horst Schrey, "Krieg. Historisch/Ethisch; 6. Die Rezeption des Krieges in der christlichen Moraltheologie," in *Theologische Realenzyklopädie*, ed. Gerhard Müller, vol. 20 (Berlin: De Gruyter, 1990), pp. 28-55, esp. pp. 35-41.

19. "War Message," in *Great American Speeches*, ed. Gregory R. Surioano (New York: Gramercy Books, 1993), pp. 137-42.

20. *Great American Speeches*, pp. 143-46, esp. p. 146.

21. Schrey, "Krieg," p. 41.

tion for peace and readiness for war can, de facto, coincide when legally protected rights that are declared to be universal — human rights most of all — come into conflict with positive law (for example, international law). I can only hint at this ethical dilemma and the political rhetoric that easily allies with it — the division of the world into good and evil.

Despite its appearance, this division is not a religious one — at least not one based on sound Jewish and Christian grounds — but it happens through the confusion of religion and moralism. The moralist knows how to relate God to the world in every given situation, and knows how to quickly make "God" a component of the world order and to be its guarantor. In this way the moralist also is able to incessantly ascribe guilt to others when he wants to make sense of godlessness there.

It is not an accident that after September 11 the smoldering debate about "just war theory" flared up again in the United States. I consider it to be a theologically promising sign.[22] Or perhaps it is a voice in the midst of a secularized world that speaks amidst the whirlwind of political instability: "For the ignorant, the superstitious and me (and maybe you), the face of the Evil One was revealed, and died; for the ignorant, the superstitious and me (and maybe you), the cross survived. This is how God speaks to us. He is saying, 'I am.' He is saying, 'I am here.' He is saying, 'And the force of all the evil of all the world will not bury me.' I believe this quite literally. But then I am experiencing Sept. 11 not as a political event but as a spiritual event."[23]

This leads us to another perception of providence, the old companion of American piety and politics. I will refer to some lines from John Irving's *A Prayer for Owen Meany*,[24] an exemplary literary account that, by the way, is based upon profound theological advice.[25] Young

22. David S. Yeago, "Just War: Reflections from the Lutheran Tradition in a Time of Crisis," *Pro Ecclesia: A Journal of Catholic and Evangelical Theology* 10 (2001): 401-27; John L. Berquist, ed., *Strike Terror No More: Theology, Ethics, and the New War* (St. Louis: Chalice, 2002).

23. Peggy Noonan, "Welcome Back, Duke: From the Ashes of Sept. 11 Arise the Manly Virtues," *Wall Street Journal*, Oct. 12, 2001, editorial page.

24. John Irving, *A Prayer for Owen Meany* (New York: Morrow, 1989).

25. Irving thanks his teacher Frederick Buechner in the acknowledgments of *A Prayer for Owen Meany*. See also Buechner's memoir *Telling Secrets* (San Francisco: HarperCollins, 1991).

Owen Meany considers himself chosen as a tool for God. While acting in a drama, he sees in his mind's eye his own gravestone. From then on he attempts to arrange his life toward this end even though his comprehension is fragmentary. He remains confident of God's providence, i.e., God's providing and caring for him, though he can catch only a glimpse of this. He cannot avoid making plans, but at the same time, in a flash he realizes that he is not able to plan his life and particularly not the heroic death he dreamed of. Again and again his efforts to bring his plans into line with the vision of his death are set back. Only at the end does Owen Meany, as well as the reader, get to see the connection. It happens through a sports exercise, a little detail, apparently without consequences and meaning, of which he could not in any way see the value. Yet, thanks to this exercise he can protect children from their would-be murderer, at the expense of his own life. The connection he had always been looking for in vain had been with him all the time without his knowing it. It was happening alongside him, simultaneously, so to speak, without visible relation to everything he saw before him. Something done without purpose turns out to play a decisive role.

In a split second Owen Meany had gotten an idea about when and how his life would end. But he does not let himself be fixed on this prognosis, even though it worries him a lot. He wants to believe: to hold on to God, to ask for God's will in the planning of his life, and to be dissuaded from the relentless self-doubts that are caused by circumstances. What he experiences with others and with himself, what he thinks and how he talks about it, does not add up. Nevertheless, the narrator succeeds in not letting the story fall apart into various fragments nor interpreting it in a psychologizing manner.

Gaps and inconsistencies obstruct every conclusive interpretation. Owen Meany's exaltations might be exposed as pathological narcissism, and the narrator indeed leaves it open whether this is possible from time to time. Or we might also read *Owen Meany* as an example of typical American consciousness of "chosenness" roused from its happy daydreams and prepared to die on behalf of others. "Chosen for suffering" — is this the new paradoxical message of success? The dying Owen Meany, after all, desires to be awarded a medal for his bravery.

Yet, this might only be another indication of the deeply entangled relationship between personal decision-making and a problematic political fate that has tormented Owen Meany for a long time. John Irving's *A Prayer for Owen Meany* belongs to the best tradition of American piety that is supported by theological depth. It does not know simple answers to difficult questions. It is far away from the know-it-alls on the Internet who attempted to answer the absurd topic "Where *was* God on September 11?"[26] It will be a long and arduous way to the question, What is God *like* in times of crisis? and even more particularly, *Who* is God, to whom we pray?

26. http://google.yahoo.com/bin/query?p=%22where+was+God%22%2c+september +11&hc=0 and www.biblrytr.com/boston.htm.

CHAPTER 9

Public Theology — Theology outside the Church?

In the last two chapters we were confronted with the question of how theology interferes in public discourse. Now we must more thoroughly work on this task, comparing it with attempts to prove "theology in public." There may be another fork in the road.

The Public Service of the Church

In 2000 a Hungarian theologian, who was the consultant in church relations to the Hungarian prime minister, told me about a terminological complication. The story he told me revealed the delicate constellation of state and church after the dark years of Communist government. The prime minister was preparing a speech for Saint Stephan's Day — a patriotic memorial day remembering a decisive point in early Hungarian history and a day loaded with religious sentiments. The politician wanted to engage as many Hungarian Christians as possible in the social and spiritual renewal of his country, since it was struggling intensely for economic reforms and the restructuring of politics. He thought it right to call for the *service of the church* in favor of the common good. But he overlooked or maybe did not know that this very term "service" was misleading and provoked extremely bad memories. In the sixties and seventies the Hungarian Protestant churches, the Reformed church even more rigorously than the Lutheran church, had called for a "Theology of Service."[1] This theology aimed to encourage

1. Cf. chap. 7, n. 6, and chap. 10, n. 7, in this volume.

the people to be faithful to the socialist movement and to engage in the creation of a new political order on all levels of communal life. This political order promised perfect social justice and was meant to shape all private interests for the sake of the community; it also aimed to support solidarity with all nations seeking the same goal, and therefore to bring peace. This so-called Theology of Service claimed to be the sound theological interpretation of God's will for history and in history, a theology to be done by the church for the sake of all people. The church's aim was understood to be the common good enriched by spiritual sources but independent from any religious interference with public affairs. The Theology of Service was ready to interpret or even to justify this new direction of history as congruent with God's will. Because of this relationship, it lost its strength to engage in the current state of affairs as an independent, spiritually constituted, and therefore self-sustaining body. Its main interest was reduced to comparing the gospel with urgent political challenges and to understanding the proclamation of the gospel as an answer supporting and adjusting to those challenges. Nearly all elements of the church had been converted into mere functions of politics. The church was seen as a useful instrument for urging people to adjust their lives to public needs already defined by the political authorities. The Theology of Service merely integrated the remaining resources of the church into a politically unified public life. Theology had been transferred to this public realm because it was transformed into a mere interpretation of history, an interpretation that was meant to be progressive. In being comprehensively relevant to the public realm, theology ultimately became absorbed by it.

The Hungarian theologian Ervin Vályi-Nagy (1924-93) marked the fundamental error of this theological usurpation of history. He stated that the church authorities demanded the obedience of faith while equating God's will with the course of history interpreted as progress toward a perfect society. History itself, no longer obstructed by reactionary forces, saves humankind because it is in conformity with God's will.[2] Even when the Theology of Service called urgently for the public service of the church, it was a theology outside the church because it was centered in an overarching justification of the politically formed life.

2. See chap. 7, nn. 7-8, in this volume.

Hungarian Protestant Christians today hearing the phrase "service of the church" associate this slogan instinctively with the Theology of Service of former church authorities. These authorities have in fact alienated many church people from the spiritual sources of the proclamation of the gospel. They were alienated from the promises of God that confront the church with God's hidden work within history and that open the church for God's providence, that is, God's acting in a surprisingly judging and saving way. Therefore, there is a growing skepticism toward or even resistance against all kinds of public engagements of the church. In Hungary, as in the other countries of the former Communist bloc, there is a widespread tendency to confine Christian faith to an enrichment of private life only. That might be quite comprehensible as an overreaction to the political usurpation of the service of the church. But that privatization would be a false alternative to any totalitarian movement that insists upon the political character of all areas of life. On the contrary, the point at stake is a well-structured personal life grounded in faith and anchored in hope in God's promises, which means at the same time a life deeply rooted in the Christian community faithful to God's promises and commandments. Furthermore, we have to ask how that kind of personal life soundly relates to the openness of granted love for the need of other people. This very relationship forges the responsibility of Christians for public life. To give account for this highly sensible relationship is the task of the *service of theology* in the church.[3] In that respect, theology serves the public domain indirectly rather than acting as a "Theology of Service" — a theology that claims to be an affirmation of political goals that are underlined by motivations derived from Christian moral traditions.

What kind of church service should the Hungarian prime minister have asked for? First, he was interested in engaging as many Christians as possible in public service. In Hungary there is a growing need for social work that the state cannot sufficiently cover. This can be observed as well in other countries, not just in the former Communist countries that had extensive social security. The Hungarian government is willing to subsidize the church for such activities. In addition,

3. Cf. Wallace M. Alston, Jr., ed., *Theology in the Service of the Church: Essays in Honor of Thomas W. Gillespie* (Grand Rapids: Eerdmans, 2000).

many social institutions, including high schools and colleges, which had been expropriated from the churches, have been returned to church control. But it becomes more and more evident that it will be insufficient for the church to merely substitute for the state in social services and higher education. The decisive question pertains to the characteristic service of the church. It might be the task of the church to indicate urgent needs, which are neglected by the society from time to time. But even in well-acknowledged social services and educational work of churches, there are often unresolved questions about the direction and value of these activities. This might be a special challenge for the service of the church. Of course, such a challenge is not to be met by the church issuing authoritative advice for society, but rather by taking account of its experiences in those areas, faithful to the essentials of church service in many forms, and contributing primarily in indirect ways.

This leads us to the second kind of public service of the church, which is often required even more urgently and decisively than the first. This service might have been explained to the liberal Hungarian prime minister by his theological consultant. *Democracy needs the clear and undistracted voice of the church,* of a church that is really independent by its genuine constitution, by its purposes, and by the pursuit of its goals. But that explanation might be insufficient and even misleading. The Christian church is *entrusted* to proclaim God's promise for his acting to, for, and with human beings and to clarify what God asks for a personal and a communal life interwoven with God's work. The church is free and independent only if it listens to that external voice. Only then may it engage public matters, an engagement that is sometimes a confrontation with the prevailing concept of the direction of social and political life. If the church neglects its witness to this ongoing work of God, it would be just a voice representing one interest group among others in a society heading toward pluralism. But the church is asked to be just the church with its specific task of questioning the truth of human existence. Therefore, the way the church sees itself in a democratic society is at stake if it is asked for its service.

Is the service of the church in public really church service, or is it instead a mere religious function of an already politically defined direction of cultural history? The answer depends on this self-understanding and even more on the way it gains clarity in this self-understanding. This crucial task was enunciated by the Barmen Declaration of 1934. Thesis 5 states that the church is entrusted to remind people to seek justice and peace,[4] essentially in its preaching and intercession. This task is crucial again today, and there are very different opinions about its meaning.

The term "service of the church" in Hungary recalls the burden of the Theology of Service as a temptation to build up a theology on a reflection of the course of past and future history. This would be a theology located outside the church while centered in an *overarching justification* of the politically formed life. In this respect there is, if you look closely enough, no difference in principle between the former so-called people's democracies in socialist countries and liberal democracies. Of course, there are significant fundamental differences between totalitarian states and democracies in defining and forming public life, and especially in communicating information about it. Accordingly, the structure of public life is quite different. However, for theology the same task remains if we understand theology as but a cultural study destined to compare certain religious traditions. Then it aims to explore a desired public life and to combine those traditions within this intention. But the theological reasoning will be clearly different if theology is constituted to serve the church and to support it to be really and truthfully the church, the people of God within society. I want to explain this distinction, often fine as a hair, later in this chapter, and then I will sketch two examples. For now it might be sufficient that, at least in central and eastern Europe, enough hot memories survive to make us aware of this distinction, even if other political circumstances prevail. These memories might serve as an ecumenical contribution to the task of reconsidering theology today. And because I was involved in the struggle for theological education in Hungary and Poland for many years, it might be fair to say that this is at least a part of my context in teaching theology and reflecting on it.

You may understand that with the background of these experiences I became very interested in the claim for *public theology* in contemporary North American theology. I invite you to look at this program in the light of questions raised under quite different circumstances. We have

---

4. *Creeds of the Churches: A Reader in Christian Doctrine from the Bible to the Present*, ed. John H. Leith, 3rd ed. (Louisville: John Knox, 1982), p. 521.

to examine what might be similar or different. Some designs of public theology were well noticed in Germany and were acclaimed by German theologians who see themselves in the same line,[5] since public theology promises to address problems and tasks worldwide, at least in cultures with similar political and multireligious cultural features.

Public Theology

The term "public theology" might be understood in different ways. If you define it as an equivalent to "political theology," it often means theology engaged in urgent affairs of social reform or even a radical restructuring of society.[6] Another, wider definition would show the manifold intersections of faith and public life,[7] especially to comprehensively reconsider and reconstruct the impact of theology for political thought.[8] The elaborate and different program of a specific *public theology* attempts to figure *out a new kind of theology*, in contrast to any strictly church-related theology. This theology declares *the public sphere as the primary space and medium for doing theology*. I would like to focus my analysis on this theology.

The new and distinctive claim for a public theology was prominently proposed by David Tracy of Chicago Divinity School in his books *The Analogical Imagination*[9] and *Plurality and Ambiguity*[10] as well as

5. Rolf Schieder, "Politische Kultur als Civil Religion," *Zeitschrift für Evangelische Ethik* 32 (1988): 107-18; Wolfgang Huber, *Kirche in der Zeitenwende: Gesellschaftlicher Wandel und Erneuerung der Kirche* (Gütersloh: Verlag der Bertelsmann Stiftung, 1998); Trutz Rendtorff, *Theorie des Christentums: Historisch-theologische Studien zu seiner neuzeitlichen Verfassung* (Gütersloh: Gütersloher Verlagshaus Gerd Mohn, 1972); Trutz Rendtorff, *Vielspältiges: Protestantische Beiträge zur ethischen Kultur* (Stuttgart: Kohlhammer, 1991).

6. For example, Benjamin Valentin, *Mapping Public Theology: Beyond Culture, Identity, and Difference* (Harrisburg, Pa.: Trinity, 2002).

7. For example, James R. Wilburn, ed., *Faith and Public Policy* (Lanham, Md.: Lexington Books, 2002).

8. Cf. Oliver O'Donovan, *The Desire of the Nations: Rediscovering the Roots of Political Theology* (Cambridge: Cambridge University Press, 1996).

9. David Tracy, *The Analogical Imagination: Christian Theology and the Culture of Pluralism* (New York: Crossroad, 1981).

10. David Tracy, *Plurality and Ambiguity: Hermeneutics, Religion, Hope* (San Francisco: Harper and Row, 1987).

in numerous articles, particularly in his essay "Catholic Classics in American Liberal Culture."[11] Following the tradition of American liberalism, Tracy seeks to integrate the progressive impact of American Catholicism into a tradition originally based on radical Protestantism.

Tracy's understanding of public theology relies not only on a fundamental interrelation of moral values that shape liberal democracy, such as tolerance, genuine freedom of the individual conscience, and responsibility for the common good shared by enlightened fellow citizens. He also adds classic Christian symbols and metaphors like "image of God" *(imago Dei)* and "kingdom of God" as resources for public discourse and conversation. He intends to integrate these resources into a consensus that supports the liberal democratic culture. This universal hermeneutics seems to be very similar to the former concept of the *corpus Christianum:* the Christian body encompassing European culture and its public life, which is shaped by Christianity even outside the church. Influential from the Middle Ages to the Enlightenment and beyond, *corpus Christianum* reflects a comprehensive social entity prior to any institutional structures. It is understood on the grounds of moral convictions and the binding, compulsory force of rationality. Therefore, public theology as presented by Tracy is essentially fundamental theology. All the specific subjects of doctrinal theology are transformed into this fundamental theology in order to make them communicable in the public sphere. They are subjected to a continuing process of evaluation for the sake of nourishing the public domain, and they are structured by politics, the academy, and the church. Theology is then judged mainly, if not exclusively, by its *effects* on communal life and the public.

It might be instructive to reflect on places where theology has already been reduced to topics related solely to the public life, to urgent common needs, and to the common good that is at stake because of unsolved social and economic problems. A young South African theologian once told me that the department of theology where he was teaching had been converted into a department of religious studies in order to do justice to the multireligious social context. After the

---

11. In *Catholicism and Liberalism: Contributions to American Public Philosophy,* ed. R. Bruce Douglass and David Hollenbach, Cambridge Studies in Religion and American Public Life, ed. Robin W. Lovin (Cambridge: Cambridge University Press, 1994), pp. 196-213.

change to religious studies, the next step was to select, according to their public significance (i.e., ecology, social justice, and so on), the subjects to be taught and studied. The theologians were asked to contribute to those topics, but the opportunity to study theology as a discipline with its own genuine subject matter and its own discourse declines as time goes by. How can students learn to argue theologically if theology is looked upon merely as a set of traditions to be compared with other traditions or new challenges? Theology loses its strength if we understand it exclusively as material for comparative interpretation even though the interpretation might be carried out for the sake of an inclusive construction of communal life.

Consider another example. Recently in Germany there was a heated debate about opening all shops on Sundays. Shops are closed on Saturday afternoon and on Sunday, with only a few exceptions. The businesspeople wanted to change these rules. They argued that working people need more opportunities to shop, enjoy the increased supply of goods, and get a better feeling for the offers. This attitude reflects the slogan I read on a shopping bag at the Whitney Art Museum gift shop in New York: "I shop, therefore I am" — the American version of the Cartesian principle: *Cogito ergo sum* — "I think, therefore I am." The Protestant and Catholic churches in Germany entered the public debate. Church leaders looked at the argument as a chance to remember the observance of the Sabbath, which is a divine gift meant to give rest for working people and which is an important part of the Christian tradition. They created the slogan "If there is no Sunday anymore, there will be only working days." With this slogan they supported the claim of the labor unions for two days off or at least one common day of rest for most of the working people. The day off was meant to ease family life, e.g., to allow one to sleep longer and have more leisure time for lunch and supper. But that slogan did not work; that is, it did not bring the commandment "Remember the sabbath day, and keep it holy" (Exod. 20:8) into the public debate. You need much more creative thinking to mediate this commandment to a public consciousness that is only partly concerned about labor conditions, but is more concerned about spending opportunities. The commandment is not only about having rest from ongoing labor, but is also about the joy of people gathering together to praise God and to hear from him the promise for his work, which is sustaining human life.

Almost nothing was said about this theological rationale for the observance of Sunday. Therefore the slogan "If there is no Sunday anymore, there will be only working days" was not a sound theological contribution for the sake of saving Sunday, even when it was considered support for an important element of the common good.

Coming back to David Tracy's program for establishing public theology, it would be unfair to suppose that he wants to abandon serious theological research and education in order to reclaim the Christian traditions for the ongoing process of public communication that structures the culture. But he overestimates the stability and enduring strength of such a tradition if it is connected to the church only as a cultural phenomenon alongside the academy and politics. This tradition resembles cut flowers — they will bloom for some days, but they are cut off from their life-sustaining roots. Tracy might be convinced about the liveliness of the American Catholic Church, which is so strong that it can set theology free to an ongoing hermeneutics of Christianity as an essential part of Western culture. But the question remains if even the Catholic Church is really so strong and vital as to go on without the continuous theological effort to comprehend church doctrine, to clarify and deepen it, and, let me say it right away, to enjoy dogmatics. But besides this question, we must be aware that the claim for public theology can be understood as a substitute for a church-related theology and might be used as a contribution for restructuring theology into religious cultural studies. The critical point would be if we can take a *comparative viewpoint* on Christian faith, hope, and love — or if we are given account for them as members of the Christian community. This account must certainly be in dialogue with other people, but must remain sensitive to tensions and strains within this dialogue that cannot be overcome by comparison, intellectual negotiation, and adjustment. A standpoint that is mainly or even totally comparative would create a theology outside the church.

This problem is not as evident with the second advocate of public theology, the Lutheran Ronald F. Thiemann, former dean of Harvard Divinity School, in his book *Constructing a Public Theology: The Church in a Pluralistic Society.*[12] (Interestingly, in an article published in the Ger-

---

12. Ronald F. Thiemann, *Constructing a Public Theology: The Church in a Pluralistic Culture* (Louisville: Westminster John Knox, 1991).

man *Journal of Protestant Ethics,* Thiemann changed the title to "Public Theology: The Moral Dimension of Religion in a Pluralistic Society.")[13] Like Tracy, he fights against a theology that nourishes only a private religiosity. In contrast to such privatization, Thiemann studies the point of contact between Christian moral values and the legal system. He shows that there can be no neutrality on fundamental issues of life and death. This idea, along with his view of a well-structured public life where both institutions and basic social entities like families play an important role, advances his thesis.

Thiemann proposes a public theology that is "communal, formative, critical, and public"[14] (i.e., "faith seeking to understand the relation between Christian convictions and the broader social and cultural context within which people of faith live").[15] But while borrowing the phrase "faith seeking understanding" *(fides quaerens intellectum)* from Anselm of Canterbury, Thiemann equates two significantly different tasks and goals of theology. Anselm asked for the rational implications of faith, particularly for understanding the relation of language (and specifically the word "God") to reality, speaking within the very limits of a given, created world. But Anselm first and above all dealt with the constitution of prayer where a human being becomes aware of his or her creatureliness. Here a person addresses God as "You" who established the "I" answering to the "You" in God's address to his creature. It is the relationality of faith that is expressed in prayer, and this constitution of the "I" radiates in everyday life.

The meaning of "faith seeking understanding" — a rational explication of the manifold human answers to God's creative work and word, as pointed out, for example, by Daniel Migliore in his fine introduction to theology[16] — is changed by Thiemann into a contextual interpretation of Christian convictions. This is indeed an important task for the hermeneutics of moral theology, but it does not characterize theology concerning the constitutive elements of faith, hope, and love. To extend Anselm's phrase into faith seeking understanding "the

13. Thiemann, "Public Theology: The Moral Dimension of Religion in a Pluralistic Society," *Zeitschrift für Evangelische Ethik* 42 (1998): 176-90.

14. Thiemann, *Constructing a Public Theology,* p. 167.

15. Thiemann, "Public Theology," p. 184.

16. Daniel L. Migliore, *Faith Seeking Understanding: An Introduction to Christian Theology* (Grand Rapids: Eerdmans, 1991).

broader social and cultural context within which people of faith live" would be to claim a prophetic insight into God's judging and saving work within history and an evaluation of the doctrine of divine providence. But if Anselm's formula is just watered down, it may turn into "faith seeking public acclamation."

I grew a bit skeptical about Thiemann's design of public theology when I read his article in the journal *Dialogue*.[17] Here Thiemann compares his program critically with other contemporary concepts of theology. Taking "theology as narrated promise" as a threshold,[18] he originally thought himself situated close to George Lindbeck's *The Nature of Doctrine*[19] and to the narrative foundation of Christian ethics described by Stanley Hauerwas of Duke Divinity School.[20] But now, Thiemann rejects these two concepts because he considers them too secluded in the internal communication of church people.[21] He fears any kind of sectarianism. But he fails to notice Lindbeck's emphasis on the process of learning the language of faith, the precondition for any approach to Christian theology and for any theological engagement. Regarding Hauerwas, Thiemann underestimates the decisive role of central church practices — especially the liturgy — as a living source for the foundation of Christian ethics, although he respects the "teaching function of liturgy."[22] He rather focuses on the church as a cultural space for a sound plurality of hopeful religious convictions. He sees the church as a model for a pluralistic interchange of different beliefs and practices, on the common ground of human limitations and openness for new insights. But because public theology is "a process of 'mutual critical correlation' between specific principles, beliefs, and practices of the Christian community and concrete issues of public belief, practice, and policy,"[23] this kind of theology intends

17. Ronald F. Thiemann, "Faith Seeking Understanding," *Dialogue* 38 (1999): 46-52.

18. Ronald F. Thiemann, *Revelation and Theology: The Gospel as Narrated Promise* (Notre Dame, Ind.: University of Notre Dame Press, 1985).

19. George A. Lindbeck, *The Nature of Doctrine: Religion and Theology in a Postliberal Age* (Philadelphia: Westminster, 1984).

20. Stanley Hauerwas, *In Good Company: The Church as Polis* (Notre Dame, Ind.: University of Notre Dame Press, 1995).

21. Thiemann, "Faith Seeking Understanding," p. 50.

22. Thiemann, *Constructing a Public Theology*, p. 121.

23. Thiemann, "Public Theology," p. 185.

mainly the comparison of truth claims and their effects within the public sphere. Public theology has to inspire responsibility for the common good, to strengthen the notion of the distinctiveness of religious beliefs as motivations, but most of all to integrate them into a permanent public discourse.

Thiemann understands the church as a part of the public sphere. Therefore he asks for the church to contribute to the public discourse by speaking publicly. He is concerned more that the voice of the church be heard in public than that the basic practices of the church, like proclamation and intercession, be known. He seems to be little interested in various social activities, particularly Christian education, which have been and remain an important factor in the public service of the church. He perceives the church as the sphere where personal religious convictions can grow and be shared before entering the public debate. This approach diminishes the church's main point of contact with public affairs even if Christians are no longer a majority within the society.

Here the late Mennonite theologian John Howard Yoder might challenge the advocates of public theology. In his last book, *For the Nations: Essays Evangelical and Public,* he contributes significantly to the public character of the church. He does not reflect on the minor role of Mennonites in American society and the denominational map; he is not concerned with the publicity of religious convictions and values. He straightforwardly reminds his readers of the letter of Jeremiah to the Jews in the Babylonian exile, quoting a passage that often guided Jews and Christians under political suppression: "Seek the salvation of the culture to which God has sent you" (Jer. 29:7)[24] — just being the people of God serving their vocation as people called by God.[25]

Now I will look quickly at a third proponent of public theology. Owen Thomas of Episcopal Divinity School in Cambridge, Massachusetts, in his article "Public Theology and Counter-Public Spheres," argues for the church as the place for a balanced representation of very

24. NRSV: "Seek the welfare of the city where I have sent you into exile, and pray to the LORD on its behalf, for in its welfare you will find your welfare."

25. John H. Yoder, *For the Nations: Essays Evangelical and Public* (Grand Rapids: Eerdmans, 2000), p. 76 n. 60; cf. John H. Yoder, "Christians and Jews Seeking the *Shalom* of the City," in *The Jewish-Christian Schism Revisited,* ed. Michael Cartwright and Peter Ochs (Grand Rapids: Eerdmans, 2003), pt. IV, pp. 181-204.

different voices, particularly marginalized ones. Democracy is about equality of chances, and the church contributes to a culture heading toward true democracy by having and raising a voice in public. Thomas concerns himself with the conditions of the public discussion of Christian convictions and the witnesses involved. Within this context he claims that the church is a forerunner for a society that represents all its members equally and gives the same attention to each, hearing and valuing their claims and legitimate interests. Thomas concludes: "This kind of conversation assumes equality among the conversation-partners, equality of power and access of self-representation, public space, and collective voice. This is something that does not exist, but it is a goal worth striving for."[26]

This task might be a vicarious function of the church. But I have experienced, at least in my home parish, that this task, if granted a superior role, can be dangerous if it leads only to an ongoing self-referential discourse and a mere exchange of particular aspects for the sake of integrating them into a communal significance. Such discourse sooner or later excludes people who are open to the transpersonal truth-claims of the Christian faith and to the promise that Christians are united in the Spirit of God and are made one. This unity does not build on social equality. Rather, it consists of different gifts that are intended to nourish the body of Christ and to connect it with the needs of other people. This discourse is a space to encounter God's judging and saving action in the world.

Relating to the church as the place for a representation of very different voices, Thomas's intention reminds me of Thiemann's remarks on the decisive role of churches in Eastern Europe "providing counter-public space for citizens to organize and protest against the ruling communist regimes."[27] But this notion is misleading. Of course, the Polish Catholic Church and the Protestant churches in East Germany provided space for protest, and they backed social critique against the totalitarian regime over public life that destroyed individuality. In Poland this protest was understood as a constituent component of pastoral care and spiritual guidance of moral life as part of the public ser-

---

26. Owen Thomas, "Public Theology and Counter-Public Spheres," *Harvard Theological Review* 85 (1992): 453-66, here p. 466.
27. Thiemann, "Public Theology," p. 180.

vice of the church. In East Germany the space for critique was seen as the task of the church for "being-for-the-other," according to a famous phrase of Dietrich Bonhoeffer.[28] But this being-for-the-other is not possible at length without Christians being "with-each-other" and being "for-each-other."[29] This tension was experienced very often within parishes; the space for protest in particular was possible only because of compromises that church authorities had made with the state. To become a counterpublic space can imply that the church is judged only according to its effects on the public, and is therefore transformed into a function of the public domain, even dialectically by its counterpublic effects. And after a change of political structure, this function is no longer needed, as in the case especially of East Germany, Poland, and the Czech Republic. The church was used, not always, but often, for purposes not essential to the church. That might be tolerable for some time, but it is not intended to define the character of the church and its public service.

This utilization of the Eastern European churches to depict a counterpublic space has been the main interest of the Western media. I remember many complaints of East German friends that Western television reported only on politically critical voices in church gatherings and synods, but not on the church affairs and the spiritual needs that were treated there as well. This persuades us to be mindful of the role the mass media plays in shaping and even structuring not only the public opinion but also the "public" as such. Recent debates on public theology have underestimated or even neglected this role. We

28. Dietrich Bonhoeffer, *Widerstand und Ergebung: Briefe und Aufzeichnungen aus der Haft,* in *Werke,* vol. 9, ed. Christian Gremmels et al. (Gütersloh: Christian Kaiser, 1998), p. 558: "Unser Verhältnis zu Gott ist ein neues Leben im 'Dasein für andere', in der Teilnahme am Leben Jesu." The American translation is not quite correct: "Our relation to God . . . a new life for others, through participation in the Being of God." *Prisoner for God: Letters and Papers from Prison,* ed. Eberhard Bethge, trans. Reginald H. Fuller (New York: Macmillan, 1954), p. 179. "The Church is her true self only when she exists for humanity," p. 180; corrected in the 3rd ed. (London: SCM, 1967), p. 211: "The Church is the Church only when it exists for others."

29. Dietrich Bonhoeffer, *Sanctorum Communio: A Theological Study of the Sociology of the Church,* in *Dietrich Bonhoeffer Works,* vol. 1, ed. Clifford J. Green, trans. Reinhard Krauss and Nancy Lukens (Minneapolis: Fortress, 1996), p. 170. Cf. Wolf Krötke, "Dietrich Bonhoeffer als 'Theologe der DDR': Ein kritischer Rückblick," *Zeitschrift für Evangelische Ethik* 37 (1993): 94-105.

have to pay attention to the method of the media: they claim to give the full picture by representing different impressions and opinions, preferably those that oppose one another. Therefore the public is often viewed only through exclusive alternatives. Do we take this structure into account as we consider church and theology in the twenty-first century? The demand for public theology, in sharp contrast to private piety with its suggestive rhetoric, can develop a totalitarian touch, even if it is correct to criticize any privatization of Christian faith, hope, and love.

Considering the impact of the media in structuring the public leads us back to the starting point for our considerations: the request of the Hungarian prime minister for the service of the church. His concern for the common good is challenged not only by statistics of gross national product, budgeted deficits, rising mass poverty, and overburdened social security, but also (and sometimes even more) by the needs created by the media and its advertising partners. They may help increase the production of consumer goods and therefore strengthen free enterprise, but they tend to undermine personal virtues, which can change opportunities into possible accomplishments. The real danger for Eastern European economies is an unlimited liberalism — both in the marketplace and in private life — as much as a hypertrophy of imminent expectations and overstated hopes. This is especially troublesome with a younger generation that views democracy only as a sphere for personal growth recast by advertising. As time passes, these hopes become more and more disillusioned and provide the source for a spiritual depression more dangerous than any economic depression.

What Dare We Hope — Facing the Service of the Church?

Therefore, the question "What dare we hope?" that shapes our everyday expectations becomes the crucial task for giving an account for theology in the public realm, even if it is a public service of the church. As "hope" is the topic of another chapter of this book, I want to touch only lightly on this theme here. Let me remind you that the message of hope as energy for overcoming particularity and ego-centered self-indulgence has been an important factor of American public theology as represented by Reinhold Niebuhr and Paul Tillich. According to Tillich, "Suffering is therefore overcome by the self-negation of the will's desire to be something particular. In Christianity the demand is made to accept sufferings as an element of finitude with an ultimate courage and thereby to overcome that suffering which is dependent on existential estrangement, which is mere destruction."[30] This message, as painted so vividly by Edward Hopper, is linked with the very idealistic and American concept of transcending limits, in heading to new frontiers and creating new spaces, even in the inner life. But hope rooted in endurance is quite another thing. The character of such a hope, experienced by so many Christians living without certain prospects of change (as was the case in Eastern Europe and is true in many parts of our global village), might be a contribution for Christians seeking the common good. But hope is not just a virtue to be transferred into public discourse. It needs to be nourished in the "we" of the Christians Paul talks about when he says: "We boast in our hope of sharing the glory of God. And not only that, but we also boast in our sufferings, knowing that suffering produces endurance, and endurance produces character, and character produces hope" (Rom. 5:2b-4). This "we" is constituted by the marks of the church, such as worship, listening to the Word of God, sacraments, prayer, pastoral care, suffering, respecting the struggle of political authorities in serving the public need, and participating in this struggle as much as possible.

Also in this regard, we must give an account of hope if we are to recognize that redemption is the very basis of life together and of our capacity to bear responsibility in any public office. Theologians of the Reformation often pointed to this impact of redemption for those who serve the needs of other people within the family, in the economy, in politics, and of course, in the church. Redemption does not mean a lax admission of mistakes unavoidable in interpersonal affairs; on the contrary, redemption is the very mark of God's continuing creation, constituting new beginnings. Martin Luther said in one of his table talks: "You cannot act as a major, as a father and a mother without for-

30. Paul Tillich, *Systematic Theology*, vol. 2 (Chicago: University of Chicago Press, 1964), p. 80.

giving and receiving redemption every day."[31] This redemption as a public mark of the hidden work of God relies on God's atonement granted as the forgiveness of sins. The mother of a Polish friend of mine, during World War Two, prayed every day that Germans and Poles might be reconciled to God in order to be reconciled with each other. Here again there cannot be any public theology outside the church, even as it points to redemption as a constitutive element of culture because redemption needs forgiveness, and forgiveness is first and foremost God's work.

The claim for public theology might be quite understandable in a democratic society where Christianity is valued within a pluralism of values and convictions. But in this case theology is in danger of being reduced to a subject of comparative cultural studies, cut off from its very roots. On the basis of experiences when theology was subjugated to an overarching justification of the politically formed life, I make a plea for dogmatics as reasoning theologically what the church is entrusted to say. This theology might serve the church preparing for dialogue with other members of the society to give account of our hope if we are asked for its reason (1 Pet. 3:15).

---

31. *Martin Luthers Werke*, Kritische Gesamtausgabe: *Tischreden* (Table talks), no. 315, vol. 1, ed. Karl Drescher (Weimar: Böhlau, 1912), p. 129: "Remissio peccatorum est in omnibus creaturis." Also no. 943, pp. 472-73: "Doctor Luther sagete einmal: 'Den Artikel von der Vergebung der Sünde hätte Gott in alle Creaturen gesteckt.' Denn die, so in der Oberkeit und in offentlichen Aemtern wären, müßten alle der Vergebung der Sünden gebrauchen. Ein Bürgermeister in der Stadt, Vater und Mutter, Männer und Frauen. . . ."

CHAPTER 10

Observations on the Current State
of Reformed Theology

In 1980 I was asked to write a comprehensive article on dogmatics for the *Theologische Realenzyklopädie,* the most extensive theological encyclopedia of our time. To get an adequate survey I called the editor some time later to ask him who would be the contributor for Reformed theology. He replied: "Who is a really genuine, typical, and representative Reformed theologian in Germany today?" Then I realized how difficult it is to answer this question satisfactorily. The editor told me just to include Reformed theology in my article, but that made my task even more demanding.

An expert characterizes: "A bewildering array of denominations — more than a hundred in the United States alone — either consider themselves Reformed or find Reformed Christianity in their active tradition. In a tradition that sees itself in constant reformation in the light of Scripture, it is impossible to determine how many of these denominations continue to teach and believe all the tenets of Reformed Christianity."[1]

In what respect can we find a comprehensive, characteristic Reformed theology, besides the fact that there are biblical scholars and church historians at departments of theology in universities and at Presbyterian seminaries who think of themselves as Reformed? Jürgen Moltmann, for example, claims to be linked with Reformed

---

1. Louis B. Weeks, "Reformed Tradition," in *The Encyclopedia of Christianity,* ed. Erwin Fahlbusch et al., vol. 4 (Grand Rapids: Eerdmans; Leiden: Brill, 2005), pp. 541-49, quotation is from p. 548.

theology and has been a speaker at meetings of the World Alliance of Reformed Churches (WARC). Still — you may ask — what is really "Reformed" in his way of doing theology? Moltmann is devoted to a kind of political theology that seeks to open the future by permanently transforming Christian traditions into a striving for social change, for peace, and for social justice. Here, the Bible is sometimes understood literally as a blueprint for new social and international structures, e.g., reconciliation conceived as reparation of distorted relationships. Such a radicalized social ethics — with an immediate biblical frame of reference including directly applied images and symbols — has often been ascribed to Calvinistic traditions. In the later sixties, seventies, and eighties the Moderamen des Reformierten Bundes (the association of Reformed parishes in former West Germany) argued for this kind of theology. This approach was the main direction of Reformed theology in France as well. In the Czech Republic the tradition of Jan Hus, which predates the Reformation, advances the social-ethical orientation of theology and stresses the involvement of church and theology in critical social engagement. Nowadays, though, many younger Czech theologians are aware that at least between 1969 and 1989 there was hardly any space for constructive voices and realistic views even in the church and in theological education, but often only subordination to the interests of the government, alongside political oppression.[2]

There is a wide range of perception about how Reformed theology can contribute to social ethics and respond to political challenges. Joachim Staedtke, who held the chair of Reformed theology in Erlangen (Bavaria, Germany) in the 1960s, emphasized a wide range of social issues, especially concerning public policy, to outline a profile of the task of Reformed theology in a strongly Lutheran-oriented faculty. Hans-Joachim Kraus, who succeeded the distinguished Reformed theologian Otto Weber at Göttingen, understood biblical and systematic theology as a constructive enterprise for interpreting the kingdom

2. Dr. Jan Štefan, who now teaches systematic theology at the Faculty of Protestant Theology of the Charles University Prague (the former Comenius seminary, which honored the Moravian tradition), calls it the renewal of the old enthusiastic dream of "reforming the deformed church and world": "Prager Notizen," *Evangelische Theologie* 55 (1995): 239-43, esp. p. 240.

of God as a historical process that produces peace, justice, and true, meaningful life.[3]

Wallace M. Alston, a Presbyterian minister and the former director of the Center of Theological Inquiry in Princeton, New Jersey, points to his teacher Paul L. Lehmann (Union Seminary, New York City) and states: "Politics is the means by which the mission of the Church is discerned and done in the formal and informal processes of its institutional life. It is the context in which the question of authority is answered in a voluntary association. . . . The politics of the church are those patterns of human association that enable the church to reflect on and to participate in the politics of God, that is, in God's renovating activity in the world."[4]

Michael Welker stresses the heritage of Reformed "covenantal theology" (God's covenants with Noah, Abraham, Israel, David, the New Covenant through Jesus Christ). He concludes that faith

> is a communally fashioned and fashioning form of life, a spiritually and culturally creative form of life which results in proclamation, spiritual communication and interpersonal love, which is perceptible both internally and externally in various forms of communal life.
>
> It has been precisely Reformed theology which has concentrated time and again on these realistic and public aspects of faith. In contrast to modern religiosity, which has excluded or at least repressed this dimension of interactive, publicly shaped and publicly shaping faith, Reformed theology should bring these central themes into the current ecumenical discussion as well.[5]

What was and what is the impact of Karl Barth's theology for Reformed theology? It would be a complicated and difficult task to seriously differentiate between the theology of Barth and the Reformed tradition. But when Barth was called to Göttingen in 1921 to take a pro-

3. Hans-Joachim Kraus, *Systematische Theologie im Kontext biblischer Geschichte und Eschatologie* (Neukirchen-Vluyn: Neukirchener Verlag, 1983).

4. Wallace M. Alston, Jr., *The Church of the Living God: A Reformed Perspective* (Louisville: Westminster John Knox, 2002), p. 97.

5. Michael Welker, "Reformation Theology and the Reformed Profile," *Bulletin of the Institute for Reformed Theology* 3 (2003): 1.4–9.16, quotation is from p. 7.

fessorship founded by American Presbyterians after World War One, first he studied the writings of Luther rather than those of Calvin or Zwingli more intensely. Barth and his friends were mainly interested in the common substance of the theology of the Reformers in general because it was not really understood, or was misread, in recent theological education. When Barth started to teach theology at Göttingen, he was forced by his Lutheran colleagues to restrict his teaching to Reformed theology. In Münster and Bonn he taught systematic theology. In his *Church Dogmatics* (the first volume was published in 1932) he claimed to focus on a biblically grounded theology that could serve the entire range of the Evangelical Church (*evangelisch,* in the German understanding: faithful to the *euangelion,* the gospel). In Bonn he became familiar with a very traditional and rigid Reformed heritage, marked mainly by Hermann Friedrich Kohlbrügge (1803-75), who had strongly emphasized the total sinfulness of all humanity, unable to face God's glory and totally dependent on God's incarnation in Jesus Christ. Despite some similarities with his own theological enterprise, Barth, I was told,[6] found himself out of line with this kind of Reformed piety, which was sometimes very conservative in political matters, too.

In the former Prussian territories, theological education and research were shaped by the merger of Lutheran and Reformed churches that formed the Evangelische Kirche der Union (Evangelical Church of the Union) in the first half of the nineteenth century. A remarkable influence of the Reformed heritage is to be found in the presbyterial-synodal constitution of this church. Now, however, the differences within theological education in Europe involve the question whether the curriculum must be rooted in the biblical canon and in the theology of the Reformation or in the neo-Protestant ("liberal") theology of religious culture.

Especially revealing, it seems to me, is the situation in Hungary with its relatively strong Reformed population, which in former times powerfully opposed the Austrian regime and its links with the Roman Catholic Church. In the convention hall of the famous old seminary in Debrecen, there is a chair in memory of the political revolutionary

---

6. My late colleague J. F. Gerhard Goeters, a Reformed church historian at the Faculty of Protestant Theology at Bonn University and editor of the Reformed *Books of Confessions,* gave me this information.

Lajos Kossuth (1802-94). Many Reformed Protestants supported the national uprising Kossuth led. After the other uprising in 1956, a so-called Theology of Service was developed mainly by Reformed church officials and theologians.[7] Karl Barth sometimes criticized this theology of history for its similarity to the German Christian ideology condemned in the Barmen Declaration (1934), but his objections are found only in personal letters. After 1948 Barth interfered in some aspects of church politics by strengthening its so-called progressive tendencies. In Hungary, however, critical voices were silenced, and even the representatives of the World Council of Churches who visited Hungary were unable, or at least unwilling, to understand the real situation, in which ministers and parishioners were estranged from church officials and theologians who approved the Theology of Service. Friends who were pushed into the background told me they felt neglected and even betrayed by the politics of the World Alliance of Reformed Churches and by the many Reformed theologians in the West who were mainly interested in the social impact of Christian faith and hope, but not in forming sound theological judgments concerning the very difficult social, economic, and spiritual issues facing the church.[8]

Today, Reformed theology in Hungary has to rebuild a reliable teaching ministry almost from scratch. Church and theology must deal with a situation in which the church has enormous opportunity, for example, in higher education, but lacks the spiritual and intellectual resources to match its responsibilities. At the same time, there is on the one hand a dangerous inclination to develop a merely private religious life, a kind of solitary personal religiosity. On the other hand, Christians today need a very individual (not individualistic!) spiritual life, embedded deeply in the life of the church while being aware of God's acting in public and personal affairs.

Now, how can we exhibit the proper characteristics of Reformed

---

7. See the documentation of Zoltán Balog: *Mitarbeiter des Zeitgeistes? Die Auseinandersetzung über die Zeitgemäßheit als Kriterium kirchlichen Handelns und die Kriterien theologischer Entscheidungen in der Reformierten Kirche Ungarns 1967-1992*, ed. Gerhard Sauter, Beiträge zur theologischen Urteilsbildung, vol. 3 (Frankfurt am Main: Peter Lang, 1997).

8. See chapters 7 on the political changes in Europe and 9 on public theology, in this volume.

theology in order to clarify and strengthen it not only in Hungary, but throughout central Europe and perhaps also in the United Kingdom, in America, Asia, and Africa, and do so without being merely traditionalist, confessionalist, and anti-ecumenical?

Recently, two instructive collections of essays were published. The first, entitled *Toward the Future of Reformed Theology*, was edited by David Willis, a retired Reformed scholar of Princeton Theological Seminary, and Michael Welker, the former professor of Reformed theology at Münster, now professor of systematic theology at the University of Heidelberg.[9] The second collection, containing contributions to conferences sponsored by the Center of Theological Inquiry in Princeton, addresses the identity as well as the ecumenicity of Reformed theology.[10]

In their introduction to *Toward the Future of Reformed Theology*, the editors regret that they were unable to present a fully representative survey of the actual state of Reformed theology throughout the world because many requests for cooperation were turned down. This may be the reason for a kind of one-sidedness: most contributions are from the United States and Germany. Regrettably, a contribution from Korea with its strong impact on Presbyterianism is missing, although the Presbyterian churches in South Korea constitute the most rapidly growing sector of Presbyterianism in the world today. Furthermore, for many of his fellow countrymen it is questionable whether John W. de Gruchy's "Toward a Theology of Liberation," as representative as it is for a prominent trend, can cover all contemporary Reformed theology in South Africa and its future.[11] It would have been instructive if more recent theologians from Hungary, the Czech Republic, Romania, and the Netherlands had analyzed the situation of the church and theological education in their countries more deeply and with greater theological reflection.[12] The second volume provides a more diverse

9. David Willis and Michael Welker, eds., *Toward the Future of Reformed Theology: Tasks, Topics, Traditions* (Grand Rapids: Eerdmans, 1999).

10. Wallace M. Alston, Jr., and Michael Welker, eds., *Reformed Theology: Identity and Ecumenicity* (Grand Rapids: Eerdmans, 2003).

11. See also his book *Liberating Reformed Theology: A South African Contribution to an Ecumenical Debate* (Grand Rapids: Eerdmans; Cape Town: David Philip, 1991).

12. For Hungary, see István Szabó, "Einige Informationen zum Verständnis des ungarischen Protestantismus im 20. Jahrhundert" and "Ungarischer Protestantismus —

and complex overview, but for a comprehensive evaluation I will concentrate on the first.

Toward the Future of Reformed Theology gives a significant impression of a new tendency in Reformed theology around the world: traditions, culture, and the church are criticized on the grounds of their reliance on the creative power of the Word of God and the integrative action of the Holy Spirit. The volume shows how biblical theology — understood as a special way of doing theology in general — will lead to a renewal of church doctrines and to transformations of ethical directives. This is a modern type of sanctification, which always has a special meaning in Reformed theology.

In comparison with former surveys,[13] however, it becomes evident that the characteristics of Reformed worship, the foundations of the parishes, and the regional church orders that replace an absent common confession[14] are hardly discussed in *Toward the Future of Reformed Theology*. Moreover, the theological derivation of ethical directives is rarely examined. Yet all these components shape the Reformed churches and their life. Everyone who is confronted with the Reformed churches recognizes at first glance *the characteristics of Reformed piety* that mark the distinctions between the Roman Catholic, the Lutheran, and the Reformed churches.

Let us therefore take up, *first*, the *structure of the Sunday service*. It should concentrate on the proclamation of the gospel. According to the order of worship, all hymns and prayers, the call to worship, the confession of sin, the prayer for illumination, the affirmation of faith,

---

heute," both in *Verkündigung und Forschung* 38, no. 2 (1993): 73-81 and 81-85; Zoltán Balog, "Beobachtungen zur theologischen Neuorientierung in der Reformierten Kirche Ungarns seit 1989," *Evangelische Theologie* 55 (1995): 217-29. For Romania, Tamás Juhász, "Zur Lage der Reformierten Kirche in Rumänien," *Evangelische Theologie* 55 (1995): 229-38.

13. For example, Ferdinand Kattenbusch, "Protestantismus," in *Realencyklopädie für protestantische Theologie und Kirche*, ed. Albert Hauck, 3rd ed., vol. 16 (Leipzig: Hinrichs, 1905), pp. 135-82, esp. pp. 165-73.

14. A certain exception is *The Constitution of the Presbyterian Church (U.S.A.)*, which contains a *Book of Confessions* (Louisville: Office of the General Assembly, 1991). This Presbyterian church is aware, as perhaps never before, that its confessional documents have a history and there is a responsibility for bearing witness to the gospel not only in continuity with the confessional heritage but also with a critical consciousness of the tasks and issues confronting the church today. This consciousness is documented in the Confession of 1967, which concentrates on theological resources for critical social issues.

the doxology, and the benediction surround the promise of the gospel and its directives. Reformed preaching has often been very close to instruction for Christian life. Mostly preaching and education were intertwined — for example, in the work of John Knox, the Reformer of Scotland. Or think of the institutions of higher education founded by Presbyterians and of the far-reaching activity of Presbyterians in the United States and their overseas missions on behalf of education until recent times. I observed impressive examples in Korea. The gospel was understood as an inexhaustible force illuminating all realms of life and thought.

What an enormously rich and precious tradition![15] But is it really alive today, not only to social needs and endangered humanity but also to promoting the challenges of liberty, peace, and the conservation of the creation? How can sound spiritual guidance in matters of everyday life be distinguished sharply enough from sheer religious information on the one hand, and from ethical indoctrination on the other? And in a culture that is overwhelmed with quasi information in the mass media, how can a preacher give sufficient attention to preaching that provides real guidance? The preacher needs to rely on an extended spiritual knowledge and a sound training in forming a well-founded viewpoint and an independent judgment.

Reformed worship cannot rely on a rich liturgy and its theological message. In some churches, in Switzerland, for instance, it consists of only a salutation, a hymn, a prayer before the sermon, another hymn, and the so-called dismissal of the congregation. How much depends on the ability to listen, to concentrate, and to meditate! Does this service really speak to the whole person, or just to the person's intellect or willpower? Can it be helped that the sanctuary could be confused with a lecture room or a room suitable mainly for performances?

Immense treasures for the Reformed service and personal piety are the prayers of the Psalms.[16] They contain the manifold forms of prayer: complaint, request, intercession, thanks, and praise. The person who prays gets in touch with the memories of God's saving ac-

15. As it is explained, for example, by Hughes Oliphant Old, *Worship Reformed according to Scripture*, rev. and expanded ed. (Louisville: Westminster John Knox, 2002).
16. Cf. Patrick D. Miller, *They Cried to the Lord: The Form and Theology of Biblical Prayer* (Minneapolis: Fortress, 1994).

tions in the history of God's people as well as with his or her own existence under God's judgment. Well-founded experiences of faith and hope are contained in the Psalms. One who prays them regularly will learn bit by bit what it means to be a person before God. This will shape human self-perception. To discover and benefit from this richness will strengthen Christian anthropology. Another treasure is the doxology: a significant contribution of Reformed worship.[17]

The *second* step: I would like to question *the administration of the church*, especially the role of the presbytery and the synod.[18] On the one hand, in Germany, in the thirties, there was the famous example of the gathering (*coetus*) of Reformed preachers in the German Rhineland, which started the theological opposition against the so-called German Christians, a group of church leaders, theologians, and laity close to the National Socialist movement. The gathering of Reformed pastors led to the Barmen Synod in 1934, where Lutherans, Reformed, and United theologians and church representatives agreed to the Barmen Declaration, the groundbreaking and pioneering consensus of obedience to the first commandment in all realms of life, action, and thought. This was a fine example of independence in reasoning theologically, rooted in well-established and reliable structures of debate, mutual clarification, and decision making. On the other hand, I have often noticed recently in presbyteries and synods the temptation to simply follow political modes of discussion and decision making. This can be decisive in periods of political oppression, as was the case in Hungary.[19] It becomes urgent whenever there are factions in moral and in political issues — such as social unrest, gender problems, and sexual ethics. How can we avoid theological judgments that are shaped by already rigid convictions that are merely decorated with theological motifs? Are there direct, immediate biblical analogies for

17. Hughes Oliphant Old, *Themes and Variations for a Christian Doxology: Some Thoughts on the Theology of Worship* (Grand Rapids: Eerdmans, 1992), esp. pp. 121-31.

18. Lukas Vischer, ed., *The Ministry of the Elders in the Reformed Churches*, Papers Presented at a Consultation Held in Geneva in August 1990 (Berne: Evangelische Arbeitsstelle Oekumene Schweiz, 1992).

19. See Bogárdi Szabó István, *Egyházvezetés és teológia a Magyarországi Református egyházban 1948 és 1989 Között* (Church leadership and theology in the Reformed Church in Hungary between 1948 and 1989), Societas et Ecclesia, vol. 3 (Debrecen: Ethnica, 1995), with an English summary.

the social and political issues of our times? What should be the theologically sound procedure in finding judgments for Christian ethics?

This leads us to a *third* marker of Reformed theology. We have to take into account the readiness to revise church doctrines by discovering the inexhaustible richness of biblical witness that is neither harmonized nor systematized. How can we think and act in a way that is shaped by sincere *biblical theology*, formed by the biblical narrative?[20] Let us discover the constitution of theological arguments by being faithful to the Scripture that is faithful to us! The Reformed tradition directs our attention especially to the Old Testament as a witness to Jesus Christ and as a treasury of God's promises.

Since Calvin, the Reformed study of the Bible has paid particular attention to the connections of biblical texts with one another and with Scripture as a whole. One form of sermon — taken over from the early church, and for a long time cultivated by the Reformed church — has contributed to the reading of the Bible. Single biblical texts were not considered in isolation but in their context of meaning and in their literary context.[21] The "homily," the exegesis of larger sections of the Scripture Sunday after Sunday, helps those members of the parish who regularly take part in the service to increasingly understand the connections. This also helps to avoid one-sidedness, which would easily arise if only a few texts of the Bible were known and always repeated. The homilies educate the congregation to listen to the different voices of the Bible and to be open to the variety of spiritual insights, which enrich the parish and encourage the continuous and mutual dialogue of the parishioners today.

There is, *fourth*, the *rational* nature of Reformed theology[22] — a rationality that, for example, comes into effect when faithful people speak of having recognized God's acting in history and in social affairs, or of God's providence directing personal life and the fortune of a church or a

---

20. Cf. Michael Welker, "Biblical Theology and the Authority of Scripture," in *Theology in the Service of the Church: Essays in Honor of Thomas W. Gillespie*, ed. Wallace M. Alston, Jr. (Grand Rapids: Eerdmans, 2000), pp. 232-41.

21. See Hughes Oliphant Old, *The Reading and Preaching of the Scriptures in the Worship of the Christian Church*, vol. 4, *The Age of the Reformation* (Grand Rapids: Eerdmans, 2002).

22. See Hendrik Hart, Johan van der Hoeven, and Nicholas Wolterstorff, eds., *Rationality in the Calvinian Tradition* (Lanham, Md., and London: University Press of America, 1983).

nation.[23] To be sure, this rationality can be in opposition to faithfulness to the Scriptures whenever it misuses biblical texts merely as information about true reality; this information — sometimes almost an indoctrination — may hinder listening to the living Word of God speaking in and through the Scripture. Sometimes the rationality of Reformed tradition conformed very well to that of the Enlightenment. There was and is also a distinctive Reformed habit of faithful dealing with its tradition while being at the same time critical of it and open to reshaping it, in order to be not only Reformed but always open to radical reform of church life and reformulation of theology.[24] How can we respect this heritage and at the same time avoid sheer rationalism and religious ideology? The Reformed emphasis on divine illumination might almost lead to identification with critical and self-critical insights, as was sometimes the case under the influence of the Enlightenment.

Another marker of Reformed theology is, *fifth*, the *awareness of God's sovereignty*, expressed especially in the doctrine of predestination and election. This awareness includes two components: the glory of God as the ultimate direction of human life in all its acting and suffering — to sum it up as John Calvin said: "What is the chief end of human life? To know God"[25] — and the complete dependence of human destiny on God's will.

Here let us again look at *Toward the Future of Reformed Theology*. *Election* has replaced *predestination*, probably under the influence of Karl Barth's doctrine of election. Thus the theological intention has changed noticeably and profoundly. Calvin's doctrine of predestination cannot be thought of without his doctrine of damnation: but everything had to be based on God's judgment and acting. Often this was seen — contrary to Calvin's intention — as drawing a clear dividing line between the faithful and the unbelievers and therefore marking

23. For corrections see John H. Leith, *The Reformed Imperative: What the Church Has to Say That No One Else Can Say* (Philadelphia: Westminster, 1988), chap. 4: "God's Providing, Ordering and Caring."

24. Cf., for example, Brian A. Gerrish in his introduction to *Reformed Theology for the Third Christian Millennium* (Louisville: Westminster John Knox, 2003), esp. p. 5, and his article "Tradition in the Modern World: The Reformed Habit of Mind," in *Toward the Future of Reformed Theology*, pp. 3-20.

25. Calvin's Geneva Catechism (1542) in his *Tracts and Treatises*, vol. 2 (Grand Rapids: Eerdmans, 1958), p. 33.

the boundaries of the church, whereas Barth considered the election grounded in Jesus Christ as a far-reaching event that transcends human divisions. In addition, Calvin's doctrine was pastorally motivated: people who wondered about their destiny, which God had decided before all time, had to learn to ask for God's will throughout their entire life. They would not be able to rule out their own damnation all the time. This could culminate in a kind of scrupulous self-examination that frequently provoked a hopeless, fearfully uneasy conscience.

In his novel *In the Beauty of the Lilies,* John Updike describes a Presbyterian minister who had studied at Princeton Theological Seminary with "the two Hodges, and Benjamin Warfield . . . sitting down there in fox-hunting country, surrounded by estates and lettuce farms."[26] Pressed by the incessant questions of a parishioner as to whether he could really die with the assurance of election, the minister begins to doubt his own faith. Had he ever had an incontestable experience of the presence of Christ? He cannot claim this, hence pure confidence in the grace of God is no longer sufficient. How can he go on preaching? How can he minister to the dying? This seems impossible to him, and he leaves his profession.

Here a man fails because of "the cruelty of a theology that sets us to ransacking our nervous systems for a pass to Heaven, even a shred of a ticket."[27] Such a misery of the soul that could mold the religious conscience shaped by Reformed theology is of course a caricature. But it mirrors a picture of Reformed piety that is prominent in western European culture and in the United States. It is foreign to Calvin's theology and would be unthinkable for Karl Barth. However, one characteristic of American Presbyterianism and its understanding of predestination is prominently reflected in *Toward the Future of Reformed Theology:* there is a strong consciousness of one's individuality, a confidence in one's ability that can sometimes certainly include earthly success-seeking and at the same time a high degree of social responsibility. I have seen these impressive traits of character especially in older American Presbyterian laypeople as well as in the Korean Bible study groups and prayer services.

But in general, Calvin's pastoral and individual-ethical approach

26. John Updike, *In the Beauty of the Lilies* (New York: Knopf, 1996), pp. 75f.
27. Updike, *In the Beauty,* p. 44.

that, at an earlier stage, influenced the Reformed doctrine of predestination is replaced in *Toward the Future of Reformed Theology* by a concept of election that will evoke trust in the creative-dynamic activity of the Holy Spirit and in the Spirit's many-faceted powers. This confidence also motivates cultural criticism by means of the Word of God: to change creatively a world that is always in danger of falling prey to human stubbornness and reactionary thinking, urgently demands a constant critical attitude.

This leads us to the *sixth* special mark of Reformed theology, an unusually far-reaching *doctrine of the Holy Spirit,* especially of his boundless presence. That differs from classic Roman Catholic pneumatology, which tends to identify the Holy Spirit with the Roman Catholic Church and its sphere of influence.[28] It differs as well from the traditionally strict and exclusive link of God's Spirit with God's Word and the mediation of the revealed Word of God to the present time and situation in the Lutheran tradition.[29] John Calvin extended the notion of the work of the Holy Spirit to the world, to society, and to culture.[30] And I am convinced that renewed attention to this topic would lead us above all to the insight that the notion of the diverse forms of God's activity helps us to understand Christ's presence as the Coming One in the Lord's Supper.[31]

Seventh, last but not least, there is the difficult and troublesome relation between *eschatology* and *history.* The eschatological course of Reformed theology began with Ulrich Zwingli and Heinrich Bullinger in Zürich, rather than with Calvin, and was fully developed by

28. For example (with helpful corrections in consideration about the Second Vatican Council and its "move toward the world" and openness to other churches and religions), Yves Congar, *I Believe in the Holy Spirit,* trans. David Smith (New York: Seabury Press; London: G. Chapman, 1983).

29. See Regin Prenter, *Spiritus Creator,* trans. John M. Jensen (Philadelphia: Muhlenberg, 1953).

30. Documented in different ways by Werner Krusche, *Das Wirken des Heiligen Geistes nach Calvin* (Berlin: Evangelische Verlagsanstalt, 1956); in the theology of the Dutch, Arnold Albrecht van Ruler, especially *Calvinistic Trinitarianism and Theocentric Politics: Essays toward a Public Theology,* ed. John Bolt, Toronto Studies in Theology, vol. 38 (Lewiston, N.Y.: Edwin Mellen, 1989), chaps. 1, 2, and 5; and by Michael Welker, *God the Spirit,* trans. John F. Hoffmeyer (Minneapolis: Fortress, 1994).

31. Cf. Michael Welker, *What Happens in Holy Communion?* trans. John F. Hoffmeyer (Grand Rapids: Eerdmans, 2000).

Johannes Cocceius (1603-69), who taught theology at Bremen (northern Germany) and at Franeker and Leiden (Netherlands).[32] This theology is based on the view that God has established several covenants, starting with the creation, or with God's initiative after the fall of Adam and Eve, and culminating with the covenant of grace of God, Father and Son. These covenants divide history, and the biblical witness to them enables us to grasp all history and to understand momentous historical events in relation to the coming of the kingdom of God. This conception of progressive salvation history is a fruit from the tree of Reformed construction of our world in light of divine revelation. It traveled from the Netherlands up the river Rhine to Switzerland. In Zürich the Reformed minister Johann Jakob Heß (1741-1828) developed a doctrine of the kingdom of God according to the course of world history.[33] It fit nicely with the idealist religious philosophy of history established especially by Georg Wilhelm Friedrich Hegel. His philosophy merged — through the mediation of the Reformed minister and professor Christian Krafft (1784-1845) — with the Lutheran theology of salvation history (John Christian Karl von Hofmann, 1810-77) at Erlangen. It became very influential throughout the nineteenth century and is similar to American dispensational theology.[34]

Failure to understand the intricate connection between eschatology and theology of history has been, as I have tried to explain elsewhere,[35] one of the deficiencies of theology in recent times. It can also become, if soundly revised, one of the most important contributions of Reformed theology to the ecumenical dialogue.

Eschatology not only intends to give a coherent account for the hope that is in us but also "opens theology up to a sensitivity for history"[36]

32. Gottlob Schrenk, *Gottesreich und Bund im älteren Protestantismus, vornehmlich bei Johannes Coccejus: Zugleich ein Beitrag zur Geschichte des Pietismus und der heilsgeschichtlichen Theologie* (Gütersloh: C. Bertelsmann, 1923).

33. Johann Jakob Heß, *Kern der Lehre vom Reiche Gottes: Nach Anleitung des biblischen Geschichtsinhalts*, 2nd ed. (Zürich: Orell, Füßli & Compagnie, 1826).

34. Clarence Bass, *Backgrounds to Dispensationalism: Its Historical Genesis and Ecclesiastical Implications* (Grand Rapids: Eerdmans, 1960); B. C. Norman Kraus, *Dispensationalism in America: Its Rise and Development* (Richmond: John Knox, 1958).

35. Gerhard Sauter, *What Dare We Hope? Reconsidering Eschatology* (Harrisburg, Pa.: Trinity, 1999), pp. 9-18, 126-59.

36. Martin Kähler, "Die Bedeutung, welche den 'letzten Dingen' für Theologie und Kirche zukommt," in *Dogmatische Zeitfragen*, vol. 1 (Leipzig: A. Deichert, 1898), p. 252.

and encourages us to ask both what is God's living will in what we experience and what is God's verdict on what happens and how it happens. The crucial point is that first we *ask* about God's will, rather than assume that we know it already, and then we may ask how this knowledge can be brought in line with the stories we combine to fashion an overall picture that we call "history."

We really need to ask these questions in the light of contingent events, predictable developments, and supposedly manageable contexts. Such a theology of history (with emphasis on theology rather than on history) can proceed neither descriptively nor prescriptively. It cannot prescribe God's activity, let alone predict it. Instead, it tracks assertive responses to God's promises of justice as the revelation of God's righteousness, of peace as becoming united with God's uniting work, of freedom as being liberated from all kinds of self-righteousness, of recognition of God in the life of Jesus Christ, of life in community with Christ, and of rest at the Lord's table as a token of the homecoming when God will dwell with mortals (Rev. 21:3b). God steps into our lives and makes us recognize God's will, often neither through shaking events not through transforming, progressive developments but exactly where we do not reckon with God.

Theology of history rests on the amazing exclamation of gratitude to God for God's contingent and everlasting activity and surprising providential activity and care that we can perceive only retrospectively as a glimpse of the unity of human life, personal and communal, because it is borne in the context of the action of God and is interwoven with it. And so we call on God to preserve our sense of time and to provide spiritual experiences of ending and new beginning, and therefore, the sense of the complexity of true hope.

These few remarks can be only a sketch, consisting mainly of open questions that call all of us to be jointly engaged in drawing a fuller and more adequate picture of what the crucial tasks of theology are today and how we might face up to them. As Blaise Pascal wrote, "The last thing one discovers in composing a work is what has to be put first."[37]

---

37. Blaise Pascal, *Pensées and Other Writings*, frag. 740, trans. Honor Levi (Oxford and New York: Oxford University Press, 1995), p. 177.

Index of Names

Adams, John Quincy, 137n.7
Ahlstrom, Sidney E., 140n.11,
 144n.17
Alston, Wallace M., 151n.3, 168,
 171n.10
Ameringer, Charles D., 138n.8
Anselm of Canterbury, 75, 158
Auerbach, Erich, 37
Augustine, Saint, 51, 70, 84, 109

Balog, Zoltán, 170n.7, 172n.12
Balthasar, Hans Urs von, 48-49
Barth, Karl, xxi, 73n.27, 88, 98, 122-
 23, 168-70, 176-77
Bartha, Tibor, 121n.2
Barton, John, 40n.10
Bass, Clarence, 179n.34
Bellah, Robert N., 132n.1
Bengel, Johann Albrecht, 35n.2
Benz, Arnold, 10
Bernard of Clairvaux, 85
Berquist, John L., 146n.22
Beutel, Albrecht, 45n.25
Bevans, Stephen B., 100-101
Beveridge, Albert, 137
Bloch, Ernst, 8-9, 17, 23-24
Bonhoeffer, Dietrich, 72-73, 125n.6,
 129-30, 162
Bornkamm, Günther, 7

Buber, Martin, 21-22, 26, 28-29, 53
Buechner, Frederick, 146n.25
Bullinger, Heinrich, 178
Bultmann, Rudolf, 6-7, 19-20, 22-23
Bush, George W., 132-36, 141

Calvin, Jean, 15, 84-85, 175-78
Coccejus, Johannes, 178
Cone, James H., 111
Congar, Ives, 178n.28
Conzelmann, Hans, 20
Cornehl, Peter, 27n.25

Davis, Ellen F., 40, 47, 56
Dunn, James D. G., 127n.11
Dutzmann, Martin, 117n.1

Eco, Umberto, 43n.17
Edwards, Jonathan, 141

Fichte, Johann Gottlieb, 28
Fischer, Rainer, 43n.17

Gaustad, Erwin S., 143n.16
Gebhardt, Jürgen, 27n.25
Gehrig, Gail, 132n.1
Gerrish, Brian A., 176n.24
Goeters, Gerhard J. F., 169n.6
Gogarten, Friedrich, 6

Index of Subjects

affliction, 2, 68, 109, 132, 141
atonement, 92, 108, 165. *See also* reconciliation

baptism, 34, 37-39, 71-72, 78, 81, 83, 89, 97
Barmen Declaration, 86-87, 98-99, 102, 126, 153, 170, 174
Bible. *See* Scripture
biblical theology, 167, 172, 175

Chalcedon, dogmatic formula of, 48, 63, 101
Christian education, xviii, 62, 72, 77, 160, 173
church: grounding of, 65-67, 72, 97, 101; hiddenness of, 66; leadership, 72, 174; marks of, 66-67, 82, 164; practice(s) of, 60, 64-66, 68-70, 72-73, 91n.16, 97, 101, 159-60; public service of, 149-53, 160-63, 168; self-enclosure of, xviii, 56, 159; and state, 79, 117, 122, 132, 137, 149, 151-52, 162. *See also* theology: and church
city upon a hill, xx, 136, 138-42, 144
civil religion, xx, 117, 132-33, 137, 144
Constantinople, Creed of, 18, 73

Constitution of the Presbyterian Church (U.S.A.), 172n.14
context, xiv-xv, 65, 75, 96-97, 102-3, 105, 155-56, 158, 180; context-related/context-dominated, 103, 110; contextuality, 97-98
contextual theology, xix-xx, 96, 103-4, 106-7, 109-10, 113
Council of Trent, 80, 88
creation, 11, 64, 178. *See also* eschatology: new creation

Dabru Emet, 30-31
Darmstadt memorandum, 123-24
doctrine, 57, 80, 82, 157, 172, 175. *See also* dogmatics
dogmatics, xviii, 58, 60-62, 64-65, 72-73, 97, 107, 110, 114, 165
Dominus Iesus, 71n.24

Enlightenment, 74, 109, 145, 155, 176
eschatology: completion, consummation, 20-21, 29-30; ending and new beginning, 2, 14, 164, 180; end of the world, 1, 4, 9-11, 18, 22; new creation, 17-18, 29-30, 32, 81, 85, 140; promise and fulfillment, xvi, 12-15, 17-18, 20, 26, 53-54, 97; resurrection of the dead,

Index of Biblical References